Killing Fame

To Maxine
Enjoy
fiona

Coming soon from Fiona Cane
WHEN THE DOVE CRIED

Killing Fame

Fiona Cane

RED SAIL

This edition published 2006 by
Red Sail Publishing
11 Compton Place Road
Eastbourne
East Sussex BN20 8AB

ISBN 0-9552855-0-X. (Paperback)

Typeset by Phoenix Photosetting, Chatham, Kent
Printed and bound by Mackays of Chatham, Chatham, Kent

Acknowledgements

This book is due to the monumental effort and enthusiasm of Jon and Caroline Haynes. Thank you for transforming my dream into reality . . . so quickly.

To Chris Barrett, for your inspiration, help and hilarious guidance, I thank you for those fun-fuelled days spent editing. The sun really did shine on Fridays.

The patient, laid-back approach of Adrian Newton is in direct contrast to his dramatic cover. Thanks Ade for your skill, speed, time and efficiency . . . but *not* your jokes.

Special thanks to Lesley Frame, Catherine Prendergast, Fran Kazamia, Roma Biltcliffe, Susie Horner, David Caffyn and Anthea Stewart for their support, humour, friendship, the endless re-rereading, glasses of wine and those pep-talks that kept me going through the dark times.

I'm immensely grateful to Dorothy Frame and her eagle eye; and to Mark Freeland, Rachel Angel, Martin Surgey, Nicky Eckert, Nettie Boutwood, Nicola King, Janie and Mathew Jellings, Sarah Cinci, Kim and Rog Carmichael, Karin Taylor, Damian Thornton, Wendy Shuttleworth and Nick Webborn for reading the manuscript in its various stages.

Love to Simon, Holly and Sam. Thank you for believing in me, for putting up with me and encouraging me over the years.

And finally I give a huge, gigantic thank you to Peter James – you showed great faith in me as a writer and led the way on this long adventure.

For Holly and Sam

PART ONE

Monday 7 May

My hand is trembling as I point the gun. He stands before me, silent, staring down the barrel, a slight smile at the left hand corner of his mouth.

'You don't really want to kill me,' he jeers.

And at that moment I see that he is, at last, afraid.

I squeeze the trigger and laugh. 'Bang, bang, you're dead!'

The bullet goes right through him. That surprises me. When it enters his body just below his left nipple, I do not expect it to come out again. I watch intrigued as it splinters the wood behind him where it lodges in the door-frame. It isn't embedded in the wood. It sticks out.

I could hang my coat on that, I think.

I shake my head in amazement and try to concentrate my attention on my silent victim. He is lying in a crumpled heap less than four paces in front of where I'm standing as though he has folded into the ground. I take a few tentative steps towards his breathless body and stare at its inert form. Blood seeps through the bullet hole in a steady trickle, glistening red, discolouring his clothes and the green grass at my feet. It is sticky and smells awful, sweet yet metallic, foul. And as I watch it darken and thicken I begin to understand that I have scorched his heart with my barrel load of gunfire. He does not scream. He does not whimper. He can make no noise at all, only stares at me, his eyes wide open, disbelieving, shot with blood.

Shocking, I tell myself, but at the same time, comforting.

He had to die. Don't you see? Because of her.

He had to die. A simple case of retribution. No more no less.

You've won, I tell myself, because that is how it feels. He is dead. And I . . . I am free to live with her . . . my angel . . . until the end of time.

Instead a nightmare rages around my head. A persistent headache, painful, irritating, it distorts reality. Years pass but it never leaves me, this blackest of clouds, my living hell. And I am left wondering if this is it.

Is this my life?

2

One

There is no such thing as bad publicity, thought Larry ruefully, straightening the cutlery on the white linen tablecloth in front of him. It was funny how he always found himself deliberating this adage whenever he was waiting for Alfie. No matter what mood he was in, sad, happy, pessimistic, optimistic, he always arrived at the same conclusion – what a load of bollocks! That hadn't always been the case. As an eager, young publicist he'd believed it implicitly, at least as long as the journalists had spelt his client's name right. He sighed, wondering if he was to be forever haunted by his occupation.

Behind him a bluebottle buzzed furiously as it crashed into the window.

'Standards at The Ivy are slipping,' he muttered to the diners seated at the neighbouring table while gesticulating at the offending insect. They nodded non-committedly then continued with their conversation. The fly, unaware of the irritation it's bid for freedom had created, persisted blindly in its quest. For a moment Larry toyed with the idea of rolling his neatly pressed and starched napkin into a suitable weapon to swat the infuriating pest before concluding that such abandoned behaviour would only lower the tone of the esteemed establishment. Besides it was not his style.

Instead he raised his hand to grab the attention of a waiter but noticed that his eyes, along with everybody else's in the restaurant, were concentrated on the latest arrival. A slight man of sixty was making his way slowly across the room, a camera slung over his shoulder. Casually dressed in jeans, white shirt unbuttoned at the cuffs and a black jacket, it was his presence that was spellbinding, the aura he exuded and his faded good looks synonymous with unparalleled fame.

'Alfie!' exclaimed Larry, leaping to his feet and grabbing his great friend by the hand. 'It's good to see you.'

'Larry Woods, international publicist, is it really you?' Alfie

3

responded, feigning disbelief as he placed his battered camera carefully on the table.

'Still carrying that old thing around?' Larry asked, ignoring the jibe.

Alfie smiled, sat down and picked up the menu. 'Still your favourite restaurant then?'

'You know I can't resist their shepherd's pie,' said Larry grinning, pulling up his chair.

'Tut tut,' taunted Alfie. 'Broad shoulders you may have and a fairly impressive muscular frame given you are fifty-nine but face it Larry, you've got a barrel for a belly. Are you sure you should be ordering pie?'

Larry smiled and patted the solid dome of flesh that had replaced the six-pack of his youth. 'I think it's safe to say it's here to stay however many times I flex my stomach muscles and hold it in. I usually manage to defy gravity for at least five minutes and almost enjoy the burn but then the pain hits me. Next year I vow I'll sign up at the local gym.'

'Next year's a good three months away Larry. Stop procrastinating. What you need are press-ups – as a matter of urgency.'

Larry laughed despite the ribbing. The waiter came over, beaming at Alfie as he took their order.

'Fish Alfie, without chips. Very healthy,' commented Larry. The waiter nodded approvingly then left.

'Charming waiter, lovely room but I can't say I'm fond of this place,' said Alfie.

'Oh really? So why did you suggest we meet here?' Larry asked, glancing over his shoulder. A couple of B-list celebrities were chatting earnestly at a table behind him while three members of the public, seated to their left, gawped openly.

'*I* didn't. *You* did.'

'I did?'

'Yes. You always do.'

'I suppose it is a bit of a celebrity grazing ground,' said Larry pensively.

'Well that goes without saying but . . .' Alfie paused to look around him, at the oak panelling, the 1920s stained glass windows. '. . . this place . . . this trendy little restaurant with all its fabulous reviews, its wonderful food, its exemplary service . . . it holds a lot of bad memories for me.'

'Really?' Larry could not disguise the astonishment he felt at this sudden and frank admission. Alfie rarely referred to his past. 'But we often eat here. What on earth's brought this on? You've never said.'

'They torment me Larry, these memories. Like time-worn spectres rising from the grave,' he added shuddering, the light-heartedness of his earlier conversation giving way to morbid sincerity.

'You surprise me,' replied Larry, rendered almost speechless by this admission from his resilient friend.

Alfie, intent on getting whatever was bothering him off his chest, seemed oblivious to Larry's shocked reaction. 'The bash for *Nausea,* my brilliant art-house film . . . Abe's film. We held it here,' he continued falteringly.

'I know. I organised it. It was a marvellous night,' offered Larry cautiously.

'It grinds me down. The guilt that is . . . about Abe . . . you know.'

Larry paused, astounded yet concerned by Alfie's candour. He was not usually prone to emotive recollections. 'Even after all these years?' he asked tentatively.

'Daily it hurts me. Subliminal torture like a dripping tap of guilt saturating my conscience with its constant reminder that Abe Cunningham and I were, once upon a time, the very *best* of friends. From the moment we met at Cambridge he took me under his wing, treated me like a brother. Nothing was too much trouble for Abe where I was concerned. I adored him.'

Larry nodded staring into Alfie's tortured hazel eyes but said nothing.

'He was by my side at my directorial debut. He held my hand at that first premiere and continued to hold it as fame engulfed me. You must remember when my second film broke box office records on its opening weekend he was by my side, celebrating with me. You remember that, Larry? Abe was there for me.'

Larry nodded again, his unease mounting. Where was this conversation leading? It was uncharacteristic, totally unheralded, freakish, if such an adjective could be applied to someone as solid and sanguine as Alfie. 'I do remember. He was a good friend to you.'

'And then I let him down. I let him down spectacularly as if everything that had gone before was meaningless. I blame myself for his death. Time has not changed a thing.'

Twenty-two years had passed since Abe's untimely death and all the grief that Alfie had felt, the agony he had gone through, the guilt seemed to have migrated to the forefront of Alfie's mind to hammer at his conscience. Larry leant forward and placed a reassuring hand on Alfie's shoulder. 'You mustn't Alfie. He would not want you to.'

'Remember Stella?' continued Alfie softly.

Larry started and leant back in his chair, alarmed by this further quiet but sudden change of subject. Now there's a name from the past, he thought. 'Absolutely as I suspect anyone who ever met her does.' His voice, though cheerful, belied his true feelings. Why was Alfie talking this way? First Abe and now Stella. And he hadn't mentioned Stella since her disappearance fifteen years ago.

'I fell in love with her here. Truly in love. Here in The Ivy, at the party for *Nausea*.'

Larry's curiosity was roused. Even though his friend was clearly melancholic, the conversation morose, he could sense a golden opportunity to ask a question that he had never dared vocalise although it was often on the tip of his tongue. He seized the moment. 'You never actually told me what happened to Stella, Alfie. Where did she go?'

'She left,' he replied flatly.

'Why Alfie? What happened?' he repeated urgently.

'She's gone that's all you need to know.'

The waiter returned with their food. Larry thanked him, picked up his fork and thrust it into his pie, one eye still on Alfie. What next? he wondered dumbfounded, casting a wary eye over his friend. He looks thinner than usual. Tired and strained. Larry watched him for a moment as he played with his food, shifting it awkwardly around the plate like a chef deliberating the perfect presentation.

'Not eating?' he asked him gently. 'Are you all right Alfie?'

'Abdominal pains,' responded Alfie matter-of-factly. 'They make it damned hard to enjoy good tucker.'

'Oh!' exclaimed Larry startled. 'Have you seen a doctor?'

At this question Alfie visibly relaxed, his shoulders retreating from his ears to their rightful place below his chin. 'Yes. Yes. In fact, Larry, I meant to tell you. I'm to undergo surgery.' He smiled as he hurriedly offered the news confusing Larry still further.

'Surgery!' he echoed, stunned.

'That's right. Nothing serious. Purely investigative. My consultant seems to think it might be worthwhile to put my mind at rest.'

'That's good,' replied Larry numbly.

'It's very common at my age, Larry,' he added reassuringly.

Our age, thought Larry staring blindly ahead. 'When?'

'Thursday. At the Chelsea and Westminster.'

'The day after tomorrow. That's quick!'

'Yup!'

For a couple of minutes neither man spoke. Alfie took his first forkful of fish and chewed labouriously without swallowing as Larry attempted to digest the facts. Abdominal pains. An operation. His obvious weight loss. Alfie had told him it was nothing to be alarmed about and yet he seemed frightened. The talk of Abe, his guilt, Stella . . .

'You know Larry, 'the nice thing about being a celebrity is that when you bore people, they think it's their fault.' I think Henry Kissinger had a valid point. Don't you?'

'You're not boring me,' said Larry. 'I'm shocked, that's all.'

'Don't be. It's just a routine operation.'

'Yes but the pain. I'm worried for you.'

'Don't worry just carry on being the great friend you've always been. How long have we been friends? Thirty years isn't it. Thirty years since I walked into your Soho office alone and unannounced and asked you to represent me as my publicist.'

'With that camera and those clothes, more or less,' recalled Larry, snatching the bait. 'You seemed taller in real life than in the photographs. Lean and athletic with wild and unruly, dark curly hair. I particularly remember the hungry look in your eyes.'

'Brooding. That's how Vogue described me back then. Eerily attractive rather than conventionally handsome!'

'Ha!' laughed Larry. 'The tosh journalists write.'

'They loved my crooked nose and the slight cleft in my chin,' joked Alfie. 'And I'll have you know I'm extremely eerie.'

'Clearly!'

'Mind you, that was before I started behaving like a multi-million pound arsehole.'

This further surprising change of tack almost floored Larry. It was as though Alfie was rewinding his life only to focus on the few dark years that had punctuated an otherwise glittering career. It was as if ... but Larry couldn't bear to contemplate the possible reasons.

'You had a few *interesting* years but what journalists never quite understood was how serious and hard-working a director you were both on set and off it. Everyone in the industry had the utmost respect for you.'

'If only I hadn't succumbed to the fame. Actors do that not directors.'

'Nonsense, everyone who lives a life in the public eye is vulnerable. Anyway I thought you'd dealt with all of this. I thought you'd lain these ghosts to rest.'

'I did, I have ... it's just ...'

'Perhaps it's time for you to write your autobiography,' interrupted Larry abandoning his pie, his appetite finally giving way to a rising sickness in the pit of his stomach.

'Never.'

'So you'll leave it to Phoebe then. Not a bad idea. She's a sensible and intelligent girl,' he added, trying to jolly Alfie along.

'My daughter has far more sense than to waste her time scribing the biography of her father. Besides, she despises fame and all it stands for.'

'She loves you,' whispered Larry, his voice cracking.

Straining the corners of his mouth until they formed a smile, Alfie placed his hand on Larry's and squeezed it affectionately. 'Look after her Larry.'

'But it's only a routine operation,' he insisted hopefully, helplessly.

'Promise me you will.'

Two

Two days later in the pouring rain Larry marched furiously down the road towards his house, a folded copy of *The Evening News* in the clenched ball of one fist, the key to his house in the other.

'Story, my arse!' he muttered angrily under his breath as he thrust the key into the lock of his navy blue front door. 'Vicious rumour, more like.'

He kicked the heavy door with such force it slammed shut behind him. The hallway shook slightly as he strode down it toward the kitchen.

How on earth am I going to explain this latest turn of events to Alfie when he comes round from his operation? he wondered as he laid the newspaper, with great precision, flat on the kitchen table. With a monumental sigh he licked his forefinger then pulled back the front page to the offending article.

There was the headline in all its unhibited glory – ALFIE MACBETH'S SECOND WIFE FLIES TO LONDON FOR TEARFUL REUNION. He shook his head in frustration and thumped the table with his left hand. Alfie's second marriage, a private ceremony in Australia, had been a well-kept secret. No one, not the British press nor public, were aware to this day that he had been married a second time. There had been no announcement, no photos, no press release, nothing. It had been quite a feat given the extraordinary fame of the man.

Long-time estranged second wife of legendary film director Alfie Macbeth (Killing Fame, The Ark, His Cold Blood, Tribulation) was sighted at Heathrow Airport yesterday having flown in on a Qantas airline from Brisbane, he read bristling with anger.

Two pictures accompanied the story. The first was a full colour shot of Alfie's beautiful first wife enveloped in the arms of an equally handsome actor, Raul Mendoza. They were standing beneath a palm tree on a sandy beach under a cobalt sky – the set of the film *Eternity* in which they had both starred some twenty years ago. It was a picture the papers still loved to publish, nothing new there.

The second smaller black and white photograph however, in contrast to the first, was out of focus and grainy. If he concentrated hard enough Larry could just about discern the outline of a woman of indefinable age, whose blurred and distant image was obscured by the upturned collar of her large overcoat and an Akubra hat.

Was it her? he wondered. Could it be her?

He slammed his right hand down hard on the kitchen table. The paper rose up a couple of centimetres in the draught created by this sudden movement and might have left the table entirely if Larry hadn't slapped it back down as if it were a prisoner undergoing interrogation.

Thomas Slater, pondered Larry, his eyes wandering over the article again desperately searching for clues. He wrote this . . . this . . . piece of shit. But how the hell could *Thomas Slater* know? Stella disappeared fifteen years ago. Into thin air, it had seemed back then. Neither sight nor sound has been heard of *her* since. Yet this journalist, this Thomas Slater, appears out of the ether to claim otherwise. Who is he? What stone has he crawled out from because I've never heard of him? And given that I'm one of the world's top entertainment publicists, *that's* a bit odd as I have the names of hundreds of journalists filed in the mental address book of my brain, certainly all those with the credentials to publish a story as sensitive and prominent as this.

He glanced at his Rolex. Where the hell is Phoebe? he wondered, redirecting his anxiety to the whereabouts of his goddaughter. It's not like her to be late. The dear child's been asbsurdly punctual all her life.

He sighed loudly and spun round on the smooth soles of his Gucci loafers and headed back down the hallway, shoulders hunched in his baggy, pink Ralph Lauren shirt. He felt anxious, angry and weary, as though he were staggering under the weight of a huge object

I feel like that poor bugger Atlas trying his damnedest to hold up the heavens. Right now I'd welcome any distraction even if it meant being turned to stone, he thought as he pressed his aquiline nose into the cold glass of the full-length gilt mirror, blurring his features. He stared at his amorphous reflection. In the savage light of day it seemed to scream *old man* at him his face, he noticed with alarm, etched with more wrinkles than seemed fair.

He stepped back and rubbed his face vigourously with his hands before declaring loudly 'I am becoming fearful of age.' Then shrugged emphatically before reminding himself that Alfie was merely undergoing tests.

A familiar gentle knocking sounded at his front door. Relieved, Larry turned to answer it. Alfie's daughter, Phoebe, was standing in the rain, her tall, willowy figure obscured by her baggy student uniform of oversized jacket and blue flared jeans. She had a large kit bag slung over her shoulder and was cold and wet but smiled prettily. Larry laughed as she flung her arms around him in the impetuous way she had done since a child.

'My dear, you're drenched,' he said as she kissed him lightly on both cheeks, her long wet hair soaking his shirt. 'You look like a drowned . . .'

'Rat?' Phoebe interrupted, a faint smile on her lips.

'I was going to say dryad, actually,' corrected Larry, helping his goddaughter out of her rain-sodden jacket. 'Dryads, naiads, gorgeous creatures darling, just like you.'

'Ah! Still the same old Larry,' she said, playfully punching him in the stomach. She dropped the kit bag to the floor and began to wring out her hair with her tiny hands.

'Absolutely,' he replied, feeling suddenly flat again. 'Let me get you a towel. Your hair's gone all straggly.'

'I'm fine. Don't worry about it,' she assured him, tipping her head forward and shaking her long dark hair. 'So, as London's top Entertainment Publicist are you going to tell me, a humble veterinary student, what's going on?'

'How is your father? Have you got his camera?' he countered, watching Phoebe busily twisting her hair into a tidy coil.

'Yes, I've got his camera.' she said, flicking the rope of hair over her shoulders. 'Apart from the fact that he's lost a lot of weight he seemed fine. He's never liked hospitals so I suspect he's covering up his nerves to protect me.' She pulled off her black hooded sweatshirt, yanked down her white T-shirt with her slight but muscular arms then glanced at her watch. 'He's due in theatre at 7pm, that's a couple of hours from now. He won't be in there long because it's hardly an operation he's having, more an exploration. It's really *very* routine. But you know that Larry. We talked about it this morning. Don't tell me you're going senile.' She narrowed her Bambi brown eyes to accentuate her sarcasm.

'Of course. Quite.'

'It's this article that I'm more concerned about and the handful of journalists camped outside the hospital lying in wait,' she explained, her good humour fading at the memory.

'They're there already? That's dreadful,' muttered Larry.

'Why can't they leave him in peace? Why must they rake up his past? Look!' She tugged angrily at the rope around the neck of her kitbag, pulled it roughly open and thrust her hand in to produce a rolled

11

newspaper. She brandished it at Larry, waving it under his nose so that for a moment he wondered if she was going to hit him with it. 'Have you read this? Because if you have you will have seen what they are writing about him? It's ... it's totally ... un ... accept ... able.' Phoebe's voice cracked. She paused and lowered her head to disguise the beginning of a tear that had pricked the corner of her eye.

Well that's an understatement, thought Larry wryly. 'The article in *The Evening News?* Yes, Phoebe, I've read it,' he told her gently, picking up her hand to lead her towards his sitting-room. It was large and imposing, painted beige and smelled faintly of vanilla. Dark red, elephant print curtains hung heavily from wrought iron poles on either side of the French windows. A cream sofa and two chairs covered in a scattering of red and purple cushions flanked an ornate stone fireplace, the main feature of the room that Larry often referred to as his *little piece of Ken Russell*. In the corner of the room, clustered together on a large, round light-oak table were photographs of Larry pictured with the rich and famous: Larry and Spielberg playing tennis; Larry beaming, shaking hands with the Princess of Wales, Prince Charles looking on; Larry laughing, holding baby Phoebe in his arms; a panoramic shot of his villa in Cephallonia. And on the wall opposite the door hung two full-sized posters framed in blonde wood of Alfie Macbeth's films *The Ark* and his Australian adventure *Tribulation.*

'Why don't you sit down and I'll make you a cup of tea,' he suggested. 'You look done in.'

'No!' said Phoebe moodily.

'OK,' said Larry at once letting go of one hand and easing the tabloid paper from the clenched fist of her other.

'Will they never leave him alone?' asked Phoebe angrily. 'It's unbelievably insensitive to chew over his marriages at a time like this. Can't you stop them raking up his past?'

'It's what they do,' said Larry gently.

'But you're so good at getting stories into the press. Surely you can keep them out?'

'He's famous, irrevocably so. This ... this ... well, this *shit* – there's no other word for it, Phoebe – goes hand in hand with success. You know that I'll do everything I can in the way of damage limitation.'

'Where is she?' demanded Phoebe, grabbing the tabloid back. 'Thomas Slater,' she said, her voice clipped as she read the name of the journalist responsible for the article, 'says she was sighted at Heathrow Airport yesterday having flown in on a Qantas airline from Brisbane.'

'So he says,' replied Larry with a sigh. 'But really Phoebe, you are an intelligent girl. Look at the picture. It's out of focus. It could be anybody!'

'Exactly,' responded Phoebe, flinging the offending article angrily towards the small steel wastepaper basket in the corner of the room. It landed with a rustle on the wooden floor in an untidy heap. 'It could be her! Come on Larry! You're the expert! This Thomas whatever his name is. Is he reputable? Does he know his stuff?'

'Never heard of him,' declared Larry, trembling suddenly as the past began to replay random images like a fast-paced film trailer in the cinema of his mind. At the time of Alfie's second wife's disappearance it had seemed prurient not to ask exactly what had happened. Alfie had been cut up, lacerated by his loss, bowed and broken for the first time in his life. Now, fifteen years later and faced with this article that had crept out of the undergrowth like a tenacious predator intent on its prey, he was being forced to ask the question, why had she left Alfie and where had she gone?

'Brilliant!' shrieked Phoebe. 'The great Larry Woods has no idea!'

Three

The lobby of the London Hilton, Park Lane was bulging with the bodies of Britain's media. Outside the hotel the heat hung over England's capital city, heavy and oppressive like a thick, grimy eiderdown. Writhing in discomfort in the sweltering temperature, their clothes splattered with sweat, the journalists jostled for space as they inched their way out of the sun and into the crowded foyer. From his relatively secluded position by the lift, Abe Cunningham watched the five bright-eyed public relations girls guide the convoluted mass towards the air-conditioned suite set aside for today's press conference. He was unimpressed by the proceedings that seemed way too lavish. At the end of the day, it was just a lousy film.

His head ached, his eyes stung and his mouth was dry. His stomach, that had been bothering him for days, grumbled malevolently. He took a deep breath to calm the cramps but the rancid smell of overheated homo sapiens that hit the back of his parched throat caused him to gag involuntarily.

Wondering why on earth this fetid pack of hacks had not made an extra-special effort with the deodorant this morning, Abe reached into his tatty canvas fishing bag and pulled out a bottle of Evian. He took a long swig of the lukewarm water, wiping away the spills on his chin with the back of his hand. The relief he felt was negligible. His mouth was less dry but so was the rest of his body, which seemed to be acting like a sieve. He could feel the rivulets of his sweat tickling his spine as they rolled down his back, the heavy moistness of the cotton of his T-shirt chafing the skin in the pit of his arm.

His mood was lugubrious but this would have been the case whatever the weather. The intense heat served only to accentuate the fact. He was stressed, hence the stomach cramps.

A camera crew lurched towards him, inadvertently bumping his skinny frame into the metal surround of the lift casing. He rubbed his bony shoulder, cursing quietly under his breath.

'Sorry mate,' apologised the sound technician. 'No space to manoeuvre.'

'Quite!' muttered Abe.

'Amazing the interest this latest film of his is generating. They say it's his best yet and that Buzz Holland gives the performance of his life. You seen it?'

'No.'

'I'm seeing it tonight. Sneak preview. Can't wait,' he said as he lugged his equipment toward the suite, his face lighting up into a massive grin, like a child in a sweet shop.

Abe groaned. It was the irony of the situation that crippled him. After all it was he who'd introduced Alfie to directing. A chance decision, as it turned out, taken in a moment of desperation at Cambridge University. He'd needed a director for his production of *Romeo and Juliet* and Alfie, his best friend and room-mate, had jumped at the chance. He'd put in a creditable performance as Romeo but Alfie had excelled in his role as director like he did when he tried his hand at anything.

When Alfie left university, armed with glowing reviews in the national press and a 2:1 in English, he waltzed into a job in advertising hungry for success. That's what separated Alfie from the rest, his intense desire to get on and achieve. Within six months he'd got behind a camera and shot some film. The mini-movies he'd created revolutionized the advertising industry and provided him with a springboard to launch his cinematic career. His big screen debut, at the tender age of twenty-eight, turned him overnight into an inspiration to millions of young hopefuls around the world. He had courage, ruthlessness, nerves of steel, machismo, good looks and charm, all the attributes required to get to the top.

Unlike me, thought Abe, flattening his fleshless form into the wall as an overweight hack, clutching his genitals, barged passed him toward the lift. With the benefit of hindsight it all seemed obvious now. Life had dealt him a bitter blow. The cruel remarks his tutor at RADA had made in his final term had left him reeling.

'Abe,' she'd told him, 'you are lamentably thin. You have fine mousy hair and a long but distinguished nose. You are interesting, certainly but handsome, no. A good actor, but not great.'

That was why he'd turned *his* hand to directing, wasn't it? Or had it simply been a question of vanity, a feeble attempt to emulate the sky-high success of his friend? He had stood on the sidelines of Alfie's life and watched his career flower from the smallest and most improbable of seeds – eight years, six critically acclaimed films, two Oscar nominations and the nation's public constantly clamouring for a word, a photograph, a glimpse, anything pertaining to the great Alfie Macbeth.

And I'm down here, a struggling theatre director, crouched at Alfie's feet as he lords it above the star-struck populace on his pedestal on the top of the world. Is he a genius or has it all been down to luck? My God, I sound like a jealous man, thought Abe sadly. This is Alfie Macbeth you're talking about here, your best mate. You should be proud of him. Instead you stand here, swathed in self-pity, lambasting his character as though he were guilty of some heinous crime. He's a successful film director, not Attila the Hun.

A tall, dark, well-built man sashaying impressively through the gridlocked crowd roused him from his thoughts. He'd been bustling around all morning, a lone calm presence quietly organizing the tumultuous throng into some semblance of order. Only now his impassive mien had given way to concern.

'Any sign of him, Abe?' he asked, straining his voice to be heard over the din.

'Nope!' replied Abe with a shake of his head.

'This really isn't like him, you know.'

'I shouldn't worry, Larry. He'll turn up. This sort of occasion will be excellent fodder for his ego.'

'Come on Abe. Don't be so hard on the guy. He's only doing his job.'

'Right! It's just I preferred him when he was humble. He never used to be like this. He was a regular guy. Fame has transformed him.'

'It's bound to.'

'Into an arsehole!'

'I think I'm going to get them seated in the suite,' said Larry ignoring the insult, his mind clearly elsewhere. 'Buzz, Mary, Burt and Chantal are already there. If I don't get started soon tempers are sure to get a little frayed.'

'Good idea,' agreed Abe mechanically.

'See you in there.'

'Sure. Wouldn't miss it for the world,' said Abe with the faintest of smiles. He liked Larry, admired his professionalism and he'd done a great job today. The turnout was immense. Everyone seemed excited. The lobby was humming with anticipation, throbbing with adrenalin. Even *he* had to admit it was exhilarating, however resentful it made him.

But where was Alfie? he wondered again. Larry was right. If he delayed his arrival too much longer the mood might turn to frustration. With so many people gathered together in such heat, a riot could break out. What the hell was he playing at?

The lift doors opened to the right of him. It had been busy all morning, clanking and groaning under the weight of journalists and photographers in need of a coffee or the washrooms on the mezzanine level, one floor up. With the lobby full the traffic had been constant – only now, all of a sudden, a spectral hush had descended on the room as if a spell had been cast striking dumb the waiting journalists, immobilising them, save for their eyes that now turned with frightening synchronicity in his direction. He shifted uncomfortably, feeling for his flies as a collective gasp left the mouths of the congregation.

Only it wasn't him they were staring at, he realised as he inclined his neck towards the open lift, but the stunning rear view of a gorgeous young model in a skin-tight, bright red dress. Alfie's right hand was under her dress, his left in the small of her back, her miniscule crimson G-string looped accusingly around his wrist.

It took five seconds before the silence broke, shattered by the sound of a 100 flashlights popping. The photographers, stirred into frenzied activity at the sight of Alfie in action, snapped away viciously like a group of hungry crocodiles presented with an unexpected evening meal.

Oh shit, thought Abe horrified. He's in full spotlight now. No chance of escape.

From behind the model's shoulder, Alfie, who must have been all but blinded by his reception committee, smiled agreeably as he relinquished his hold on the model to straighten his tie and adjust his open cuffs before striding out into the lobby, suave, handsome and confident. Abe watched impressed in spite of himself as Alfie with an uninhibited flourish passed Larry, who was standing open-mouthed and frozen to the spot in the doorway of the suite, handing him the offending piece of underwear.

'It must be awfully hot in here Larry. You look a little flushed,' he said loudly and with an undisguised wink.

Larry laughed nervously as he stuffed the G-string into the pocket of his tailored jacket, his face vermilion. Blinking rapidly but without a backward glance he followed Alfie into the conference room just as the terrified model pressed the door close button and disappeared.

Perhaps a psychiatrist would describe what I'm doing as a form of self-torture, thought Abe morosely as the flashbulbs continued to explode, blinding him while his head pulsated in time to the whirr of the camera motors. Why else would I stand in the shadows and watch a man indulging in an obscene display of self-promotion? Although after his unbelievable entrance what occurs in the next half hour might even be beyond Larry's mediating skills. There's no way they'll focus on the film after the mind-blowing stunt Alfie's just pulled.

He was leaning against the wall at the rear of the room, the cold white plaster refreshingly cool against his back. Some 20 metres in front of him on a spotlit stage surrounded by life-size posters of their film, the four stars of *His Cold Blood* sat with their director and the seemingly unflappable Larry Woods like half a dozen fresh-faced victims before a tribe of blood-hungry cannibals.

Alfie's arrival on the stage had been greeted with wolf whistles and cheers that had stopped immediately the first question was asked.

'Alfie, you have come a long way in eight years. You have given us romance, sci-fi, historical drama and now your first thriller,' proffered an immaculately dressed journalist. 'You are a world-wide success story. How do you feel about that?'

Larry beamed. Abe and several of the journalists groaned. It sounded less like an enquiry and more like a eulogy. Given the stunt Alfie had pulled in the lift, it had to have been a plant.

'Naturally I feel elated. Of course I'm indebted to producer David Palmer,' Alfie replied as though he were at an award ceremony and not a press conference. 'He backed my first project. Who knows, without him I would still be pacing the streets today, looking for the cash.'

This was followed by a general murmur of approval and several other questions relating to Alfie's brilliant and unblemished career.

'What is it exactly that enables you to cross all genres?' asked a researcher for the television show Film '80.

'I have a strong visual style and an understanding of art,' replied Alfie quickly.

'I would agree and yet it is directly because of your strong visual style that critics accuse you of being cine-literate, a moneymaker pure and simple, with *no* knowledge of art. What would you say in response to such criticism?' he continued.

'I am very much aware of my critics though I take it you are not one of them.'

'Indeed, I am not,' he replied with a wry smile, ignoring the tittering that had broken out around him.

'I would agree that my films put a smile on the face of my bank manager, which is great news for Hollywood. However they are wrong to assume that I have no knowledge of art. My films push the boundaries of filmmaking. They are contemporary masterpieces, which is presumably why some of the more established critics refuse to accept them as art.'

And so it continued, Larry fully in control, expertly orchestrating questions from the reliable journalists in the crowd and Alfie fielding them with panache and intelligence until a pretty, serious-faced young

18

reporter whose mousy coloured hair was pulled off her face by a black velvet Alice band, was given the floor.

'Do you often indulge in sex in public places?' she asked coolly, her face dead straight. A cacophony of laughter filled the room.

'Venetia, we are here to discuss *His Cold Blood*,' interrupted Larry quickly, angry at being caught off guard.

Abe groaned and buried his head in his hands. It was the question he'd expected at last.

'Was that your girlfriend or just some *professional* you picked up for the ride?' continued Venetia.

'No comment,' barked Larry, his cool turning icy as he glared ferociously in Venetia Johnson's direction. 'And I would appreciate it if you stopped wasting everybody's time.'

Abe looked to Alfie expecting to see an expression of horror, embarrassment, regret ... anything other than the smile he was flagrantly brandishing with what appeared to be genuine pride.

What was he thinking of? he wondered, astonished. Tomorrow the tabloids would be full of pictures of the explicit sideshow. Did Alfie not realise how damaging that would be for his career? Over the next few weeks, journalists would trawl through his life exposing every sordid detail for the gratification of the general newspaper-buying public.

'OK Larry,' said Venetia sweetly. 'I have a question for Buzz.'

'Yeah,' Buzz blurted out, roused from his stupor, flashing an instant A-list Hollywood smile at the glamorous young *Express* reporter.

'Are the rumours true that you and Mary indulged in a passionate affair on the set of *His Cold Blood?*' she asked.

'No comment.' Larry rolled his eyes. Buzz stopped smiling and cast a nervous glance in Mary's direction.

'Would that be because Mary is happily married?' continued Venetia, who was clearly enjoying herself.

'Alexander Baker. Yes,' said Larry pointedly.

'Alfie, you are often bracketed with Steven Spielberg because the films you make are commercial successes. Many critics would have us believe that because your films have such broad public appeal, you will never win an Oscar. Do you think this a fair comment?'

'Absolutely not.' Alfie glowered in the esteemed critic's direction. 'A comment like that suggests popular films are in some way inferior. I strongly believe that I push the limits of filmmaking, that my films move people. I have already been nominated for two Oscars. I see no reason why I shouldn't win one in the future.'

'So I presume you find the tag *Movie Brat* abhorrent?'

'Next question!' prompted Larry brusquely.

'Your professional . . . in the lift . . . was she any good?' teased a *Sun* journalist. 'Great tits, I'll give you that! I hope you got your money's worth.'

'Please!' exclaimed Larry.

A general muttering punctuated with much laughter broke out amongst the journalists. Abe, from his place at the back of the room, could not detect even the tiniest flicker of shame on Alfie's face. In fact, thought Abe, he was grinning inanely. He must have known he would be seen. Perhaps he had planned the whole sordid stunt. But why? What could he gain from it? A savaging from the tabloids! Is that what he wanted? Was he simply growing bored of all the adulation?

'We've heard rumours that you are about to direct a film called *The Ark,* your first attempt at action adventure. Is this true?' asked an eager young journalist at the back of the room.

'Yes it is,' confirmed Alfie happily.

'Can you tell us the plot?'

'It's set in Egypt and Turkey. The comic style hero, a leather-jacketed, globetrotting explorer armed with a kukri, is appointed leader of an expedition from Egypt to Mt Ararat in search of Noah's Ark.'

'Is it also true that Katherine Katz is to star in the movie?'

'Yes.'

'And presumably the budget will be huge.'

'Presumably,' repeated Alfie.

'And you won't have the worry of G-strings with Katherine,' said the *Sun* journalist. 'It's well known that Miss Katz waltzes through life unhampered by the constraints of underwear.'

The room erupted into laughter once more.

'Ladies and Gentlemen, I'm sorry we have run out of time,' said Larry abruptly, bringing an end to the proceedings.

Four

Life is good, thought Alfie as he stepped from the taxi onto the pavement outside Abe Cunningham's flat, inhaling a deep breath of the cool September evening air.

In two days' time he would be on a plane heading for Egypt to make another film and this one was going to be special. Pushing boundaries, that's what he'd been doing these last eight years. It was what he was all about. And yet *The Ark* was his boldest idea yet.

He sauntered towards the iron staircase that led to Abe's basement flat, then paused, one hand on the railing and stared up at the star-dusted sky feeling almost supernaturally confident. 'This is it,' he whispered. 'The big one. The movie to launch me into the firmament.'

Preparation for *The Ark* had kept him busy for the last six months. As well as scouting for locations, he'd been hard at work developing the script. He'd storyboarded the movie, worked out the camera angles and, after days locked in a small, airless room with his stunt co-ordinator, had meticulously planned a series of action sequences, hair-raising stunts, pyrotechnics and thrilling special effects. Then, moving heaven and earth, he'd secured Katherine Katz, arguably the most celebrated star of the moment, in the lead role. Even before one frame had been shot, his film was being heralded as the potential blockbuster of the year.

He smiled another self-satisfied smile and was just about to rap his fisted hand on Abe's faded blue front door when he noticed what a terrible state of disrepair it was in. What appeared to be a urine stain in the corner at once hinted that perhaps his friend had fallen on hard times.

Alfie sighed. Abe was an outstanding director. There could be no denying that. It was his business skills that were to blame. He ran his own theatre but instead of putting on plays with wide commercial appeal he preferred those that had great intellectual significance.

21

Although brilliant in substance, these productions did not attract large audiences. His theatre wasn't making money and consequently neither was Abe.

Disturbed by his train of thought, Alfie sighed again and sank down on the bottom step. The stone felt cold and damp beneath the fabric of his jeans but he remained seated, his head in his hands.

Abe had been the most loyal of friends from the moment they'd met at Cambridge. He'd discovered Alfie was an orphan and, like the Good Samaritan he was, he had insisted on taking him home for Christmas. His mother Mary had accepted him with open arms. And his gothic-looking sister, Imogen ... what was it she'd said before she'd fucked him under their Christmas tree? Ah yes ... 'I love your eyes. You will have beautiful children.' Happy days.

He stood up. Bugger, he thought, rapping loudly and briskly on Abe's front door.

One painful minute later it opened with a pathetic creak to reveal Abe's drawn, gaunt face. In the low lamplight of the flat, his friend's pale skin was luminous, ghost-like. His usually thin cheeks looked hollow to the point of emaciation.

'Oh, it's you,' said Abe, his tone projecting both surprise and disappointment.

'Who were you expecting?' asked Alfie jovially. 'Father bloody Christmas?'

'That would have been good,' admitted Abe.

'Well sorry to disappoint you my dear friend. You'll have to make do with me, so be a good chap and let me in. I've got a gorgeous bottle of Margaux about my person. Looks like you could do with a drink.' Determined not to be deterred by Abe's lack of enthusiasm, he pushed breezily past him into the tiny, sparsely furnished sitting-room. Two mangy, uncovered armchairs sat on a worn woollen rug in front of a small television that was perched precariously on a dilapidated table in the centre of the room. There was a larger, more substantial table to one side with a broken jointed reading lamp on it and a pile of much thumbed copies of *The Stage*. The wallpaper was peeling from the damp, bare walls, which explained the rank, fetid smell that permeated the room. Shit, he thought appalled. This place is not a home. It's a hovel.

'Are you sure I can't lend you some cash, mate?' he asked carelessly. 'You need the decorators badly.'

'No,' Abe replied tersely, closing the front door behind him with a loud bang. 'Thanks.'

'It's just ...'

'I said NO.'

Alfie took a pace backwards, startled. This was not the Abe Cunningham he knew. Where was the ready smile, the brilliant wit?

'Abe, what's up?' he asked him as he tried vainly to catch his friend's eye that appeared to be focusing on the dog-eared corner of his threadbare floor rug. 'You seem out of sorts.'

Surprised by Alfie's genuine concern, Abe's face relaxed into a half smile. And he looked up. 'Sorry. Just a little tired.'

'You want to take a bit more care of yourself,' said Alfie kindly.

'That's easy for you to say,' mumbled Abe, staring down at his hands.

'You could get out a bit more, perhaps. Invest in a girlfriend, that sort of thing.'

'Invest! Invest!' said Abe sharply. Alfie jumped a second time. 'You don't invest in women. Sorry, *real* people don't invest in women.'

'OK, OK. Poor choice of words but honestly Abe, I mean it, I really think you should get laid.'

'And that's your answer to everything isn't it?'

'Most things,' he answered with a sage nod of the head. 'I find it helps, certainly.'

'And so very easy since your face became as famous as your films. I mean you're a celebrated hero, a household name. Stunning young actresses and models are desperate to be seen with *Britain's latest golden boy*,' he sneered.

'There's something in what you say,' said Alfie good-humouredly, though he was finding Abe's resentment difficult to ignore. In fact his continued sniping was beginning to grate on his nerves.

'Only the great Alfie Macbeth could get away with the little stunt you pulled at the press conference for *His Cold Blood.*'

'Steady on Abe. Let's keep everything in perspective here.'

'Your entrance was the biggest piece of exhibitionism I've seen in a long time.'

'You obviously haven't been getting out much,' retorted Alfie.

'Your head is so far up your arse you can't tell whether it's night or day.'

'Now hold on a minute. The press had a field day,' he remonstrated. 'At my expense.'

'Of course they did,' said Abe, his eyes flashing angrily. 'And the papers flew off the shelves. Not the best kind of publicity for your new film, as I'm sure Larry would agree, but publicity none the less and lots of it and, oh my word, what a surprise, *His Cold Blood* soars to number one. For Christ's sake Alfie, it's like you planned the damn thing.'

'Is that why you're pissed off?' asked Alfie, relieved.

Abe said nothing but merely stared at him in disbelief.

Alfie smiled. 'Bit of a stunner, don't you agree? And a real laugh, too. Tell you what, Abe. I'll introduce you. She'd do you the world of good.'

'Are you so high on success that you've waved goodbye to morality?' asked Abe quietly.

'That is bullshit!'

'Why else would you sleep your way through such a gruesome array of B-list actresses and models then? I can't open a paper these days without seeing your ugly mug grinning at me, your arm draped around another mindless, nameless beauty.'

'Because, my old friend, they are so easy to take advantage of. They smile and they are eager to please,' he replied, digging his friend in the ribs.

'You're nothing more than a Tinseltown playboy. You wade through filth, Alfie. Admit it.'

'You're jealous!' exclaimed Alfie, although taken aback by Abe's continued onslaught.

'No I'm not. I'm worried for you if you must know. It's as though you feel you're beyond morality, suspended in a star-lit dimension, which, of course, being of your own creation, is lawless. One day you'll be held accountable.'

'Spare me the philosophy, Abe. That's bollocks! The press worship me. They are fanatical about every breath I take.'

'In all the years I've known you I've never criticised you Alfie but I honestly think that you are displaying all the signs of a weak man. It's not surprising really. I mean you were quite literally chucked into stardom like a grenade into a crowd where you, duly and predictably, exploded. But fame has corrupted you. Face it Alfie, your life bears all the hallmarks of Sisyphean futility.'

'Oh how wrong you are, Abe,' Alfie said, disdainfully. 'I'm not the guy pushing the ball up the hill. I'm the one enjoying the free ride down. I'm having the time of my life. Now shut up, there's a good chap and get me a couple of glasses and a corkscrew. This bottle of vintage wine is going to waste.'

One hour later and feeling totally dispirited, Alfie made his excuses and left. Try as he might he had been unable to relieve Abe of the shroud of despair that he'd draped himself in, transforming him from lovable clown to laboured cynic. He'd never seen him depressed, for that was what he appeared to be. Never known him as critical.

Sure, it's true that fame has altered me, he reasoned as he flagged down a taxi. It hasn't corrupted me as Abe claims. It has hardened me. And that has been absolutely necessary, a conscious decision to bury my sentimental approach to life.

Naturally there had been times when he had stopped to think what his mild-mannered parents might have thought had they been alive. These occasions however had been rare, the guilt he'd felt insignificant. If he was to succeed, he'd told himself time and time again, he had to be bullish, single-minded, determined. There was no room for wimps in this business. Abe in his dark, dank flat was living proof of that. Anyway he was, he truly believed, a better person for it. As his career had escalated, his gentle manner had been replaced by a hardness that formed the outer shell of his being. Alfie Macbeth has skin of steel, a colleague had once remarked to the press. That had pleased Alfie. He liked the idea that however hard the blow, he would not crack.

I am, he thought as he sank into the warmth of the taxi, invincible.

Five

The set was humming with activity. In front of him the dolly grip was finishing laying the railings that would guide the camera during the tracking shots he had scheduled for the morning. The man's face was red with his exertions. It obviously hadn't been easy laying the tracks in the sand. Alfie nodded his approval and received a huge grin in return. From behind him came the sound of the generator being fired up. He turned round, shading his eyes from the sun to see the best boy carting the heavy lights into position, the many snake-like coils of cable trailing behind him in the sand. He sniffed the air. It was heavy with heat and dust. There was not a breath of wind.

Just as well, thought Alfie, a sandstorm would only delay matters further and I can't afford that.

Frustrated, he wandered towards the tables, director's chairs and large canvas umbrellas that the caterers had arranged outside the stars' air-conditioned trailers, giving the appearance of a mobile cafe. In the blistering heat of midday this will be a welcome oasis, he mused as he sat down stiffly on the chair bearing his name. In front of him he caught sight of the one labelled, *Katherine Katz*.

Another fifteen minutes and she will be officially late, he thought as he yanked back the loose cuffs of his pale blue cotton shirt to study the Tag Heuer on his wrist. It was 7.45am and already hot. By midday yesterday, as he oversaw the finishing touches to the set, the sun blazing down from a cloudless azure sky had scorched the sand, engulfing the desert in heat so intense Alfie had felt as though he were standing in a convection oven.

He kicked angrily at the sand with a battered brown desert boot. He needed to get on but that was not possible until Katherine Katz made her grand entrance. The crew had been around for hours setting up for the first day of filming and the last member of the cast had arrived at least 30 minutes earlier. But Katherine Katz, superstar and prima donna, was nowhere to be seen.

He barked an order to the clapper-loader who was dawdling around the caterers' trailer. At the sound of Alfie's voice he stood to attention, smiled sheepishly, then scampered off toward the cameraman, his clapperboard under his arm. Alfie looked after him, approvingly. To direct was to command. He'd realised that early on in his career. Respect from the cast and the crew was everything. He would make it crystal clear that he was in charge and that he knew how to budget time. Tonight the sunset was due at 17:34 and he would make damn sure that the actors were in place for the scene by 17.32. That is if Katherine ever showed up. Where the hell was she? This was taking the piss. Time on location was money. His impatience, like the patch of sweat on the pale blue shirt on his back, was growing as every second ticked by. If he didn't get rolling soon, he'd have his producer breathing down his neck. That would be a first, he thought, as he glanced over at the lighting crew who had huddled under a lone and bedraggled palm tree, desperate for shade.

Alfie closed his eyes, trying to compose himself. It had seemed such a brilliant idea to sign her. Big star meant big money. The piece of the equation he'd forgotten was her accompanying ego. Katherine Katz had arrived on celluloid in a blaze of glory, her face loomed down large on her public on billboards around the globe and last month *Time* had declared her *The Most Desired Woman* of the year.

Christ, he thought, as the penny with a loud clang dropped into his brain, the next two months are going to be pure hell.

'Hello, Mr Macbeth. I'm Katherine Katz,' came a quiet voice from behind him. 'May I say what an honour it is to be working with you?'

Bristling with controlled rage Alfie turned slowly round to face her. But as his eyes came to rest on her gorgeous form he realised that nothing had prepared him for the havoc her actual presence would wreak on his senses, like a pop star walking into a room full of fans that turn mad with hysteria. It was her beauty that hit him, right between his thighs. Not the saccharine beauty of some overly made-up beauty queen, or the fake beauty of a model dressed for the catwalk. No this was real, mind-blowing beauty, the type confined to an exceptional few that steals your breath from your lungs and leaves you gasping.

Around him the set had ground to a silent halt. All eyes had turned to stare. She was moderately tall, about 5' 7" with long, perfectly groomed hair the colour of raw sienna that matched her eyes. Her face, that featured high cheekbones, a bee-stung mouth and a tiny nose with a fine sprinkling of freckles, seemed to Alfie an impossible work of art. Her scantily clad figure, an array of sublime curves, was perfect. Protruding from the skimpiest pair of white shorts he'd ever seen, her tanned, slim legs looked endless. The crew, like their director, were captivated. Alfie could not help but wonder whether they assumed she was knickerless?

Pull yourself together, man! he screamed inwardly, as the piquant, musky scent of her body drifted towards him. He cleared his throat that had become a little dry and thrust back his shoulders.

'You're late,' he barked, glowering down at her in a macho attempt to assert his authority. 'If you want to continue to keep a place in my team, you had better look sharp and get punctual.'

There was a collective intake of breath, the sound loud like a typhoon sweeping through the streets of a beleaguered city, followed by an eerie quiet as Katherine walked off to make-up, meek as a lamb.

*

It was Sunday and Larry was sitting at his desk, attempting to wade through a *Sunday Times* article on the advent of video and its effect on the cinema.

It would be a fair observation should anyone wish to make it, he thought as he struggled with the article, that it has taken a whole month for the aftermath of Alfie's shenanigans in the lift at The Hilton to die down. He shook his head, recalling the memory. Shenanigans, perhaps, is the wrong word. Debacle, performance, rebellion might be more appropriate. Or folly! Now that is spot on. He groaned again, burying his face in his hands, his elbows resting on *The Sun*day *Times*. 'And after all we've achieved in eight years,' he moaned out loud.

Alfie's second film had generated record revenue at the box office on its opening weekend. That had caused a furore of epic proportions. It had seemed to Larry that every single journalist the world over had wanted a piece of the young director – requests for interviews, transparencies, black and white stills, items of clothing, strands of hair, anything to do with Alfie Macbeth. And Larry had planned every appearance, every interview and photographic opportunity with the necessary caution, precision and flair to ensure his image remained intact.

Now it seems he is determined to run out of control, he thought ruefully.

Moneymaking Playboy! Hadn't that been the headline in *The Mirror* the day after the Hilton experience? Which is a shame because more than anything, Alfie longs to be taken seriously as a filmmaker. And it's true that, like a fine wine, Alfie is maturing with each film he makes. I

can only hope that his critics will one day wake up and taste the
difference

Just over four weeks had passed since his quiet word to Alfie,
warning him to be careful after his Houdini-like escape.

'You got away with it this time, Alfie, though God knows how. Put a
foot wrong again and I can assure you that the press will come down on
you like the biggest pile of bricks you have ever seen. You'll be lucky to
come out alive!'

He only hoped Alfie had been listening. Still, for the moment at least,
he was certain that he had nothing to worry about. Alfie was filming in
Egypt and therefore, for the time being, he was safe from the press. Not
only that but when Alfie was filming he was totally focused. There was
no time in his nineteen-hour day for frivolity of any kind, beyond
keeping the members of his cast and crew comfortable.

The phone rang.

'Larry Woods Associates.'

'Larry. Thank God you're there. It's Minnie. Minnie Cooper.'

'Hi Minnie. What's up?' he asked his unit publicist as breezily as
possible, though his heartbeat, in response to the anxiety in her voice,
had begun to accelerate. 'Everything OK in Egypt?'

'Alfie Macbeth is soft on his female lead,' replied Minnie, rushing
straight to the point.

This bold pronouncement from the otherwise taciturn Minnie Cooper
sent his heart into overdrive. 'Are you sure you've got this right?' he
asked, trying his damnedest to appear calm.

'No, it's true. He can't take his eyes off her. And I'm not the only one
who's noticed. There's a lot of giggling and nudging going on whenever
they're together.'

'I bet that annoys him.'

'I don't know about that. He's done nothing to assuage the gossip on
the set. He hasn't backed off. In fact, if anything I would say that he was
engaging her in conversation more and more.'

'And that is your opinion on the matter,' he replied a little testily.

'Well, yes, put like that, I suppose it is.'

'Right!'

'I'm sorry, Larry. I just thought you should know. In case . . .'

'OK. OK. Very good. I'm sure you're just doing your job but Minnie,
make sure none of this gets out. I do not want the press involved in such
gossip. They'd go crazy at the news and well, Alfie would blow a gasket.'

'Don't worry, Larry. This is a secure set.'

Trembling, Larry put down the phone, his mind reeling. He took a
deep breath and closed his eyes but the image of Katherine Katz and

Alfie Macbeth wandering hand in hand across the desert sands, like the stars in a sodding Bounty advert, flashed into his brain.

No. This is taking celebrity too far, he decided. Alfie can't mess around with stars of Katherine's quality. If and when he ditches her there'll be a public outcry, the like of which hasn't been seen since the Beatles split up. He groaned recalling the excitement he'd felt when Alfie had told him the news that Katherine Katz was to star in *The Ark*.

'The publicity you'll get with her on board is going to be great,' he'd told Alfie. 'I'm going to get started on it right away, before production begins. I've heard *Vanity Fair* is desperate to secure an exclusive with her. I'll make sure my unit publicist hones in on the right journalists to bring to the set. And by the time you get into post production, the articles will be writing themselves.'

So why the stunt, first of all, followed by the trophy girl? he wondered helplessly before reminding himself that what his unit publicist had told him was probably pure fantasy. I mean, for Christ's sake, let's put it another way, what on earth would Katherine Katz see in Alfie Macbeth? Yes, he told himself as he folded the newspaper, this was pure fantasy, born of the boredom of an isolated film crew.

Six

For the third day in succession, Abe lay on his bed in the dark, motionless save for the occasional flickering of his eyelids. Behind the mouldy, splintered skirting board, the mice scratched away at the rotten wood.

Abe's head, which ached almost as much as his stomach burned, groaned on and on, repeating its weary mantra over and over, tirelessly, like the speaking clock on the end of a phone line. He had eaten nothing since his self-imposed incarceration. Not a drop of water had passed his lips. He was fast approaching a delusory state. That was why it now seemed that the mice were talking to him, telling him to take the gigantic leap into the abyss.

And then he'd caught a glimpse of the man in black. It was he who was whispering demonically, telling him to jump? A black-hearted man, knife poised, reeking of death? A black man singing softly?

Was there someone in the room? Alfie?

'Alfie? Alfie?' he called out weakly. No. No. Alfie wasn't there.

There was no one there, only darkness. Coal-singed blackness. Funereal cold. It surrounded him, obscured him until the bed he lay on in the black-locked room took the form of a charcoal sketch hanging on a wall in an eerie chamber of his mind.

'Get a grip, Abe,' he whispered as the tears poured painfully down his sunken cheeks like blood from an open wound. 'Get a grip. You're not finished yet.'

*

It was unnaturally hot even for Egypt. The mercury had hit 45 degrees at midday. During the morning one of the runners had been hurried to hospital suffering from dehydration but that was nothing in comparison to the incident with the monkey. One of a pair had escaped from its cage

31

and had found it's way into Marjorie Wells' trailer. It had sat on the co-star's head as she slept, searching her hair for nits, Alfie had presumed. She had woken to find the primate's yellow eyes staring solemnly into hers and she had screamed. There had been much debate about who was the most terrified but, as his assistant director had so eloquently explained to Alfie, Marjorie had gone bananas. An hour later and she was still being counselled to recovery in Katherine's trailer from which she refused to move.

Infuriated but resigned to the chaos, Alfie called a halt on the day's proceedings. It was only 4pm but he was ahead of schedule. I could do with a break, he thought as he leapt into a jeep and headed off to his hotel.

He opened the door to his room, turned on the air-con and pulled off his baseball cap, noticing the salty tidemark of sweat that stained the fawn coloured crown. He untied his battered desert boots, removed them and his socks to reveal two white feet at the bottom of two dirt-encrusted legs. Like his clothes, his boots were damp. He yanked off his heavy khaki shorts that had begun to chaff his inner thigh noticing as he did so an unpleasant smell. He sniffed his T-shirt. It reeked of stale body odour.

He wandered into the bathroom, stepped into the shower cubicle and turned the temperature dial to cold. He braced himself for the shock but the jet of water that shot out with a loud clunk was tepid. Relieved, he sighed with pleasure and told himself to be more tolerant. Marjorie obviously did not feel at ease in the presence of monkeys. She had many assets, though right at that moment he felt hard pressed to think of any. She was such an odd looking woman, the features on her face appeared to have been slapped together in haste, her eyes, nose and mouth an alarming mismatch. Then there was the vastly more annoying fact that her incredibly pale, translucent skin was not suitable to long periods in the sun.

'And yet some muppet had had the brainwave of casting her in a desert movie,' he muttered, frustrated once more.

He snatched at the bottle of shampoo in the soap dish, spilling a little as he squeezed it roughly onto his hand. With unnecessary vigour he attacked his hair, pummelling it as though a week's worth of dirt was lodged in its roots.

It's like the time at Cambridge when I was directing Abe as Romeo, he recalled fondly as he rubbed his scalp. He'd fallen asleep in the sun one afternoon after a particularly liquid lunch, mouth open, dribbling, snoring. Naturally I'd taken a picture. If I'd guessed he would have burned I'd have woken him up. His face was so blistered we couldn't put his make-up on without him screaming. Alfie laughed at the memory. I hope he's feeling better, he thought, remembering the last time they met. I must give him a call soon, check that he's back to his old self again.

Fully refreshed, he stepped out of the shower, his irritation at Marjorie's inadequacies wholly forgotten. He grabbed one of the hotel's coarse white towels and began to dry himself, the fabric rough on his sun-scorched skin. The phone on the small, rickety desk opposite the bed rang. Wrapping the towel around his waist, he wandered over to answer it.

'Hello.'

'Alfie!'

'Hi Larry. Good to hear from you,' he said, grinning at the sound of his friend's voice.

'So what's happening, Alfie?'

'I've wound up for the night and as you rang I was preparing for bed in my delightful hotel room, which, as I think I may have mentioned before, is a ten-mile, bone-rattling jeep ride from the set.'

'Great. And how's filming going?'

'All good. We're bang on schedule. Producer's happy. Stars are coping with the heat, well ... mostly,' he added with a wry smile. 'The last journalist has been and gone. Larry I have to tell you, your publicist has been a revelation. The press that we've allowed on set have behaved impeccably and it's all thanks to her. It's going swimmingly – apart from Marjorie's unfortunate incident with the monkey an hour or so ago but then I suppose these things happen,' he said, his feelings toward Marjorie more charitable now.

'Oh? I'm intrigued.'

'You had to be there,' laughed Alfie. 'Then there are the camels, of course. Why do they have such bad breath?'

'That's excellent,' said Larry, ignoring the question. 'And I gather there's a bit of romance in the air too. That'll be a great notch on your pencil, Alfie!'

'What are we talking about now? Not the camels, I trust.'

'The living goddess, Katherine Katz, she of the come-to-bed eyes, heavenly limbs and pneumatic ...'

'I'm very busy, Larry. I have a demanding schedule to keep,' Alfie interrupted crossly.

Larry, however, seemed intent on needling him. 'But filming is going well. You said yourself that you are due to finish production on schedule. And this is, of course, entirely due to the fact that you have flogged the crew into submission. Come on Alfie, there's time for a little romance, surely?'

'With Katherine Katz. Don't be ridiculous, lead actors would be more her style. Besides I haven't got the time or the energy Larry,' he replied tersely, sucking air through his teeth. 'I'm completely fucked after a day's filming. Often I work through the night. It's not like your cushy little desk job. Out here on location we work our balls off. And when I do take an evening off, which is rarely, it's as much as I can do to have a beer with the crew after filming.'

'Right! I see!' Larry said. 'Afraid I can't help you with the camel problem but I suppose you could try cleaning their teeth.'

'Piss off! I've got today's rushes to study.'

Alfie slammed the phone down, fuming. He ripped off his towel and flung it angrily in the direction of the bathroom. Grabbing a pair of jeans from the back of the chair, he pulled them on roughly. He picked up a crumpled white shirt off the floor and forced it over his head without undoing the buttons then, slipping his bare feet into his loafers, he stomped out of his hotel bedroom to the bar.

I need a drink. No, I need several drinks. How could Larry be so flippant? Really it's preposterous. Where did he get the idea? he wondered, suddenly recalling the many conversations he'd instigated with his leading lady over the past few weeks.

'Minnie Cooper,' he muttered, spitting out the publicist's name venomously as he headed towards the bar. 'I shall have words with dizzy Minnie Cooper the moment I set eyes on her.'

'Large scotch with ice,' he told the eager barman as he perused the establishment for familiar faces. The wicker tables and chairs that normally creaked under the weight of a full house were empty. Marjorie must be holding things up, he thought, relieved. He caught the barman's eye. 'Make it a double,' he added with a sigh.

After his second double a certain confidence began to take hold of him. Perhaps the idea wasn't so ludicrous after all. Beautiful women – models and fans – flung themselves at him regularly. He'd got used to that sort off attention. It was part and parcel of being famous, a far cry from his barren days as an undergraduate. At Cambridge he'd been painfully shy. He'd certainly fancied lots of his fellow undergraduates but he'd never had the confidence to ask them out, terrified that they'd say no. He'd been truly grateful to Imogen Cunningham for taking it upon herself to relieve him of his virginity that Christmas at Abe's house. Even so, she hadn't become his girlfriend. In fact he'd never had a proper relationship. As Abe had so rightly pointed out, he'd made a habit of appearing in public with a different nameless beauty by his side. It was fun and it was easy. None of them had been the stars of his films though, that was out of the question.

He took another swig of his whisky, draining his glass. Why is that? he pondered anxiously. Is it a question of respect? . . . Possibly . . . Or some sort of inferiority complex on my part? Hmm, that's sounds more likely. However ... *Katherine,* the star in question here, does seem to like me. We've formed a great working relationship these last few weeks. She's shown me a great deal of respect and has accepted all my directions with a generous smile. We've had the odd drink together and I've got to know her a bit but let's face it, she's impossibly beautiful, a dark, modern-day version of Julie Christie with freckles. I have to admit I've been so knocked out by her beauty I've fallen completely under her spell. Why even now just thinking about her I can picture myself as a lascivious cartoon character, my tongue lolling out the side of my mouth, eyes glazed.

But hell, why not give it a go? I'm a good-looking guy, he reminded himself with renewed enthusiasm. I'm photogenic and in pretty good shape for a man of my age. And we get on well. It would be idiotic not to take the opportunity to at least invite her to dinner. I'll ring her from the privacy of my room. That way, if she turns me down, I won't make a spectacle of myself. Nobody will be any the wiser. If she says yes ...

'You are a big star, Katherine,' Alfie told her, appalling himself with his hammy use of words. They were sipping vintage Bollinger, reclining in luxurious leather chairs in the Justine restaurant in Cairo where he'd flown her for the evening, waiting to be called to their table. 'But this film could launch you heavenwards.'

'I'm not so sure, Alfie. I think you may be getting an over-inflated opinion of me,' she answered demurely, staring at his groin.

'Oh I don't think so, Katherine,' he said, clearing his throat and crossing his legs, wondering if she'd intended that as a pun? 'And I think perhaps you may have a slight inkling yourself.'

'No, really!' she insisted, but the knowing smile on her glossy lips gave her away. Alfie was impressed. Encouraged, he blundered on.

'My dear, I have big plans for you.'

'I can see that!' she purred. Alfie felt a tingle travel the full length of his spine. He shuddered before he could control himself. Get a grip, he thought, shifting in his seat. He hoped she hadn't noticed.

'You're very different away from the set, Alfie,' she said, licking her lips. 'Not so hard, definitely more congenial. I am beginning to think you may have a soft centre.' She was looking intently at Alfie now. Her brown, almond eyes wide open, her wet lips temptingly parted, leading him on.

'Katherine, I would like to apologise for your first day on set. I treated you shabbily.'

'Not at all. You have been lovely. So attentive.' And as she said this she lightly brushed his hand.

Seven

It was a cold Monday afternoon in late February. Pretty as a picture postcard this morning, the crisp white snow that had fallen over London the previous night had turned to mushy, gun-metal grey. It lent the capital a dull, depressing air that would have been demoralising to anyone but Alfie whose ebullient mood was resolute. Taking a break from editing *The Ark*, he had decided to pay Larry a visit in his Soho office down the road from his suite to discuss his publicity agenda for the next few months before he jetted off to Australia to shoot his latest film *Tribulation*.

That Alfie relied on Larry 100% was common knowledge. He'd hired him nine years ago after the success of his first film. Media interest in him had seemed to be running out of control and Alfie had realised that to keep his good name intact and his head above water, he would need help. Larry was his safety net. He knew that and Larry knew that. Their respect for one another was mutual. Though confident in his dealings with the press, Alfie relied on Larry to map out the route down which he would travel. This was the best way. Unlike Alfie, Larry knew which journalists to encourage and which to avoid.

The man is obviously perverse, thought Alfie, as he climbed the four flights of stairs to Larry's office, the white walls to the right of him eclipsed by posters of movies framed in shiny stainless steel. Why else would he inhabit an office on the top floor in a block without a lift? And if it belonged to anyone other than Larry, mused Alfie as he knocked on the black painted door, it would be referred to as a lair with its state-of-the-art black desk, suite of black leather with zebra-striped and leopard-print cushions, fully-stocked bar, TV and stereo. In fact all that's missing is a strategically placed magic button that releases a double bed slowly and silently from the wall. Utter nonsense of course, he thought smiling at his friend as he opened the door, arms wide in welcome, because Larry is a man who keeps his trousers firmly zipped.

'This is great publicity for *The Ark* and my forthcoming film,' said Alfie, grinning as he caught sight of the day's copy of *The Sun* open on Larry's desk. He sauntered across the room, picked up the paper and read the headline TEN THINGS YOU NEVER KNEW ABOUT ALFIE MACBETH!

'You better believe it.' Larry snatched the paper from Alfie. 'My God, if *The Sun* is writing lists about you then you've made it. I never knew your favourite position was the starfish or that you liked your eggs fried.'

'Neither did I,' said Alfie, grabbing the paper back. 'It's cowgirl.'

'Pardon?'

'And I always scramble my eggs. And those are *not* mine,' he added horrified, pointing to a model pictured in what was supposed to be an imitation of his underwear.

'Really?' asked Larry, raising his eyebrows. 'I imagined you always wore Union Jack boxers! But you are punctual and you do wear a Tag Heuer!'

'Yeah! Everybody knows that. They pay me to.'

Larry laughed and picked up *The Mirror*, its headline CHEERS ALFIE simple in its offer of congratulation for Alfie's forthcoming marriage. He, along with every newspaper reader the world over, had been stunned when two months after his return from Egypt, Alfie and Katherine had announced their engagement. The papers referred to it as a whirlwind romance. To Larry, the coupling of these words was an understatement. *An act of God* would, he felt, be more appropriate.

Bound up in the romance of the story, journalists meanwhile, were having a field day. Daily the papers were loaded with articles featuring the happy couple. It was the depth of interest that amazed Larry. This latest development in the life of Alfie Macbeth was not a subject confined to the news and celebrity pages. Fashion editors' had jumped on the bandwagon detailing which designers the couple favoured, diarists revealed whom they'd been seen partying with and even the food critics joined in, listing the names of restaurants where they had been spotted dining together.

Larry had seen and known nothing quite like this. Alfie's alliance with Katherine had created a national hysteria on a scale normally aligned to Princess Diana. He was living his life in a giant bubble, the daily focus of everybody's attention. Yet, fact or fiction, he appeared to love every minute of it.

'I can only congratulate you, Alfie. You are a publicist's dream,' said Larry, his eyes twinkling. He slapped Alfie on the back. 'Sit down and I'll get Audrey to bring us some coffee.'

'Marvellous,' said Alfie, landing in his chair with a squeak of leather.

Audrey, Larry's secretary, was a fairly formal, sensibly dressed twenty-four-year old, pleasant to look at but by no means attractive. She had a neat little room off to the left of Larry's. Alfie considered her the mother figure to Larry's little boy character. She was tidy and efficient. She always knew exactly where Larry was, where he should be and made sure she could always contact him whatever he was doing. Together they made a great team.

'Thank you Audrey, you are an absolute gem,' Alfie said, taking the coffee that she handed him.

'Congratulations on your engagement Alfie,' enthused Audrey.

'Are you still planning to get married in Australia?' Larry asked him.

'Yup. We're flying out a week before I start filming *Tribulation* to get married barefoot on the beach.'

'Very romantic,' cooed Audrey.

'And your honeymoon?' asked Larry.

'I suggested we spend our honeymoon in a tent in the rainforest like love-struck savages.'

'You didn't?' chorused Larry and Audrey together.

'Of course I did.'

'What on earth was Katherine's reaction?' asked Larry.

'Let's just say we harbour different fantasies. Anyway, I've since booked the exclusive and very luxurious Lizard Island. It's a stunning place.'

'Lucky lady,' said Audrey. 'But I have to admit your engagement took me rather by surprise.'

'Audrey!' exclaimed Larry.

'I'm sorry but I always thought of Alfie as the happy bachelor type,' continued Audrey, never one to be deterred from her opinions.

'That will be all,' admonished Larry, ushering his secretary out of the room. For all his light-heartedness on the subject, he felt exhausted. This latest announcement of Alfie's that had appeared like a genie out of thin air had shocked him. It had been unlike Alfie to make such a spontaneous and impulsive decision. Though he was relieved that the relationship hadn't ended acrimoniously, he was unsure why Alfie seemed determined to make it permanent. He was doubtful of his motives and concerned about the outcome. Sure the story was like manna from heaven as far as the press were concerned but did Alfie really know what he was doing? Marriage was a huge commitment in itself but a celebrity marriage was about as hard as it could get. He was concerned for Alfie as a friend but as his publicist, his finely tuned mind foresaw potential disaster and that was something that Alfie, long-time darling of the media, had never had to deal with before. Had he really thought this thing through?

'Audrey's right, of course,' agreed Alfie, placing his coffee on the table beside him. He stretched his arms above his head and yawned. Larry sighed and sat down behind his desk. 'But with Kate it's different. She's not like all the rest.'

'I can imagine,' muttered Larry with a slight shake of his head as he picked up *The Daily Telegraph*. Perhaps he was wrong. Perhaps Alfie knew what he was doing. Perhaps he really was in love. He certainly hoped so.

'There are certain things that I have got used to with Kate,' continued Alfie in an altogether softer tone, like an uncle talking fondly about a favourite niece.

'Oh?' replied Larry, intrigued at this sudden unexpected show of tenderness. This sounded altogether better.

'What I mean, Larry, is that with Kate I feel I've scaled new heights. You know, like conquering Everest without oxygen, that sort of thing.'

'Yes, well, she's a very beautiful, talented woman,' affirmed Larry sagely.

'Not only that!' exclaimed Alfie, relishing the moment. 'She makes the entire Russian gymnastic team look stiff.'

Larry groaned and dropped his paper.

'Just kidding, Larry.' Alfie winked. 'What I meant to say is, I love her. It's as simple as that.'

'That's ... that's ... Alfie I'm delighted for you both, I really am,' declared Larry, leaping to his feet to shake Alfie by the hand.

'You hopeless old romantic,' replied Alfie with a grin.

Tuesday 8 May

*I used to lie awake and watch her sleep, silent, motionless, a tranquil
smile on her pretty lips, one arm bent and raised, both legs folded to
the left, her dark blonde hair strewn about the white cotton pillow save
for a few strands that fell across her face. Or lying on her side,
seemingly breathless, one arm hooked over my chest, the smell of our
love on her buttery brown skin half-covered by a sheet. And I thought
then how warm, enchanting and content this perfect being was even
while she dreamed. But she won't remember that at all.*

*And memories. She kept them in a biscuit tin. Lengths of ribbon from
presents I had wrapped, postcards, matchboxes, hastily scribbled notes
I'd written, three champagne corks, a pebble from a beach, a thistle
from a field, rose petals, a half-filled jam jar of white coral sand, a torn
and crumpled paper napkin from a picnic by the lake. These were her
memories, her meaningful things, trinkets, tokens of her happiness
stored away in a brightly coloured tin, a picture of an English cottage
on the lid.*

*I have no such tin though I have memories. Free as a bird, there
wasn't a cage on earth that could contain her spirit. She would not,
could not be controlled although I never even thought to try. She was
independent, fiercely so. And passionate, positive, devoted to her many
dreams, not one of them too great to conquer. And she was always
right. She really was, except one time. And that was on the day she said
she thought she loved me.*

But she was wrong.

*I saw him first, down by the lake, alone. He had his back to me. Bent
at the waist, he was picking something up that he'd dropped on the
sand in front of him perhaps, knees locked, legs straight. That was
when I had the idea. You see, I hadn't meant to do it. It wasn't planned
or anything. It was as if he was saying. Go on. Here's my arse. A gift.*

*I had my shotgun with me. An over-and-under Beretta SO-6 EELL
12- bore with 28" barrels and a coin finish receiver magnificently
engraved by F. Ferrante. He knew it well. It was the gun I used when
we went shooting together. He often admired it, particularly the gold
inlay Pintails in flight on the left side of the receiver.*

'It's a very expensive gun,' he told me. But I already knew that.

*It was loaded but broken, the two and a half inch cartridges sitting
snug and ready in the shiny metal barrels. Green translucent plastic
tubes full of hundreds of tiny lead balls. The shot.*

I snapped it shut and pushed the safety catch forward. I laughed. He had no idea I was standing some thirty metres behind him pointing a loaded gun at his doubled form. This is too easy, I thought as I lifted the gun to my shoulder. A cinch.

I knew I wouldn't kill him from this distance. That was not my intention. Oh no. All I wanted was to pepper his arse with lead. That would teach him not to tamper with other people's playthings. I wouldn't kill him but I would severely wound him as he had wounded me.

And that is what I did. I ripped the skin off his arrogant butt, filling his bony buttocks with shot. He was prostrate in the sand, whimpering in pain as I turned to leave, his faded blue jeans ripped by the blast, splattered in blood and traces of his scorched, fragmented flesh. I'd nailed his arse.

Now that should render him impotent for a while, I thought.

And so I left him by the lake.

Lacerated, as I had been by him.

Eight

Phoebe collapsed into Larry's sofa with a frustrated groan. She kicked off her unlaced navy Adidas trainers and hoisted her feet onto the oak coffee table. Larry handed her a mug of tea. She took it without thanking him, frowning furiously.

She's scared, he reasoned. It doesn't matter that everyone is telling her not to worry about her Dad. He's in hospital. That's enough. He sat down next to her and placed a comforting hand on her knee. She turned to him and managed a wan smile. It's hardly surprising, he thought as he sipped his tea. She adores her father. She always has, ever since she went to live with him.

Phoebe had been nine years old when her mother and her mother's second marriage had fallen apart simultaneously. Larry never would get over how quickly the screaming, drinking and fights that had been the wallpaper of her world had faded to nothing in Phoebe's mind the moment she became the focus of her father's life.

Alfie had been the most indulgent parent. It was blindingly obvious simply in the way he looked at his daughter that she was his greatest love. That was why he'd tried so hard to protect her from the glare of publicity, shielding her from the paparazzi and journalists who shadowed his every move. *Spirits of the damned,* Phoebe called them.

'They want to photograph you,' Alfie had tried to explain to her, 'Because you are beautiful, just like your mother.'

But Phoebe knew better. 'They are like a pride of lions in search of their prey, hungry for any information to do with Alfie Macbeth,' she'd told Larry on one of her Sunday visits to his Chelsea home. 'And anyway I have no desire to be like *her*. She was an utterly useless parent parading me, her pretty child, like a fashion accessory wherever she went, dumping me with nannies when she was out of the spotlight. Maternal instincts? She didn't have a clue!'

42

'Feeling better?' he asked her, his mind switching back to the present. She nodded silently, unconvincingly.

'I just want some answers,' she whispered.

'Phoebe, darling, I don't know this man, this Thomas Slater. I've never heard of him.'

'No. No. I don't mean about him.'

'So what's the question?'

'What did Dad do?'

'He made brilliant films.'

'Larry. I'm serious. He must have *done* something back then. He didn't make a film for seven years. Why? Nobody has told me the real reason, I'm sure of it. It can't just be because Mum left him. I can't believe that any more.' She shook her head and stared at her hands, despondently.

Larry cleared his throat. He felt nervous, awkward. He knew that Alfie had not wanted to discuss the less savoury aspects of his life with his daughter. As far as he was concerned the past was dead and buried. There was no reason to relive it. He had wanted to start afresh, overhaul his life and that is exactly what he had done. But on the other hand he knew the press had kept a file on Alfie. It was the price he'd paid for his chequered past. These new revelations held no real fear for him and yet his instincts reminded him it was never wise to take anything for granted in this game. Most of the time the press could be relied upon – reporting events, delivering the news, divulging the facts he painstakingly fed them, but the downside to his job was that embellishing the truth, regurgitating the past and pure libellous invention also happened. It was inevitable. Sensational stories were irresistible to editors. They sold papers.

Dejected, Phoebe lay back on his sofa, eyes closed, hands firmly clenched, a mug of hot tea steaming on the table in front of her. He was, he knew, faced with a tricky choice. Should the press decide to dig the dirt then either Phoebe could spend the next few days reading about her father's life in all its gory details or he could begin to break it to her gently now.

A tear trickled slowly down his goddaughter's cheek. Of course she wants some answers, he reasoned. She worships her father. And that is why, sadly, I have no option. I owe her an explanation.

'It's important that I explain the climate of the time,' he began falteringly.

'What! Dry, arid and hot ... an emotional desert?' Phoebe muttered opening her eyes and angrily flicking away the tear.

'NO, no ... no of course not,' said Larry flustered. He paused, unsure of where to begin. Outside, the rain, which had turned to hail, lashed at the tall bay windows, the sound as it clattered onto the glass like hobnail boots on a concrete floor. Two minutes passed before either of them spoke.

'Dad always says that his first film was his dream project, the one he was most passionate about,' said Phoebe quietly, breaking the silence but still scowling.

'Yes. He worked his butt off to get that one made. Failure was not a word in his vocabulary.'

'He's often told me that making films gave him the freedom and the challenge he'd always craved,' she continued, her mood thawing a little as she picked up the mug of tea and clasped it in both hands.

'You're a lot like him, you know.'

'Thanks,' said Phoebe, tucking her legs beneath her. 'But I have a long, long way to go yet before I even begin to match up to him.'

'Maybe. But you're driven, Phoebe, in the same way that he was. How long have you wanted to be a vet?'

'Oh years!' answered Phoebe laughing. 'Since I first set eyes on a possum on Dad's Australian ranch. I was about five, I think. But we're not talking about me, Larry. We're talking about Dad.'

'Yeah. Your Oscar-winning Dad! Do you remember your trip to Los Angeles? You must have been about twelve then.'

'I'll never forget it,' she said enthusiastically. 'His critics had labelled him a lucky contender. He really hadn't expected to win. The expression on his face when he went on stage! Do you remember, Larry? It swung from bewilderment to satisfaction and back again for about five minutes. I was so embarrassed. I thought he'd developed a nervous twitch.'

'That was twelve years ago, twenty years after his first film,' said Larry almost to himself.

'Why are people so critical of him?' asked Phoebe, slapping the arm of the sofa with the flat of her hand.

Larry sighed, stood up and walked over to the large oak cabinet in the corner of the room. He'd asked himself the same thing a million times until the question itself had become meaningless and he had ceased to care.

'His critics accused him of abandoning Britain and pandering to Hollywood. Industry pundits the world over gave him, along with several other brash, young and innovative directors, the tag of *Movie Brat* because they made films they *wanted* to make. His films were commercial successes,' explained Larry. He opened the door of the cabinet and took out a bottle of whisky. He unscrewed the cap.

'You?'

'Yuk. In tea? No thanks.'

'Sure?'

Phoebe nodded silently as Larry poured a generous measure of whisky into his mug of tea. A necessity, he felt, to steady his nerves. PR was a synch compared to godparenting. He took a large gulp, shut his eyes and sighed with pleasure as the warm mixture hit the back of his throat.

'Your father was passionate about his films Phoebe, and so was his public. But the critics kept on accusing him of making films totally devoid of deep intellectual content. You're smiling Phoebe, that's good.'

'Well it's ridiculous isn't it? It smacks of jealousy.'

'Quite right and best ignored. It was the public who made him. They flocked to his films.'

Larry looked at Phoebe waiting intently for him to proceed. The sixty-year-old man she called Dad was completely different to the bold young film director, Alfie Macbeth. Perhaps she'd heard a little about the antics of his early thirties, his womanizing and partying. Maybe her mother had told her.

'The popular press on the other hand couldn't get enough of him,' he began, hesitantly.

'Thanks to you,' said Phoebe grinning.

'Well, not entirely. He was doing well before he met me. You see Phoebe, he was successful, good-looking and boisterous. He made brilliant films but away from the camera he led a somewhat glamorous lifestyle.' Larry paused as the image of Alfie and his model in the lift at The Hilton sprung into his mind. Would he ever rid himself of the memory? he wondered wearily.

'You've gone all red,' interjected Phoebe. 'What were you thinking?'

'I was just ...' said Larry slowly, trying to compose himself. He cleared his throat. 'You know Phoebe, sometimes ... well sometimes your Dad could be as subtle as a piece of raw meat in a vegetarian's kitchen.'

'Tell it like it is why don't you!'

Her mother hasn't told her, thought Larry as he blundered on desperate to convey the information yet determined not to shatter her illusions.

'He got away with it because the press adored him at the time. Why, even his colleagues paid lip service to him. It would have taken a very strong man, Phoebe, not to become arrogant and selfish. And at that point in time your Dad was as weak as the next man.'

'It's odd to think of him like that. It's as though you are describing a complete stranger, not my Dad.'

'Phoebe, your Dad led an enchanted life, full of glamorous women, late night drinking at bars,' confided Larry. 'Feted by Hollywood, adulated by an adoring public, he had reached the pinnacle of his career by the time he was thirty-seven. That's the age most directors start out. He wielded great power, especially since his second Oscar nomination. The world was at his feet.'

'So he married my mother! And together they proved irresistible,' said Phoebe sadly. '*Sex and stardust!*' she added cynically.

'They oozed romantic appeal. Darling, they were the couple of the early '80s.'

'I know, I know. It's just that it seems so irrelevant now.' She stopped, chewed the end of her forefinger while looking Larry directly in the eye, then said, 'Yet this same journalist, this *Thomas Slater*, goes on to say something totally unbelievable.'

'Oh?' queried Larry raising his left eyebrow.

'He implies my father killed a man!' Larry's right eyebrow sprung upwards, joining the left in alarm. 'I thought you said you'd read the article.'

Larry sprang out of his seat. Aware of his sudden movement, he made a show of gathering up the tea things. It wasn't lost on Phoebe.

'At last I get a reaction!' exclaimed Phoebe.

'It's nonsense, Phoebe. The man is clearly insane.'

'If it's obviously nonsense, please explain why he's allowed to get away with it? I thought there were laws about this type of thing,' she persisted dryly, fully aware of Larry's discomfort.

The telephone rang. Larry bounded into the hall like a dog after a rabbit. 'Who was it that coined the phrase *saved by the bell?*' he muttered under his breath, pulling the receiver from its stand.

'Larry it's me.'

'Hi, Alfie!' Larry exclaimed, his heart turning somersaults inside his chest. He coughed hoping to recover his equanimity quickly like the publicist he was. 'How are you? How did it go?'

Nine

'A film. And with *Hamlet* opening next month?'

'Yeah. I know. Hopefully I'm about to get really busy.'

'That's terrific Abe.' Larry meant it, although he was surprised.

'Thanks,' replied Abe, his voice full of the confidence of someone who has been born again.

'What made you change your mind? You're always swearing the theatre is your only love.'

'It's sounds corny, Larry. Really corny but I had a dream.'

'Well no one said Martin Luther King had the exclusive rights to those. Good on you, Abe. So you're in Cannes? Have you got a backer?'

Down the other end of the phone Abe took a deep intake of breath. 'Yeah, I'm in Cannes but no I haven't got a backer. That's why I'm in Cannes.'

'Here to hustle.'

'Something like that. I gather Alfie's here.'

'Yeah, yeah with what I like to call his honeymoon film *Tribulation*. He and Katherine are staying in Juan Les Pins at the Eden Roc Hotel. It's a safe distance from the gangs of media that patrol the Croisette. I can assure you that over the next ten days Alfie's ego will be well and truly massaged.'

'But I trust it won't affect him?'

'I wouldn't bet on it,' said Larry with a groan.

'But he's been married a year? Surely Alfie has calmed down.'

'Yes. You're right,' agreed Larry laughing. 'Though it sounds as though you've yet to see it for yourself.'

'I was hoping to catch up with him.'

'Well, they're at the Eden Roc. He's very busy but I'm sure he'll find time to meet up with a friend. Now if you'll excuse me Abe . . .'

'You're busy too. Sorry Larry.'

'Something to do with 450 films on tap for sixteen hours a day. It's hard to keep tabs on the ones I'm supposed to be publicising. Take care now.'

From his temporary office deep in the bowels of the Majestic Hotel, Larry Woods was the figure central to the success of the Film Festival. His company ran the publicity at Cannes with the efficiency of a well-oiled machine. His staff placed stories in the daily publications of *Variety*, *Screen International* and *The Hollywood Reporter* with the utmost care and to full effect. Film stars were chaperoned about town discreetly and intelligently, his fashionably dressed girls accompanying them to interviews with international journalists who had been painstakingly hand-picked. This had earned him the respect of clients, stars and the press alike. If there was a story to be had then the press made straight for Larry.

Larry was up to his neck in it. Cannes was never an easy fortnight. The gruelling days were endless. The floor of his office was awash with press releases, biographies and invitations – a sea of paper amongst which a handful of his girls sat, cross-legged, stuffing envelopes. Other members of his staff manned the phones, one the fax machine, the rest charged up and down the Croisette with various stars in tow or met with clients at restaurants, keeping them sweet. Nights were packed with screenings and parties. Last night he had found himself praying that the marquee he had dared to erect on top of the Old Palais for Panama Pictures' all-star party would not blow off during an evening of freak wind. He could not afford to relax for one minute. His clients needed his protection – journalists could hurl questions at stars, directors and distributors alike with the deadly accuracy of a Zulu warrior lunging his spear into his enemy's heart.

Larry was stressed. His head buzzed with the sound of ringing phones. Stretched to their absolute limit attending screenings and interviews as well as party planning, his staff had been rushed off their feet. Last night's arrival of Jack Nicholson in Cannes to promote his film *The Postman Always Rings Twice* had thrown his office further into chaos. Despised by the US critics, the film had been well received in Cannes. Everyone wanted to talk to Jack. Every time they did Larry had to supply two of his girls to escort him in a chauffeur-driven car to the interview. It was an absolute necessity to prevent him being mobbed. There could be no question of him strolling casually down the Croisette. Crowds were drawn to Jack like iron filings to a magnet. The short walk from the Majestic Hotel to the Carlton would result in total carnage. Still, at least for now he was safe having been delivered to Barry Norman for an interview.

Larry was now totally out of staff, apart from his secretary, Audrey, who was manning the phones. Even Stella Armstrong, the seventeen-year-old girl he'd recently hired as a favour to her mother, had been dispatched on an errand. *Although I'm not at all sure she's up to it*, he thought worriedly. *Perhaps it would have been better if I'd gone. Stella is very young, after all and totally green.*

He shook his head to dispel the thought and reached for the unopened manila envelope that contained the action stills from Alfie's film *Tribulation*. They'd just been delivered by bike from Panama Pictures's office in the Carlton Hotel. He ripped it open and smiled with relief. *Tribulation* was undoubtedly another potential money earner. The story of Captain Cook's discovery of the East Coast of Australia was being touted as the favourite to win this year's coveted Palme d'Or. These should appease several hundred picture-editors, he thought happily as he glanced his professional eye over the glossy 10 × 8 black and white photographs.

'Larry!'

'Audrey!' replied Larry startled as his usually unflappable secretary careered into his office without her customary sharp little knock.

'Larry!' she repeated, her face ashen.

'Whatever is the matter?' he asked, his pulse beginning to race.

'It's Alfie,' she replied.

'Is he hurt?' He leapt to his feet. 'For God's sake woman, speak.'

'No. No. Well not yet, anyway. Oh Larry, try and be calm about this.'

'I *will* try very hard if you would do me the honour of letting me in on your secret,' he laboured, already struggling to reign in the panic he was feeling.

'It's not her fault. I mean she's very young . . .'

'Stella!'

'Yes, that's right, Stella.'

'What the fuck has she done now?' he yelled, banging his fist down on the desk with such ferocity that Audrey jumped.

'Well I suppose it would be a fair to assume that she was acting on her own initiative. Only I do think it would have been kind for someone to have warned her that it would be unwise to wander, without a chaperone, down the Croisette . . .'

'Oh shit,' said Larry, grabbing his jacket. 'Call me a driver!'

*

'It's a stone's throw away!' he exclaimed.

'No. I insist we take a car.'

49

'That's a preposterous suggestion. We'll sneak out the back. No one will notice,' he assured her as he looked into the strange green eyes of his elfin-faced companion. She was small, about 5′ 5″ with a boyish frame, long dark blonde hair and an olive complexion, unblemished save for a large freckle under her right eye. 'Trust me,' he added as he cast his eye over her tiny, tight white T-shirt and short, royal blue skirt that revealed a surprisingly impressive pair of legs.

'I don't know,' she protested determinedly. 'Larry is very strict about this.'

'Don't be chicken,' he taunted before making a dash for it, Stella in hot pursuit.

'Alfie, where's Katherine?' screamed a fan recognising the director and attracting the attention of a large group of tourists hovering outside the hotel, directly in Alfie's path.

'Alfie, I love you,' yelled one of the women as she took giant strides towards her idol.

'Marry me Alfie,' shouted another as the crowd began to deepen and close in on them.

'Let me shake your hand.'

'Al-fie! Al-fie! Al-fie!' The chanting was gaining in volume. The noise, like clashing cymbals, reverberated round Alfie's brain disorientating him for a moment. He turned to Stella whose terrifed face was chalk white.

'If we try to keep moving we might be able to squeeze through them to The Bunker. We'll be safe there,' yelled Alfie above the din.

'The Bunker?' asked Stella, blinking rapidly like a rabbit caught in the headlights of a juggernaut – a further 70, 80, maybe 100 fans had closed in on them in an hysterical frenzy.

Not one of my better ideas, thought Alfie, half-pulling, half-pushing his terrified companion in the direction of the Palais des Festivals.

The screams were deafening, the crowd swelling. Stella had her hands over her ears, staring ahead, eyes wide with fright. He grabbed one of her hands and pulled it away from her ear.

'Don't worry, we'll make it,' he yelled. But she just shook her head and covered her ear with her hand again. Then, as if by magic, the crowd began to part. A chauffeur-driven Mercedes was inching its way towards them. Hanging out of the front window, was Larry's face, puce in colour and dripping with perspiration.

'Get in,' he screamed, gesticulating at the open door.

'But we were having such fun,' replied Alfie, grinning as he dived into the back seat. 'Jump in Stella.'

'Alfie, I'm sorry,' continued Larry when Stella had closed the door. 'Honestly Stella, what were you thinking of?'

'I . . .'

'Have you any idea of the dangers of a mob.'

'One heart, one mind,' interjected Alfie unhelpfully.

'Disorderly and therefore bloody dangerous,' said Larry angrily. 'And you . . .' he said now turning on his friend, '. . . should have known better.'

'He . . .' began Stella.

'You were under specific instructions, if you remember, to make the short trip to the Palais by taxi.'

'Did you just say *trip*?' asked Alfie who was not concerned in the least. 'My God you're right Larry, that was some trip. Totally surreal and wonderfully psychadellic. I had no idea I was so popular in France.'

'Honestly, Stella, I thought you had more brains.' Larry glowered at Stella, ignoring Alfie. 'Have you anything to say for yourself?'

'No. I . . .'

'Like an apology?' growled Larry, glowing red.

But Stella, who showed no sign of remorse, said nothing, simply turned her head in Alfie's direction, then dissolved in a fit of hysterical laughter.

Ten

'Come in!' Larry barked in response to the gentle knocking on the door of the temporary office in the corner of the large, open-plan room. It opened slowly, hesitantly. 'Come in, come in,' he repeated impatiently.

'You called for me,' said Stella, marching into his office with sudden boldness.

'Ah yes, Stella,' sighed Larry. 'Listen, Stella. I've got a problem. We are incredibly short staffed again today what with Jack, Gerard Depardieu ...' he paused and rubbed his face with his right hand, his mind racing. Eager to get it over with, he leapt to his feet, walked across to Stella and put his arm around her. 'Thing is Stella, I can't spare Audrey. I absolutely have to have her here to man the phones. She's the one person who knows exactly what goes on. And I have a meeting in 20 minutes. Once again you are the only person available. Do you understand?'

Stella nodded. Pleased with the way things were going so far, Larry wandered back to his chair and sat down, resting his elbows on the desk in front of him. He placed his head on his hands and stared at Stella.

'It's absolutely vital you listen to everything I am about to tell you.'

'OK!' said Stella, who appeared to be trying to look as confident as possible under the circumstances, which, after the debacle of four days previously, were strained to say the least.

Her face, set in a concentrated frown, was determined in a youthful way. Girlishly pretty, her slim androgynous body, not yet fully matured, was covered today in a skimpy white T-shirt and skin-tight jeans. Her translucent eyes that were fixed on Larry as she waited patiently for instruction were mesmerising, impossibly green, like bottle glass. He looked at her mouth, the lips slightly parted.

For God's sake Larry, he castigated himself. You knew her mother! He cleared his throat. 'Good!' he croaked as he reached for the glass of water on his desk and took a large gulp. His composure recovered, he pointed to the card hanging from Stella's neck. 'You've got your accreditation with you, I see.'

'Well you are always insisting that we never leave these offices without it.'

'Quite,' said Larry, relieved that at least one instruction had filtered through the fog of her naivety.

'I sleep in mine,' she added.

'Really!' he replied dismissively. 'I want you to take a taxi to the Eden Roc Hotel in Juan Les Pins where Katherine Katz is staying. We have arranged for a photographer from *Tatler* to take some pictures of her down by the pool at 11am. It should make a stunning back drop. She and Alfie Macbeth . . .' he paused, momentarily panicked. Stella blinked but her expression remained set. Encouraged by this apparent show of confidence, he continued. 'They are in the Presidential suite . . . ask at reception. A porter will take you there. Knock on her door and remind her as politely as possible that she has a photoshoot in . . .' he looked at his watch, '. . . by the time you get there, she'll have half an hour to get ready. She's a notoriously late riser, so she'll want some time to get dressed and made up. That is why you must hurry now. Try very hard to appear professional. I know it's a lot to ask. And try to keep the photographer off the subject of Alfie and fully on her film *Desperate Remedies*. Katherine is a bit sensitive about that at the moment, probably because *Tribulation* is up for the Palme d'Or and *Remedies* isn't. That is very important Stella.'

'Right.'

'And beware of any stray press lurking about. They're dying to get a shot of Katherine and Alfie together. It's a huge bonus to have them both in Cannes but it is vital that we moderate the media circus. It must not be allowed to run out of control. The staff at the Eden Roc are extra vigilant. Unless a journalist has an appointment he or she won't get past the security at the gates but even so, you cannot afford to be complacent. Think you can manage it?'

'Definitely,' said Stella, smiling. 'It's not exactly rocket science is it?'

Startled by her sarcasm, Larry was speechless for a moment.

'I'll be off then?' she suggested, raising her eyebrows questioningly.

Gathering himself together and recovering control of his jaw, Larry said, 'Yes. Hurry. And remember, I'm relying on you. Katherine Katz is a huge star. Her well-being is very important to me. Stuff this up and we'll have to think long and hard whether this is the right career for you.'

Frowning at the back of the departing girl, Larry's thoughts turned once more to the conundrum of Katherine Katz. Unlike her ebullient husband, she was not enjoying Cannes and this was giving him great cause for concern. Her latest film, a Hollywood adaptation of Thomas Hardy's passionate first novel *Desperate Remedies,* was competing in Directors' Fortnight. It was the debut movie of young director Bradley Tyler and starred Katherine in the role of the heroine Cytherea Graye.

The film seemed to Larry to be a mess of corsets, wigs and breeches. The fault lay indisputably in the casting of Leighton Graham, a typical American beefcake actor, in the leading role. It was painfully obvious to Larry that he had been cast on the strength of his looks rather than his talent. Maintaining an English accent for the duration of the film had ultimately proved impossible for the young star. In the final cut he was lost somewhere in mid-Atlantic. While this added a touch of humour, if nothing else, to an otherwise long-winded production, his ineptitude had infuriated Katherine.

Larry likewise was under no illusions. The film would bomb. Directors' Fortnight was dedicated to screen work from new and cutting-edge directors. It was a miracle this film had made it so far. But now that it had, he saw his role in this case as one of damage limitation. There was not a lot he could do for the film but he was determined that Katherine, at least, should come out of it unscathed.

So why on earth have you sent an inexperienced teenager to such an important shoot? he asked himself as the alarm bells of his mind began to clang.

'Audrey,' he called to his secretary who was seated at her desk right outside his room. 'I know I promised I'd sort out the Goldcrest business but I have this nasty feeling I should be elsewhere.' He grabbed his briefcase with one hand and his accreditation with the other.

'But . . .'

'I simply cannot allow Katherine Katz's guts to be spilled across the Eden Roc Hotel's 25 acres of picturesque gardens. It's too ugly a concept to contemplate. I'm sorry darling. You will just have to find a way to cope. John will be back in a minute. His screening was due to finish at 11am.'

'Don't worry, I'll manage . . . somehow.'

'I'm sorry, Audrey. I won't be long.'

Alfie was dozing next to Katherine who was in a deep sleep. They had been guests of honour at Larry's swish all-night party on top of the Old Palais, last night. Everybody who was worth knowing had been there, including Jack Nicholson. It had been quite some time since he had last been to the festival and he was enjoying himself. This was the first time he'd been up for the Palme d'Or. Panama

Pictures had pulled out all the stops. He and Kate were being treated like royalty with a chauffeur-driven limousine at their disposal that, after the incident outside The Bunker, he had taken to using as a matter of course. This provided a certain amount of superficial privacy, the size of the car naturally attracting the interest of the press and public alike.

'It's like being in a goldfish bowl,' Katherine had complained.

'But you wouldn't be without it,' Alfie had replied. Silly money, silly lives, he'd thought as he'd waved goodbye to Larry at 5am. 'You'll be up and working in a couple of hours then Larry,' he'd said.

'Naturally. Don't forget you've got interviews from noon and Kate has a photo shoot at 11am with *Tatler* by the pool. I'll send someone over.'

'Relax, Larry. It'll run like clockwork. With you at the controls working these monkeys, how could it go otherwise?'

Through his alcohol-induced semi-conscious state, Alfie heard a gentle knocking. He rolled over dreaming of clog dancing. The knocking became louder. 'Clog dancing?' mumbled Alfie incredulously, now wide-awake. 'I'm losing it!'

The knocking persisted, waking Katherine. 'Who's that?' she asked, bleary with sleep.

'Someone at the door?' suggested Alfie, amused. He sat up expecting his head to pound after the excesses of last night. There was nothing – no headache, no furry tongue. Yet again he'd got away with it. 'Aren't you expecting someone?' he enquired, nudging his wife.

'Oh God!' groaned Katherine. Angry at having been woken, she glanced at the clock by her bed. The red light flashed 10.30. She had had a mere five hours sleep. That was not enough. She groaned again, covering her head with a pillow. 'Oh Alfie, why couldn't Larry have postponed this shoot? The pictures will be dreadful,' she said, her voice muffled.

'You look gorgeous darling,' Alfie assured her. He rolled over, pulled the pillow off his wife's head and kissed her on the back of her neck.

'Get off, you idiot. That's the last thing I need.'

The knocking persisted, louder this time. Katherine rolled onto her side pulling the crumpled white sheet off Alfie as she got out of bed. Draping the sheet around her, she dragged her weary body out of the bedroom to the door of the suite, muttering obscenities under her breath. Alfie sprung off the bed and pulled on a pair of boxer shorts. He followed her into the sitting-area and grabbed the day's copy of *Variety*. He sat down in a chair and began to flick through the pages, fully aware of his wife's growing anger. Fascinated, he watched as Katherine, the sheet clutched to her throat, tossed back her thick head of hair in preparation for the film-star rage she was about to throw.

'Who the hell do you think you are?' she screeched as she opened the door.

Yes, thought Alfie from the comfort and safety of his distant chair, Kate is definitely not in the mood.

'I demand to know your name,' yelled Kate ferociously.

'Stella Armstrong,' the girl replied stepping into the room.

Remarkable choice Larry, thought Alfie, leaning forward to get a better look. Like sending the savage to the Brave New World.

'Stella Armstrong!' repeated Kate. 'Don't you realise you should have phoned us?'

'I'm sorry,' said Stella jutting out her small, pointed chin with a hint of defiance.

'You are obviously not trained in the finer points of your chosen occupation,' screeched Katherine. 'I intend to tell Larry of your ineptitude. Larry runs a tight ship and you have let him down.'

'I'm sorry,' insisted Stella. 'But you are urgently needed for a photo shoot on the terrace by the pool. You've got ten minutes to get ready. I'm extremely worried that we'll lose the photographer. I'm to escort you there.'

My God, thought Alfie, surprised. *She's* annoyed with Kate. 'She'll be with you in ten minutes,' he said, lowering his magazine and startling Stella, who hadn't noticed him sitting there, quietly observing. 'Won't you Kate?' he added firmly, though not taking his eyes off Stella.

Kate groaned again. She hoicked up the long sheet like a haughty bride gathering up her train and flounced off to the bedroom, slamming the door behind her.

Stella's strange, green eyes that had been set in a steely gaze relaxed. Alfie winked at her but she glanced away, embarrassed.

'Why don't you run down to the pool Stella and tell your photographer Kate is on her way. Order the guy a coffee and compliment him on the size of his zoom lens! That should do the trick,' he continued, beaming at the girl. 'I'll bring her down to you as soon as she'd ready.'

'Of course. Yes. Thank you Mr Macbeth,' she said formally as she turned to leave.

Eleven

Cut into the edge of the bluish-pink rocky coastline, the seawater swimming-pool overflowed into the ocean below. Abe could see Stella sitting in the warm May sunshine at a poolside table, writing. Her face was totally obscured by her dark blonde hair. It had fallen forward, down to the barely perceptible swell of her breast. Opposite her on the other side of the pool, a pony-tailed photographer was fiddling with his camera strap.

Stella! Hi!' he yelled, waving vigorously.

Stella looked up, caught sight of Abe, smiled and rushed over and hugged him. 'Abe. Abe Cunningham. Boy is it good to see a friendly face.'

'It sounds like you really mean that,' said Abe, pleased at the reception from this gorgeous girl whom he'd met four weeks ago at Larry Woods' offices. In two weeks time she would be assisting Minnie Cooper with the publicity on his stage production of *Hamlet*. He was delighted because they'd hit it off immediately and had met subsequently for a drink. Her inexperience was of no concern to him. It would be a golden opportunity to get to know her better.

'Of course I do,' said Stella kissing him fleetingly on the cheek. She grabbed him by the hand, dragging him over to the table where she'd been writing. 'Sit down and have a cup of tea.'

'Are you sure I'm not interrupting anything?'

'Not at all. I'm waiting, as usual.'

'Anyone I know?'

'I believe her husband is a very good friend of yours,' she said laughing.

'Oh!' exclaimed Abe.

'Presumably that's why you're here?' she asked, reaching for his hand which she held for a moment, squeezing it before letting go to concentrate her efforts on pouring tea.

'Yes. As a matter of fact it is. It's exactly why I'm here,' said Abe robotically. Stella passed him a cup, glancing at him quizzically.

'He's not at all how you described him though. He's much more approachable than I'd imagined, if a little crazy.'

'Oh yes. Alfie is all charm,' replied Abe. The sarcasm was not lost on Stella.

'Are you OK, Abe?'

'Me? I'm fine. Never better. First rate.'

'Have a biscuit,' she suggested, shoving the neatly arranged plate in his direction. 'In fact have lots of biscuits.'

'Thanks,' said Abe taking one.

'You look a little pale Abe,' she said quietly, holding him by the arm now, staring into his tired eyes, her own eyes alive with vitality. He smiled, hoping to assuage her concern.

'And you're very beautiful, Stella,' he replied without thinking. She groaned, relinquishing her hold on his arm.

'Blah, blah, blah,' she retorted, moving her head from side to side and rolling her eyes.

'It's true Stella. You may not realise it now, I mean, for Christ's sake, you're only seventeen but mark my words, you will drive men mad.'

Stella frowned, screwing up her mouth. Abe looked away silently admonishing himself for his tactlessness but caught sight of Alfie and Kate approaching.

'They're here,' he said, rising to his feet. 'I'll go.'

'But you wanted to see him,' protested Stella.

'Later,' said Abe disconsolately as, without a backward glance, he scuttled away.

'Doesn't she look magnificent?' Alfie asked loudly, who appeared not to have recognised Abe. The photographer grinned mawkishly, unable to hide his delight that Alfie had shown up too.

'Gorgeous!' he replied, his eyes momentarily alighting on Kate's cleavage, revealed to great effect in the strappy white sundress she was wearing.

'So few people can get away with wearing white. Wouldn't you agree?' probed Alfie placing his own camera on the table. Stella glanced nervously up at him and nodded dumbly in agreement. Alfie winked at her and she giggled suddenly, unable to stop herself, placing her hand in front of her mouth as her eyes widened. 'I must say, you are very lucky with the weather er ...?' continued Alfie, now thoroughly enjoying himself.

'Brian.'

'Exactly. A cloudless, blue sky. Couldn't be more perfect,' he declared, grinning at Stella who giggled again.

Kate said nothing.

'I'd love a picture of the two of you,' prompted the photographer hopefully.

'I don't think . . .' began Stella, attempting to control herself.

'Love to!' interrupted Alfie. Beaming, he turned to Kate who was red-faced with anger. 'Wouldn't we darling?'

'Yes, of course,' replied Kate through gritted teeth.

'Fabulous!' effused the photographer, clapping his hands in glee.

'Isn't it though?' remarked Alfie just as Larry arrived, hot and panting.

'Everything OK?' asked Larry breathlessly as the photographer ushered his prized couple towards the rocks. Alfie looks pleased, he thought relieved as he watched the photographer arrange him and Kate in a suitable pose. Stella must have come up trumps, thank goodness.

'Actually, I'd like a word with you after this,' snarled Kate, glaring in his direction.

'Oh! Right!' Larry said, his heart sinking.

Oh God, thought Alfie sadly, his fun over. Married life!

Twelve

Live jazz blared out of the speakers from the deck of one of the massive yachts moored off the sandy beach. The photographers and paparazzi flashed away at the elegant figures that graced the red carpet area as they glided up the impressive staircase of the grey concrete Palais into its hallowed halls.

Business, that's what Cannes is all about, Abe told himself. And these well-dressed, well-connected businessmen have the luxury of multi-million dollar budgets to play around with. But they're not interested in my screenplay. Oh no! It's too arthouse. An American audience won't understand it because they're Philistines! It's pretentious, the critic's will say. Well that's a laugh. They should take a look at themselves – trussed up VIPs riding on the back of true talent. What the hell am I doing here? I must be mad!

A strange, hollow feeling overcame him as he caught sight of Alfie striding manfully down the carpet. His cool demeanour and seemingly choreographed swagger exuded infallible positivity.

It's hardly surprising, thought Abe. Tonight is the night.

There had been the usual rumours flying around about horse-trading within the jury but with the reliable and respected director Joss Farman at the helm the critics had mainly dismissed them as ludicrous. The considered opinion was that *Tribulation* would win fair and square and that was great news for Alfie.

Tremendous news, thought Abe chewing his lip with such aggression he drew blood. 'Fuck,' he muttered under his breath.

The well-heeled lady standing next to him tut-tutted loudly before turning to her husband to ask, 'Where's Katherine Katz?'

'I've no idea,' he replied. 'Hopefully she'll be along a little later.'

'They'd hardly arrive separately. They're newly weds,' she remarked knowingly.

'Good point. He's hardly been able to keep his hands off her these past ten days. What a shame. She always lights up the carpet.'

'The poor girl must be ill.'

Abe shuddered. It was these kind of conversations that shook his belief in mankind's credibility. These opportunists didn't know either Alfie or Kate, nor were they likely to meet them, yet their opinions on their life and philosophies were as real to them as the lives they believed their heroes led. Mind you they have a point, thought Abe extracting himself from the crowd. It is odd that Kate's not with him. What's he done now I wonder?

'Hello Abe.' The voice was friendly, upbeat, the hand that grabbed his arm to gain his attention, small but insistent.

'Stella!' he exclaimed turning round to face her, his mood lightening immediately.

'Come on, Abe. We're off to the Le Petit Carlton for some well earned vodka tonics before the real partying begins.'

'Sounds great,' said Abe, his heart pounding as he took in Stella's short, tight, white mini dress. This was just the sort of distraction he needed. There was something different about Stella, the centrepiece of so many of his dreams lately. 'You look amazing, Stella.'

'And you need glasses,' she countered punching him playfully in the stomach.

He laughed. 'Come on then, lead the way,' he instructed as he linked arms with his adorable companion. After a couple of drinks he'd find the confidence to tackle Alfie with his proposition. Everything is going to be all right, he thought happily.

*

Having a movie selected to run in competition at Cannes is a great honour, thought Alfie as he wriggled nervously in his seat. He was struggling to focus on Joss Farman, the chairman of the jury of eight judging the Palme d'Or.

Joss was standing on the stage beside the podium making a serious and heart-felt speech about the integrity of all the films that had been screened in competition this year. A mild-mannered man, his speech was unusually emotive and it came as no surprise to Alfie when the audience greeted its conclusion with thunderous applause.

Earlier, Alfie had tried to affect a sauntering walk down the red carpet towards the Palais that was lined with barriers and flanked with appreciative fans. Assured rather than arrogant was the look he'd hoped to achieve. And he had managed this well until Barry Norman and his camera crew had leapt out at him, shattering his concentration.

'Win or lose tonight I would like to congratulate you, Alfie.

Tribulation is one of your finest films. You must be feeling fairly confident.'

'I don't know about confident,' he'd replied, trying to appear precisely that. 'But I am very happy with the film.'

'And is this the sort of occasion that makes filmmaking worthwhile?'

'I'm certain that I am not the first director to maintain that he doesn't make films for the awards but rather for the audiences they might attract and the enjoyment they bring. However, it's fantastic when your film is appreciated by the industry, especially when the jury in question is made up of one's peers. Recognition on this scale you cannot buy.'

'Well said, Alfie and thanks for your time.'

'It's a pleasure Barry,' he'd said, forcing his dry lips into a smile.

And now here he was waiting. Jack Nicholson was holding the envelope in his hands. He was grinning maniacally at the audience, the lights reflected in his Wayfarers, milking the moment, tying Alfie's gut into knots.

Come on Jack, be a good fellow and open the bloody thing, willed Alfie barely able to contain himself as he watched Jack slide his finger under the seal. That a boy. Nearly there.

But Jack had stopped and was cracking another joke. The audience was laughing.

Please, please put me out of my misery, beseeched Alfie silently, certain that if this ordeal didn't end soon, he would cease to breathe.

'And the winner?' Jack paused, raised his eyebrows and grinned expansively once more. 'Ladies and Gentlemen, I have very great pleasure in announcing that the winner of 1981 Palme d'Or is my very dear friend Alfie Macbeth for his film *Tribulation*.'

Relief that the waiting was over surely explained the feeling of total euphoria that swept over him as he walked up to the podium to take the Palme d'Or from Jack. He turned to the audience who cheered and clapped thunderously as he held it aloft in his right hand.

An hour later and he was on Panama Pictures's yacht with the bouncers balanced on the gangplank, for a reception thrown in his honour, clutching the Palme d'Or in one hand, a glass of Veuve Clicquot in the other. The industry bigwigs swarmed around him. A crowd of people queued to speak to him. He felt like the most popular kid in school.

Vainglorious? he asked himself as he excused himself from a group of French dignitaries. No way. There's nothing to be smug about. I've worked hard and I've won. It's as simple as that.

'You're *acclaimed* Alfie,' said Larry, interrupting his thoughts. 'Everyone is saying so.'

'Wow!' exclaimed Alfie, satisfied. 'There's nothing like admiration from your peers.'

'You deserve it. You've worked hard.'

'Life is rosy.'

'Make the most of it,' advised Larry patting his friend on the back. 'See you later.'

Alfie smiled. My fortunes are on another upward curve, he marvelled. I've got good health, a great job and a stunning wife. He sighed. Yeah Kate is stunning all right but she's in a filthy mood thanks to that turkey *Desperate Remedies*.

He'd left her in their room with a face as long as a Disneyland queue after she'd thrown a film star rage and refused to leave. She'd been unable to accept Alfie's explanation that filmmaking was precarious and involved risk. He'd tried to explain that one dead duck of a movie for an actress of Kate's calibre would not affect her career in the long run but she hadn't listened.

She's jealous, he reasoned. And perhaps I would be jealous of her if the situation was reversed but I like to think that I would at least try and make an effort to bask in her glory. I hadn't realised that she was this selfish. She hadn't appeared that way when we made *The Ark*. I expected better from her. That was why I married her. But she's fallen, no jumped, at the first hurdle and I am left with the feeling that after just over a year our marriage has descended into mediocrity.

It's tragic really, thought Alfie, draining his glass. She should be here tonight. It's her duty, surely? Being married is all about sharing the highs and offering support through the lows. I've done my fair share of cajoling Kate through the ignominy of these past three days but she's repayed me by behaving like a petulant child. I'm damned if I'm going to let her ruin my night, he decided swapping his empty glass for another. This is my party and I'm gonna enjoy it.

'It's absolutely fine. I'm a friend of his. A very good friend.'

'And we've never heard that line before.'

'So sling your hook pal.'

'We were at university together. Cambridge. And unless I am very much mistaken I am not your pal.'

'Fancy a swim, wanker!'

'Later. Possibly. But as I think I may have mentioned, I am hear to see Alfie Macbeth, winner of the Palme d'Or, my best friend.'

'And he's expecting you is he?' asked the shorter of the two bouncers, as he gripped the lapels of Abe's jacket with hands that resembled a bunch of bananas.

'Er . . .' But now that his legs weren't touching the ground he couldn't think of a suitable response.

'Abe!! Is that you?'

'Yes,' he affirmed weakly, from behind his right lapel.

'Put him down please,' he heard the man say. 'This is no way to treat an honoured guest.'

'Terribly sorry Mr Woods,' apologised the bouncer lowering Abe gently to the ground. 'We thought he was an interloper.'

'That's OK,' said Abe as nonchalantly as possible as he looked into the eyes of his rescuer. 'And thank you Larry.'

'Looks like I arrived in the nick of time,' muttered Larry. He took hold of Abe's arm and steered him away from the bouncers. 'You idiot. I'd have given you an invitation if you'd asked.'

'But that's just it Larry.'

'What?'

'If I'd asked.'

'That's what I said.'

'But I didn't ask.'

'Clearly.'

'Exactly.'

'And your point is?'

'I would have thought that was obvious.'

'Abe. It's been a very busy ten days and you are trying my patience.'

'Larry, I'm sorry. What I meant to say is it would have been good to have been asked.'

Larry released Abe's arm, stopped walking and screwed up his eyes. 'Jesus. I'm sorry Abe. I . . .'

'You're busy, Larry. I understand.'

Alfie felt sure he recognised her – blonde hair, blue eyes and a spectacular chest. She looked more porn than movie star in her tight, black leather mini-skirt, pink lycra top and thigh length patent leather boots.

I'll have a chat with her the moment I extricate myself from Dick Shepherd, he decided as he smiled and nodded at Panama Pictures's senior vice president, who was busy congratulating him.

'It was good but not your best.'

Disorientated, Alfie turned round awkwardly to face the speaker. 'Good heavens!' he exclaimed barely able to contain his surprise. 'Abe! Abe Cunningham.'

'It's good to see you old friend,' said Abe, holding out his hand. Alfie took it and shook it. It felt like a limp lettuce leaf.

'Dick, I'm not certain you've met Abe Cunningham.' Oh dear, he thought. This is bad timing.

'I'll leave you friends to it,' suggested Dick much to Alfie's relief.

'Good to see you,' said Alfie not quite believing what he was seeing, if indeed it was Abe and not his ghost? He looked thinner than ever, on the point of emaciation in fact. There were dark circles under his eyes, his cheeks were gaunt and his fine, mousy brown hair had thinned.

'You haven't been taking your vitamins old chap,' said Alfie slapping him on the back with such force that Abe lost his balance momentarily. He staggered sideways then corrected himself. 'What can I do for you?' Alfie asked him feeling suddenly anxious. He had no idea Abe was in Cannes. This kind of shock could kill a man. 'Are you after a drink, an introduction? Eh?' he added, his voice charged with false jollity.

'I thought it would be good for two old friends to catch up,' replied Abe brightly. 'How are you, Alfie?'

'As you can see I am fine,' he declared, holding up his award. 'In fact, things just couldn't be better.'

'I'm pleased for you, I really am. Mum sends her love.'

'Oh, right,' responded Alfie sheepishly. He lowered his arm and looked down at his polished shoes. His frowning face stared back 'That's great. Yes, lovely. Say hi to her from me when you next see her.'

'I will. She'd like that,' said Abe breezily. 'And I gather you're married now? To a Hollywood superstar, no less? Is she here?'

'Er ... no. She ... er ... she's overtired, got a headache, couldn't make it.'

'Oh! That's a shame. I was looking forward to meeting her.'

For a moment an awkward silence prevailed.

'Actually,' began Abe slowly. 'I am trying to get backing for a screenplay I've adapted and I'm looking for a director.' He winked conspiratorially at Alfie and nudged him in the ribs. 'Perhaps we could collaborate. What a great team we'd make. It would be like old times. Maybe the time is ripe for the great Alfie Macbeth to spread his wings and delve into the mysterious world of arthouse films.'

Alfie took a step back, appalled by the audacity of his friend. What was Abe thinking of. He'd just won the Palme d'Or. Was he out of his tiny mind?

'Sorry, Abe, no can do,' he blurted out. 'I'm afraid you don't quite match up to Hollywood standards!'

Abe stared back at him, stunned into silence.

'I can, however, get you a drink,' Alfie said, smiling again, relieved to have spoken his mind. He'd find a waiter, give Abe a glass of champagne, then he'd make his excuses and leave.

'Christ!' replied Abe, ignoring Alfie's offer of a drink. 'Is that what years of success brings you, the ability to shit on people from a great height?'

A hollow laugh rang from Alfie's opened mouth. This brusque and pained reaction had startled him. Still if that's how Abe felt then fine, it was one way of getting rid of him. 'You'll be going then,' he said dismissing Abe as if he were a bad script that had landed on his desk.

'Don't worry, I won't trouble you again,' whispered Abe as he faded away.

'Alfie!'

'Hi!' said Alfie turning to face the voice. 'You look familiar.' He grinned on sight of the body of the voluptuous young actress in the tight black mini-skirt and thigh length boots.

'It's Chantal! You remember. Chantal Tardy. I had a tiny part in *His Cold Blood*. You must remember me. You told me I had a lot of talent,' she said, her accent pure Essex.

'I bet I did,' said Alfie staring directly at her breasts, delighting Chantal who squealed with pleasure.

'Where's Katherine?' she asked coquettishly.

'Poor old thing's not well,' explained Alfie making no attempt to hide his lack of disappointment. This is altogether better, he told himself. In fact this could be just what I need, a little light distraction. A couple of hours spent in the company of the voluptuous Chantal might even reinvigorate my waning enthusiasm for my far more beautiful wife. He made an on-the-spot decision. This would be a one off, a consolatory reward for Kate having let him down. 'Why don't we go back to your room for a nightcap? I've had about as much adulation as I can stand for one day.'

Thirteen

Larry heaved a huge sigh of relief. Cannes had reached its glorious end after two frantic weeks. Apart from the little contretemps between Kate and Stella, the fortnight had gone swimmingly. And Alfie winning the Palme d'Or had definitely been the climax. He had been wrong about Alfie. Marriage had not altered him one little bit. The press seemed to adore him all the more and certainly his work hadn't suffered.

'What does it feel like being so powerful?' Larry had asked him.

'It's one hell of a rush!' Alfie had replied.

It had become customary for Larry to wrap up the Cannes fortnight with an all-night party at his spectacular villa situated on the hillside overlooking the bay. The caterers were already busy preparing a feast that would be served on the large paved dining area at the back of the villa. Purple clusters of trailing bougainvillaea spilled down the whitewashed wall that bordered the terrace, which was decorated with terracotta pots full of pink oleander and flaming red geraniums. Beyond the terrace was the crescent-shaped swimming-pool, around which were scattered a dozen or so teak sunbeds and to the right of that, where the garden dropped steeply away toward the sea, was the bar.

This year he was looking forward to the party more than ever. He had, he felt, earned a little bit of relaxation.

'Hi! Larry.'

Larry turned to see Alfie walking across the pale stone terrace, two palm trees reflected in the Ray-Bans he wore. 'Ah! The maestro! You're early so you must be on for a big night. Am I right or am I right?'

'You are not wrong, if that helps,' said Alfie traversing the length of the crescent shaped pool. He too was casually dressed in long khaki shorts, a long-sleeved white cotton shirt, unbuttoned at the cuffs and a pair of brown suede loafers on his bare feet. He walked over to the poolside bar and helped himself to a can of cold beer from the fridge.

'I feel that I should be bowing and scraping,' declared Larry, opening a large packet of dry-roasted peanuts. He poured them into a bowl.

'Quite right!'

'But where's your beautiful wife?' Larry asked as Alfie lobbed the ring pull into the plastic bin next to him. 'Great shot!'

'Sadly she has returned home.'

'Oh. Why's that?'

'I think she needed a remedy, desperately!'

'Ha, ha! But you're OK?' he added, his publicist's antennae roused.

'I can't say that I'm that upset. Her mood has been shocking the entire week. It made it very difficult for a guy to have fun.'

'I meant you and Kate . . .'

But Alfie wasn't listening. 'Tonight, my friend, I intend to enjoy myself for tomorrow I fly to the States and my new project.'

'To be idolised by the American press and public no doubt!' suggested Larry with a sigh. He pushed the bowl of peanuts in Alfie's direction.

'Marvellous, isn't it?'

'Yes. Yes it is marvellous,' repeated Larry lamely.

'So why the long face, Larry?'

'I'm sorry Alfie. I was just wondering whether Kate's disappearance had anything to do with Stella?'

'Stella?' he asked, taking a handful of peanuts.

'My youngest member of staff. She pissed Kate off at that photo shoot by the pool.'

'Ah yes, Stella.' Alfie smiled recalling the seventeen-year-old and her nubile limbs.

'In her defence she was only trying to do her job. I'm afraid I haven't sacked her though Kate insisted I should. You see, I think she has real potential.'

'Really?'

'Really!' insisted Larry.

'You know what, I think you're right,' agreed Alfie, amused. 'And I can tell you that Kate's grand exit has nothing to do with Stella.'

'She's a feisty little character,' continued Larry enthusiastically, forgetting his concerns about the Macbeth marriage. 'Calls her Kitty you know. Says she looks like a cat. Kitty Katz! Funny, don't you think?'

Alfie smiled. He'd last seen Kate three days ago when she'd stormed out of their hotel bedroom in tears because he wouldn't take her shopping in Nice. He'd been pleased to see the back of her. He'd had enough of her petty tantrums and frankly not enough sex. Chantal had been a revelation, double-jointed, energetic and filthy. It wasn't so much that he was being unfaithful, he'd reasoned, more that he was mourning the hedonistic lifestyle that Kate had once provided for him. He missed the passion. That was all. Chantal simply fulfilled a need, filled a gap. There were no long-term complications to consider. Kate was his wife, this . . . this other actress was just a bit of fun. And anyway, she seemed unconcerned that he had used her and totally unfazed by his fame . . . unlike Kate. Fame and notoriety was the oxygen she breathed and yes, her sensual features certainly had a feline quality. Kitty Katz! He turned to Larry and grinned, 'Yes. I like that. I like that very much.'

Larry cleared his throat nervously. 'I'm going to approach her tonight, as it happens.'

'Larry! You old devil!' exclaimed Alfie, slapping him on the back. 'I always knew you had it in you.'

'I shall invite her out to dinner. Wine and dine her, isn't that the way?'

'Careful,' warned Alfie laughing at his friend's old-fashioned approach. 'You'll be getting a reputation next!'

Later Larry, having fortified himself with a bottle of whisky to aid him with his quest, stumbled upon Alfie lying unconscious beside Carla, one of his more mature publicists, behind a sofa on the floor of the sitting- room. Her turgid breasts were exposed, an empty bottle of champagne on its side on the floor. Oops! he thought, recalling that earlier an amused guest had stumbled upon them going at it like steam trains in the jacuzzi. Things must be bad with Katherine.

Too drunk to be concerned about tomorrow's headlines, he fumbled his way through the room, colliding with the furniture until he reached the dimly lit corridor. His befuddled mind was intent on his mission. He'd thought of little else all night. The last couple of whiskies he'd sunk around 2am had broken down the final barriers providing him with the courage necessary to carry it through. 'Here we are,' he mumbled, tottering to a halt outside a closed door. As he adjusted his position, straightening his back and bringing his legs in line, a sudden and alarming sense of urgency overwhelmed him. For a moment, he felt light-headed. He took a deep breath and leant against the door-frame to steady himself. Another deep breath and he felt better. His composure regained, he smiled blearily and knocked on the door.

'Who is it?' asked the female voice.

He coughed, unsure of what to say, then knocked again louder, still leaning against the frame. Seconds later he heard the soft pad of bare feet on the wooden floor behind the closed door. A strange fluttering sensation, like a fast down-ride in an elevator, gripped his stomach. The door swung open.

'My god you're ... you're ... you're naked,' said Stella, laughing. Larry glanced down impressed by the sight of his own erection.

'Can I come in?' he asked, leering drunkenly at the young, virginal apparition clad in a white silk, knee-length nightie. His hard-won prize!

'Go to bed you lecherous old bastard. You know you're old enough to be my father.'

'That's bloody unoriginal!' Undeterred, Larry took a step closer. The door slammed in his face. 'Ow! Bloody, fucking ow!' he yelped and, grabbing his deflating genitals, chastened, disappeared into the darkness.

Fourteen

The house was quiet and, after the warmth of Cannes and Los Angeles, cold and morgue-like. Odd, because he was sure Katherine had said she'd be home when he'd phoned her last night from his hotel. He dumped his Louis Vuitton suitcase on the limestone-tiled floor of their spacious hallway and wandered into the kitchen.

'Hi Kitty, I'm home,' he called as he scanned the large, light room for signs of his wife. It was empty apart from a vast glass vase full of pink lilies on one of the granite work surfaces. Their strong, heady scent filled the room.

'Kitty!'

There was no reply, no sound, nothing, apart from the ticking of the stainless steel-rimmed clock on the wall above the long, marble table.

She must be out, thought Alfie, glancing with adoration at the Hockney that hung on the far wall. He'd never regretted buying that. From upstairs came the sound of the john flushing. Turning a quick 360, Alfie made for the stairs, narrowly avoiding his suitcase as he crossed the hall.

'Alfie, is that you?' Kate called out weakly from above him.

'Yes, Kitty darling. I'm back.'

'Oh thank goodness. Alfie, I'm so glad you're home.' Her pale face appeared over the wrought iron banisters.

'What on earth's wrong? Have you been crying?' Alfie asked, worried by the sight of his obviously distressed wife. He bounded up the stairs two at a time and reached the landing where Kate, still in her dressing gown though it was almost 4pm, fell into his outstretched arms.

'Alfie, I've been really sick. It's awful. If I'd known it would be like this I would never have done it.'

Alfie's stomach lurched guiltily in his abdomen. Perhaps she'd heard about his womanising in Cannes and LA. He was in no mood for a row.

He was exhausted. All he wanted was to make love to his beautiful wife and then fall asleep.

Gently she pulled away from him, took him by her elegantly manicured hand and led him to their bedroom a little way down the landing. His spirits lifted a little.

'Darling, it's all so awful and I just keep on being sick,' she repeated as she sat down on the side of their king-sized, steel-framed bed.

'Why, honey, why?' asked Alfie, tugging gently on her ponytail.

'How silly of me,' said Kate, her face flushed. 'I haven't told you yet. How funny. I've told so many people, you know, family and friends, but not my own dear husband. Grab some champagne and come to bed.'

Fantastic! That's more like it, thought Alfie. He flew from the room, down the stairs, hurdling his suitcase into the kitchen, opened the three-doored Herculean fridge and pulled out a bottle of his favourite Veuve Clicquot Champagne. It was ice cold. He reached for a couple of champagne flutes from the maple corner cabinet, leaving the door open in his haste to return upstairs and touched down in the bedroom, pouring the drinks in seconds flat. He handed Kate a glass and knelt before her on the cream carpet like a dog awaiting a treat.

'So what's the film?' he asked, panting slightly.

'It's not about a film darling,' she purred, pulling out her pony-tail so that her hair cascaded dramatically about her face.

'It's not?' echoed Alfie.

'No silly,' she said, laughing. 'I'm pregnant.'

'You're what?' repeated Alfie, distracted suddenly by a tickling sensation on his right hand. A spider was creeping over his fingers. He flicked it away absent-mindedly.

'I'm going to have a baby.'

'Sorry darling, what?' asked Alfie, glancing back at Kate.

'Alfie darling, I wish you'd listen. I'm trying to tell you that I'm pregnant.'

'You're pregnant?'

'Yes, Alfie. That's what I said. Isn't it wonderful?' she added with a shallow laugh.

'What?'

'You're going to be a father,' explained Kate, the smile on her mouth collapsing at Alfie's reaction.

'You mean you're pregnant?' asked Alfie bemused.

'Yes!' exclaimed Kate emphatically.

'And you're happy about this? I mean you actually want to be a . . . a . . . a . . . a mother.' He sat back on his heels, incredulous as the information dropped into his mind, tangled and nonsensical like an incomprehensible mathematical formula. It was totally shocking. He never would have guessed that Kate would want all the baggage of a conventional marriage. Marriage! The full, awful truth sat up and hit Alfie right between the eyes. He was a husband. Kate was his wife. In a few months he would be a father.

'Yes, darling. I do. It couldn't be more perfect.'

'But how?'

'Alfie, really!' said Kate as though she were scolding a child. She smiled mechanically this time, showing perfect teeth.

'But why weren't we more careful?' he said out loud then, 'Was it me?'

'Alfie!' exclaimed Kate, appalled.

The last year of his life flashed before him, a confused pattern of accelerated images: *The Ark*, a whirlwind romance, his brief engagement, marriage, *Tribulation*, the Palme d'Or, Cannes, LA. How had he, Alfie Macbeth, disciplined filmmaker and ferocious womaniser got into this mess? The truth came crashing down on him, crushing him like a hundred ton weight. He wished he had seen this coming because he would definitely have dodged out the way.

'Alfie, aren't you pleased for me? For us?' Kate asked hopefully, forcing a smile.

Alfie sunk to the floor, falling forward on his hands and knees as though praying to Mecca, struck dumb with the surprise.

'Of course, you're shocked,' she reasoned, her smile, as she stared at his folded form, a thin and wavering line.

Still Alfie said nothing. And now he rocked slowly, back and forth from head to heel.

'Alfie, say something!' she shrieked.

Alfie lifted his head to look at her. Unable to respond in words he knelt before her, staring at her, watching her talking to him. Finally with a huge exhalation of air he managed to mutter the words that were spinning around his head in a wild confusion of panic. 'Kitty, what the hell have you done?'

'Why do you keep calling me Kitty?' cried Kate, the tears falling readily. 'Why aren't you happy? Alfie! Stop being silly! Come here and kiss me!'

The phone on the square, glass-topped bedside table began to ring. Neither husband nor wife moved, just stared in its direction. It rang four times before Alfie saw it as a means of escape. He sprang to his feet and ran to answer it.

'Leave it, darling,' she sobbed. 'I need to talk to you. This is important.'

Alfie ignored her. He picked up the handset and held it to his ear. 'Yes!' he answered sharply, his head pounding.

'Alfie?'

'Larry?'

'Hi! Sorry, for a moment I thought I'd dialled the wrong number. Listen! I'm not going to beat about the bush. I've got some ... er ... I've got some terrible news.'

'Oh?' asked Alfie doubtfully. He could think of nothing worse at that moment than the news he'd heard only seconds before.

'Your old mate Abe is dead!'

'What?'

'Abe! He hanged himself!'

Alfie stood stock still, the phone frozen in his hand, his mind mesmerized by the sound of Larry's voice, his body paralysed by his words.

'His sister found him yesterday. She's with her mother, trying to recover from the shock of seeing him hanging from a tree in his garden. Seems he couldn't stand the pressure, felt he'd failed or something. Poor bastard. Anyway his funeral is on Friday. Alfie? Alfie are you there?'

'Yes I'm here,' said Alfie unable to respond to the shocking, real and immediate news. What is happening to me? he wondered. Am I losing control? Suddenly my life has been turned on its head. Five minutes ago I was invincible, a superstar. Now I'm being shot at from all angles.

'Alfie are you all right?'

'No, Larry,' Alfie croaked. 'I'm not all right. I'll see you on Friday. Bye.'

For a moment he stood there, immobilised, silent and unblinking. He shut his eyes to try to compose himself but his mind's eye threw up pictures that made him reel in horror. Images of Abe's thin and broken body hanging limply from the horse chestnut tree whose enormous bulk dominated his tiny London garden. He could see him, swinging from the branch, lifeless, a twisted rope toying with the thread of Abe's life. Then dead. Abe. His friend. Dead.

'Alfie? What did Larry want?' asked Kate who was clinging onto her husband's arm like an anxious child, her face ghostly pale.

The horror of the moment ignited a fuse inside Alfie's aching, living body. Without answering Kate, he exploded into high-speed action. There was no method to his movement. He buzzed around the house like a fly sprayed with repellent, his instincts screaming at him to get out of that hellhole.

Kate followed yelling, 'Alfie? What's happened? Where are you going? Alfie, speak to me?'

He ran downstairs, vaulting the suitcase into the kitchen to the sink and turned on the cold tap. He poured himself a glass of water, drained it then ran back upstairs where he lurched from room to room. And in his maniacal frenzy he began to pack a few things into an overnight bag, Kate following, panic-stricken, demanding answers. But Alfie couldn't speak to her. What could he say? He didn't want a baby. Right now he didn't want her. For God's sake, he thought, I've just killed someone. That was how it felt. Abe had approached him for help and he had ignored him.

What have I become? he asked himself while his life flashed in front of his eyes, screaming his crimes. I have to get out of here.

He felt Kate's hand on his arm and cringed, repulsed by her proximity but forced himself to look at her. He could see how frightened she was but he couldn't hear a word she was saying. Her mouth was working, her bee-stung lips forming shapes. And as he stared at the tears pouring down her beautiful cheeks he felt himself being dragged down to low echelons of despair that he had never visited before. Then she started to shake him. Alfie pulled away.

'Abe's dead.'

'Who?'

'Got to go!' he said picking up his bag. He hurtled downstairs, jumped over the suitcase and left the house, closing the front door behind him.

*

The West End was bathed in gloom or so it seemed to Alfie. Nursing a bottle of whisky he wandered through the rain-sodden streets, drunk and jet-lagged, his mood in sympathy with the Stygian July evening. Staggering under the weight of his grief he listed from street corner to street corner thinking about Abe. Andrew Cunningham. His friend.

There was a time, thought Alfie ruefully, when he would have described Abe as his best friend.

'As you can see I am lamentably thin with fine mousy hair and a long but distinguished nose,' he'd said on their first meeting. 'Yet I feel sure that you will refer to me as interesting when you mention this meeting to your friends.'

What had gone wrong between us? he wondered hopelessly. No! That's a ludicrous question. How did I allow things to slide? Am I really, as Abe put it succinctly, so far up my own arse that I am blind to reality?

In the beginning, when Alfie had taken his first step on the road to success, Abe had telephoned him to keep up with his news, offering his support, selfless and encouraging. More often than not he'd called him at his hotel when Alfie was away on location. On one occasion after the success of his second film when he'd just turned thirty and fame was sitting happily on his shoulders, like a mink fur on a wealthy lady in grand society, Abe had rung him, out of the blue.

'Hi Alfie. It's me. Abe! Remember me? Haven't seen you in ages,' he'd said with his usual enthusiasm.

Alfie cringed, remembering his reply. 'Sorry mate. I'm just so stretched these days. You know how it is?'

'No I don't,' he'd replied, trying to be funny.

'Listen mate, I'm sorry but I'm incredibly busy.'

'Some other time then?'

'Yeah. I've got the hottest babe here. I'm worried she'll get bored and leave. Later, OK?'

What must Abe have thought? he wondered, horrified at the memory. After all he'd done for me. Did I forget somewhere along the line that it was Abe who'd introduced me to directing in the first place?

They had been at Cambridge. Abe, on seeing Alfie's camera, had suggested he join the Amateur Dramatic Club. Six weeks later and Alfie had found himself at the helm of *Romeo and Juliet*, directing Abe in the lead part. He'd thrown himself into this new role quickly and enthusiastically. The wooden balcony he'd had built for the set had been a work of art. And then he'd suggested that it should be high enough for Abe to climb it via a rope ladder, concealed in vines. Abe had been sceptical.

'In Elizabethan clobber, in front of an expectant audience?'

'Yeah, why not.'

'It'll be bloody difficult, that's why not.'

But Alfie had persuaded him and Abe had done it with the energy and dexterity of an eager mountaineer until the last night when, his mother and sister in the audience, he'd fallen off. Too many ales in The Pickerel at lunchtime, recalled Alfie fondly.

They'd left Cambridge determined to stay friends. Abe had abandoned his dreams of becoming an actor, *too ugly* and had gone into the theatre to direct.

Alfie took another swig from his bottle. His world was spinning as he made his way into Soho Square. Struggling to balance he slumped his weary body on to a wet park bench. 'Art mirrors life, that's what the great Ted Hughes says,' Abe used to tell me. Does that make me responsible for Abe's death? Have I driven my friend out of life's game? Am I, in fact, a murderer? God, I've got to pull myself together. I'm going crazy out here.

Knowing that he couldn't face Kate again, he yanked himself to his feet, deposited his half drunk bottle of whisky in a green bin and, clutching his holdall, headed for The Ritz. The walk will clear my head, he reasoned as he marched purposefully forwards unaware that he was soaking wet.

'Good Evening Mr Macbeth,' said the thin, immaculately dressed manager who stood, pen in hand, leaning over the dark mahogany desk of the ornate lobby as Alfie staggered in.

'Oh James, yes ... er ... How are you?' Alfie slurred, shifting his weight uneasily, his feet squelching in his rain-filled shoes as he did so. He tried to focus on the manager in his dark suit and silver waistcoat, but the lamps at either end of the desk were too bright for his blood-shot eyes.

'I am well and how is Sir?' replied the manager in an annoyingly gratifying way.

'Fine, thanks.' Then, by way of explanation it being 11pm, added, 'Work being done on the house. Kate away. You know how it is?'

'Quite,' replied James, raising one eyebrow as he took in Alfie's, soiled and sodden clothing.

But I bet that's not what your bloody well thinking, thought Alfie.

'Will sir be wanting one of our deluxe suites?'

'Er ... yes. That will do fine,' replied Alfie squirming, suddenly self-conscious. It was as though he'd temporarily left his body and was looking down from the ceiling watching this grotesque display and seeing it in all its debauched glory, the behaviour of a multi-million pound arsehole.

'Will you be expecting anyone Sir?'

'No! Absolutely no! I do not wish to be disturbed at all. By anyone!'

'Absolutely Sir!' he responded, raising the other eyebrow.

Smug git. I saw your eyebrows rise. Fucking self-righteous dick, thought Alfie, angry as much with himself as he was with the manager. He made to grab the key that James held out to him, missed it, then closed one eye and tried again. This time he succeeded. Pleased, he turned away and muttered drunkenly under his breath, 'Sod off!'

'Bless you, Sir!'

Head pounding, he opened the door and glanced around the gilded room. A pair of floral drapes, swagged and tailed, hung from the tall window. They matched the pale gold bedspread adorned with cornflower blue and yellow roses. On the dark marble fireplace opposite the bed sat a large but incongruous bronze sculpture of an Irish Red Setter.

Is this what I've become? he asked himself, staring at the room with great distaste. He flung his holdall against the floor in anger, then turned and yanked back the bedspread of the double bed. Walking back a couple of paces, he screamed as he took a running dive at the bed, his face landing on the cold white linen of the goose down pillows. He gripped the corners of one tightly with both hands, willing himself to sleep.

'Aargh!' he cried. 'I am worth little more than a piece of dirt you pick up on your shoe. Difficult to remove, smelly, irritating and loathsome.'

Wednesday 9 May

She was beguiling. Did I mention that? She loved to joke and tease me wherever we happened to be – in the shower, on the boat, in the garden, in our bed. No situation could escape her humour. And she was funny, vivacious, playful with it. Her carefree mind brimful with absurdity. Hilarity flowed from her like water from a tap. And every day she wore a smile, wide-eyed, cheerful, bathed in sunshine.

And sometimes she was capricious. I must not forget that. That was when her wit turned cruel, trifling with my emotions to the point of ridicule. She would take her point, razor sharp and accurate, and spear me with it ignoring how I writhed and squirmed in shame.

You see she was never afraid to step out of line. She was honest, loyal and she was passionate. This was her real beauty. It came from within, was reflected in her actions. So that all the moments spent with her, good or bad, were diamond times.

She told me none of it was my fault and I understood, I really did, but have you ever wondered what goes through the mind of a suicide before they jump to their death on the end of a rope? What if they suddenly change their mind? I mean they might suddenly feel uncomfortable, have a premonition of death so terrifying that they want to stop the process.

Only it's too late, they've already jumped and the knot they've tied in the rope just won't give no matter how hard they struggle with it as they fall. And when they find him with fingers burnt by the fibres of the rope he fought, they have to ask the question,'Did he want to die?'

Someone must have upset Abe badly. Who could do a thing like that? He was a good bloke. He was kind and clever, thoughtful too. We were great friends, Abe and I. We were inseparable. Charles and Sebastian, that is what they called us.

Why did you do it, Abe? You must have known how much it would hurt me. I already had to cope with my parents' dying. That was hard for me. And now you!

But my life goes on. Full of nightmares that have left me deeply scarred. I have stood alone and felt the searing pain of a heart that is shattered into a million pieces. I have seen my life slip through my fingers like grains of sand. Impotent, I have stood by and watched my memories dissolve like crystals in the water of my tears.

Did I really never give a thought to your feelings, Abe?
Did I really stand by and watch you fall?

Should I hold up my hand and confess that it was I who led you to the gallows?

Oh Abe, that person, dying, dangling on the end of that twisted rope, well don't you see?

It should have been me.

Fifteen

'Larry, are you alone?'

'No. Phoebe's with me. We were just talking about you,' replied Larry, worried by the urgency in his friend's voice.

'I have something to tell you which I don't want Phoebe to know about.'

'OK.'

'When I said I was undergoing tests, I wasn't exactly telling you the truth.'

Alfie's voice was familiar – the resonance warm and deep like the hum of a double-bass, sentences flowing from his mouth easily and lazily like honey from a comb, sweet and soothing to the ear and yet his words, in total contradiction to the sound they produced, were hard, repulsive, frightening. Larry felt his toes curl and his shoulders stiffen.

'Pardon?'

'The truth,' Alfie repeated calmly. 'And that, Larry, is what I am about to tell you now. The truth. Phoebe is with you so I want you to react as if you are receiving good news.'

But Larry was too shocked to speak.

'Larry?'

'That's fantastic,' Larry mumbled eventually while he forced his mouth into a rictus grin.

'I want you to promise that you won't tell Phoebe.'

'Absolutely, old chap,' he replied, feigning an enthusiasm he did not feel.

'Right! Well. Here goes!' Alfie coughed to clear his throat, further prolonging Larry's agony. 'Tonight my consultant, Arthur Sutton, is going to attempt to remove the tumour in my colon. Mr Sutton, who incidentally is a brilliant man, quite the best Larry, I can assure you, is 80% certain that he will be successful.' He paused, perhaps to allow the awful news to sink in.

'When you next see me I shall be very weak. I may have a colostomy. Whilst I'm under they are going to take a look at my liver to check for something they call metastases. And that's about it.'

The information, like a heavyweight's hook to the side of the head, had Larry floored. He wanted to ask his friend all kinds of questions like *how long have you known this?* And *why didn't you tell me?* But he couldn't. He was gagged by his own fear. Taking a huge breath he said, 'So it's nothing at all to worry about then. That's excellent.'

'I need another favour, Larry.'

'Anything!'

'I need you here at the hospital. I want you to deal with the press. There's about half a dozen of them camped outside the hospital.'

'So I gather.'

'It seems they're getting heated up about my being here. Anyway, they are upsetting the nursing staff.'

'Of course. That's my job.'

'Tell them anything apart from the truth. That I've got wind, constipation . . .'

'If that's what you want.'

'It is. Oh and Larry, I want my camera.'

'It's under control.'

'Thanks Larry. I'll be seeing you. Could you put Phoebe on? I want to say . . . I need to . . . you know how it is?'

'Sure. Bye Alfie.'

Larry was under no illusions as he passed the phone to Phoebe, Alfie was scared and who could blame him? And it was his job now to protect Phoebe. For how long? he wondered desperately. One day would be possible, maybe two at best? But what if he died tonight? No! Now I'm being ridiculous, melodramatic. He smiled at Phoebe, his face cracking with the pain of his pretence, as she chatted happily away to her father, oblivious to his fate. Turning away almost choking on his tears, he walked, with measured steps, upstairs.

'Exquisite timing, as ever!' Phoebe called up to him five minutes later with no hint at concern.

'I'll be down in a minute,' yelled Larry. 'I just need to get a few things together for your Dad.'

Oh shit, oh shit, he thought sadly. This really is turning out to be a shocker of a day. He'd managed to sidestep Phoebe's question about Thomas Slater's accusation, thanks to Alfie phoning only to have leapt out of the fire into the fucking furnace. He moaned as he let himself fall backwards onto his bed, his eyes shut.

'Larry! Come on,' Phoebe yelled from the hallway.

Larry heaved his weary body to its feet and shook himself. He picked up the small holdall full of books, papers and magazines that he'd somehow managed to pack for Alfie and traipsed slowly downstairs. Phoebe was waiting patiently in the hall, adjusting her makeup, peering into the gilt mirror.

Not that she wears much, he thought fondly. He watched her apply her mascara, transfixed by the way her mouth formed a perfect O as she brushed her eyelashes. Beautiful long, dark lashes, he mused sadly, just like her father's.

'How do I look?'

'Like a shining light!'

'Larry! Honestly! You do overdo it sometimes.' She smiled and flung her duffle bag over her shoulder, blissfully unaware of the strain her godfather was under. 'Come on. We want to be there when he wakes up. He's desperate for his camera, though I can't imagine who or what he wants to take pictures of. Knowing him, he probably wants to photograph his eminent surgeon whom he has nothing but praise for. He always says he is lost without it. And don't look so mournful, Larry. It's nothing more than an exploratory operation. You've convinced me he's going to be all right, clever you.'

Phoebe opened the front door and strode out into the street, arm raised, saluting a black cab whose orange light she'd spotted with her hawk-like eyes. Sickened by her last remark, Larry shuffled after her silently praying, I hope to God he's OK.

*

'So how does he get away with it?' asked Phoebe.

They were sitting side by side on chairs on the light airy landing outside the private wing of the Chelsea and Westminster Hospital, Larry sipping coffee from a plastic cup, Phoebe fingering her father's camera. Initially Larry had been amused that Alfie had favoured this particular hospital. It was not exactly a safe refuge for the rich and famous. But Alfie had muttered something about the skill and tenacity of his esteemed consultant, which translated meant that Alfie, having delved deep into the man's personality, had formed an attachment to him. He admired him and he liked him. That was typical of Alfie.

Larry stared mournfully at his fawn-coloured, plastic cup, swirling the festering remains of the coffee. He felt emotionally bereft and dull, disorientated by the smog of reality that had descended on him, grey and thick as porridge.

'Phoebe, you know how the press works,' he said, trying his best to sound casual. 'They seize upon a story, true or invented. In this case it is quite clearly idle conjecture. The subject however is a sensational one. People are curious and fascinated. They want to know more. Papers fly off the shelves.'

'So you're telling me it's untrue? Even though they've named names.'

'Really?' said Larry disinterestedly. He threw back his head and stared at the vast transparent plastic roof. It lent the hospital its natural light. A giant mobile of rainbow coloured leaves tumbled down the five storeys of the atrium in a leafy autumn shower.

'Yes!' said Phoebe sharply, startling Larry. He sat up, giving her his full attention. 'Somewhere in his article, this journalist accused my father of being directly responsible for the death of Abe Cunningham. And I ... well I've never even heard of him! Can you explain that to me?' asked Phoebe, her voice staccato-like as she pronounced the words, her eyebrows knitted in a perfect frown, arms firmly crossed.

Larry sighed and shook his throbbing head. That's what had irritated him the most about Thomas Slater's article. It was another pop at Alfie about Abe. That was cheap, by anyone's standards, especially if the other papers followed suit.

'Yes Phoebe, I can,' he said softly, touching Phoebe lightly on the arm. She pulled it away, the frown still firmly in place. Larry drained his coffee cup and sighed again as he lobbed the empty cup into the bin a short distance to the right of his chair. 'Abe Cunningham was a friend of your father. He died years ago. Before you were born, in fact. He killed himself. Your father blamed himself for his death.' He put it succinctly, not wanting to dramatise.

'But why? That's the most selfish thing a person can do. Dad can't be held responsible for that. Who was he?'

'Your Dad and Abe had been friends since university. Best friends. They did everything together.'

'But Dad has never mentioned him.'

'Well perhaps the memories are too painful,' said Larry patiently, focusing on the leaves again.

'Did you know him?'

'I met him, certainly, several times. I did some work for him, though I doubt that qualifies as knowing him.'

'Did he support Dad?' persisted Phoebe.

'Like a rock. He was by Alfie's side at the premiere of his first film. They were good friends then. Abe was working as a theatre director but he was a huge support to your Dad at that time. He selflessly enjoyed Alfie's run of good fortune. I remember being very entertained by him the night of Alfie's second film. That was granted a Royal Premiere. I could see he was a funny guy. He came up to Alfie, bowed extravagantly and said, *The queen hath happily receiv'd Macbeth, the news of thy success.*'

'Sounds a bit corny to me,' said Phoebe, arms still tightly locked in front of her chest.

'Maybe. But I can assure you, he was Alfie's number one fan.'

'So why is Dad blamed for his death. No! Don't tell me! He failed, right? And he blamed Dad for his failing? Is that it?'

'No, Phoebe. You have to remember that your Dad was different back then. For a while he and Abe carried on as before, distant friends who got together whenever they could to have fun. But then your Dad changed. He stopped returning Abe's calls. He began to think of Abe as inferior and a bit of a pain.'

'And that led him to kill himself.'

'No, of course not. It's a lot more complicated than that.'

Larry stood up, walked over to the galvanised steel railings and absently leant on them. Beneath him the ground floor was bustling with activity. Doctors, patients and visitors clutching floral offerings marched purposefully in different directions, circumnavigating a vast multi-coloured, steel sculpture of an acrobat.

'You were saying?'

'I'm sorry Phoebe,' he said turning to face her, his back against the railings. His mind was throbbing. Was there really any point in going into detail?

'Please Larry. I need to know.'

Larry rubbed his face with his hands and sighed loudly. Phoebe didn't blink. 'We were in Cannes. Abe wasn't making much money at the time and had decided to make a go of it in films. He'd adapted a screenplay and was intent on approaching Alfie to direct it. He knew that with Alfie on board as director, he'd find it easier to raise the cash. Your Dad, you see, had just won the Palme d'Or. Anyway, I'm afraid your Dad was not impressed and instead of letting Abe down gently he pointed out how much higher in the firmament his star was than Abe's. He coldly dismissed him. Three months later, Abe was dead and Alfie was forced to draw his own conclusions.'

'And he chose to blame himself.'

'Exactly,' said Larry almost to himself.

'Poor Dad!' said Phoebe, unfolding her arms. Larry watched her. Her head was bowed, her eyes staring intently at her newly bitten fingernails. He wondered what was going through her mind. Without lifting her head to look at Larry she said in a quiet voice, 'It seems so unbelievable that he could have been so arrogant. I always think of him as a modest man. This picture you paint of him as a young man comes as quite a shock to me.'

'I know, my darling. And you mustn't worry about it. There really is no point. It happened years ago.'

'Yeah.' She stood up and wandered over to the railing, next to him. 'But tell me anyway. How did he deal with it?'

'Well, it was a terrible time. I remember taking him to the funeral,' Larry paused for a moment, thinking of Abe. Minnie Cooper and Stella Armstrong had been publicising his production of *Hamlet* when he died. They had told him what a decent bloke he was, quiet and disarmingly modest. Abe's tiny budget meant that he could afford little in the way of PR, which was a shame because it had been an excellent interpretation of the play.

'I insisted on driving him to the crematorium in Oxford. Abe's mother, Mary, who had taken on the role of surrogate mother to Alfie, asked him to make the address. She adored your Dad.' Larry paused, remembering their arrival.

'You two were such good friends over the years', Mary had said, clutching Alfie's hands as he stepped out of Larry's chauffeur-driven XJS. Alfie had blushed visibly, embarrassed by her selfless appreciation for his ostentatious presence. Not so Imogen.

'How dare you show your face here?' she had screeched. Larry had jumped and Alfie, he'd noticed, had trembled visibly. It had not been surprising because Imogen Cunningham was terrifying to behold, attractive in a quirky Mortitia Adams kind of way with raven hair and a porcelain complexion. Larry had been aware that she was a doctor of English Literature. Standing before them, hands on hips, eyes flashing, an air of intense intellect about her, she had been horribly intimidating. How she must dissect Alfie's films to pitiable little shreds, Larry had thought with a shiver.

'Imogen control yourself, please,' Mary had said, sternly. 'Alfie was Andrew's greatest friend. It can't be easy for him. He's a very important person now, aren't you dear?' she'd said, casting a fleeting, bemused smile at Larry's personalised number plate, 14LWA.

'Er . . .'

'Darling Alfie, it's just so wonderful to see you. I've felt so awful. Just seeing you here is a precious reminder of Andrew.' Her words, overflowing with gratitude, had been more punishing than the lashes of a cane.

'Tell me,' said Phoebe, interrupting his thoughts. Larry ran his fingers through his hair and exhaled deeply.

'Abe had a very intense, very clever older sister called Imogen. She tended to pull Abe's strings. Their father left them when Abe was ten. He ran off with a friend of Mary's. He died a couple of years later, a stranger to his kids having not made contact with them again.'

'But what about Dad? How did he cope at the funeral? It must have been awful for him.'

'Yes. It was. When Mary praised him for his address she told him that he'd got Andrew just right. She said she was glad that they'd remained such good friends – another twist of the knife! And then Imogen laid into him. She asked him if he was feeling guilty.'

Larry closed his eyes. Imogen had rushed towards Alfie in front of the assembled guests. Everyone had thought she was going to hit him but somehow she had controlled herself.

'How could you turn him down?' she'd asked, tears pouring down her cheeks. 'Did it make you feel good? Did it make you feel important? Superior? Did it turn you on?'

Larry opened his eyes. 'She cried. That surprised your Dad. He told me later that he had not thought her capable of tears. Then he tried to empathise with her, told her he knew how cut up she was and that believe it or not, so was he. But all she could say was, 'How very inconvenient for you!' And then *he* began to cry. I remember how she looked at him. It was with a mixture of hatred and disgust. She turned on her spiked heel and left him to his misery.'

'She'd lost her brother. She was bound to be upset.'

'I know, Phoebe,' said Larry softly. An uncontrollable frisson of nervous apprehension shook his body. He pulled back his shoulders and tried to recover his composure. Phoebe, staring directly ahead, did not notice.

'So then what happened?' she asked, her voice cold and unaccommodating.

'I drove him back to the office. Stella was waiting.'

'Stella?' asked Phoebe, surprised.

'Yeah. It was late. She and a few of the staff had been at the funeral. She'd gone back to the office and was waiting for us.'

'Why?' demanded Phoebe, her eyes flashing angrily.

'She had something for Alfie.'

'Really!'

'Really! She had a diary. Abe had given it to her just before he died. She was helping out with the publicity on his production of *Hamlet*. It was a diary he'd written during the rehearsals and performance of that play, his attempt at mainstream. It was full of his thoughts on life. Your father featured in it quite a lot apparently.'

'Larry Woods?'

Phoebe and Larry turned toward the female voice. A nurse, her blue and white striped uniform neatly pressed, had joined them on the third floor. She looked flustered.

'Larry Woods?' the nurse repeated.

'Yes. I am he. What is it?'

'There's the most dreadful commotion going on downstairs. The journalists waiting outside for news of your friend, Mr Macbeth, are making a lot of noise. They have begun chanting and it is upsetting the patients and visitors coming and going. I'm sorry to intrude on your privacy at a time like this but I was instructed to find you if there was trouble.'

'Yes. Yes of course.' Larry felt a strange sense of relief. Unlike the enigma of the bowel, the press held no mystery for him. 'I'll be right down,' he added. He hugged Phoebe in what he felt to be a futile gesture of reassurance. 'You'll be all right here, won't you darling?'

'Yes. You know I will. Don't fuss over me. In fact I'm going to the cafe to grab another coffee.'

Larry watched her sadly as she strode off towards the elevator without a backward glance, her father's camera slung over her shoulder. I think I'll take the stairs, he thought.

The atmosphere outside the hospital was raucous. The nurse was right. The six journalists had swelled to a dozen and were chanting, quite what, he couldn't hear.

'Gentlemen. Can I help you?' he asked loudly, appealing for control.

'Well if it isn't Mr Congeniality!' bellowed one journalist above the din. The others quietened down.

'What seems to be the problem gentlemen, and indeed ladies,' he added, ignoring the jibe and catching sight of the indomitable figure of Venetia Johnson who had worked these last twelve years for *The Daily Mail*. A man he did not recognise, dressed in a grubby fawn mackintosh was standing at the front of the small but rowdy group. His eyes that seemed too far apart narrowed as he smiled maliciously at Larry. Irritated, Larry asked, 'And you are?'

'Thomas Slater, freelance,' he lisped while at the same time attempting a sneer. His nostrils flared as his tongue protruded through his teeth. He looked ridiculous rather than threatening. 'And I have here a copy of today's *Evening News*!'

'Thank you,' said Larry amicably as he clocked the Australian accent. He held out his hand for the paper. The lizard-like journalist thrust it into his outstretched palm and took a step closer.

'You'll enjoy that,' he whispered into Larry's ear. Trying not to look repulsed by his acrid breath, Larry glanced down at the copy. The picture on the front page was instantly recognisable. James Bond dressed in black tie, pointing a loaded gun. The body belonged to Pierce Brosnan but the face was Alfie's. Above the picture in big, bold, black letters the headline screamed its accusation, the words the journalists had been chanting.

MR KISS KISS BANG BANG!

Sixteen

'Would you come to dinner with me?' Alfie stared at the book he gripped in his hands, avoiding eye contact with the girl who was standing self-consciously in front of him. He did not want to alarm her. He thought she looked anxious enough already. 'Now!' he added emphatically.

'I'm er . . .'

'Please,' he insisted, interrupting her attempts at an excuse.

'Yes,' she said, after a short pause. 'Yes. I'll come to dinner with you. I'd love to. I'll just grab my jacket.'

'Excellent!' He raised his head to smile at her but Stella had turned round, the action so sudden, her long, dark blonde hair swung in a glossy swirl behind her leaving a slight breeze in her wake. He watched as she disappeared through one of four black doors into an office off to the right of the red walled reception area. She should advertise shampoo, thought Alfie fascinated, Abe momentarily forgotten. The director would have a field day playing around with that hair. He opened the diary and began to flick through the pages, his heart sinking with every word he read.

'OK?'

Alfie, who'd become absorbed in the book, jumped at the sound of her voice.

'Are you ready?' she repeated.

Forced into the present, he nodded in her direction. She'd slung a faded denim jacket over her shoulder, and her small bow mouth that had been stern had now formed a hint of a smile. Strangely optimistic, Alfie opened the heavy, oak door of Larry Woods Associates and waved her through.

The cool evening air washed over him as he stepped out onto Wardour Street, soothing as a flannel to a feverish patient's brow. He breathed in deeply and felt the rush of oxygen to his lungs. His dulled brain began to recharge.

'What do you fancy?' he asked his young companion. She was standing patiently on the pavement, waiting for him to take the lead, busying herself putting on her jacket over her short black cotton sundress.

'Pizza?' suggested Stella, buttoning up her jacket.

'Well that's easy. Any particular pizzeria take your fancy.'

'Kettners. In Romilly Street. If we're really lucky, Alfredo might sing for us.'

'Sounds good.'

'It's one of our favourite places. We often take Larry there.'

'Meaning it's good enough for me.'

'Oh . . .' began Stella embarrassed, pulling her hair out of her jacket.

'You just carry on,' said Alfie laughing, his troubles temporarily forgotten. 'I can't tell you how refreshing it is to be with someone so young and yet so unimpressed by fame.'

'I'm not . . . it's just . . . you see . . .'

'No need to explain, Stella.'

A group of women enjoying a girl's night out stared open-mouthed as he followed Stella into the restaurant. They giggled behind their hands, nudging one another. Roused from his thoughts, Alfie shot them a generous smile that sent them swooning. He hailed a waiter. 'A table for . . .'

'Of course, Mr Macbeth,' the waiter interrupted, rushing over and grinning widely and obsequiously. 'How lovely to see you here. Will this table in the window do?'

'Actually, no. I'd rather have one in the back,' he replied with a frown.

'No problem sir,' said the waiter unabashed, delighted to be of use to his eminent visitor. He ushered another group of curious customers out of the way as he led them to a more private table. 'Here you are.'

'Thank you,' said Alfie, pulling out a chair for Stella. The waiter did the same for Alfie.

'Can I offer you and your *young* companion a bottle of champagne, compliments of the house,' he asked, head tilted to one side, beaming like a demented fan.

'A bottle of Pinot Grigio will do fine,' replied Alfie, waving him away with his hand, irritated by the waiter's protracted pronunciation of the word *young*.

'Certainly sir!'

'I'm sorry,' he said, leaning toward Stella, his arms on the table. 'It's how people react to fame!' Stella said nothing, just smiled knowingly. She had a small gap between her top front teeth, he noticed, a second imperfection to go with the freckle under her right eye. 'So what's a nice sweet girl like you doing working in the film industry?' he asked, blundering on, small talk never one of his talents. He sat back confidently in his chair, awaiting her reply.

'My mum was friends with Larry,' Stella said, glowering at the tablecloth, her hands nervously pulling at her paper napkin.

'Really?' asked Alfie, unable to hide his amusement. Mother and daughter, eh? Why Larry, you old rogue!

'They go way back, not that it is any of your business.'

'Does your father mind?' he asked, bullying her a little.

'I have no idea. I haven't seen my father in seven years,' said Stella, looking him directly in the eye.

'Stella, I'm sorry,' replied Alfie embarrassed.

There was a pause while Alfie, like a college student out on his first date, contemplated how to placate his pretty companion. Hostility was a totally new experience for him. Sitting like a dumb mute, incapacitated, all he knew was that he had to keep her there. There were so many things he wanted to ask her about Abe. That was all. He wasn't interested in flirting with her, though she was pretty enough. She was just a kid he'd taken out to dinner because she had been a friend of Abe, a loyal one at that. He had no designs on her. None at all.

A piece of red paper fell to the floor. Stella's hands were working overtime on her napkin.

'I was never much good at origami myself,' he said.

Stella looked down at the shreds of her napkin. As she screwed the sorry remains into a ball it seemed to Alfie that she was trying to suppress a smile. With renewed confidence he asked, more delicately this time, 'So you worked with Abe, then?'

'Yes.'

'And you got to know him.'

'Over a very short time, yes I suppose I did ... well ... sort of. I was very lucky,' she said, glancing at Alfie from beneath her fringe again. The light from the single white candle in the centre of the round table caught her eyes. Hauntingly green, clear as marbles, Alfie thought, staring at them intently. She blinked her dark lashes, as she held his gaze.

'Tell me about him? I mean the things he told you, his hopes and dreams perhaps. I knew him well ... of course,' he added awkwardly.

'Well we both know he was keen to break into films,' she began, her tone sharp, her back a ramrod. Alfie nodded sadly. 'Beyond that he wanted children. Lots of them,' she continued, softening.

'Really? He never told me that.'

'It was his dream. Lovely wife, house in the country, big garden and lots of screaming kids.'

The waiter returned with the wine. Alfie signalled to him to open it. They placed their orders: American for him, Napoletana without capers for her. Alfie took a large swig from his glass, draining it.

'Did you sleep with him?' he asked carelessly as he poured the wine.

Stella's eyes narrowed and she shot him an intensely ferocious look, Alfie was unsure whether to be impressed or terrified. Her eyes may be bewitching, he thought, but they're like blades. And what with a tongue that cuts like a knife, I'd better watch myself or I'll be severed!

'I'm sorry. I'm sorry, it's really none of my business.'

'I visited him in his flat in Clapham a few times,' she continued through clenched teeth, smothering her anger. Perhaps she'd remembered she was with a client. 'Abe would open a bottle of wine and we'd sit down and discuss poetry, the theatre, sometimes philosophy.'

'Don't tell me that a pretty young thing like you is interested in Kant and Wittgenstein?' asked Alfie dismayed.

'Actually, I prefer the existentialists,' she retorted.

'Of course,' he said, humbled a second time. 'Stella, I'm sorry. Forgive me. I'm not myself.' The meagre apology appeared to appease her because her body that had been as taut as a yacht stay relaxed visibly. She leant forward, picked up her glass and had her first sip of wine.

'He told me about you. About Cambridge and the trouble you used to get into together. I liked the story about *Romeo and Juliet* and the rope-ladder.'

'You had to be there,' said Alfie, relieved that her equanimity had been restored a little more easily this time.

'He told me about how you revolutionised the advertising industry. How you got offered a job directing a feature on the strength of that. Abe was very proud of your instant success you know.'

'I know. And he was good too, at what he did. I suppose it was only natural that he should gravitate toward arthouse films. I er ...' he paused, embarrassed at his openness. Stella said nothing. Alfie shifted uneasily in his seat as the memories of his crimes against his friend ran screaming to the front of his mind once more.

'I think he was disappointed that you lost touch with him,' she continued gently, sensing his discomfort.

'I know he was.' Alfie sighed. 'And I really should have helped him. Did he tell you how I humiliated him in Cannes?'

'No he didn't. But the last time I saw him, it can only have been last week, he looked tortured, in pain. It was an excellent screenplay.'

'I'm sure,' said Alfie, wiping his face with his palm. 'If only I . . .'

'None of this is your fault, you know,' Stella blurted out, interrupting him.

Startled by this passionate outburst, Alfie sat back in his chair, with a jolt.

'You mustn't beat yourself up about this. Abe was an adult. He was completely responsible for his actions.'

'I know, I know,' said Alfie, grabbing his arms helplessly 'But it still hurts when I think how irresponsible I have been.'

'Abe pulled the hardest punch and hurt the most people by committing suicide.'

Alfie shook his head.

'Mr Macbeth, you have achieved great things.'

'Alfie,' said Alfie, with a weary smile.

'Alfie!' replied Stella, trying it out. 'You're greatly admired, Alfie. You're healthy, handsome.'

Alfie felt his eyebrows rise.

'You have a beautiful wife!'

Alfie laughed. His pain eased. He looked at the innocent creature sitting beside him, trying to console him with wise words, the language she used far beyond her experience. She knew his reputation. She must do. It was public knowledge that he was a womanising, arrogant, self-centred bigot. Judging by their conversation with its multitude of peaks and troughs, he obviously was not her sort of man. Yet she had endured his company, taken him on. Sycophantic she was not but caring, certainly, serene, in a way. And although tonight her presence was like a nurse to his tortured soul, he was in no doubt that he appalled her. So why, he wondered later, did he do such a very stupid thing, even by his cavalier standards? It was not so much trigger-happy as lemming-like. Leaning towards her, he picked up one of her tiny hands, gazed into her eyes with the sincerest look he could muster and asked, 'Will you come to bed with me, Stella?'

The eyebrows went down and she glared at him. Alfie held on to his smile, armour against the daggers threatening dismemberment. He hadn't bargained on the counter attack that she unleashed with undisguised fury. Six words clear as day that left him feeling disembowelled.

'Alfie, go back to your wife!'

Seventeen

'*Tribulation* is doing well. Have you seen the reviews, Michael?' Alfie spoke with confidence. Under the large, beech conference-room table, his hands, which he clasped together, were sweating fear as he stared at an aluminium-framed and mounted poster of *Tribulation,* which hung in glorious, ironic majesty on the wall behind Michael Fenning, the president of Panama Pictures. 'I read an article in today's trades that it was Panama's most profitable film this year.'

'Yes. Damn right, it is. It took 18 million dollars on its opening weekend. Congratulations, Alfie! Another winner,' said Michael, puffing out his ample chest with pride. 'You got real class.'

Alfie beamed, eager to project a confidence in his manner that he did not feel. He glanced around the well-lit room with its corporate smell, absorbing the positive reactions from the assembled gang who were seated round the oval table. This boded well for his pitch. Dick Shepherd, the senior vice president of production, sat at the far end, smiling profusely. He appeared to be in an uncharacteristically good mood, his chubby face glowing, his bald pate shining in the strong light.

Not the most attractive of men, thought Alfie.

Dick's sidekick and second in command, the head of film production and the executive at the very bottom of what was, in reality, a very greasy pole, nodded along in pleased agreement.

'So what have you got for us this time?' Michael asked, slapping the table enthusiastically with the open palms of his hands. 'Another film with a ton of action, bursting with special effects, barrel loads of guns and a healthy smattering of sex?'

'Not exactly, Michael,' said Alfie wincing. 'I have here several copies of the screenplay as it stands at the moment.'

'I'm intrigued,' said Michael, peering over the steel rim of his spectacles at Alfie. 'Let's take a look.'

Tentatively, Alfie took the wad of screenplays out of his large, battered brown briefcase and handed them all a copy. He watched nervously as they removed the elastic bands that held the papers in place. Never had he been more aware of what he was up against. Fresh out of Harvard Business School, these guys were equipped with an agent mentality. They were not schooled in production, only finance and economics. They knew all about cost and applied their financial finesse to any creative decision they made. He was lucky to be here. Without his impeccable reputation as a moneymaking film director, he would have been shot on sight by the studio gatekeeper. He leant back in his chair, taking out his handkerchief to wipe away the beads of sweat that had formed on his forehead.

'*John-Paul Sartre's Nausea!*' exclaimed Michael, flinging his suited body backwards in his chair, slack-jawed. There could be no doubt that he was astonished – his voice imperious, his bushy eyebrows raised in disbelief.

'In theory . . .' said Alfie, his tone slow and measured, '. . . the idea is simple.'

'Simple? It's a college French text, goddamn it!'

'In practice, I admit, the project is ambitious.'

'An accident waiting to happen, more like,' replied Michael, his face reddening with anger. Having adjusted his tie, he yanked his jacket forward in exasperation. 'What's got into you, Alfie? Or have I missed something here? Perhaps you are about to tell me that Arnold Schwarzenegger is taking the lead!'

'Er . . . no Michael. That would be poor casting,' responded Alfie, trying to make light of the situation, which, as quick as the flick of a switch, had become highly charged.

'Is this some kind of sick joke . . .' asked Dick, confusion spread across his furrowed forehead, '. . . that yet again I've missed the punch line of?'

'Kamikaze!' interrupted Michael. 'That's what it is. Utter madness. Totally lacking in the ingredients necessary for a spell-binding evening at the cinema.'

'Of course, I've adapted the story to suit today's audience,' enthused Alfie, leaping to his feet. 'I have added a couple of sex scenes. Safe sex, naturally. Antoine Roquentin . . . er . . . I don't know if you've read the book . . .'

'Never mind about that!' barked Michael.

'Well, Antoine is the hero of the story,' began Alfie. He began to circle the table, his hands making animated gestures as he lead them through his pitch. 'In the book he comes across as a solitary kind of guy. He spends far too much time thinking. So I thought I'd beef up the story a bit.' Alfie paused, alarmed by an unexpected noise that was emanating from his body. A squeak, that's all it was but how noticeable? Would Michael Fenning see that he'd forgotten to put on his socks? Could he hear the sweaty skin of his feet as it rubbed against the leather of his loafers?

'Go on,' growled Michael.

Alfie stood up straight, as though standing to attention. Refocused, he parted his lips and, flashing his teeth, gave them his most brilliant of smiles.

'In *my* film, Antoine cheats on his long-suffering girlfriend Anny to embark on a raunchy affair with a gorgeous, very sexy black singer,' he continued, hovering behind Dick's chair afraid to move for fear the squeak would betray his inappropriately shod feet. Dick tried to crane his neck to look at him but soon gave up in discomfort.

'And?' insisted Michael, unimpressed.

'Her lover finds out. A chase on motorbikes across sand dunes results in a white-knuckle fight with knives. Macbeth mastery, I call it.'

'Gratuitous violence more like,' piped up the sidekick. 'It's nothing like the book!'

'I don't recall anyone asking your opinion,' bawled Michael, turning to glare at the young man. Alfie, who by now had reached Michael's end of the table, was treated to a full frame shot of the President's ears. An unsightly bush of grey hair sprouted from them, holding him spellbound.

'Get to the point . . . *please,*' begged Michael.

'I'm sorry. Yes. Where was I?'

'Macbeth mastery,' said Dick with undisguised sarcasm.

'Ah yes. Well, inevitably, the singer's lover's death is bloody and gruesome. The film rises to its happy but emotionally charged climax, Antoine and Anny, the quiet but gorgeous love of his life, getting it together in the Bois de Boulogne . . . Oh!' exclaimed Alfie, as though he'd been about to forget the single most important aspect of the movie. All the faces turned to stare at him, hopeful, expectant. 'I really think the film score should be big!'

The heads drooped back into their scripts, the spell broken.

'It certainly won't be the sort of film only watched by college or indeed A-level students. I've strayed too much from the original text,' implored Alfie.

'But it *is* art!'

'Well, yes. Yes it is. The fundamental theme of a man desperate to justify his existence is the pivotal point about which all the action takes place.'

97

'And you were part of the juvenilisation of the movies, Alfie. Your films make us money. Those people who try to imitate you make money. Are you telling me that this ... this literary masterpiece will reach 80 million people on its opening day?'

'Never mind the quantity, it's the quality I'm after with this picture. I'm thinking of it as meat and two veg cinema!'

'I'm sorry, Alfie,' said Michael, non-plussed. 'Now you've really lost me!'

'I suppose what I'm trying to say ...' Alfie took a deep breath, his last shot to blind them with words, '... is that film is also a literary medium and not simply an audio-visual extravaganza. As you have said yourself, Michael, Hollywood has a history of marching to false drums. All I'm doing with *Nausea* is moving out of the bigger game, for one film only.'

'And I am meant to be impressed by that. So impressed that Panama Pictures will cough up the necessary millions. Have you forgotten that we are slaves to numbers, Alfie? Big bucks require big audiences. I'm not sure your fans will see it your way. They are young and impressionable, not the type of audience who would root for a fucked-up existential crackpot like Roquentin. And who the hell will play him? No, let me guess, you're hoping for Dustin Hoffman.'

At this the assembled executives let out a ripple of laughter.

'I'm not asking for 30 million. This kind of film can be made on a shoestring. I'm after 1 or 2 million dollars tops. It shouldn't be too difficult to bring in the necessary 20% profit. A certain amount of people will be drawn to it out of curiosity.'

'1 or 2 million' said Dick incredulously. 'What film can be made for that? It's chicken feed.'

'A film like this. I know for a fact that that was all Abe Cunningham was looking for!'

'Abe Cunningham! Abe Cunningham!' parroted Michael, removing his spectacles. 'The guy who hanged himself, you mean?' he added triumphantly as he made the connection. 'He was a pal of yours. I'd forgotten that.'

'Perhaps you should think more along the lines of *Nausea* as a requiem for a friend, Michael,' said Alfie hastily, as Larry's banner-touting image came bounding into his mind. 'Think of all the publicity that would generate.'

'Remember, Alfie, we are looking for our next *Tribulation.* I do not think you would be so naive to assume that your films will be blockbusters no matter what,' cautioned Michael.

Damn, thought Alfie. This is like selling sex to nuns!

'I don't think you should worry about the title or the type of film this will be,' said Alfie, desperately treading water like a swimmer way out of his depth.

'Really, Alfie, why on earth not?' asked Dick derisively.

Alfie could only watch and listen as the last grains of sand began to slip slowly through his fingers

'You see, Alfie,' continued Michael, his voice heavily accented with condescension. 'We are slightly concerned about this need for a change in your career. This *J-P's Sartre's Nausea* is hardly mainstream, Alfie. In my mind it is not suitable for adaptation to the silver screen. It's not a good piece of business, Alfie.'

'And the requiem idea . . .'

'Oh. Alfie Macbeth turns Saint. Is that what you're thinking? I don't know whether the American public would swallow that, Alfie. But I admire your tenacity.'

Michael's mood that had been simmering away cooled. Now that he had made his decision, his job still intact, he felt agreeably disposed to Alfie again. He got up from his chair, walked over to the other end of the table where Alfie had finally ground to a halt and slapped him fondly on the back.

'You're one in a million, Alfie!'

'That's a no then is it Michael?'

'For now, Alfie, for now. See how you get on elsewhere . . .'

The project, like Kate, went pear-shaped.

Eighteen

Alfie was up to his elbows in *Nausea*. It had taken him three years but he had done it. Not only had FilmFour had the nerve to stump up the cash to get the film rolling but he had also succeeded in cajoling Buzz Holland to take the starring role. A Hollywood idol, Buzz's last film had bombed at the box office. He was disillusioned.

'It's a motherfucker!' he had been quoted as saying. 'Hollywood doesn't so much chew you as swallow you whole, then spits you out semi- digested without so much as a hallelujah. Man, it stinks. Next film I make is gonna to be deep and meaningful. A work of art, I hope.'

Sensing a golden opportunity, Alfie had reached for his address book.

Now *Nausea* is in post-production, he thought with satisfaction as his phone rang. It was Larry. He had incredible news.

'The BFI love the rough cut. They think *Nausea* is going to be a massive hit. Something reflective of, get this, *today's troubled souls*,' he said, his voice pumped with excitement.

'Shit!'

'You are not going to believe this but they've granted your film a Royal Premiere. That's one in the eye for Panama Pictures, eh Alfie? Michael Fenning may yet lose his job over this snakebite if it goes on to be a success.'

Alfie was struck dumb by the news, his body trembling, his mouth paralysed.

'Alfie? Alfie? Are you there?'

'Shit!'

'You must tell Buzz. He'll feel thoroughly vindicated. This is exactly the sort of break he was hoping for.'

'Larry, I . . .'

'What, Alfie?'

'I . . . I . . . I feel like I've just emerged from a darkened room. Really! This is beyond my wildest imaginings.'

'Let's hope the critics like it,' said Larry, suddenly realistic.

'You know what Larry? I don't give a fuck what they think.'

'Excellent Alfie, so get on to your editor.'

'I've done it,' he said as he put the phone down. 'I've only gone and done it. I've done it,' he repeated, loudly this time. From next door in the kitchen came the sound of a young child crying. He charged out of his study, yelling at the top of his voice.

'It's a miracle, Kate, a bloody miracle.'

'Alfie be quiet,' scolded Kate who was sitting at the kitchen table, a toddler on her lap, her head buried in her mother's apron. 'You're upsetting Phoebe.'

Grabbing his daughter beneath her armpits, Alfie spun her around wildly. Phoebe giggled with delight.

'Be careful Alfie!'

'She loves it, don't you Phoebe?' said Alfie, ignoring his wife's pleas. 'Look Mummy, Phoebe's flying.'

'Well are you going to tell me what the miracle is?' Kate asked. She was smiling now, infected by his enthusiasm. 'I haven't seen you so happy or relaxed for months.'

Alfie hugged Phoebe to his chest with one arm and dragged Kate towards him with the other. 'It's *Nausea*. It's going to be a success after all.'

'How can you be so sure?' asked Kate, alarmed by this sudden confidence after months of gloom and despondency.

'Because, my darling, that was Larry on the telephone. *Nausea* has been granted a Royal Premiere. Don't ask me how or why, all I know is that the interest this will create will provide us with the ticket sales needed to cover our costs. And who knows, if the critics like it, I may actually have another success on my hands.'

'Alfie, that's incredible,' said Kate, astonished. She wrapped both her arms around her husband's waist. 'After all your hard work over the past three years. Oh darling, I'm very, very pleased for you.'

'I think I need to sit down,' said Alfie suddenly as the shock struck home.

Still smiling, Kate took the chattering child from his arms. 'I'll open the champagne,' she said, taking a bottle of Veuve Clicquot out of the fridge. 'This calls for a celebration.'

Alfie sank into a chair and placed his hands face down on the plastic tablecloth that now protected the marble table from Phoebe's sticky fingers, crayons and glue to steady his shaking self. The fog had finally lifted. Fighting to raise the finance and being slammed repeatedly against the wall in the process had taken a lot of the stuffing out him.

There had been times when he had been so bogged down in despair, the bills stacking up, that if it hadn't been for the birth of his daughter he had thought *Nausea* would drive him insane. He looked at Phoebe and smiled. She was driving around the kitchen in her red and yellow plastic Little Tikes car, talking animatedly to her parents.

Two and a half years' ago Phoebe Macbeth had arrived kicking and screaming, hands clenched, into the safe confines of London's Portland Hospital. Alfie still cringed with embarrassment when he recalled how much he had dreaded, perhaps even resented, her arrival. Yet when he had first set eyes on the tiny baby with the dark spiky hair, his heart had turned a somersault.

'Isn't she beautiful?' Kate had whispered. 'Aren't we clever?'

'Yes!' he'd replied, overwhelmed by this little bundle of humanity's ability to tug so immediately at his heartstrings. 'Yes she is.'

'Alfie, you're pleased,' she'd said happily but he had been too choked with emotion to reply because the moment Kate had handed him their child it had seemed to him that he held the universe in his hands.

The arrival into his life of his daughter had taken him completely by surprise. He could laugh at it now, how it had turned him silly with devotion. If he wasn't taking pictures of her every movement and gesture – her first smile, her first mouthful of food – he was out walking with her in Kensington Gardens, every inch the proud father. The feelings her arrival had stirred in him were colossal. It was as though his monochrome existence had turned Technicolor, iridescent like the rainbow's sunlit archway across a rain-drenched land. And she was entrancing, with large round dark eyes like chocolate truffles and thick dark hair. Her godfather, Larry had told him she looked like Kate. Mary Cunningham had said, with great tact, that she was the image of her Dad but all he knew was that she had altered him. She had made it possible for him to knuckle down to what had been, without doubt, the hardest work of his life. And she had affected his conscience. Sexual peccadilloes were a thing of the past. He had grown to love his wife. Life was good. Phoebe had cleansed his soul.

'To Abe!' said Alfie raising his glass.

'To Abe,' repeated Phoebe, solemnly raising an invisible one.

*

Morning limped slowly into consciousness the day of *Nausea's* premiere. It was February and very cold. London was buried under an oppressive, heavy blanket of charcoal clouds. The weathermen were predicting snow but so far London had escaped. From his offices in the heart of Soho Larry prayed that the turnout would be good.

A little over three years had passed since *Nausea's* conception and Alfie had just turned forty-one. Larry had called him in the morning to go over the plans for the evening ahead. He'd arranged various interviews. It was vital that Alfie be brought up to speed.

'Are you OK, Alfie?'

'Fine. I'm fine.'

'It's just that you sound a little nervous.' He seems edgy, Larry had thought, unable to concentrate on the simplest instructions.

'Of course I'm nervous. Have you any idea what I have done.'

'You've made a film.'

'If it works I intend to think of it in terms of a bloody miracle.'

'It will work, Alfie.'

'How can you be so sure?'

'Faith, Alfie. I have faith.'

At which point Alfie had laughed hysterically and Larry had made up his mind. He had to be with him.

He arrived at 5.30pm. Kate was sitting at the kitchen table calmly sipping tea. Larry kissed her on the cheek and sat down next to her. Alfie, who was almost dressed in black tie, the buttons on his white shirt all undone, his feet bare, managed a smile in his direction before fleeing the room.

'Where's he gone?' Larry asked after ten minutes had elapsed.

'The bathroom,' replied Kate impassively, flicking through the March edition of Elle. 'He's been in there most of the day.'

By the time Alfie emerged some 40 minutes later smelling strongly of Listerine, Larry's own nerves had begun to wobble.

'It looks like the pair of you could do with a drink,' said Kate, putting down her magazine. She went over to the maple cabinet and reached for a couple of tumblers and the bottle of whisky.

Half a bottle of the finest malt later, the chauffeur-driven limousine rolled up outside the front door. It was 7.30pm. Kate, the epitome of self-assured calm, having tied Alfie's bow tie and helped him on with his shoes, was attending to her hair-do, teasing it into shape with a comb. Larry, slumped over the table sipping whisky, had relaxed visibly, unlike Alfie who, having given up trying to secure the cuffs of his shirt, was pacing the kitchen like a condemned man when the doorbell ran.

'Come on guys, time to go,' instructed Larry. He stood up and began to shepherd his charges toward the front door. Kate obliged by getting into the back of the car immediately. Alfie, however, hung onto the banisters. Alarmed, Larry, who usually had a word for every occasion, began to pull at his arm.

'I feel as though I've lost control of every single muscle in my body, Larry,' he said, suddenly letting go his hold on the banister so that the pair careered towards the door like characters in a Harold Lloyd film, faster than anticipated.

'Nonsense. It's just a bit of stage fright,' Larry replied, rubbing his shoulder that had hit the doorframe with some force. 'You'll be fine when you get there.'

'Say if I collapse on the red carpet?' Alfie asked Larry, who still had a firm grip on his arm and was now steering him toward the car. Having reached the car, Larry placed his hand on Alfie's head and pushed down hard. Sensing it was pointless to object further, Alfie allowed himself to be bundled onto the back seat next to Kate where he sat, trembling visibly, hugging his knees to his chest.

'You won't. Trust me,' said Larry getting in behind him and slamming shut the door.

'But you don't get it do you? The rest of my career is hanging in the balance. If I fuck up tonight, that's it, curtains, the end of the Alfie Macbeth show.'

'They'll love it,' said Kate, squeezing his hand. 'You'll be fine.'

The car travelled towards Leicester Square, Larry and Kate on either side of Alfie, a reassuring hand on each of his arms. No one spoke. And as the car inched ever closer Alfie longed for the ability to press the pause button on the remote controls of his life.

'They're here!' screamed a woman delirious with excitement on catching sight of the limousine. She was standing in the cold at the front of the madding crowd, waving a Union Jack. At the sound of her voice it seemed as though ten thousand eyes turned in their direction. Alfie was amazed. He had not expected this.

'Alfie! Alfie Macbeth! Katherine. We love you,' the fans hollered effusively.

At last, instinct took over. Larry is right, Alfie told himself. I know what to do, how to act. However absurd the situation might seem, Kate and I are stars. This is how the public treat us, with pride and adoration. And as for *Nausea,* there is nothing I can do about that now. This enormous crowd seem unaware of anything extraordinary. I may as well just go with the flow.

'Come on Alfie. Let's go get 'em,' said Kate, grabbing his hand. 'And remember whatever happens tonight, I love you.'

'I love you too, my darling,' he said sucking in a lungful of air.

Kate alighted on to the red carpet first. There was a collective gasp of admiration from the expectant crowd. She looked every inch the movie star in her full-length bottle-green velvet frock coat, hair piled high on her head and offset with a dazzling diamond and emerald tiara that Tiffany had lent her for the occasion.

I'm a very lucky man, thought Alfie as he followed her, cuffs flapping.

'Sex and stardust!' yelled a particularly exuberant fan.

The press will love that, thought Alfie with a wry smile as a hundred notebooks, hats and T-shirts were thrust hopefully in his direction.

'Alfie, my mother would die a happy woman if you'd sign her pants for her,' said a buxom blonde waving the skimpiest thong Alfie had ever seen.

The press, blinding them with their flashbulbs, were out in force as were all the major television stations. Larry, standing by a television crew near the entrance to the cinema, was gesticulating wildly in Alfie's direction. It was Channel 4 and, as FilmFour, its theatrical arm, was the film's backer, Alfie had agreed to a short interview with them before the screening.

'It's good to see you in the public eye again, Alfie. How does it feel to be back?' he was asked as the cameras rolled.

'Incredible!' replied Alfie.

'Are you surprised by the reaction?'

'Absolutely. As you know, I haven't made a film for almost four years. And . . . well *John Paul Sartre's Nausea* is a bit of a departure for me. I am thrilled that the public seem to be embracing the change.'

'I gather you were inspired to make this film by your late friend Abe Cunningham's love of the arts.'

'Yes, I was. In fact I have dedicated the movie to his memory.'

'A memorial for a friend, in a sense.'

'Exactly.'

'You have set an admirable precedent for your colleagues, Alfie. May I be the first to wish you luck?'

'Thank you. Thank you very much,' said Alfie hoping he appeared confident although his legs were shaking. With some difficulty, he strode over to where Kate was captivating the press and public alike.

The film ended to the audience's thunderous applause. Alfie felt his ego swelling to something resembling its former size. No way could Abe have done such a good job, he thought smugly. Any doubts that *Nausea* could have been anything other than a success were drowned like dust in a rainstorm under the shower of compliments that poured down on him from every quarter. He felt ecstatic, triumphant and important.

'You are a great maker of films, Alfie Macbeth,' said Larry slapping his friend on the back as they formed a line in preparation to meet the prince. 'You deliver what the public want and in this case what the public didn't know they wanted! That old rogue Sartre owes you one. A whole new fan club has arisen out of your success tonight.'

Nineteen

The Ivy had been a favourite haunt of Lawrence Olivier and Vivien Leigh in their day, which was why Larry had chosen it for the premiere party. The press were always drawing comparisons between the two couples. Alfie, Kate and Larry had dived into the waiting limo and had been delivered to the door of the Covent Garden restaurant, a short drive but vital to avoid the clamouring fans.

'*It's like an elegant Hollywood eatery without the sunshine,*' quoted Larry as they handed their coats to a waiter.

'You got that line straight from a book,' said Alfie nudging his friend in the ribs. 'So what's for supper, then?'

'Seared scallops with bacon and spinach, followed by roast poulet des landes with truffle jus and dauphin potatoes,' replied Larry quick as a flash.

Kate smiled as she removed her coat. She winked at Alfie.

'Blimey!' said Alfie. 'FilmFour has really let you push the boat out.'

'I've just caught sight of a friend,' said Kate heading off into the adjacent wood-panelled room that was heaving with happy partygoers. 'See you later!'

'Have fun!' he told her.

A ball of excitement was bouncing off the walls. Out of the corner of his eye Alfie noticed Buzz Holland standing beneath a stained glass window, laughing and joking with the head of FilmFour. He set off towards them but a sharp and sudden pain in his arm stopped him in his tracks. Someone had grabbed the limb and was squeezing it, stabbing him with long, polished blood-red fingernails.

'Do not think for one minute that I condone this film,' hissed a familiar voice.

Alfie spun round to face the speaker. 'Imogen?' he gasped. Dressed head to foot in black silk, save for the red nails, the ghoul-like apparition of Abe's eerily attractive sister was staring at him malevolently.

'This is just another example of how low you will stoop to save your good name,' she said, circling him.

'Now hang on a minute, Imogen. That's a bit strong isn't it?'

Ignoring his protests, her beady coal-black eyes gleaming with disgust, she continued, 'You may have succeeded in brainwashing my mother into believing that you are some kind of saint so that daily she worships the very ground you walk on. You and I, however, know different. We know that you are in fact the lowest form of life that lives and breathes upon this planet and I am determined to reveal you as such. However, now is not the time. I do not wish to debase the memory of my brother. I intend to let you go through with this, your grand but petty act of grieving but beware Alfie, when the time is right I will sell your soul to the press. And believe me, they will deliver *you* to the devil.'

It was as though she were a snake and Alfie her prey. She circled him three or four times, enveloping him in her coils, delivering her venomous sermon, until she stopped suddenly. Was she going to squeeze the life out of him? he wondered in alarm, rooted to the spot. Their eyes locked. Then Imogen sniffed and tossed back her head in disgust. Without a backward glance she slithered out of the restaurant like the serpentine villain of a pantomime, minus the puff of smoke and the hissing audience. Alfie, rendered insensible, stared after her.

A waiter passed by him bearing a full tray of champagne. He snatched a couple of flutes and downed the contents of both glasses in seconds. He could feel the effects of the tiny bubbles of alcohol immediately. They fizzed, pricking the back of his throat as he swallowed them greedily. He relaxed slightly and shook his head, trying to dispel all thoughts of Imogen. His eyes, keener for the shock he had received, travelled warily around the room eager to catch sight of a friendly face. About two feet away Kate was talking animatedly with Raul Mendoza, the smouldering Spanish icon, who was looking his usual dashing self, if a little over-dressed, in white tie and tails. They made a spectacular centrepiece to the room. It was hard to judge who was the better looking.

No doubt he's trying to grab the headlines again, thought Alfie wryly, turning his attention instead to his wife's fantastic body. The velvet fabric of Kate's dress clung to her form, accentuating every curve. He watched as Raul placed his hand on Kate's lower back. She smiled at him, leant forward and whispered something in his ear then laughed loudly as he pulled her towards him. Alfie felt a pang of jealousy. Morbidly fascinated, he watched Raul's hand slip down Kate's back to settle on her left buttock. Kate made no attempt to remove it. Irritated,

Alfie thrust his hands in his pockets and stared at the cosy duo helplessly until he caught sight of Larry out of the corner of his eye. He was sharing a joke with a stunning girl in an ankle-length, elegantly tapered, silver dress. Bouncing from foot to foot and fiddling with the signet ring on the little finger of his left hand, Larry was obviously working up to something. He saw Alfie and gesticulated to him to come over. Relieved at the distraction, Alfie inched his way through the crowd toward them. By the time he'd reached Larry, the lovely apparition had gone although he seemed far from disappointed. He wrapped his arms around Alfie, giving him one of his famous bear hugs.

'This evening has been huge,' he told him.

'Yep, Larry. It was worth all the blood, sweat and tears.'

Another waiter passed by bearing a tray of champagne. Alfie reached out for another glass and poured it down his throat. He could feel his heart pounding as adrenalin coursed through his veins. First Imogen, then Kate! Was he losing control?

'Did you see that vision in the silver dress?' Larry asked him, wide-eyed.

'Yes. Hard to miss,' he replied tetchily. 'You obviously didn't impress her.'

'Not yet but I will. Stella and I go way back.'

'Stella?'

'Yup! The gorgeous, ever lovely Stella Armstrong. She used to work for me,' crowed Larry, slapping Alfie on the back. 'And tonight I know she is ready for me.'

Alfie searched around his tired and inebriated brain for a picture of Stella. It was there but the two images did not equate.

'Are you sure, Larry?' he asked, surprised. 'I remember Stella as a mousy girl, boyishly pretty but nothing special.'

'That was then and this is now,' he said, lapsing into the vernacular of the drunken male.

He's pissed, thought Alfie amused, remembering the whiskies Larry had downed before the screening.

'I'm afraid it shows what three years and a decent wage can do for a girl. She'd never have been able to afford that dress on the salary I paid her. It's got to be Chanel! Wouldn't you agree, Alfie?' Larry asked, his cow eyes bulging with lust as he wandered off in search of his prey.

Stella Armstrong, thought Alfie, recalling the image. She's done a lot of growing up in three years. I'm sure her hair is fairer than before and longer, definitely.

'Congratulations, Alfie!'

Alfie turned round to see John Goode, Buzz's agent, beaming at him. 'Thank you, John.'

'You've resurrected what appeared to be an ailing career.'

'You're too kind!'

'I don't know if you've met Stella,' said John, gesticulating to the girl standing beside him. 'She's been with me a couple of years now and has all the makings of a very good agent.'

'Yes, we've met. Hello Stella. You're taller,' he said clumsily, grabbing her arm roughly as he admired her figure that had developed a rather wonderful array of womanly curves, her breasts more pronounced. Aphrodite, thought Alfie happily. 'What are you doing here? You look great.'

She glanced at the hand that tightly gripped her arm before averting her gaze to his face to reply without smiling. 'Hello Alfie and thank you. You look good too. How are Kate and Phoebe?'

The barbed comment delivered with customary finesse took Alfie momentarily aback but still he did not relinquish his hold on her arm.

'They are both very well. Kate's here and looking more divine than ever.'

Unheeding, Stella looked from her arm to Alfie's face again, frowning. Taking the hint at last, Alfie released his hold.

'Thank you,' she said, her firmly set mouth breaking into a smile. Unprepared for the effect this would have on him, Alfie took a step backwards and trod on the toes of a lady behind him. 'Ouch!'

'I'm sorry,' he apologised, taking out his handkerchief to wipe the spilled champagne off the lady's hand. When he turned back, Stella was laughing openly at him. 'So let me ask you Stella,' he said with renewed confidence. 'As a confidante of our late friend Abe Cunningham, what did you think of my tribute to him?'

'I liked you better when you were humble, Alfie,' she replied with a withering stare. John Goode coughed loudly, covering his mouth with his hand. 'Er, it was good. Very good. Abe would have loved it,' she added a touch too politely. Alfie beamed. 'In fact I feel compelled to tell you how honoured I am, talking to such a brilliant man.'

'Stella!' said John crossly. Alfie looked down at his shoes.

'On the contrary Stella, it is *I* who am honoured to be talking to a talent as rare and as beautiful as yourself.' Peering up at her he could not help noticing the beginnings of a true smile forming at the corners of her mouth.

John Goode sighed and took his leave. 'I'll leave you to it,' he said resignedly.

'So. Have you got a boyfriend? Are you married?' Alfie's question, delivered as it was as a total non sequitur, had the effect of startling Stella into answering.

'Yes. Thank you. I do.'

'Marvellous,' replied Alfie, feeling a strange twist of jealousy. 'Is he an actor?'

'No. He's an accountant actually, called Neil.'

'Really?' replied Alfie, gobsmacked. 'How interesting.'

'Not that it's any of your business.'

'Quite! How's the new job going?' Alfie asked, changing the subject. 'Does John treat you well?'

'Yes he does,' she said coyly.

'Kind of him to let you out for the evening.'

'I insisted on coming.'

'Really?'

'I don't mind admitting I was very interested to see the film. Sorry, tribute,' she added, rolling her eyes. 'It's a whole new take on *La Nausee*, a total rewrite in fact. Still, judging by the audiences' applause, I think you just about got away with it. Not sure that Sartre would've approved though.'

'Thanks, Stella,' said Alfie, lapping up this the faintest of praise.

'For what?'

'For coming.'

'I knew Abe. I liked him.'

'And that's why you're here is it? Nothing to do with me.'

'Well, I've been reading about your abandonment of Hollywood and how you've thrown yourself into this project. I was interested to read about it all. I suppose I wanted to see it for myself.'

'And are you perhaps just the tiniest bit interested in me?' he asked, half-joking. Stella did not smile.

'I was interested to hear about the obstacles you faced getting the film made. I mean this *Nausea*, well it's a bit of a departure for you.'

'Yes, it is.'

'Buzz told me about the intense time you had filming. That half way through shooting you had to borrow more money to keep it flowing. It seems to me you were driven to succeed.' She stopped, embarrassed, perhaps because she felt she had talked too much.

'I was,' he said smiling at her. 'You helped me. You know that don't you?'

'Don't be silly.'

'I'm deadly serious, Stella. That evening . . .'

'The BBC are waiting to talk to you Alfie,' interrupted Larry staggering towards them. 'And then we must seat the guests and . . .'

Larry paused, burped, grinned stupidly then continued, '... eat. I apologise for tearing him away Stella, but it's what I'm paid for.'

'Don't go!' Alfie implored her as he was led away. 'I have to see you before you go. Promise me you'll stay?'

'OK, Alfie.' She waved him away, laughing, like a queen dismissing an amusing courtier.

Later, after dinner, Alfie left his agent fielding questions from all quarters about his availability over the next few months, to scour the room for Stella. He was determined to find her but it was to be a fruitless search.

'Where the hell has Stella gone?' Larry asked Alfie whom he'd found staring forlornly into space.

'Only wish I bloody knew,' replied Alfie.

'It's actually quite typical of her,' added Larry drunkenly not noticing the look of dejection on Alfie's face, unaware of what had passed between them. 'C'mon man,' he said, grabbing Alfie by the arm. 'Stop moping. It's time for the serious partying to begin.'

Twenty

'What time is your flight?'

'6pm.'

'I'll drive you to Heathrow. It'll mean leaving at 3.30pm.'

'Thanks.'

'Don't forget to take your malaria tablets every day.'

'Alfie, stop fussing. It doesn't suit you.'

'Will Joss meet you at Bangkok?'

'I doubt it. I've got to catch a connecting flight to Koh Samui and then it's a short boat trip to the island.'

'Well he should.'

'I'm sure something will have been laid on.'

'Joss should meet you himself. I would.'

'C'mon Alfie. A man of his reputation?'

'He might send Raul.'

'Alfie!'

'How do you feel about Raul, Kate?'

'He seems OK.'

'Whaddya mean? The guy's a sex god. Women come out of his films drenched in their own drool. It's a well known fact.'

'He seems OK,' she repeated.

'OK? You were all over him at The Ivy.'

'We were talking. He'd heard I'd been offered the part.'

'Talking. Huh! I'd call that a very physical chat. The man's an octopus.'

'Alfie! Go and take Phoebe for a walk. I've got to pack.'

I'd be blissfully happy for my wife, if Raul was not in the equation, thought Alfie. He pushed the chair carrying Phoebe, who was chattering happily, towards the swings and snapped open the belt that kept Phoebe secured in her chair. Once released, she made a beeline for the swings, blissfully unaware that her mother was about to leave for Thailand later

113

that day. Kate had hired a nanny to help Alfie look after Phoebe for the next three months. Rachel was more than capable, but even so Alfie was struck by how unconcerned Kate appeared to be, leaving her precious daughter for the first time.

She must be excited, reasoned Alfie as he pushed his daughter in her cage-like swing. I mean this is the big time. Kate knows that even if she doesn't fully appreciate it.

'Higher Daddy, higher,' shrieked Phoebe.

'I'm trying,' he said, his mind still racing with thoughts of Kate. Raul and Kate. Kate and Raul, two icons of the silver screen filming together on an island paradise. The press had been apoplectic at the news. And with Joss Farman, the single-minded maverick as director, no wonder Kate had been excited. She'll be made to work hard over the next few months. I read somewhere that Joss is prepared to gamble his house on a film. Now that's commitment! I'll miss her though, he reflected sadly. I really will.

'Slide now!' exclaimed Phoebe.

'OK darling. Let me help you out of the swing,' he said, hoisting his daughter up over his shoulders.

'Down Daddy!' she ordered and he duly obeyed.

The Jungle Book was being screened at the Odeon nearby. Alfie decided the time was right to take Phoebe to see her first full length Disney feature. Phoebe was mesmerised. On the way home, from the confines of her pushchair, she chattered incessantly about Baloo and Mowgli.

'And next time I eat lots more popcorn. And I sit on pop-up seats. Phoebe go tomorrow?'

'Why not? Then I'll take you for trips down the river and to castles in the country. 'And at night time, when you're a worn out little Phoebe, I'll read you some more of those *Just So* stories you like so much.'

'Yes. Yes. *Just So* stories,' she said happily, clapping her hands.

*

Kate had been gone ten days and he'd been in regular contact with her. Brief phone calls late at night. Kate was full of enthusiasm for the film and described it as a powerful and epic love story. She seemed in awe of the director who, she told Alfie, had this amazing ability to delve deep into his characters souls. Filming was exhausting, which is why she couldn't chat for long but she was distant too. Alfie could sense that. As the days wore on her aloofness towards him began to take its toll. He felt lonely and deserted.

It was a warm afternoon in May, the forget-me not sky dotted with cartoon clouds. Alfie was back in the park. Phoebe was busying herself in the sandpit making mud pies with a remarkably attentive five-year-old boy. Sitting in the sun on a bench in the playground, he watched his daughter enjoying herself, an unopened John Grisham paperback on his lap. He sighed, took out his wallet and pulled out a picture of him and Kate. It had been taken at the premiere of *Nausea.*

The reviews of *Nausea* had been sensational, the critics applauding the emotional depth that had been lacking in his previous films. FilmFour had been deluged with offers from the US. Eventually they had sold the rights to Warner Brothers who were now talking about the US premiere, much to the amusement of Alfie who could not help wondering at what cost to Michael Fenning.

Alfie's agent had been bombarded with scripts from all the top film companies now he was once again back in favour, or *King of the Screen* as she liked to call him. For the past few months she had read them, weeding out the better ones for Alfie's close inspection. This had been fine for a while but Alfie was growing tired of reading them, his motivation dulled by the pressures *Nausea* had imposed on him. With Kate now gone and the joys of single parenting fading fast, he had grown bored and restless. Kate, Phoebe, everyone it seemed, was having fun, except him.

He glanced back at the picture that he held in his hand. Kate had looked magnificent that night but not as good as Stella Armstrong. Proud, defiant but ever so slightly self-conscious, she had stood before him, bright-eyed and bewitching in her silver dress.

Remarkably self-assured for a twenty-year-old, he recalled approvingly. She had a profound effect on me that night although I suspect she was toying with me? Perhaps it's just a game to her, playing with the big boys. Right now, he thought idly, what I'd really like to do is spend an evening out with her. She's good fun and a friend so it would be OK, he reasoned. I'd love to see her again. I like her. That's all. There's no harm in that.

*

Alfie's heart was thumping as he made his way across London to the John Goode offices deep in the heart of London's West End. Wine and dine her, that's what Larry had told him he'd intended to do in Cannes. Good old-fashioned chivalry, that was the way to get through to Stella. And he wasn't going to beat about the bush, he'd ask her straight away. Then maybe, over dinner at some unpretentious Italian restaurant, she'd relax a little. Open up, perhaps. Even let slip that she was as mad about him as he was about her.

'I'd love to come to dinner, Alfie.'

'That's fantastic. How do you fancy a quiet little Italian somewhere nearby?'

'I've always wanted to go to *Aubergine*.'

'Er . . .'

'You know, the really fancy place with the fabulous French food . . .'

'And fantastic prices,' interrupted Alfie who could hardly believe what he was hearing. It was uncharacteristic. Stella was usually unpretentious.

'Well?' asked Stella, drumming her fingers on the polished surface of her desk behind which she sat, suited and upright, a matronly air about her pretty form that was quite unsettling.

'Fine. In fact, more than fine. I'd be delighted. I haven't been there in ages.'

'Not since that last time with Kate,' said Stella, sticking in her point with as much accuracy as an acupuncturist's needle. 'Her birthday or perhaps your anniversary? But it's a sweet idea,' she said not quite able to disguise her sarcasm.

'And it was yours!' countered Alfie. 'Are you sure though, Stella? I would hate to force you.'

'I'd like to,' she said, her eyes narrowing.

'I'll meet you there at 8pm. Don't be late,' he said, leaving the room. Touché, he thought thrilled with the way he'd handled her. Two can play at that game young lady.

'How about if you choose the starters and I choose the main course,' suggested Alfie helpfully after Stella had spent five silent minutes hidden behind the menu. The faint sound of air being exhaled, a bit of movement, the table shifting slightly and Stella's face appeared around the menu. It was unusually pallid, her expression resolute. Alfie wondered if she was feeling OK, whether she was trying to put a brave face on a case of indigestion or something. It was unlike her to dither. She was usually so forthright.

'Great idea,' she said with a sigh, and pulled the menu in front of her again obscuring Alfie's view of her completely.

'OK so what'll you choose for starters?' Alfie asked gently. He was worried. Should he ask her if she was feeling all right? His concern might embarrass her. He didn't want to do that.

'Er . . .'

'Do you need more time?' he asked carefully. Another exhalation of air followed, only louder this time.

'No. It's fine. I know exactly what we'll have,' she said bringing the menu down onto the table quickly and with such force that the glasses shook in the breeze.

'Great,' said Alfie steadying the crystal with both hands. He looked at her quizzically but she avoided his gaze by staring at a point just above his left shoulder. He signalled to a waiter who whizzed to their table with admirable French efficiency.

'You are ready to order?' he asked, his accent richer for the slight American twang.

'Yes. Thank you,' said Alfie. 'Fire away, Stella.'

'To start we will both have the salad of roasted langoustine with candied aubergine,' said Stella peering at her now horizontal menu.

'And to follow we'll have the filet de boeuf with shallot confit sauce Hermitage.'

'Beef?' interrupted Stella, a horrified expression creeping across her face.

'Yes!' replied Alfie, alarmed.

'Oh!'

'You don't like red meat?'

'Er . . . not as a rule,' she said quietly.

'I can change the order you know. It's not impossible,' he reassured her.

Stella's face suddenly broke into the most radiant smile, taking Alfie completely by surprise. She laughed. 'But tonight I do.'

'It is delicious,' said the waiter putting his hand to his lips to blow a dramatic kiss. 'Ze chef cooks it to perfection. It well be verry tender.'

'Marvellous!' enthused Alfie. 'And could you tell the wine waiter we'll have a bottle of Margaux.'

'Any particular year?'

'Tell him to choose the vintage,' said Alfie, instantly regretting the comment as Stella's eyebrows shot skywards. 'You think I can't help myself,' he said, pre-empting her attack.

'I said nothing,' replied Stella feigning innocence.

'But you are feeling OK?' he asked before he could stop himself.

'Of course I am,' she retorted. 'Why wouldn't I be?'

'It . . . I . . . well . . . Stella, I'm sorry. Why don't we begin again?'

'Fine,' she said her voice still prickly, her eyes boring into him.

'How's Neil?'

'Neil?'

'The accountant!'

'Oh, Neil. Er it ended.'

'I'm sorry, Stella,' he said sweetly, silently celebrating his good fortune.

'That's OK. I'm seeing Martin now,' replied Stella with a triumphant smile.

'An actor?'

'No. Solicitor.'

'Ah! Young, talented, handsome and rich, no doubt?'

'Talented, yes, thirty-five and balding.'

'Really?' said Alfie worried by the reference to age. Did this place him in a more positive position? Probably not. At five years his junior, Martin sounded the safe and comfortable type, the sort of person it was hard to give up.

'Alfie!' she said shrilly thus putting an end to the conversation. Alfie changed tack.

'I've often wondered ... do you have any brothers or sisters?' he asked, startled again by the intimacy of his question. Where did that come from? he thought appalled. By a strange freak of fortune, Stella's face relaxed into a slight smile.

'Why on earth would you want to know that?'

'To be honest Stella, I was at a loss how to proceed.'

'Alfie, why must you always joke with me?'

'I'm not. I really am interested. You are something of an enigma to me.' He stared at the freckle on her right cheekbone and thought how lovely she looked tonight in a burnt orange shift dress, her skin the colour of milky coffee *and* she smelled heavenly. 'What perfume are you wearing?' he asked forgetting himself.

'Cartier,' she replied laughing. 'And I can tell you I am very dull and very ordinary.'

'Please, Stella. Indulge me. It would mean a lot to me,' he implored. The waiter returned with their starters. She was silent while he served them. Then, like a shy Catholic at her first confessional, she began to talk about her childhood.

'I was born and brought up in Oxfordshire. I have no idea what my father did. I didn't care because before he left home for good he and my mother were usually abroad. Ned, my brother, and I were pretty much looked after by our grandparents.' She stopped and took a sip of her wine. Enthralled, Alfie sat quietly, watching her, hoping that she would continue. 'When he ran off with his secretary, my mother retaliated by running off with the husband of his best friend. Ned and I were completely abandoned.'

'Stella, that's awful.'

'The last thing my mother did was to get me a job with Larry.' She stopped and looked Alfie directly in the eye. 'Very caring, wouldn't you say? Most parents would protect their seventeen-year-old daughters from a lech like him.'

'Larry, lecherous! He's more saint than sinner,' said Alfie. He had found the brief tale sad. Perhaps it explained her cynical manner.

'Maybe, but his clients are!' she retorted but she wasn't angry. 'Anyway, I enjoy what I do now.'

'Thank goodness for small mercies!' he exclaimed.

'Aren't you shocked though? I mean I left school at seventeen with two A-levels and six O-levels. It's well known that you're a Cambridge graduate.'

'So what? It's what you do after that counts. Do you keep in touch with your brother, with Ned?'

'I try to, by phone anyway. He lives in Australia, in Brisbane. You've been there.'

'Yes, when I was filming *Tribulation*. Have you? Been there, I mean.'

'No but I'd like to.'

'You'd love it.'

'I gather,' she said wistfully just as his leg accidentally brushed against hers. She didn't say anything, just shifted her position.

'And anyway,' he added determinedly. 'We do have something in common.'

'Oh?' she asked, her interest genuine.

'I too was left alone at a young age.'

A wash of colour spread rapidly across her face turning it crimson. 'I'm sorry, Alfie. You must think I'm a bundle of self-pity. I'd heard . . .'

'That I was orphaned at fifteen?'

'How awful to lose both parents so quickly.'

'Yes but I have much to thank them for,' said Alfie in a low voice, almost to himself. This was a subject he never discussed, but now, sitting here with this earnest young girl, it suddenly seemed the most natural thing to do. He looked across the candlelit table at her elfin face and saw the sad, dejected look she wore and immediately felt embarrassed. 'Enough on the subject,' he said sternly, holding up his hand. 'I promise you I had no intention of embarrassing you. Stella I'm sorry.' And, because his feelings were in total disarray he made a dramatic change in subject. It was Stella's turn to be surprised. 'Tell me about Buzz.'

Twenty-one

The beach, which was accessible only by sea, was about a mile long, trimmed with coconut palms and flanked by two pillars of craggy, grey limestone rock that stood tall and majestic like the posts of the gates to paradise. The delicate ripples of the brilliant cobalt blue water barely made an impression as they gently stroked the creamy white sand of the shore. Behind the plantation the hills that were covered in a tangled jungle of trees, many of which were rusted and covered in vines, rose steeply. As Alfie alighted from his long-tailed boat, he could see Joss Farman studying the rushes with a select group of crew, their conversation drowned by the loud metronomic throbbing of the generators. Judging by the amount of backslapping that was going on and the beaming faces, filming appeared to be going well.

At vast expense Joss had managed to get three trailers ferried to the island – two to be used by the actors, one for wardrobe and makeup – in addition to the vast amount of film paraphernalia. Alfie could see two cameras and the familiar dolly track. The gennys provided the power for these, the sound and the lighting.

Kate had told him over the phone how much trouble the art director had had persuading the Thai government to allow them to cut down a few palm trees. The beach was part of a large conservation area so permission had been vital. They'd got it after months of legal wrangling and the set was now big enough for the action.

Alfie breathed in deeply, anticipating the sweet, delicious smell that would befit such a Garden of Eden but instead his olfactory nerves were treated to the rancid smell of burning oil. He coughed uncontrollably, inadvertently attracting Joss's attention.

'Ah Alfie,' he said, stepping over the coils of cable littering the sand, hand outstretched in greeting to his guest. 'Are you all right?' He was about 5' 7" with thick, salt and pepper hair that sprayed out from under his fawn baseball cap and small grey eyes that disappeared when he smiled.

'Tip top,' said Alfie, clearing his throat.

'You've moved onto headier heights since we last met.'

'It's kind of you to say so,' said Alfie, flattered to be receiving a compliment from a director he held in such high regard. 'How did you find this place?' He pulled out his camera from his small rucksack and began to snap away. 'It's a stunning choice.'

'Weeks of scouting,' he replied, grinning blindly. 'Hard work, Alfie! Not so very alien to you now. I gather you worked your butt off for *Nausea.* I am encouraged to hear that you are taking filming a bit more seriously these days.'

'That's a bit rich coming from a yank,' he countered, not minding the jibe. 'I'll have you know I pride myself on hard work.' He looked at his watch. 'Shouldn't you be getting on? Time is money and all that!'

Joss laughed and gestured to Gareth, his second assistant director, to get his guest a chair. He placed it under a rickety bamboo canopy.

'I made it myself,' he said with pride as he made his way over to the cameraman. 'It does a fine job keeping the sun's rays off.'

Kate appeared from one of the trailers dressed in a cotton sundress, her dark hair piled on her head. Stirred by the sight of her fabulous body, Alfie sauntered over.

'Darling, how wonderful to see you. You look more beautiful than ever. I've missed you honey.' He placed one hand around her waist, pulled her to him, pressed his lips against hers and attempted to kiss her.

Kate pushed him off, irritated. 'My make-up Alfie. You'll wreck it.'

'I'm sorry darling. It's been so long since . . .'

'Alfie!' said Kate glowering. 'Later! I'm working!'

Raul Mendoza emerged from out of the second trailer, a white towel wrapped around his waist, his hair tousled. He was yawning profusely and stretching, as though he had just woken up.

'Don't worry old chap,' Alfie yelled. 'I promise I won't lay a hand on you when you seduce my wife.' Raul shot a startled look in Alfie's direction. I bet the bastard didn't know I was coming, thought Alfie, amused. Kate glared at him. 'I'm joking,' said Alfie, holding up his hands in surrender. 'See you later.'

'Scene seven, Take two,' shouted the clapper loader.

'Lock it down,' said the assistant director calling for quiet.

'Speed!' The camera operator indicated he was ready.

'And action!' said Joss.

Joss's approach to his actors was far more passive than Alfie's energetic, autocratic style. He held them on a longer rein, which allowed them room to improvise. Alfie watched Kate, fascinated. She was oblivious to his presence and was totally engrossed in her work. If Joss called *Cut!* she would stop and discuss her ideas with him. Each question, each answer met with the same placid but concentrated concern.

The first scene completed, the crew prepared for the next. It took place in a wooden hut, one side missing, the main feature of which was a rickety double bed. Shit, thought Alfie, suddenly wishing that Raul were less chiselled and handsome.

Raul, however, seemed to have no reservations about performing love scenes in front of his co-star's husband. As the action unfolded and the on-screen chemistry between the two semi-naked actors began to spark, Alfie began to feel strangely disconcerted. Their passion was more real than he could bear. When Kate removed the towel from around Raul's waist, Alfie stood up, shaking.

'Cut!' said Joss. Filming ceased and the director strode over to the actors.

'I'm a bit thirsty. I think I'll take a break,' said Alfie hoarsely. His throat was parched. A bi-product of gawping in the heat, he thought testily. I feel like a voyeur.

'The girls in make-up will look after you,' Joss said, returning to his monitor. Alfie thanked him and shuffled off to the third trailer. It was cool inside, the air-conditioning humming along to a tape of Bryan Adams singing *Heaven.* How apt, thought Alfie shutting the door.

'Gareth got as far as lying on the beach with *her* under a palm tree when he caught sight of the bulge in *her* knickers,' gossiped a large blonde make-up girl, clutching at her ample belly.

'What did he do?' asked another, smaller red-haired girl, intrigued.

'What could he do but yelp in fear and make a dash for the bar,' said the plump girl, wobbling as she doubled up with laughter. 'He was white with shock let me tell you.'

Hysterics broke out. Alfie smiled. He took a plastic bottle of mineral water out of the fridge. As he returned to the beach he cast Gareth a furtive glance to see if he was bearing any emotional scars. He didn't seem to be. Like the rest of the crew Gareth was absorbed with the action. The love scenes had been completed and Joss was filming what looked like breakfast the following morning. Kate and Raul, now dressed, were talking across a bamboo table laid with white crockery, a bowl of fresh fruit in the centre.

'I was very impressed with the day's filming,' Alfie casually remarked to Kate. They were preparing for bed in their small bamboo-lined, rush-matted, wooden bungalow located in the adjoining bay.

Apart from the large vase of orchids on the wicker dressing table, it was sparsely decorated with a couple of wicker armchairs and a wooden wardrobe in one corner. 'I'd forgotten how professional you are. Joss is lucky to have you.'

Kate looked pleased at this effusive praise from her husband.

'Perhaps we should work together on a film again. It might be fun,' he added. Kate laughed, which was not quite the response Alfie was expecting.

'I don't think it would be a good idea, but thanks for the compliment anyway,' she said, settling down for bed.

Rocked by this emphatic rejection, Alfie disappeared into the tiny, adjoining washroom to clean his teeth. She's exhausted, he reasoned, mind on other things. Her schedule is gruelling, especially in this humidity. I'm sure she'll think differently in the morning. He slipped under the white cotton sheet beside the perfect form of his sleeping wife. Pity, he thought. She hasn't seen me in ages.

It was thirst that woke him. Reaching for the tumbler by his bed he noticed Kate was no longer beside him. He rolled over, closed his eyes, resentful that he'd been deserted. Where was she? Why hadn't she woken him? he wondered as he lay there in the dark. He felt frustrated, let down for a second time. He pulled the sheet up tight to his chin and sighed.

An hour later and sleep still evaded him. Is it jet lag or Kate's continued absence that's keeping me awake? he wondered. Damn it! I'm wide-awake, now and I'm not sure whether to be worried or angry. I can't just lie here. I'll get up and find her.

He pulled on his shorts thinking that perhaps he'd been snoring. Unable to sleep, she would have got up and gone for a walk. He was sure to find her on the beach, asleep under the stars.

As he shut the door of his bungalow, he heard a noise behind him. He turned round toward the direction of the beach and saw two figures approaching out of the darkness. They were walking hand in hand. He watched unnoticed as the pair disappeared into a nearby bungalow.

Intrigued, Alfie crept toward the bungalow, his bare feet noiseless in the sand, and crouched below the open window. He could hear the low tones of a man talking, his voice identifiable by the thick Spanish accent. Raul? What was El Gringo up to now?

He stood up silently and peered in over the window-sill. Nothing could have prepared him for the shock of what he saw. Raul was lying on the wooden floor of the bungalow, naked, beneath Kate, semi-naked, who was writhing on top of him, her hands moving frantically over his body. He watched in horror as Raul removed Kate's silk camisole expertly with one hand, rolling her onto her back with the other. The last thing Alfie noticed as he moved away from the window was the expression of euphoria on his wife's face.

He felt sick.

Steadying himself, he leant against the wall of the chalet as Kate began to moan.

Alfie's initial reaction was to charge up the steps of the bungalow, rip the door off its hinges, haul Raul off his wife and thump the living daylights out of the bastard. It was only the idea that every member of the crew would see him as a pathetic cuckolded husband that prevented him. Instead he began to talk out loud, admonishing his wife in a furious whisper.

'How dare she treat me in this way? How dare she have an affair and with this . . . this . . . this . . . Spanish playboy!'

Tugging furiously at his hair he strode through the complex of bungalows to the wooden bar situated at the top of the beach. He grabbed a bottle of whisky from behind the counter, unscrewed the cap and took a long swig. For a while he just stood, bottle in hand, staring vacantly out to sea, his mind numb. Then he became aware that he was whimpering like a tortured animal. He doubled over involuntarily, as if he was in physical pain.

Five minutes passed before he regained any sort of composure. Straightening his body, his mind still blank, he held the whisky to his lips again and took a deeper more satisfying swig, clenching the fist of his free hand as he drank. As the alcohol began to kick in, thoughts began to form in his mind, wild, uncontrollable thoughts that lurched from hatred to despair and back again.

'I hate this. I hate this,' he muttered under his breath. 'This kind of thing doesn't happen to me. No! This is the kind of thing that happens to sad losers, bald guys, wimps! This does not happen to successful, good-looking, award-winning directors. It's not happening. It can't be. It just can't be. Can it?'

He chucked the top of the bottle of whisky away and took another long slug of whisky. It felt as though a lifetime of confidence was seeping from his brain. He took another longer swig and shuffled through the sand back to his hut. He fell through the door and into the wicker armchair that rested against the opposite wall where he sat glowering into the silent darkness, until a new sensation started to overtake him.

He felt hot. Agitated. His mind, that had been spinning and reeling, was at last beginning to focus but what it centred on was a terrible anger. He could feel it stirring deep within him like a malignant tumour. A little voice inside his head kept telling him to calm down but the rage inside him was growing. He put the bottle to his lips but in a sudden fit of disgust flung it ferociously against the door. It smashed into hundreds of pieces.

How dare she?

How Dare She?

He was boiling now. Sweat trickled down the back of his neck, the side of his face. He wiped it away, furious, with the flat of his hand and clenched his teeth, his mind set on revenge.

But then reason began to take hold. What was he thinking of? What was happening to him? He couldn't do that. He wasn't like that. He wasn't a violent man. Was he going completely out of his mind? He leant forward and buried his head in his hands.

'I must calm down,' he said, his voice muffled. 'I'm angry. I need to rationalise my thoughts.' He lifted his head and stared through the darkness. 'I will try and appeal to her. Cajole her. She loves me. With Raul it's lust. That's all.'

He was unsure how much time had elapsed when Kate slunk in. He heard the crunch of broken glass under her kitten-heeled mules. No doubt expecting to find her husband fast asleep, she froze when she saw him sitting in the gloomy corner of the room. Alfie said nothing just stared at her unblinking, a fierce expressionless stare. The sight of her was sickening, knowing what she'd done. He could feel bile at the back of his throat. He swallowed hoping to contain it.

'Hello,' said Kate attempting a smile.

His stomach churned at the insult. How could she do this to him? Had she no feelings whatever? he asked himself as his anger deepened. He could feel it tugging at his reason, goading him to act. Kate took a step towards him, still smiling. That was it. The final trigger.

He leapt from the chair, his temper bursting out of him, out of his control, grabbed his wife by the throat and pinned her against the wall. Kate screamed in horror.

'Whatever is the matter?' he asked her, aggression flowing though every vein and artery of his body, red-hot like fire burning him from the inside. He was breathing heavily, his nostrils flared. She's putty in my hands, he told himself. I am in command. He squeezed her neck a little to prove his point.

'Ow, Alfie! Stop it! You're hurting me!' she exclaimed, abject terror reflected in her bulging eyes.

He laughed. He could hear the sound reverberating in his ears, long, low and eerie as though the noise was coming from some other being. Kate turned her face away, screwing up her eyes, her body trembling with fear. Shocked, Alfie stopped laughing and let go.

'What on earth is wrong with you?' she asked him as she rubbed her neck.

Covering up his ears, he turned and retreated to the other side of the room. Had he imagined this? Was he going mad? He reached the dressing table. Kate's bottles were arranged in a tidy row. He stared at them fingering a bottle of perfume, trying to collate his thoughts.

'Where have you been Kate?' he asked her.

'I couldn't sleep, so I went for a walk.'

'On your own?'

'Of course on my own.'

His fingers clenched the bottle, tightly, his knuckles white. Why was she lying to him? For fuck's sake, how could she? Did she think he was an idiot? Had she no respect for him at all?

He spun around explosively and hurled the bottle at the wall. It smashed above Kate spraying her with fragments of glass filling the air with its sickly sweet smell. She ducked, covering her head with her arms. Alfie grinned at her maniacally. He could see she was petrified and that amused him.

'Tell me the truth, God damn you woman!'

Crying now she slipped down the wall until she sat on the glass-splattered floor, her arms hugging her legs. Alfie strode towards her. He knelt down in front of her, his face about six inches from her own. He began to fire questions at her, lacerating the silence of the night with his insults, short and sharp like the lashes of a cane.

'Is it because lover boy does it better than me? Or maybe it's because he's rough? Do you like it rough Kate? You dirty little bitch! You scheming whore!'

Large round tears of self-pity ran slowly down his cheeks as he placed his hands gently on her shoulders.

'I saw you together, Kate. I saw you. I saw you fucking him. You and Raul. Together,' he sobbed, trying to explain his hurt. 'Why did you do it Kate? How could you do this to me? You loved me. That's what you told me. And I believed you Kate.'

Kate's head was bowed. Appalled by the sight of her husband's tears she had stopped crying.

'Oh!' she said. That was all.

Alfie stared at her, confused. 'But it's going to be OK,' he said softly, his anger dead. He leant towards her and kissed her on her cheek. He tried to kiss her mouth but she pushed him away.

'I'm sorry Alfie,' she said coldly. 'I didn't mean to upset you. I didn't think you'd care.'

'How can you say that?' he asked, horrified by her insouciance.

126

'Because, Alfie, you don't love me. You never have.'

'What are you talking about? Of course I love you,' he implored, reaching for her hand. She sighed and let him hold it.

'It's no longer enough.'

'But we've been so happy. You and I and little Phoebe. We are a happy family.'

'Please!'

'I'm sorry,' said Alfie, chastened by Kate's single-mindedness. 'Have I missed something?' This information was a total bolt from the blue and yet the strength that she displayed was astonishing. It was as though she had prepared for this. Sensing that it would be futile to further deny her allegations he lifted her hand to his lips and kissed it.

'I'm sorry if you feel I've let you down. But Kate, I love you. You know that. And you love me.'

'For God's sake Alfie,' screamed Kate. She yanked her hand free and leapt to her feet, brushing the glass off the back of her legs, cutting her left hand on a fragment. She pushed past Alfie, as she marched over to the little wooden wardrobe. Ignoring the pain she opened the wardrobe and pulled out her clothes, splattering them with her blood as she piled them on the bed.

'What are you doing, Kate?' he asked, standing helplessly behind her.

'I would have thought that was obvious,' she said angrily, sucking her bleeding hand. 'I'm leaving you. I'm moving in with Raul.'

'What? Just like that. Surely you want to at least try and save our marriage?'

'What? Carry on living with a man who has never loved me?'

'Kate that's rubbish.'

'So why do I feel like I'm covered in shit then?'

'I don't know Kate.'

'You mean you don't know that you treat me like a doormat?'

'All I can tell you is that I do love you.'

'Oh please! Spare me the poetry,' she said raising her hands in exasperation.

Alfie was at a loss. I'm the injured party here, aren't I? he asked himself. So why is Kate yelling at me? 'OK, I admit, perhaps I didn't at first, but now ...' he dithered, unsure of what he was trying to say. The life that he had made for himself flashed in front of his eyes. A good life, a happy life, shred to ribbons. He had been such a fool. He had to keep her. He knew that now. 'Kate I don't think I could live without you.'

'That's the biggest load of bullshit I've ever heard come out of your mouth. And that is saying something.'

'We were happy together, Kate.'

'Yeah, Alfie, we were. I adored you. I thought the sun shone out of every natural orifice of your body. That's how deluded I was and that's why I put up with you and your selfish ways,' she said with a sudden laugh. 'And then I met Raul.' She pulled the suitcase down from the top of the wardrobe and sighed. 'He's altogether different to you. He's young, he's handsome, he's reliable and he's incredibly attentive. When I'm with him he makes me feel that I'm the centre of his world. I'm in love with him. It's as simple as that.'

Stunned, Alfie sank onto the bed as Kate bundled her clothes into the case. 'But our daughter, Kate. Phoebe?'

'Phoebe will be fine. You'll be going home now. She'll have you to look after her. When I've finished filming I'll come and collect her,' she said, snapping the suitcase shut.

'She's not just a fabulous accessory you can pick up and discard at random, Kate. She's a little girl. A piece of you and me. Doesn't that mean anything to you?'

Kate said nothing, just stared at her case.

'And what about me?'

'What about you?'

'Don't tell me you don't care. Don't tell me you've just stopped loving me because of an on-screen romance with some pretty Latin loverboy. He's got a history of philandering as long as his dick.'

Kate turned to look at him, her face filled with contempt. He'd witnessed the look many times but never experienced it himself. 'You want me to spell it out for you? Is that it?'

'YEAH, KATE. I DO! I THINK THAT'S FAIR,' he shouted.

'Well Alfie, here it is in language that I know you'll understand,' she said, stabbing his chest with a long painted fingernail. 'You're a lousy fuck!' And with that she grabbed her suitcase and strutted out of the hut, out of his life. Only she caught her heel on the rickety steps, tripped and fell.

'Kate!' exclaimed Alfie running to her aid. There was blood above her right eye. Concerned that she was badly injured he touched her gently. 'Are you OK?'

'I'm fine!' she replied testily.

'No you're not,' persisted Alfie. 'You're bleeding! Come back inside and I'll clean it up for you.' He held out his hand to her.

'Will you please leave me alone,' she yelled. She stood up, shaking. 'I don't want your help. Can't you understand that? You should never have come here. Go! Please. Go home!'

Thursday 10 May

She had a silver dress, ankle-length, elegantly tapered. It clung to her body like an outer layer of skin. That is something I will never forget. She was all grown up by then, had lost something of her innocence. I watched her sparkle unaffected as she sipped champagne in a room full of stars. Dazzling, incandescent, she shone in that dress like the midnight sun, far brighter, more vivid than her stellar companions though I doubt she realised that. My heart turned somersaults that night but that was all.

I can still recall the first time I made her angry and in doing so scared myself. Will never forget the ferocious glare that shot like laser fire from those eyes of hers. Startlingly green, clear as glass, she used them as weapons, narrowing them into slits like two beautiful razor-sharp blades. A look that cut me to pitiable shreds. That was when I knew that all I wanted was to please her, make her happy. And this I managed, for a time.

When I close my eyes I see her breasts, two golden orbs with nipples hard as amber beads beneath the touch of my fingers, her ribs, like the ripples of a river, her belly soft as a feather pillow. Can smell our love on her soft, silken skin. Aphrodite, Venus brought to life. Like a drug I have absorbed her beauty through my skin, like an addict I am hooked.

And still I am nervous though I've seen such things a million times in the movies. They are my inspiration. The thug picks up the axe and flings it over his shoulder. The poor helpless victim kneels before him, blindfolded, nervous, awaiting his fate. He's praying like crazy. Hoping beyond hope that the psychopath behind him will change his mind. Yet you, the audience, know that nothing is going to save him.

Everybody wants to get it over with. Everybody, that is, except the murderer. He pauses. Perhaps he is relishing the moment. Fear emanates out of the body in front of him. He can smell it. It is pitiable.

Or maybe he pauses because he has second thoughts about the vile act he is about to commit. I mean, essentially, he is not a bad man. He's been hard done by. His most prized possession has been wrenched from his grasp. He loved her. Life was sweet.

The murderer stifles his conscience. His nostrils flare as he wields his weapon. Up goes the steel blade, flashing in the bright light, then down into the skull of the uncomprehending victim with a bone-splintering CRACK. No movie prepared me for that. The noise of the skull as the axe smashed into it was deafening. It rent my eardrums. CRRRAAACKK.

It's a bit like when you top a boiled egg with a spoon. You remove the shell to reveal the thick, yellow yolk. His brains though, they were like jelly.

I could spread them on my toast, I thought.

And the blood oozed thick and dark.

In the silence of that moment there could be no doubt that I regretted what I had done.

Twenty-two

'Come now, Thomas,' said Larry with his usual bonhomie. 'This story has been done to death. Alfie cannot be held responsible for the suicide of Abe Cunningham.'

'I know,' he replied, smiling menacingly and flicking his top lip with his ophidian tongue.

'Well then, I suggest you stop this nonsense and go home,' suggested Larry cringing, repulsed by the proximity of this slimy man.

'The truth will out. Have no fear about that.'

'It will indeed.'

'You see I'm not talking about Abe Cunningham's death. Oh no. Alfie Macbeth killed a man. In cold blood,' said Thomas, his mouth set firm as he folded the newspaper. 'I intend to expose him for what he is, a murderer and a coward. He'll die in prison. And I shall be the one who puts him there.'

'I'll have you for libel, you detestable little man,' shouted Larry, unable to contain his anger.

'He killed a man, in cold blood,' repeated Thomas, undeterred by Larry's threats.

'He made films,' snapped Larry.

'OK, OK, so he made fantastic movies. His drive was relentless. He worked the system with admirable finesse. But perhaps you have forgotten his rampant ego. He would have done whatever it takes to win. Like his Shakespearean namesake, Macbeth has broken all the rules. He wanted everything and he got it no matter who or what stood between him and success.'

'Rubbish! You're deluded,' said Larry, reddening with anger.

'I have the facts,' he sneered.

'Oh really?' said Larry, trying the sarcastic tack. 'And who is it he's supposed to have murdered anyway? Tell me! I'd like to know.'

'You'll find out soon enough the moment I've unearthed the body. It's hidden you see. Been hidden for fifteen years.'

'How very inconvenient for you!' exclaimed Larry with a derogatory snort.

'He's a clever man, Alfie Macbeth,' continued Thomas, ignoring him. 'But then you'd know that, wouldn't you? Been friends with him a long time, haven't you? Funny he's never confessed his guilt to you.' He took a step closer to Larry and peered at him, the whites of his eyes yellowed and bloodshot.

He's like some sort of reptilian alien straight out of *Men In Black*, thought Larry, staring back at him checking for signs of a nictitating membrane. Thomas blinked both eyelids slowly, threw back his head and laughed, revealing a set of pointed yellow teeth.

'But then again, maybe he has.'

With that he evaporated into the darkness leaving Larry shivering in his wake.

Venetia Johnson of *The Daily Mail* wandered over. 'That sounded ominous,' she said jerking her thumb in the direction Slater had disappeared. 'He seems determined to make a name for himself.'

'Quite! And you obviously believe him. Really Venetia, how can you stand out here and chant rubbish like that when Alfie's ill inside? Haven't you stopped to consider what this might be doing to Phoebe?'

'So what exactly is wrong with him then?' asked Venetia, fishing.

'He's got wind,' said Larry, angry at not being able to appeal to her better nature.

'Appendicitis?' probed Venetia, 'Or something far more sinister.'

'Nothing to worry your pretty little *Femail* head about,' said Larry dismissively. He was in no mood for a fight. 'Now if you and your vociferous colleagues could just pipe down a little, the staff and patients of the Chelsea and Westminster hospital will be truly grateful.'

*

'Something's wrong,' whispered Phoebe. 'I know it is.'

'Let's not jump to any conclusions,' Larry replied weakly.

'I'm a vet,' said Phoebe irascibly. 'A three hour operation is not purely exploratory. Dad hasn't been telling us the truth. I'm going to stay with him tonight, in case he comes round.'

'The surgeon won't be visiting him until morning. He'll explain the operation then. The nurse suggested we go home and get some rest. There's no point staying up all night.'

'You go Larry. I want to be here when he wakes up. He hates hospitals so it's the least I can do.'

132

Relieved at the composure she was showing under such adversity, Larry said goodbye, leaving Phoebe by her father's side.

If Alfie is seriously ill there's no way he can hide it from his daughter now, he thought sadly as he climbed into a waiting taxi. As she had so rightly pointed out, she was a vet ... well almost. And Alfie? He was a complicated animal under any circumstances. Phoebe, more than anyone, seemed to understand his eccentricities. Maybe she'd suspected that he was ill all along.

*

Larry lay corpse-like on his bed in the dark staring at the ceiling, his unblinking eyes hypnotised by the faint feathery cracks in the plaster above his head. Sleep eluded him. He was waiting for morning.

Swathed in guilt at his complicity in the crime, he hoped that Phoebe would bear the consequences with equanimity. His mind was numb, overloaded by the drama of the day.

'Macbeth, you are a very foolish, fond old man,' he whispered as he tried, for the fiftieth time that night, to make sense of Thomas Slater's allegations. He hoped that by meeting the facts head on he would be able to understand them. To his tired and shattered mind it was like trying to decipher the wall paintings of an ancient and forgotten civilisation. He was dealing in non-sequiturs. A life spent feeding stories to the press, signposting journalists when they lost their way or rejecting those that were pure fabrication, had not prepared him for the information that he'd received earlier that day. It had been hurled at him with pinpoint accuracy, a bull's eye that had hit him square between the eyes and left him reeling, much to the obvious delight of the perpetrator. He was under no illusions. Thomas Slater was a man with a mission.

What's Slater playing at? he wondered bitterly. The idea that Alfie's a murderer is so ludicrous it's a wonder that I can't just laugh it off. An Aussie journalist casting deluded allegations against one of Britain's finest directors. It doesn't add up. Unless ... unless he knew Alfie and Stella. After all there's that out of focus picture to consider. Could it be her? Does Thomas Slater know Stella? Surely that's impossible? As Alfie's publicist I have files on all the journalists he's ever spoken to. I've kept a record of every interview, every article, every mention of Alfie in every newspaper and magazine that's appeared worldwide. And I'm certain, absolutely 100% certain that I've never heard of Thomas Slater.

He closed his eyes and groaned. Sooner or later Phoebe would get to hear of this latest story in all its grotesque detail. It would be impossible for him to keep these allegations from her. True or false, this was sensational news. The journalists at the hospital hadn't taken much convincing. They had embraced the idea, chanting away like the deranged followers of a religious cult. By tomorrow morning accusations of this terrible crime would be splattered across the front page of every national paper.

How will Phoebe cope? he wondered sadly. The poor child will be faced with a stack of gory facts while trying her hardest to attend to her sick father. Oh God, how will I broach the subject with him? Phoebe's right, news like this could kill especially when the victim is an ill man. As Larry lay in the darkness he clung to the hope that the media, along with everyone else, would dismiss it as nonsense.

'It is nonsense,' he said out loud. 'Pure pantomime. Thomas Slater manipulated them into chanting. It was easy for him. They hadn't embraced his idea, they had simply been bored.'

*

The papers arrived early. They always did. It was something Larry had insisted upon when signing with the newsagent at the end of his road. He liked to flick through a tabloid and a broadsheet before he set off to work. That way he felt he started each day ahead of the game, aware of what was going on.

Sleep had eventually overcome him some time after 4.30am. The sound of his letterbox snapping shut a couple of hours later had woken him, the strength of the iron springs' recoil louder and more effective than an alarm clock. He sat bolt upright in bed. The memories of the previous day careered into his head just as the blood drained to his waist leaving him light-headed. He took a deep breath to fully oxygenate his brain, swung his legs out of his bed then set off downstairs, taking the steps two at a time.

The papers lay face up on the doormat set into the parquet floor of the hallway, three paces in front of him. *The Daily Mail* headline was therefore clearly visible.

MY LIFE AT THE HANDS OF THE RAPIST ALFIE MACBETH.

'What?' screamed Larry. Staggering backwards, he collapsed on the bottom stair almost dropping the paper. 'Who at *The Daily Mail* is responsible for this disgraceful piece of journalism? Venetia Johnson!' he read, in disbelief. '*Femail*'s answer to Oprah bloody Winfrey! The conniving little bitch! No wonder she looked so smug last night. And that fake show of concern. Shit! How on earth did I allow this to happen? I'm losing my touch,' he said, letting the offending front-page article fall to the floor. 'Oh God! Phoebe!' he shouted, leaping to his feet.

He bounded back up the stairs. Pulling off his pyjama bottoms, he hopped into the bathroom, walking out of his pyjamas as he struggled into the shower. Then, without bothering to shave, he dressed quickly, grabbed his wallet, mobile phone and electric razor and dashed downstairs, out onto the street, his arm already raised in a taxi salute.

'What were you thinking of, Venetia?' he yelled into his slim silver mobile from the back of his cab, his razor poised in his other hand. However bad things had become he could not neglect his personal appearance. It was vital he project a united front.

'Who is this?' came the confused reply.

Good, thought Larry, he'd woken the cow up. 'Larry Woods!'

'Ah Larry!' she said sounding pleased. 'I was expecting to hear from you today but perhaps not this early. What's the time? Has the dawn broken?'

'You should be ashamed of yourself making up stories like this!'

'Making up?'

'It's total fabrication and you know it,' he growled. 'Alfie Macbeth did not rape his wife.'

The cab driver smiled and slid closed the window to the back.

'That's not what Katherine told me yesterday.'

'What? You'd believe the rantings of a sad old drunk with three failed marriages behind her? This is real life, Venetia, not Eastenders!'

'Don't have a go at me, Larry. I'm just reporting the facts. Alfie raped her.'

'STOP!' screamed Larry. The cab driver, unsure of whom Larry was instructing, brought the taxi to an abrupt and screeching halt. Larry was flung off his seat into the window. 'OW!'

Feeling the thud the cabbie turned around and opened the window. 'Sorry mate,' he apologised. 'I thought you were talking to me. I'll carry on now shall I?'

'Thanks,' said Larry, rubbing his nose.

'Trouble?' asked Venetia. Larry ignored her.

'I insist you publish an apology on the front page of tomorrow's paper.'

'Why?'

'Because otherwise I'll take you to court!'

'Go ahead! You haven't a leg to stand on. I have reported Katherine's exact words. She claims that *Alfie grabbed her by the throat, obscenities spewing from his mouth, as he rammed her against the wall. Pulling her by the hair he threw her face down onto the bed . . .*'

135

' ... *and raped her from behind like the beast he'd become,*' interrupted Larry reading from his paper. 'I know exactly what you said. I've got the offending article in front of me. You go on to say *Ignoring her screams he turned her over and slapped her across her face to silence her. Eventually she gave in, her body went limp and Alfie finished his vile and disgusting act like a man demented.* The highly charged over-explicit words of a sensational and desperate woman journalist, Venetia.'

'Hence the bruise on her face,' she retorted. 'That's on film Larry, remember. Oh and the red marks around her neck. Don't forget those.'

'This article is 100% libellous as you will learn to your cost unless there is a full apology in the paper tomorrow. For God's sake Venetia, I thought you had a conscience. How the hell will Phoebe feel when she reads this rubbish? She's got enough to deal with'

'But he's not seriously ill?' asked Venetia, probing again.

Larry ignored her. Right now she was the last person he was going to confide in about Alfie's health.

'Why Venetia? Why did you do it?'

'I think you should ask Katherine Katz that, don't you? After all it was she who came to me with the story.'

'Lies Venetia! It's all lies! You paid her, naturally!'

'Whether we did or we didn't, you've got to admit that this violent streak of Alfie's goes some way to corroborate Thomas Slater's story that Alfie killed a man.'

'Which man?'

'That's what I'd like to know. Which man?' she said slowly and with great satisfaction. 'Tell me Larry, have you ever wondered what actually happened to Raul Mendoza?'

Larry groaned, infuriated by the irrationality of the woman's argument. Sometimes dealing with these hacks was like having one's head repeatedly hit against a brick wall. The world and his wife had all read how Kate had risen out of the ashes of her marriage to Alfie like a magnificent phoenix straight into the outstretched arms of Raul Mendoza. For five years the stunning and talented couple had the world eating out of their exquisite hands. Then disaster had struck. Raul made a couple of dismal movies. The starring roles dried up and his golden career had taken a nosedive. Abandoned by Hollywood he'd become disillusioned with life. Living in the shadow of his successful, glittering wife he had filed for divorce and then disappeared. The last anyone had heard of Raul Mendoza was that, having immersed himself in Buddhism, he'd upped sticks and decamped to Northern India.

'He's licking the arse of the Dalai Lama. It's common knowledge,

Venetia. Why even now they are probably discussing reincarnation over a cup of green tea. Where have you been hiding?'

'Ah but has anyone actually seen him. Is there any proof? Perhaps Alfie sought revenge on Raul.'

'Will you shut up, woman!' yelled Larry as the hospital came into sight. 'I really haven't got the time for this. Apology, tomorrow, that's all I have to say to you. Goodbye Venetia.'

'Bye Larry. Take care of that blood pressure now.'

A small gathering of the press had already arrived. They stood in a huddle outside the Chelsea and Westminster Hospital. Larry paid his fare through the connecting window and switched off his mobile phone. The driver gave no indication that he'd heard anything, though Larry was in no doubt that he had. And he was in no mood to speak to the journalists. They appeared to be engrossed in conversation.

Perhaps they're discussing Venetia's article, he speculated miserably. Without deliberating further, Larry saw his chance. Head bowed he walked briskly towards the rotating doors of the hospital, into the atrium. Once inside he glanced nervously behind him. The press pack had not moved. He'd escaped unnoticed. He breathed a huge sigh of relief.

A couple of minutes later he knocked on the door to Alfie's room.

'Come in,' said Alfie, his voice hoarse and weak.

Phoebe was sitting up by Alfie's head, her hands clasped in his. Like her father, she too looked pale and exhausted, her eyes puffy from lack of sleep, her hair untidy. A strong smell of antiseptic pervaded the room. By the side of Alfie's bed, the heart monitor beeped at a steady pace. The plastic tubes of the drip, the pain relieving drugs, the drain and the catheter that entered and exited his body looked like a tangle of colourful snakes. But the scene was a peaceful one, father and daughter in close union, existing together in a private and exclusive world brimming over with unconditional love. At this moment in time they had need only for each other, safe, secure and ignorant of the chaos that was building in the world outside their own.

Larry smiled, moved Alfie's camera from the chair opposite them and sat down heavily. He knew that the surgeon had not been on his rounds, that Phoebe did not know how ill her father was, though she had guessed all was not right. His heart ached with the thought of what was to come. How would the allegations affect Phoebe? And how would she react to Alfie's illness?

Will I be able to protect them from the flak? he wondered. And for how long?

Twenty-three

'Could you put me through to Larry, please?' Alfie asked the receptionist who had finally answered the ringing phone.

'I'm sorry you'll have to speak up,' she said vacuously.

Was she trying to infuriate him on purpose, he wondered? 'Larry-Woods-please,' he said, annunciating the words clearly.

'Who's calling?' she asked tartly.

'Alfie Macbeth!'

'Oh! Hi, Alfie. Sorry he's not here. I'll put you through to someone else.'

'No!' he yelped, before adding in a more controlled voice, 'No, put me through to Audrey, would you? It's really Larry I need.' The thought of placing this delicate matter in the hands of anyone other than Larry was ridiculous. Where was he? Alfie wondered in alarm. God I hope he's in town. I really need his help with this.

'Hello. Larry Woods' office.' The well-intoned voice of the redoubtable Audrey sang out like music to his ears.

'Audrey, it's Alfie, I need to speak to Larry,' he said urgently. 'Now,' he added, for confirmation.

'He's not here at the moment. But don't worry, I'll get hold of him and get him to phone you. Where are you?'

'I'm at home.'

'He'll call you as soon as he can,' she said, the epitome of calm efficiency.

'Thanks Audrey, you are one in a million,' he told her before replacing the handset. Thank God she's there, he thought breathing a sigh of relief. She always knows exactly where Larry is. She'll get on to him straight away. Then, not knowing what to do with himself, he began to pace the tiled floor of his kitchen padding barefoot across the room like a caged tiger.

He'd returned from Thailand the previous evening feeling completely

138

disorientated, as though he was in a tumbrel awaiting execution. Phoebe had met him at the door. She'd run into his outstretched arms and had demanded at once that he take her to see the *Jungle Book* again. She'd kissed him on the cheeks and had chattered away as he'd carried her into the kitchen, hugging her warm body hoping that it would heat his heart which had ached and hurt like frozen hands on an ice-cold day. Then Raul had phoned him. That had been the ultimate insult.

Later he'd lain in bed, failure looming over him like a black cloud. He'd struggled to collate his thoughts that had swung rapidly from Kate to Phoebe and back over and over again. It was the idea that Raul and Kate might tell their cosy little story and the media frenzy that would erupt on both sides of the Atlantic if they did, that had finally driven him to wake the nanny. He'd told Rachel that he and Kate were separating and that he was worried about what was going to happen when the news broke out. She'd asked no questions, had set about packing then had taken Phoebe to Kate's parents where she'd agreed to lie low and to speak to no one.

Two hours later the house was surrounded. Thank God Phoebe's not here, he thought as he continued his pacing. It's amazing how the paparazzi can sniff out a story. The whole world seems desperate to know what's happened between Kate and me. I only wish I knew. Have I really taken Kate for granted all these years? And if I have, how come she never complained before? Now I stand to lose Phoebe. I doubt there's a court in England that will grant the father custody of his child. I feel as though I've embarked on a journey. A long, lonely one that goes on and on but I never arrive.

Ten minutes later the phone rang. Alfie pounced on the receiver.

'Hello!'

'What's up, Alfie? Is there a problem?'

'Larry. Thank God you've called. I need your help.'

'I thought you were in Thailand.'

'I was. Kate and I had a bit of an argument.'

'Well that's perfectly normal for married couples. I must say, Alfie, I did wonder whether you were wise visiting her on set. You of all people should know how frenetic filming is.'

'LARRY, SHE'S LEFT ME!' bellowed Alfie. There was silence for a moment before Larry spoke again, quietly this time.

'Oh Alfie. Christ. I'm sorry. Do you want to talk about it?'

'Not particularly. Right now I'm more concerned about how to deal with the army of paparazzi stationed outside my home.'

'Shit! I'm sorry. I hadn't heard.'

'Then how the fuck do they know?'

'Someone must have tipped them off. I'm so sorry Alfie. I can't think how I didn't pick up the whispers. Where are you now?'

'In the kitchen, stressing out. I really don't want to talk to them right now.' Alfie swallowed with difficulty. His throat was dry. His tongue, like sandpaper, kept sticking to the roof of his mouth.

'What happened?' Larry asked.

'Raul Mendoza ran off with my wife!'

'Jeez! I'm sorry mate, you must be choked.'

'Yeah Larry, I am. And somehow the press have found out about it. I can't face talking to them.'

'I wonder who it was who spilled the beans?'

Bizarre choice of words, thought Alfie. His pulse had begun to race, his heart was hammering his ribs, his breath coming in short bursts. He breathed in slowly through his nose, out through his mouth, once, twice, three times, trying to calm down. This kind of press intrusion was a whole new experience for him. He felt trapped.

'I don't know. Raul called me from the beach last night. He told me he wants to marry Kate. Can you imagine it, Larry? That playboy. What must Kate be thinking of? They want Phoebe to live with them. He told me they are going to announce their relationship in the press tomorrow.'

'It's important that you remain calm, Alfie,' said Larry as impassively as possible because, on the other end of the phone, he was trying his hardest to come to terms with Alfie's mind-blowing news. Kate leaving Alfie was the last thing he had expected. Over the years she had appeared to be utterly devoted to him, no matter what he did. The way Alfie played around he'd presumed he would tire of Kate sooner or later, trade her in for a better model. He'd been wrong. Alfie must love her after all. Why else would he be so obviously shell-shocked? It really wasn't like him. Still, he thought, thinking of the job he had to do, let's look on the bright side for a moment, at least Alfie's reputation will remain intact. He'd get a load of sympathy from the public for this.

'I want damage limitation, Larry. Can you understand that? I don't want to lose my daughter.'

'Of course you don't want to lose Phoebe,' Larry said slowly. 'Now listen, Alfie. Everything is going to be fine. Kate is the one committing the crime here, not you. It's important you don't panic. I'm going to try and control things as much as possible.'

'Thank you, Larry,' said Alfie, relieved.

'I'll start by arranging for you to stay in a country hotel. I'll book you in under the name of Guy Jones. I'll send my driver around in a hire car. He drives like a maniac. He'll lose any press that try to follow you. I'll announce your separation from Kate to the Press Association. No other comment, though I doubt that will get the press off your back. At least Kate and Raul's story will be less sensational tomorrow. The media will go to town on the romantic side of it all ... Thailand ... the film set. Obviously they'll want to talk to you. I'm afraid you'll have to sit tight and let the storm blow over.'

'Thanks Larry. You are a true friend.'

'It's what I do. Now sit tight and don't turn on the TV.' And with those words of encouragement, he put down the phone.

Alone again, Alfie felt uneasy, disgruntled. How long would he have to wait before Larry's driver arrived? he wondered. The waiting was making him feel nauseous. He was completely on edge. Forty-five minutes passed. He was tense beyond belief. He needed distracting. Forgetting Larry's advice he got up from the table and turned on the television. It was 11am already.

'The acclaimed director Alfie Macbeth is to split from his wife of four years, the film star Katherine Katz,' announced the newsreader clinically.

My God, thought Alfie appalled, my marriage bust up is one of the headlines on national television. There was a picture in the right hand corner of the screen behind the newsreader's head of him and Kate triumphant at the Royal Premiere of *Nausea*. How apt, thought Alfie cynically, clutching his abdomen. The television cut to a live film of Larry. He was standing outside his office surrounded by hordes of press, flashbulbs popping, questions firing.

Above the din the reporter's voice asked: 'Do you have any information as to why the golden couple are separating? Is anyone else involved?'

'I'm afraid I have no more details at the moment. I'm sorry,' said Larry.

Outside a horn tooted. He grabbed his bag knocking over a kitchen chair in his haste. It clattered on the tiles behind him. Ignoring it he paused by the front door to turn up the collar of his shirt and put on a baseball hat and shades that he'd left in readiness on the table beside the door. He braced himself, opened the door and ran. He could hear the whirr of the cameras and the noise of journalists demanding answers to their questions as the flashlights popped. Head down he jostled his way through the crowd, pushing away the many notebooks and microphones thrust in his face, until he reached the car. The driver had opened the rear door for him. Alfie dived in. It sped off before he had a chance to shut the door. The press, like frenetic rats in a sewer, scattered in his wake as, with all his strength, he somehow managed to seal himself in. Out of the back window he watched as the excited crowd headed for their cars. In the past he would have been amused. Today he just felt empty.

Next day he woke in a cold sweat to the reality that was the isolation of his unfamiliar hotel bedroom. Demoralised he glanced at his Tag Heuer. It was 8.45am. Somehow he'd managed six hours sleep, his first in over two days. He got off the bed still fully clothed, picked up the remote controls and turned on the small television on the desk opposite the bed. Breakfast TV was in full flow on all the channels. He opted for GMTV who were charting the weather. It was going to be a gloriously sunny day across the UK. The news headlines followed.

'Katherine Katz and Raul Mendoza fall in love in paradise,' announced the newsreader.

Alfie fell back on the bed, panic-stricken. It seemed that ITV had deemed it worthwhile to dispatch a film crew, undoubtedly based in Bangkok, over to the island. The footage was pure theatre with Kate and Raul standing arm in arm under a coconut palm on the ivory sand beaming at one another. Kate looked a million dollars, apart from the bruise above her right eye and a bandage on her left hand. Encouraged by the interviewer they kissed for the cameras. Alfie felt a bitter twinge of jealousy.

'I gather Alfie was visiting you on set when the news of your romance with Raul got out.'

'That's right,' said Kate solemnly.

' How upset was he when you told him?'

'He was more angry than upset.'

'Understandably!' interjected the interviewer. 'He'd just learnt the earth-shattering news that he'd lost his beautiful wife to another man.'

'Quite. But that is no excuse to hit a woman,' interrupted Raul with a growl.

'I'm sorry?' The interviewer seemed genuinely surprised.

Alfie's heart skipped a beat. What the hell was going on here? What was Raul playing at?

'Kate has the bruises to prove it. The one above her right eye is clearly visible as is the cut on her hand. And if you look closer you can see the red marks on her neck where Alfie pinned her to the wall with his bare hands. The man is an animal. He does not deserve a woman like Kate.'

'No. No. This isn't happening. I'm dreaming. Hallucinating,' Alfie whispered as he stared at the screen.

Kate said nothing. She stood beside Raul and stared at the camera, her expression unflinching. The consummate actress, she had produced perhaps her finest performance ever live on TV.

'Why Kate? As if you haven't hurt me enough already. Why are you doing this?' he shouted at her image.

The pictures cut to Larry once again standing outside his office surrounded by newsmen. He looked anxious.

'What's going on Larry?' the newsreader asked him. 'This is a very serious allegation. What's all this about an assault on Katherine?'

'Yes, Larry. What *is* going on?' beseeched Alfie.

Larry strode purposefully towards the cameras to make his statement. Alfie held his breath. He could see the sweat on Larry's brow. He was not prepared for this.

'Alfie Macbeth and Katherine Katz's marriage collapsed under the intense strain of the producing and filming of *Nausea*. I was not previously aware of the allegation. At present I'm sorry I have no further comment to make. Thank you for your time, ladies and gentlemen.'

Feeling sick, Alfie staggered into the small bathroom and bent down over the lavatory. He retched into the bowl but nothing came up. It was no wonder, he hadn't eaten for over 48 hours. Prising his weary body to his feet, he shuffled back into the bedroom and over to the mini bar. He pulled open the door and grabbed a miniature bottle of whisky, poured the entire contents of the bottle down his throat then fell backwards onto the bed.

He had been big news many times but until now he had never been a target for the press's hatred. He'd thought he was immune to their displeasure, that he led an enchanted life. He'd seen it happen to colleagues. With bait like this to tuck into, the press, like sharks, would be relentless in their attacks. They would have great pleasure in circling their bleeding prey and as their victim bled, so at first they'd nibble, their teeth like pinpricks on the skin. Not until their dupe was writhing in agony would they sink their teeth into his flesh and gorge themselves. When their hunger was fully satiated they would spit out the remains and all that was left would be humiliated, broken, dead.

Sweat pricked his armpits and the nausea returned. The phone rang.

'Alfie, tell me none of this is true,' implored Larry.

'What? Are you saying you believe this bollocks?'

'All I'm saying is that they were very convincing. And the bruise . . .'

'She fell down the stairs to our hut as she was leaving me. I tried to help her but she refused my help.'

'Right! I'm sorry Alfie. I didn't doubt you. I'm a bit shocked that's all. He's got a bloody nerve announcing a thing like that on national TV. I'll have him for defamation of character.'

'I did cause the bruising to her neck. I did do that,' confessed Alfie.

'What?'

'I was angry. I grabbed her by the throat for a fleeting second.'

'Why, Alfie?'

'I was out of control. Mad for a moment. But it was only a moment, Larry.'

'But, Alfie, don't you see? That's enough.'

'I'd had a shock. I overreacted. I was wrong. I know that. What am I going to do?'

'Deny it, Alfie.'

'I don't know, Larry. I don't think I can. I think I should be honest about this.'

'I strongly advise you against taking that course of action. The press will crucify you.'

Twenty-four

Larry sat at his black wooden desk, a half-drunk cup of cold milky coffee in front of him, nervously anticipating the arrival of the papers. He'd dispatched Audrey, who had stayed late and come in early, downstairs. He couldn't sit in the lobby and wait himself. He was already fighting off the urge to chew the curtains. The moment they arrived she'd bring them up to him. In the meantime he simply had to remain calm.

Never had he been as wary of the news they might bring. He'd been on the phone all yesterday afternoon and well into the night trying to convince Fleet Street that Raul and Kate had invented the story to protect their own careers.

'It's obvious,' he had told them. 'Kate is leaving a good man for a playboy and miscreant. She has her career to think about. It's vital that her previously untarnished reputation remains intact. She and Raul are simply trying to frame themselves in a better light. After all, it will do Raul no harm to be seen as a romantic hero for once in his debauched life. And do not forget,' he'd reminded them, 'That Alfie is an honourable man with an impeccable track record.'

This was crisis PR and he was exhausted, living on a wing and a prayer, hoping that his protestations of Alfie's innocence had made an impression on the battle-hardened hacks of London. Provided that Kate did not press charges, he knew that the very worst that could happen was a severe mauling from the press. And if she does Alfie is a tough guy, he reasoned. He of all people will be able to sail through a public humiliation. He might feel a bit battered and bruised for a while but time is a great healer. After a well-deserved holiday he'll be back on his feet inside a year for sure. At least I'll be able to stand in front of Alfie with my head held high knowing that I've tried my hardest to fend off the flak. This is mud slinging and from every quarter of the country.

'Here they are Larry,' said Audrey, panting slightly from the climb with her heavy load.

'Thanks.'

'I'll make another coffee. That one's gone cold.'

'Thanks,' he said, reaching for *The Daily Telegraph*. The tabloids for once could wait.

The first encouraging sign was that the story had been relegated to page three. The journalist covering the story was harsh in his criticism of Alfie the *alleged* wife-beater. The magic word, thought Larry, feeling altogether better. He read on. The journalist was sceptical and questioned the validity of Raul's claims. It seemed so unlike Alfie. After all, he was a national treasure. Relieved, Larry flicked through the remaining broadsheets. They all followed the same tack. It appeared that he had done an excellent job defending Alfie's good name.

'You look happy,' said Audrey, returning with a steaming cup of coffee.

'That smells delicious,' said Larry smiling broadly. 'There's nothing like the smell of freshly brewed coffee to put a man in a good mood.'

'It's good news then,' said Audrey. 'As I always suspected. You are the best there is, Larry. I never doubted you.'

'So far, but now for the tabloids,' he said frowning.

'I'll leave you to it,' said Audrey tactfully.

He could hardly believe his luck. *The Mail* and *The Express* had taken the same route. *The Sun* had vilified Raul, dragging out a gruesome array of pictures of his sordid past. They poured scorn on the relationship and begged Kate, the darling of the silver screen, to see sense. GO BACK TO ALFIE, SWEETHEART. HE'S A REGULAR BLOKE, the headline read.

This is some achievement, Larry, he thought. You should be extremely pleased with yourself.

He picked up a copy of *The Mirror* with confidence. Chantal Tardy's face was grinning at him broadly in full colour on the front page under the headline OH ALFIE, HOW COULD YOU?

What? thought Larry horrified. What on earth has this got to do with anything? Chantal Tardy is a B-list actress going nowhere fast. His eyes bored into the article.

The voluptuous actress, Chantal Tardy (Larry snorted. Tart more like!), *yesterday confirmed that the rumours surrounding her brief affair with Alfie Macbeth during the 1981 Cannes Film Festival are true.*

'What is this?' yelled Larry, the blood rising to his cheeks. Audrey rushed into the room.

'What's happened?'

'The little bitch,' groaned Larry. 'Alfie, you idiot. If this is true you're dead meat.'

The telephone rang. It was Alfie. 'What the fuck do I do now?'

'Sit tight,' advised Larry. 'Say nothing.'

'But what else will they find?'

'You've been discreet, haven't you?'

'I always thought so.'

'Well then, you've nothing to worry about. Chantal is a tart.'

'And that makes it all right?'

Larry said nothing.

'Perhaps now's the time to take your advice and publicly deny the assault,' said Alfie, alarmed. Larry was never lost for words. 'The press will leave me alone and concentrate on Raul and Kate.'

'Say nothing, Alfie. That is my advice today.'

Alfie really couldn't blame Larry for the mayhem that followed. It wasn't Larry's fault that he had made such a monumental cock-up of his life. He had tried his hardest to prevent it but somehow the proverbial shit had hit the fan and all of Alfie's skeletons came crashing out of the cupboard, one after the other. The next few days of his life made very ugly reading indeed.

After a night of fitful sleep on the leather sofa in his office, Larry was woken to the sound of a ringing telephone.

'Hello. Alfie?' he asked, his mind a blur.

'No. Actually it's Joss Farman.'

'Joss?'

'That's right. I'm calling from Thailand, so I'll be brief.'

'Of course,' said Larry, sitting up abruptly in a subconscious mark of respect.

'What I want to know, Larry, is when all this garbage is going to stop? I'm trying to film an epic love story out here. This, this publicity, this trash, is making my life very difficult indeed. This is why I avoid the machine!'

'Yeah I know,' said Larry, embarrassed. It was well known that Joss avoided publicity like the plague to the extent that he never employed a unit publicist on set, gave barely any interviews unless forced to by the marketing department of the distribution company and encouraged his actors to do the same. The TV crew must have stormed the island. But what could he do? 'Do you want me to send someone over to run things your end?'

'Damn it. Don't you understand? I want this thing finished.' He paused. Larry froze. 'That's your job, isn't it?' he added ferociously, slamming down the phone.

A more solemn-looking than usual Audrey arrived weighed down with newspapers.

'Shit!' said Larry. 'Doesn't time fly when you are having fun?'

Like a cat on a mouse, the tabloids had pounced on the story. Alfie had made headlines on the front pages of all the national newspapers.

'I may as well start with *The Sun*,' he said gritting his teeth.

'I'll get you a coffee right away. You look done in,' said Audrey.

'Thanks,' replied Larry distractedly. He was trying to make sense of the explicit picture beneath the headline ALFIE'S NO ANGEL. Two unrecognisable bodies were grappling in an outside spa. *Not only is it fact that Alfie Macbeth committed adultery with Chantal Tardy but, after Kate had returned to London, he thought nothing of screwing an ageing PR executive in the outside spa of top international publicist, Larry Woods' villa,* he read horrified.

First Alfie and Chantal, then his own name mentioned and now Carla and Alfie? But where had this picture come from? No press or cameras – that was the rule at his star-studded parties. Ah, but Larry, he remonstrated. You were drunk and on the rampage. It was obviously taken by a guest when you were otherwise engaged. And now with money passing hands he must have thought it too good an opportunity to miss. A picture like this would collect a high price. God, it really is a most unflattering picture. Poor old Carla, she's attractive but no spring chicken. Wet and drunk, she looks like a tired old turkey.

Larry picked up *The Mirror* and stared open-mouthed at the front page. It ran a similar piece but with three pictures. The first was of the serene and beautiful Kate, the second of the voluptuous but naughty Chantal and the third of the sloshed and sagging Carla. The headline: THE GOOD, THE BAD AND THE DOWNRIGHT UGLY!

He flung down the offending article in disgust and dared to reach for another paper. On the front page *The Daily Mail* ran with the headline MACBETH AND HIS THREE WITCHES! They too had bought the picture of Carla and Alfie, which together with a picture of Chantal and Kate completed the headline.

Someone has been making a fortune out of this photograph, thought Larry ruefully. He picked up *The Daily Star*. Their headline was so inevitable that had his world not been so rocked he would have felt like laughing: WHEN SHALL WE THREE MEET AGAIN? He flung it down next to *The Sun*, *The Daily Mail* and *The Mirror* and reached for a broadsheet expecting an easier ride. Relegated to page four, Alfie's face stared out at him, *The Daily Telegraph* asking its readers: TOMORROW AND TOMORROW AND TOMORROW, WHAT WILL MACBETH DO TOMORROW? The report that followed concluded that Alfie was a cad, sanctimoniously defining the word as the most dishonourable of men.

Larry leant back in his chair, his body aching with fatigue, his spirit shattered. If they hadn't already guessed it, the public would now know that Kate truly deserved to be with the gorgeous Mendoza. Overnight this once errant playboy had been promoted to knight in shining armour. All that had been missing in these stories was a gleaming white steed. There could be no escaping the fact that Raul was standing by poor misused Kate, estranged wife of the wife-beating, serial adulterer Alfie Macbeth.

*

Stranded and alone in an anonymous hotel room, Alfie's world that had been balanced precariously on a cliff edge had finally crumbled, to tumble slowly and painfully into the sea below. The fall hadn't killed him. He was still alive, if you could call this living. No more the hero, Alfie's pedestal upon which he had lorded it for so long had been unceremoniously pulled from under him. Vilified, mocked and parodied by the press, he was just another victim to do with as they pleased. For the first time in his life Alfie felt exposed and vulnerable.

The phone rang. It was Larry.

'The press are on to you. Seems a chambermaid recognised you and has tipped them off, for a price, no doubt. I'm sending my driver. I've got another hideout organised.'

'Where Larry? Tell me, because I cannot believe it'll be somewhere they won't find me.'

'Oh they won't find you, Alfie! Have no fear about that.'

'Where, then?'

'I won't tell you over the phone. Too risky. My driver will pick you up and try his hardest to lose them.'

'Them? What? They're here? Already?'

'Yup, 'fraid so, hundreds of them. Oh and Audrey's telling me the car has arrived. You can go.'

'But . . .'

'Leave everything to me.'

His coat over his head, Alfie scurried out of the hotel into the back of Larry's chauffeur driven car. It zoomed off down the road with a screech of rubber, the press in hot pursuit. Larry's driver, however, knew all the back routes. It wasn't long before he lost the last Golf, screaming down a narrow country lane, the needle of the speedometer firmly set at 75mph. At any other time Alfie would have feared for his safety. Not now. His life had crumbled away. All that was left was in ruins. Questions teased his aching brain. Would Kate press charges? Where was he going? And what would he do when he got there? But more terrifying than anything was not knowing the answer to the question – would he ever see Phoebe again?

The following day as Larry attempted to nurse his own wounds while strolling amongst the debris of Alfie's broken life, Imogen played her trump card. Obviously deciding the time was ripe she had gone through with her threat and sold Alfie's soul to the press. With a sinking heart Larry read the article that Imogen, sanctimonious to the last, had offered exclusively to *The Times*, which began with the declaration, *Not only is Alfie Macbeth a cheating mass adulterer but he was also integral in the death of my brother. For the past three years I have held him wholly responsible.*

As she had so astutely forecast her bald accusation had Alfie's reputation well and truly buried. All Larry could do was to phone the Press Association and make another announcement:

Abe Cunningham's death was an unfortunate accident brought about by the stresses that exist within this industry. Alfie Macbeth has mourned long and hard for his friend. Please could you respect his privacy at such an awkward time.

PART TWO

The effect of power and publicity on all men is the aggravation of self, a sort of tumor that ends by killing the victim's sympathies.
Henry Brook Adams (US Historian 1838–1918)

Friday 11 May

She told me she was born lucky, that nothing really bad ever happened to her. I'll always remember that. She believed that life was good. I knew she was an optimist. She had a special talent, could make the right choices in life, laughed in the face of danger. And so I told her she was an angel but she didn't like that at all.

She spoke the truth, always. She never lied, not once in all the time we spent together. She was honest, sometimes painfully so, could not disguise the way she felt although she'd often try to. And her smile, the way it eased across her cheeks in tiny lines like a flickering torch to her clear green eyes that would shine and sparkle, radiating happiness, was the light that I followed in those days when I lived upon her cloud.

But I don't believe in luck. I never have. And how I wish I could have frozen time, for I was in heaven then until the day the light went out as I had always feared it would. The day I fell back down to earth.

You see I hadn't meant for it to happen. I wasn't sure beforehand that I wanted to kill him. The thought was provoked by a simple action of the victim that I really wasn't prepared for. I hadn't plotted or planned. It was a spur of the moment thing, ironic in its simplicity, committed with my bare hands.

His face turns very red as I cling to his throat with the tightest of grips. His eyes begin to water. They look as though they might pop out of his head. And the noise he makes as he frantically tries to loosen my hands, his legs buckling as he struggles for air. It is like something is stuck in his throat.

Stop making such I racket, I think. I don't like it. It's upsetting me.

But I will not let go. I squeeze and squeeze as though I am trying to get the last drop of juice out of an orange.

He takes ages to die. I want him to hurry up. I want to get it over with. And just as I think of giving up at last his body goes limp. I let go my grasp and his body slumps to the ground, a pile of bones and flesh.

A dead body.

The idiot. He must have known I would kill him. So why does his corpse continue to stare at me with a question in its eyes?

That is when I realise that now I have another problem to deal with. I have to hide the body. I have to bury him where nobody will find him.

I panic. It will take me ages to dig a hole.

And then I have my brilliant idea, another spur of the moment thing. I shall bind him with ropes, weight him with stones and throw him in

the lake. We have a lake at the bottom of our garden upon which a
family of ducks like to swim.
    That is what I did.
    I threw him in the lake, much to the annoyance of the duck family.

One

'Months?'

The surgeon cleared his throat and looked directly into Alfie's drugged, dazed eyes.

'I have to be honest with you, Alfie,' he said, his mouth set in a firm, thin line. 'I consider three months to be optimistic.'

Alfie's body throbbed with the agony of surgery. He was struggling to focus on the man who delivered this earth-shattering news. His groggy mind, in tune with his body, ached with the strain of mortality. He was going to die. That was what the man had said. He had reached the end.

A spasm of pain stung his body. He took a sharp intake of breath, clenching his fist into a ball. Death, at least, would put an end to that. Right now that seemed a pleasant alternative. At the same time death seemed so final to him. He loved life, at least the pain-free version, he decided, as the wave subsided. He wasn't ready to give up just yet.

'But what about chemotherapy?' he suggested hopefully.

'Chemotherapy at this stage would be, at very best, palliative. Of course there's a possibility that your life may be lengthened by a month. I see no point in putting your body through it. You've lost so much weight. I don't think you're strong enough.'

'But the operation to remove the tumour in my colon was successful?' Alfie asked him, grimacing as another wave of pain hit him.

'Yes. The operation to remove the tumour was a success.'

'So what was the point? Why bother?'

'It was high enough to be excised without formation of a colostomy. And in my belief the surgical removal of the tumour will alleviate your pain up to a point, once you have recovered from the trauma of the surgery. However, in addition to this tumour and the many smaller tumours in your lymph nodes, we found metastases on your liver. These are secondary tumours that indicate your cancer has progressed to the fourth stage. Most liver metastases are asymptomatic. If we had found them while they were small we might have been able to operate. However, the metastases on your liver are large and extensive. In my opinion your cancer is too advanced to be curable. I am very sorry, Alfie.'

'There is nothing you can do, nothing at all?'

'We can manage your pain.'

'I am going to die!' said Alfie, in a hollow voice.

'I am terribly sorry, Alfie. I wish I had better news.'

'But Phoebe!' exclaimed Alfie. 'I can't die. I can't leave her. What will happen to Phoebe?'

*

The press were vying for space outside the hospital. It had begun to rain and tempers were beginning to fray. Larry could see them through the large glass windows as the escalator descended the atrium, a huge crowd of tired and news-hungry hacks jostling for space. It was no more than he had expected. Thomas Slater and Venetia Johnson's revelations had kicked up a storm of interest. The entire British media were demanding answers to their questions.

Larry had left Phoebe outside her father's room where they had been anxiously waiting for the surgeon to reappear.

It's bad, isn't it?' she had asked him.

'I don't know, Phoebe. We must try to be patient,' he had said, trying desperately to reassure her.

'Mr Woods. Larry Woods?' The voice had been high-pitched. The woman, tall, grey-haired and dressed in a suit, had a business-like air about her.

'Yes?'

'Hello. Grace Smith, from the PR department.'

'Oh! I see. Pleased to meet you,' Larry had said, offering her his hand.

'Yes. Quite. But look here, we just can't cope with this amount of press intrusion.'

'Er ... could we go somewhere else and discuss this?' he'd asked quickly, nodding his head towards Phoebe.

Now, on his way to face them, it felt as though his stomach was playing leapfrog with his intestines. Roadkill! That was what he was about to become. The moment he set a foot outside the hospital the press would attack with questions, recriminations and accusations and he would stand alone before them and try to abate them. But what the hell could he tell them? Like the journalists, he was totally in the dark. All he had to go on was a gut feeling that Alfie was innocent.

I'm getting too old for this, he thought wearily. He took a deep breath, straightened his aching back and walked, head held high through the rotating doors of the Chelsea and Westminster Hospital. The steady hum of the media's conversation rose to an angry crescendo. Larry held up his hands and appealed for calm.

'Is it true that Alfie raped Katherine Katz?' demanded a correspondent from the BBC.

'No!' answered Larry categorically. 'That allegation is false.'

'The article in *The Evening News* claims Alfie killed a man. What does Alfie say about that?' piped up a journalist whom Larry recognised from *The Independent*. He hesitated, trying to contain the panic he felt rising in an acid stream from the pit of his stomach.

'Where's Raul Mendoza?' a woman's voice interjected, before he had time to answer.

Venetia, thought Larry. Bloody busybody.

'What's wrong with Alfie?' someone at the back of the crowd asked.

Larry, counting slowly to ten, took a moment to compose himself. There was only one choice open to him, an escape route from all the terrible storylines, the derisive front-page headlines that had haunted him all night.

'Alfie Macbeth has cancer,' he annunciated. There was a collective intake of breath, followed by a rumble of loud muttering. 'His surgeon is with him at the moment,' continued Larry, silently praying that he had acquired their sympathy. 'I shall know more later. In the meantime could I ask you please to respect his and his daughter's privacy, go back to your offices and leave them in peace. I will issue a full statement when I am in receipt of all the facts.'

'How bad is it?'

'Will he die?'

'Ladies and Gentlemen, I have told you all I know. So please, put an end to this rumour mongering. Now is not the time to go stirring up trouble. Naturally we must make allowances for Katherine Katz's attention seeking tactics. I am afraid her conversation with Venetia Johnson was very much the ramblings of a sad and lonely drunk.'

This news was received with a combination of loud laughter from the men and horrified gasps from the women present. Larry clenched his teeth, hoping that he'd said enough. A scaly hand tapped him on the shoulder. He jumped, turned round and came face to face with Thomas Slater.

156

Taking his chance he grabbed the journalist by the arm and dragged him into the atrium. 'I hope you're satisfied!' he snarled through gritted teeth.

'I am just reporting the news,' Thomas replied with a laconic smile.

'For God's sake man, you're rewriting history!' exclaimed Larry, barely able to contain his anger.

'I know where the body is.'

'I'm sorry?' spluttered Larry. 'What did you say?'

'I know where the body is,' repeated Thomas.

'Oh please!' said Larry, irritated by the man's persistence.

'Come on Larry you must be just a little bit interested.'

'If you must know, I think you are deranged. I mean, for God's sake, how many times do I have to tell you, there is *no* body?'

'But that is where you're wrong, Larry,' he sneered. 'There is a body and I know where it is.'

'Where, then? Go on, tell me.'

'In Queensland, Australia. At the bottom of a lake.'

'Really? Would you care to be more specific?'

'If you like. The lake is situated in the garden of a house called The Rocks, just north of Millaa Millaa on the Atherton Tablelands.'

'Tell me that you are making this up,' demanded Larry, recognising the name immediately. He was horrified by what he was hearing. 'You've had your fun, your fifteen minutes of fame. Admit you're joking and we'll forget the whole sorry business.'

'Larry,' he said slimily. 'This is no joke. The Queensland Police divers are searching the lake for the dead man this very moment.'

'Man. You are sure it's a man?' asked Larry. The mention of The Rocks had forced the memory of Stella into his mind. Christ! What was he thinking? He must not allow himself to believe this man.

'Goodbye, Larry. For now,' he said creepily and without answering the question turned and slithered away.

*

What do you do when you've just been told you are going to die? wondered Alfie as he stared at the closed door of his hospital room through which the surgeon had just departed back into the real world. How different to *his* new world that seemed to him a weird, surreal, painful suspension that fell some way short of existence. Should he shout? Scream? Cry? Break things? Slam his fist into a wall in anger at having his life snatched from him in an untimely and unceremonious fashion? Or laugh, perhaps, at life's sick joke! For that was what this surely was.

What if the wise consultant was mistaken? he asked himself. Stranger things happened. Positive thinking, that is what I need right now. Mind over matter, isn't that what my mother used to tell me? Smile in the face of adversity. Whistle a happy tune. Yes. That's what I'll do. I'll beat this thing with the power of my mind. Alfie Macbeth is a winner. He does not lose.

Another wave of pain overwhelmed him. He closed his eyes, trying to control his breathing as it seared his body. Clenching his teeth he felt for the nozzle on the tube that controlled his painkillers waiting for the relief that a higher level would allow him. After a while he felt his body relax a little.

That's better, he thought weakly. Christ, this is worse than being at the mercy of the press all those years ago. I feel utterly helpless now. How could I even entertain the thought that I could fight this thing? I should face facts solemnly and responsibly. After all, it's not as though I hadn't suspected as much for some time what with the constant pain, the weight loss, my loss of energy. The moment Mr Sutton had suggested surgery to remove the tumour in my colon, the shedding of my life's mortal coil seemed horribly inevitable.

No, Alfie! he remonstrated. Get a grip. Think of Phoebe. You have got to fight this thing. If only I had more time. However much I am resigned to my fate, I'm not ready to go. I cannot leave Phoebe. How will she cope without me? How will she take the news? I have to think of Phoebe, not me. I must concentrate my thoughts on her and her alone. For a start I have minutes, maybe seconds to work out how I'm going to tell her that her daft old Dad is going to die. What the hell am I going to say?

A nurse entered the room, bustling with efficiency and professionalism. 'I'm just going to change your drip,' she said, her perfect smile a tribute to her training. 'And then I thought I'd bring you and your daughter a cup of tea.'

She's right, thought Alfie sadly. I can't keep Phoebe waiting any longer. The poor girl must be going mad with worry. 'I don't suppose you've got a bottle of champagne?' he asked her, jovially. 'On ice?'

'Oh Alfie, really! This is not The Ritz you know,' she scolded, though she was smiling.

'Really? You do surprise me. The decor is remarkably similar.'

'It's good to see you haven't lost your sense of humour.'

'Isn't it?' he said with a frivolous wave of his hand. The nurse giggled.

'Before I send your daughter in, are you comfortable? Have you adjusted your pain relief to the right level?'

'Yes. Thank you. The pain is bearable at the moment and my head is fairly clear.'

'Good. Call me if you become the least bit uncomfortable,' she said, heading towards the door, the old plastic drip casing in her hand. 'I'll get your daughter, OK?'

Alfie frowned but she had her back to him and did not notice. 'That would be ...' he paused, momentarily breathless as he choked on this indigestible slice of reality. 'Yes. Please.'

It can only have been ten seconds before Alfie heard a gentle knocking on his door. 'Come in,' called out Alfie, his voice croaky.

Phoebe's wan face appeared.

'Darling,' said Alfie, making a monumental effort to open his arms to her as he stretched his dry lips into a smile. 'Come here and give your old Dad a hug.'

Two

Larry's driver had deposited Alfie at Heathrow Airport with a small bag, packed by Larry himself, containing a change of clothes, some washing things, his passport and a one-way ticket to Cephellonia with instructions how to get to his villa. Peaceful, private and discreetly nestled in the hills above Fiskardo, it was a haven for the beautiful people of the world as well as the damned.

Larry is right. The press will never find me here. So they'll give up looking and focus their attentions on dear old Larry instead, back home, selflessly raking through the muck, thought Alfie cynically as he climbed the dozen or so steps to the freshly painted turquoise front door. Poor bugger, no one deserves that kind of shit even if he is always at pains to point out to me that that's what I pay him for. He must have had to ask himself some very tricky questions about my integrity over the past few days.

Alfie had been relieved at the chance to escape the crossfire. The last couple of weeks had been diabolical. His reputation was in shatters. The press, with every article they had penned, had assassinated his good character. He felt savaged to his very soul. And everything he had worked so hard to achieve over the past decade had been destroyed. Could this really be the backlash of a moment of madness one night in Thailand? Or had Abe been right? Had his been a life careering out of control for years, feckless and lawless? Well, one thing was for certain, the narcissistic bubble in which he had lived so happily for so long had burst and here he was with a whole lot more than egg on his face. He felt degraded, alienated, rejected and alone.

The first day on the idyllic island of Cephellonia had passed Alfie by totally. He had reached for the nearest bottle of whisky and drunk himself into hapless oblivion.

On the second day he woke from a tortuous night of sleeping and waking, nightmares and panic, with a hangover from hell. Lurching from his bedroom to the bathroom he encountered his reflection in the mirror. Frankenstein's monster it was not but then neither did it bear any resemblance to his former self. The pitiable human being reflected in the glass was a far older, craggier version of the accredited, happy-go lucky film director of one month back. His face was red and unshaven, the whites of his eyes were yellowed and bloodshot and his lips were chapped. On close inspection his hair that seemed wild beyond control was flecked with grey.

I'm an old man, he thought. An old man with nothing but madness to contemplate. I shall descend into madness living out my days in a holiday destination. I'll become a tourist attraction. Tour buses will drive past the villa hoping for a glimpse of Bad Mad Alfie. He sat down on the toilet, slumped forward on his elbows and buried his head in his hands. Or maybe it would be better to end it all, right here and now. No one will have the bother of clearing up the mess that I have left in my wake. Kate can run off with Raul and Phoebe ... and ... well she will grow up thinking that she had a loser for a father.

He leapt up, flung open the bathroom door and strode out into the garden. Squinting in the brightness, he shielded his stinging eyes from the blazing sun, his head pounding. First of all I must drink water, he decided, trying his hardest to adopt a purposeful approach. Lots and lots of water. He glanced at the oleander bush to his left and the bougainvillaea trailing over the white terrace wall to his right. Then I'll sit down in this magnificent garden and think things through because the one thing I am sure of is that Phoebe shall not grow up without a father. It's bad enough that her guides for life will be a *mother* whose vanity could outshine Venus and a Spanish Lothario with balls for brains.

He re-entered the villa with renewed vigour. Phoebe was the reason why his life must have purpose. Quite what that would be he'd no idea right now but he'd figure it out. He'd make damn sure of that. He'd think things through, formulate a plan to salvage something from the ashes of his life. He wandered into the cool white kitchen, took a bottle of water out of the well-stocked fridge and drank until his stomach, flooded with fluid, sloshed as he walked. Then, bottle in hand, he returned to the bathroom, placed the water on the floor and set about shaving, his resolve strengthening as his appearance improved.

'So my hair is flecked with grey,' he muttered to himself. 'So what? I'm in my forties.' He smiled grimly, went outside and looked around absorbing his surroundings as if he'd found the perfect location for a film.

The days wore on and Alfie continued to battle with his emotions

161

refusing to give in to the grief he felt at being hounded out of the country he called home. Most days as he rummaged through the stuff that littered his memory banks the Sisyphean futility of his life would cause him to cry out in anguish. He could see it through Abe's eyes now. Fame and success had totally corrupted him. Standing on his pedestal with the world at his feet a badness had begun to rot away inside of him. And he'd flaunted it, titillating the press and public alike. He'd thought that he was having the time of his life but the reality was he'd been deaf to his conscience growing more selfish and inconsiderate by the day. And now he was paying for his mistakes. Why hadn't he found the strength of character to wade through the filth? Why hadn't he held onto his morality like other people had? Life presented you with choices, didn't it? Yeah, Alfie, that's right, he'd reproach himself, and you consistently made the wrong ones.

That was when the mantle of darkness descended, overpowering him, smothering him in it's heavy black folds, telling him there was no way out, that there was no point to his life but to crawl into bed and hide under the covers and sleep, sleep forever. And this he would have done if his mind had not turned time and time again to Phoebe. She was his ray of hope, his saving grace, the only reason he did not give in to the endless and empty days that stretched before him. That cheeky grin of hers she used when she wanted to get her way. Her laughing eyes. Brown puppy dog eyes. Kate's eyes. He shuddered at the reminder of his wife. How vain, weak, self-centred, ignorant and beautiful she was – beautiful like a diamond, sparkling but intransigent. Men were drawn to her like moths to a flame to sizzle and burn. Only her kind of beauty, the beauty of the body, accessorised with expensive clothes and glistening jewels, was skin deep. She'd had no dreams, no desires, no aspirations beyond self-satisfaction. Could anything that shallow provide fulfilment?

Alfie knew now that he didn't love her. He never had. Together they had been part of a crazy world of fame and unreality. They had both worked hard but deep down they were little more than a pair of self-obsessed narcissists who had indulged in a life of orgiastic hedonism and he hated that. Yet out of this mess, this tangle of egos had sprung the most wondrous thing. And she belonged to both of them. She was their darling girl, their daughter Phoebe whom he loved more than any living creature on this earth. But will Kate press charges? he asked himself time and time again. And if she does, will I ever be allowed near my daughter again?

He wondered if Phoebe missed him or whether, in fact, anyone back home in England missed him? He could think of no one he particularly missed apart from Phoebe and Larry, his good friend. He'd received a card from Stella, also, passing on her regards. Smiling, tantalising, clever Stella Armstrong. What must she think of him now? How right she'd been about him all along. How pleased she must be to have kept him at arms length. She of all people seemed able to read him like a book, a hopeless tragedy complete with tragic hero and equally tragic ending. It hurt him to think of that. If only he could turn back the clock. He'd give anything to sit with her and listen to her views on the whole sorry situation. Still, the card had been a kind gesture though he doubted she was unduly concerned for his welfare.

Somehow he had to forget the past. There was nothing he could do about it. It had been and gone. He'd fucked around, fucked up and been told in no uncertain terms to fuck off. He couldn't change that. He had to get over it. Better to think that he hadn't been destroyed, just shown an escape route. The future was what mattered now. Life was all about the survival of the fittest. What he needed now was strength of mind, vital if he was to pick up the pieces of his shattered life. He had to begin again, start afresh in the hope that he could alter the public's opinion of him. It was not going to be an easy thing to do but it was something he had to do or else he would descend into insanity.

*

It was September. Alfie had remained successfully hidden away in his idyllic Greek refuge for almost three months. Cephellonia was winding down. The holidaymakers that had arrived in droves in August had all but left the island. It was warm and quiet – maddening to a man of action.

'I've bought the ticket already, Larry. Don't waste your breath trying to dissuade me. It's a done deal.'

'But it's such a long way away. I can't believe you've thought this through,' said Larry who, on the other end of the phone, was unable to hide his genuine surprise. 'And more importantly, what about Phoebe?'

'Don't worry. I shall continue to fight to see my daughter. At the moment my solicitor tells me I'll be lucky to be granted access for more than one weekend a month, though he also tells me that Kate has no intention of pressing charges.'

'Well that is good.'

'Good? Yes. It's good she's still got something of a conscience.'

'But Australia, Alfie. It's such a long way from everything and everybody.'

'I know. It's about as far away as I can go. I've given this a lot of thought Larry and as far as I can fathom, it's the only thing I can do. I've found a ranch through a friend of a friend. It's in Queensland, just north of a place called Millaa Millaa in the Atherton Tablelands. Not quite in the Outback but just as remote. I'll be able to live a life of total anonymity up there. I've been granted temporary residence for four years and I intend to fill my time writing.'

'Your memoirs, you mean? Put the record straight. Good idea, Alfie.'

'No! I can't abide the self-congratulatory air that goes with autobiographies. I really have no intention of seeking self-justification. I'd rather run naked down the cloisters of a convent than try to reveal my damaged inner soul on paper. I don't need that kind of therapy, quite honestly!' He laughed then added in a slow, confident voice. 'Larry, I'm going to write a screenplay.'

There was a pause on the other end of the line while Larry absorbed this latest piece of information. 'Well that makes sense.'

'Quite!'

'With a view to directing it one day, perhaps?'

'Let's hope so,' he said with a sigh. 'When the mayhem has settled down.'

'Well four years in the wilderness should do the trick!'

'Exactly!' Then, with forced jollity and changing the subject, he asked, 'How's things back home, Larry? Are you getting any peace from the press?'

'Well, the media explosion is at last showing signs of abating,' replied Larry who could think of nothing he'd like more than to draw a line under the whole sorry episode. The last three months had left him drained, the press sucking the life-blood out of him like ravenous vampires. He'd stood tall and faced them, trying to defend his client and friend but their desire to defame and disown Alfie had been irrepressible.

'What you need is a holiday, Larry. Come and spend some time out here. The swallowtail butterflies and cicadas would welcome the company!'

Three

The ranch was old and rustic, made of timber, painted white, surrounded by wooden decking and went by the name of The Rocks. It was situated in Millaa Millaa, Aboriginal for plenty water, a quaint dairy town boasting six waterfalls in 15 kilometres on the plateau of Queensland's Great Dividing Range that separates Cairns from the vast emptiness of the outback. This was the Atherton Tablelands, the garden shire of the state of Queensland and a welcome refuge from the tropical humidity of the coast.

Sitting pretty in a hundred acres of pasture, The Rocks boasted two creeks and a lake that was surrounded almost entirely by lush vegetation – tree ferns, palms and eucalyptus woodland. At the head of the lake, tumbling over a narrow bank of rock, was an elegant waterfall that showered down into water that was transparently clear apart from the middle, which was rocky, muddy and overgrown with pondweed. It played home to a great many animals, the quirkiest of which was a family of six platypus and the most vocal, a family of ducks. It was hidden from view and yet only about 500 metres from the house, so that to stumble upon the lake was like discovering a beautiful secret.

He'd arrived four months ago, tired and tetchy from the long flight from Greece, his mind cluttered with fear and regret. He had marched with little purpose up the wooden steps to the front door of his new home, fumbling with the large iron key as he'd unlocked the door, acutely aware that he'd travelled half the way round the world, the furthest possible distance from his old life and his precious daughter. He'd sighed heavily at the thought of Phoebe, then with a furious shake of the head he'd grabbed the rail and dragged his weary body up the stairs to a light and airy bedroom at the back of the house. It had a pale oak wooden floor, a large iron bedstead in the centre of the room and French windows leading onto a small balcony. He'd opened the windows creating a breath of fresh air that caused the white muslin curtains to flutter in the breeze.

*

Alfie sat at the long pine refectory table in the vast bright kitchen at the back of the house working flat out on his screenplay. He was living like a fugitive, a recluse with a mission, content to lead this life oceans apart from his glorious past but far from happy. It was February and still very hot. The French windows that led to the back garden were open. Sheets of paper covered in his scribbles were strewn, in ordered chaos, across the kitchen table. He was half way through the second draft and on a roll, oblivious to the world around him, when a loud urgent knocking sounded on his front door. He jumped, startled by the unexpected interruption.

I shall ignore that, he thought, annoyed that his concentration had been broken. The fleeting silence that followed was shattered by a burst of violent hammering that caused the door to reverberate in its frame. Furious but not in the least bit curious, Alfie prised his stiff and aching buttocks off the wooden chair, wandered through the hall and opened the door. A large, powerfully built lady in her late fifties and her diminutive husband were standing in the doorway.

'G'day mate,' she said, beaming widely. 'Thought we'd finally come and introduce ourselves. We're your nearest neighbours. I'm Jesse Buchanan and this is my husband, Stumpy.'

'Oh! Pleased to meet you. I'm ... er, Alfie Macbeth,' he replied lamely, offering his hand.

'We thought we'd let you settle in before we came to visit,' Jesse told him as she shook Alfie's hand with an alarmingly vigorous shake he felt the flesh of his cheeks wobble foolishly with the force of it.

'I suppose you'd better come in,' he volunteered reluctantly, rubbing his right hand and trying to disguise his disappointment. 'Would you like some coffee?'

'Love to, darlin',' said Jesse. She brushed passed him, marched through the door and into the kitchen as one who knew exactly where she was going, her husband following in her tracks.

The outsized woman, Jesse, seemed completely oblivious to the mess. She pushed aside a wad of papers and pulled up a chair, which disappeared as she carefully lowered herself onto it, then launched into a lengthy preamble on Millaa Millaa. Alfie found himself staring at the mismatched couple in awed fascination as he waited for the kettle to boil. It had been a long time since he'd entertained company, least of all such untypical human specimens as Jesse and Stumpy.

Jesse was vast. He'd already noticed her enormous hands when she'd proffered one for that bone-rattling shake. They hung from the end of two large, roly-poly arms. A pair of huge, round blue eyes bulged out of her elephantine head that was crowned with an unruly bundle of long grey curls. He watched, mesmerised, as she rested the cup of coffee he handed her on the shelf-like bust that jutted out beneath her many chins. Stumpy, her dwarfish husband who was a third of her size sat in silence, nodding his approval from time to time as his wife rattled away.

'By the way, in case you were wondering, my husband was actually christened Jim but is known as Stumpy because he's slightly lacking in the manhood department,' she announced suddenly. Breaking into a huge bellyful of laughter, she began to wobble like a giant pink blancmange. Alfie gaped at her. Thinking that he must be confused she leant towards him and added conspiratorially, 'I mean he's insufficiently endowed.'

'Oh my God,' uttered Alfie in disbelief.

'Obviously not a problem you're familiar with?' she shrieked, tears streaming down her face.

Well, this is certainly one way to break the ice, thought Alfie, embarrassed. He glanced at Stumpy who was smiling, nodding his head in tacit agreement with his wife.

'Stumpy and I would like to invite you to dinner tomorrow night,' he heard her say. 'We want to introduce you to your other neighbours.'

Alfie inched to the edge of his chair, his attentions refocused. He felt uncomfortable at the suggestion. This wasn't what he wanted at all. He'd tell them he was busy. That way he wouldn't hurt their feelings.

'I'd love to. Thank you.'

*

Troy Thomas was fidgeting profusely as he waited nervously for the arrival of the Buchanans' new neighbour. He was standing in their porch out of the hot sunshine watching the chooks searching for food in the dusty yard, clicking his fingers, scratching his nose, adjusting his belt, checking his watch as the seconds ticked slowly by. He couldn't remember ever having been as excited, except perhaps as a child lying awake all Christmas Eve night desperate to see what Santa Claus would deposit in his stocking while the thought that he might not have been good enough that year nagged at his conscience. He had never met a real live celebrity if this person whom Jesse had visited yesterday really was *the* Alfie Macbeth. He'd asked her if she'd recognised him but her eyes had glazed over.

'He's come from the back of Bourke, you know,' she'd replied vacuously, as if that grand pronouncement explained it all. All he had to go on was the description he'd managed to coax out of her after five minutes of intense interrogation.

'Is he tall?'

'Er ... give us a sec. You see Troy, we were sitting down so it was hard to tell.'

'What, he didn't answer the door?'

'Of course he did. Strewth, wait a minute,' she'd screwed up her eyes for a minute. 'Yup. Tall, certainly.'

'And what colour was his hair?'

'Er ...'

'Was it dark?'

'Dark, yup.'

'And was it straight or curly?'

'Aw! Tricky. Let me guess.' She'd paused and screwed up her eyes again.

'No Jesse, don't guess, remember, please it's important.'

Jesse had raised her eyebrows bemused. 'I had no idea you were so interested in hair, Troy,' she'd chortled. 'Curly. It was curly.'

'Excellent!'

'So you thinking of going into hair?'

'Don't be ridiculous Jesse. Can you remember anything else?'

'I think he's a bit of a ... what's that name you young 'uns give to upstarts? Er ... F.I.G.J.A.M.?' she'd asked him earnestly.

'Yeah.'

'What's it mean again? Fuck ...'

' ... I'm Good, Just Ask Me.'

'Oh and I'd say he was a bit wild looking,' she'd added, screwing up her nose into an alarming concertina of flesh.

Still, it sounded hopeful, if a little vague. He wasn't sure about wild but Alfie Macbeth was tall, dark and handsome, that much was obvious from all the photographs he'd seen, all the interviews he'd watched. So he'd hung his hopes on the fact that there probably weren't too many tall, dark men alive that went by the name, Alfie Macbeth.

It has to be him, it just has to be, he told himself, fiddling with his belt one last time as the blue Toyota Landcruiser rocked up the Buchanans' bumpy drive.

Just at that moment Jesse, who had been busying herself in the kitchen, appeared and bustled past him, obscuring him and his view with her plump and undulating girth. Damn! he thought as he tried to peer round the aproned form of his outsized neighbour. The door of the four-wheel drive slammed shut.

'G'day Alfie,' boomed Jesse.

'Hello again,' said Alfie, his English accent music to Troy's ears. 'Lovely place you've got here.'

'Been in the family the last thirty-five years,' replied Jesse beaming broadly.

'What is it you farm?' he asked her.

Troy, inching out from behind Jesse's skirts, watched impressed as his hero leant forward over her vast belly to kiss his hostess politely on both cheeks, no mean feat.

'Sugar cane!' replied Jesse triumphantly, grabbing Alfie by the forearm to pull him into her house. Troy giggled.

'Hello there,' said Alfie noticing Troy for the first time.

'Hi,' said Troy, grinning to reveal a set of evenly spaced white teeth.

'Troy,' gesticulated Jesse, jerking her thumb at the tall but slight teenager. 'Millie and Harry's son.'

'Good to meet you Troy,' said Alfie, wrenching his arm free from Jesse's iron grip.

Troy grinned but said nothing. Triumphant in the extreme that a real live legend was indeed gracing the topsy-turvy Buchanan home, he turned and bounded off in the direction of the sitting-room.

I wonder what he'll make of this place, he thought, glancing around at the tattered settees, the chipped wooden coffee table laden with magazines, the threadbare rug in front of the brick fireplace with its heavy oak mantelpiece covered in silverware and the walls that were groaning with artwork. And what will he think of Jack's paintings?

'Millie and Harry Thomas, Alfie Macbeth,' announced Jesse as she strode into the room, arm outstretched in introduction. 'Afraid Stumpy couldn't be here. He's out in the fields.'

'I gather you're my other neighbours,' said Alfie offering his hand, not the least bit sad that Stumpy couldn't make it.

'Loosely speaking,' answered Harry, a big, sturdy sun-dried Australian, with soft grey eyes and a head of thick brown hair, coarse in texture yet incredibly straight. 'We live about five kilometres in the other direction.'

'But this is Australia, Alfie,' explained Jesse as she turned to leave. 'I'll be back in a mo with some beer.'

'You look taller. In real life, I mean,' said Millie, a cursorily youthful woman who blushed into her beer as she spoke.

'It's often the way,' replied Alfie politely, praying that his reputation did not precede him here.

'Not many celebrities appear in the Tablelands,' Millie said quietly, struggling to look Alfie in the eye. 'I've always thought of them as people to be admired from a distance.'

Oh God, groaned Troy inwardly. Why do mothers have to be so embarrassing?

'Well I can assure you I am not a god and I don't bite,' responded Alfie good-naturedly. If they had heard of his exodus from England, it appeared that it held no real concern for them. 'Well almost never,' he added, baring his teeth. Millie giggled.

'We're dairy farmers,' said Harry suddenly, 'We own a herd of Friesian cows.'

'The black and white ones,' translated Troy helpfully. Alfie smiled.

'He's eighteen and very eager,' explained Harry unnecessarily.

Annoyed by his father's fatuous remark, Troy looked away.

'But he loves films,' interjected Millie hurriedly. 'Absolutely adores them, don't you Troy?'

Humiliated beyond belief, Troy glared at his mother.

'I have a twenty-one-year-old daughter who's away at university at the moment,' Millie continued, flustered by her son's behaviour. 'She's reading history.'

'You don't look old enough to have a daughter that age,' replied Alfie, blanching at the gross predictability of his reply.

'You're a smooth-talker, Alfie,' squawked Jesse, who had reappeared with the beer and a huge bowl of tiger prawns. 'Grab a prawn darlin'.'

'Thanks. Delicious.'

'Now what would you say to the fact that I have three boys, the two eldest of whom are married with children?' continued Jesse.

'I just wouldn't believe it,' replied Alfie, trying manfully to appear surprised at Jesse's revelation.

'Well do, Alfie,' said Jesse warming to her theme. 'Why, I am a grandmother to seven little Australians.'

The image of Jesse, a vast sow nuzzling her brood of tiny piglets, popped into his mind and before he could stop himself, Alfie said, 'You must be as happy as a pig in muck!'

Troy laughed. His father glared at him. Feeling awkward, he stared down at his shoes.

'Aw, Alfie, if I didn't know you better, I'd think you were being a little cheeky, darlin'.' She turned to Millie and said as she wobbled with mirth. 'He's a raw prawn this one!'

'He makes movies,' Millie told her, her face reddening.

Oh God Mum, not again, thought Troy.

'Oh!' said Jesse not comprehending.

'He's a very famous British director, Jesse,' pressed Millie.

'My youngest son is in England,' Jesse told Alfie with a nudge in the ribs, ignoring the allusion to his celebrity, proud to have made her own connection.

By now he must be sure that we are all mad, thought Troy dismayed, trying to contain his irritation.

'How is Jack?' Millie asked her.

'Well, now that you ask, sweetheart, I'm very excited. He's coming home next month.' At the pronouncement of the news she began to quiver with anticipation.

'Oh that's wonderful, Jesse,' said Millie, giving the trembling woman a big hug. Troy rolled his eyes in exasperation.

'Reckon!'

'He's been away four years,' explained Millie.

'So, what's he been doing in England?' asked Alfie half-heartedly.

'He's been studying art at St Martin's College,' said Jesse, proudly wafting a large arm in the direction of the walls.

'Art! Of course!' exclaimed Alfie, glancing around at the pictures on the wall.

'I know, shocking isn't it? We're such an Aussie family. All beer and brawn! When he finally came clean and told us, I think he thought we might spit the dummy. I must admit we were quite shocked at first, but then he showed us the paintings he had secretly stashed away in his room. Most of them are on the wall. Stuff he drew as a child and some of his most recent work. Things he was working on before he left.' She pointed toward a large canvas in pride of place above the fireplace.

'It's very good,' said Alfie, impressed by the charcoal sketch of a naked woman. Jack obviously had talent.

'Aye he's a ripper that one, a ripper. I just can't believe he's finally coming home.'

'Oh Jesse, I'm so very pleased for you,' said Millie.

'Alfie, Mr Macbeth,' said Troy suddenly, unable to contain himself any longer.

'Alfie will do fine,' Alfie said smiling, turning his attention toward the fidgety youth.

'I've always wanted to know something . . .'

'Don't bother the poor man with your nonsense,' scolded Millie with a shallow laugh.

'Who is the best boy?' asked Troy, ignoring his mother, desperate to find out as much as he could from this superstar who had improbably stumbled into his remote life.

171

'The one that's the best behaved on set,' Alfie replied, with a raise of an eyebrow.

Troy looked back at him, uncertain. His mother giggled stupidly. He frowned. He hadn't bargained on Alfie taking the piss. He didn't feel comfortable with that unless ... unless it was the way of the English.

'No really, Alfie. I'm interested,' he said, his frown breaking into a large grin.

'He's an electrician. The gaffer's right-hand man.'

'So the gaffer, he's an electrician as well? The top one?' he asked, riveted.

'You got it. He's the director of photography's right-hand man,' said Alfie. 'So you like the movies young Troy?'

'Yes,' said Troy with a self-conscious nod. Now that he had the great man's full attention, he was not at all sure what to say.

'Seen any of my films?'

'All of them,' he confirmed, his eyes widening.

'Any good?'

'Oh Mr Macbeth, Alfie I mean, your films are totally brilliant. It's true what the critics say.'

'Oh! And what do the critics say?' asked Alfie alarmed. He would prefer to steer well clear of them.

'That you have never made a bad film,' said Troy proudly.

'Well ...'

'*John Paul Sartre's Nausea* was a real hit out here. Amazing don't you think?'

At the mention of *Nausea*, Alfie shuddered. Troy didn't notice. He was off and running now.

'My favourite was *His Cold Blood.*'

'Ah, the thriller.'

'Will you make another thriller, Alfie?'

'Shh,' interrupted his mother. 'Don't bore the poor man.'

'Don't worry Millie, he isn't,' said Alfie, warming to his young fan. It had been a long time since he'd received such ardent adulation. 'As it happens I'm working on a thriller at the moment.'

'Been taking a break then?' asked Jesse who'd reappeared with a plate laden with sausages. 'Have a snag.' There was an awkward pause, just a few seconds but long enough for Troy to notice Alfie's discomfort.

'He's on a sabbatical,' answered Troy quick as a flash.

'That's right,' said Alfie gratefully. 'How about you come round to my place for a chat on films sometime soon young man.'

'Ace!' replied Troy. My life is changing, he thought, as his adrenalin soared.

*

Later that night, back at The Rocks, Alfie sat on a teak chair on his decking under the stars and reflected on his unexpected and somewhat weird return to society. He'd liked Millie and Harry and had been greatly amused by their son Troy, a tall, dark lad, with long slim legs, brimming with the energy of a frisky young colt.

The telephone in the hallway started ringing. It was Larry.

'Alfie, I've got some incredible news.'

'What's up, Larry. Are you OK?' Alfie asked him, jolting back to reality in alarm at the urgency in his friend's voice.

'Tip top and dandy,' replied Larry.

He can't be drunk, thought Alfie worriedly. It's only 8am back home.

'*Nausea* is up for three Oscars,' continued Larry. 'Including one for best director! First of all I can't believe *Nausea* is even being considered for this year's Oscars. I suppose they went on the US release dates. Whatever, you're lucky! You've got stiff competition with *Platoon, The Mission, Children of a Lesser God, Hannah and her Sisters* but the press are saying that *Nausea* has real emotional depth. Sure, it's quirky given all the adverse publicity but hey, Hollywood is a crazy place. Isn't that great? You must make travel arrangements immediately. We'll go to the ceremony together.' There was a pause. 'Alfie! Alfie! Can you hear me?'

'Of course I can,' replied Alfie, holding the receiver away from his ear. 'You're screaming at me.'

'Well, why didn't you say anything?'

'I would have thought that was obvious.'

'What on earth do you mean? Aren't you going to come?'

'No!'

'No?'

'Yes. That's what I said. No!'

'I can't believe this Alfie. This is the biggest honour a filmmaker can receive.'

'I know that Larry. I was nominated before, remember?'

'Of course I remember.' He paused again. 'I know! You're worried you'll be disappointed a second time.'

'No.'

'What then?' He sounded exasperated. He'd been expecting Alfie to shout for joy. His friend's muted reaction had shocked him.

173

'I want to forget about *Nausea,*' he replied. 'And I'm not ready to be crucified by the press again. Give me time, Larry. I need more time.'

'I don't believe that,' retorted Larry. 'Not the great Alfie Macbeth! You've got skin of steel.'

'Or so I thought,' said Alfie cynically. 'Listen to me Larry. I'm totally and utterly grateful to you for everything you've done for me. You've gone way beyond the duties of a friend.'

'I wasn't doing my duty,' interrupted Larry. 'I wanted to help. Anyone would have done the same thing in my position.'

'I doubt it Larry,' said Alfie, certain that *he* would not have. He took a deep breath. 'And what I want to say is that I miss you. I miss your friendship, your smiling face, your company and your advice.'

'You should try and get out more,' said Larry laughing.

'You know what I mean,' he said quietly before taking another deep breath. 'How's Phoebe?' he blurted out.

'Last time I saw her she was dancing in a little white dress with wings on her back.'

'You mean you haven't seen her since Christmas?'

'No. She's been away with Kate on a shoot I think.'

'Oh God.'

'Don't worry, Alfie, she's fine. I'll keep an eye on her. I'm her godfather remember,' he told him, trying his hardest to reassure Alfie, understanding his concern because he too was worried.

'But it hurts so much not being with her. I hardly get to speak to her. Kate always makes an excuse when I phone, tells me she's in bed, out at a party. I can bear anything but the lies. What did I ever see in that woman? She's nothing more than a perfect pair of breasts and legs. I did not think it possible that one person could inflict so much pain on another. Losing my daughter is unbearable. She calls herself a mother, Larry, but the woman is pure evil.'

'Alfie . . .'

'When I lie awake at night all I can do is think of how she robbed me of my child. It's as though she and Raul are playing catch with my heart. Raul! I mean for God's sake. He's no father. He's the vainest most self-centred person I have ever met and yet he's taken my place. Poor, poor Phoebe. Raul doesn't deserve that position. I get angry when I think of him, Larry, really angry. I seem to lose the ability to reason and my resentment turns to fury so that before long I am weeping with rage, crying into my pillow. And that's when I think if I could get my hands on the man I would kill him. That's what I'd like to do, squeeze the air out of his body with my bare hands, beat his brains into a pulp, fire a bullet through his heart.'

'It's understandable that you feel angry. You've been through a lot.'

'Murderous, Larry. I feel murderous. My God if I ever set eyes on the man I'm terrified that I'll kill him.'

'Have you thought about talking to someone about this?' Larry asked him. Was Alfie having a break down? he wondered. Or was venting his spleen a natural and healthy reaction to all that he had suffered?

'That's exactly what I am doing, Larry. I'm talking to you,' he cried.

'That's not what I mean. It's just you're so isolated. It must be a huge shock to your system. It would be good for you to take a break. Come to the ceremony, Alfie. It might do you the power of good to be among friends.'

'No, Larry. I don't want to.'

'I don't believe you,' he said, hoping that by teasing him he could calm his friend down. He felt helpless and distanced.

'Try to,' said Alfie sardonically and, with a hurried goodbye, put down the phone.

Four

There had been a lot of rain the past couple of months that was at last showing signs of abating, though Alfie was not worried in the least. The rains kept Troy away and he could continue his writing undisturbed. That was not to say that he didn't enjoy the young man's company, more that Troy had become a much too regular feature at the house and his presence, however entertaining, was distracting.

Often he would stop by for a chat with a four-pack of ice-cold tinnies under his arm. Never one to say no to a cold beer, Alfie would invite Troy to pull up a chair on the wooden decking at the front of the house. And Troy would accept the invitation with unmasked enthusiasm, a broad grin stretched across his sunburned face. He reminded Alfie of himself as an eighteen-year-old, an eager bundle of testosterone straining to unleash itself on an unwitting world. It had become a habit. Troy would turn up and Alfie would put down his pen. And as the hours passed languidly in the warmth of the evening sun Alfie, fuelled by Troy's energetic and relentless questioning, would recount his life to his enthralled audience of one.

At other times Jesse would call by uninvited and bearing gifts. He found these unexpected visitations from his thick-skinned neighbour irritating and debilitating. She was opinionated to the point of rude and would barge in, intent on grilling him about his past, like a monstrous Nazi interrogator from the Second World War.

It was late March. The Oscar winners had been announced. Larry had phoned Alfie two days previously to commiserate his losing out to Oliver Stone's *Platoon*. Alfie had been unconcerned about the outcome. He had felt sorry for Buzz who had dreamt of holding the golden statuette aloft since the night of *Nausea's* premiere. It had been widely reported that Alfie would not be travelling to the ceremony and therefore it seemed inevitable that he would be spurned by the Academy for a second time. He hadn't minded in the least but what had troubled him was Larry's reaction on the other end of the line. He had sounded tense but wouldn't say why. So Alfie had asked if something had happened to Phoebe and was not convinced by Larry's feeble attempt at reassurance that everything at home was fine. He'd put the phone down feeling empty and alienated from his past. This is it, he'd thought, life at The Rocks, a solitary existence on the opposite side of the globe to all that I hold dear.

A large banging sounded on the front door. Judging by the thunderous knocking, the visitor had to be Jesse. The last thing he needed right now was an interrogation from Queensland's very own Oberführer.

'Here you go Alfie, some lamingtons to keep your strength up when you take your next smok-o,' she barked, thrusting a greaseproof bag of cakes into Alfie's hands as she strode through the hallway to his kitchen. Alfie sighed as he resolved to summon up the energy to respond politely to her kind, neighbourly but totally unwelcome offering.

'Thank you Jesse. Delicious. Though I'm no smoker.'

'Tea break Alfie!'

'Oh, right, tea, fine, I'll go and make some,' he said absently.

'Strewth, Alfie! Smok-o, tea break!' she told him, slapping him playfully on the back.

Alfie looked at her blankly. Jesse laughed. 'No worries, I'd sooner have coffee.'

'Fine!' said Alfie clutching desperately to his sense of humour.

'So. No wife then, Alfie?' Jesse asked him as she balanced her coffee with three sugars on the bench that was her chest. 'That's a bit of a shocker for a good-looking man of your age?'

Alfie stared at her incredulously.

'Millie mentioned that you were married once,' she added with a smirk.

'And Millie would be right!'

'To some bonzer goddess of the silver screen. What happened, Alfie, she trade you in for a younger model?'

Alfie glared at her in silence.

'Why you look as cross as a frog in a sock, Alfie. Touched a raw nerve, have I? No drama. Not the full quid I suspect, that Katherine Cat. I mean, who in their right mind would leave a clever, hard-working bloke like you?'

Alfie managed to force a smile.

'Grinning like a shot fox, that's better!'

'Jesse, much as I'd love to spend the afternoon listening to your banter in what must surely be one of the world's most delicate of languages, I really have to get on.'

'Holy Dooley, I can see you're cranky today. I can take a hint! No hard feelings, Alfie. We can have our little chat another time. G'day mate. You take care now.' And with those reassuring words she was off, wobbling towards her Holden Estate like a megalithic steamed treacle pudding.

Alfie was incensed. She's got a bloody nerve, he screamed inwardly. What gives her the right to saunter, no waddle, into someone's house and sound off in that coarse, probing manner of hers? I pity Stumpy. God! Stumpy! Just thinking about his name makes me cringe. He shuddered violently. Well there is no way I can concentrate now. He sighed and wandered over to the fridge in search of a consolatory beer. 'I need some fresh air,' he muttered.

The French windows that led to the garden at the back were open. Beer in hand, he walked through them heading towards the rickety old cedar-wood bench on the back decking. It was a fine place to sit and admire the view. He sat down, leant back, stretched out his legs and stared at the rolling countryside beyond – a multi-coloured patchwork of green, rust, purple and brown rolling fields. Relieved to be on his own once more he shut his eyes, allowing his mind to drift. That was when he heard the footsteps on the decking, small, rapid steps of someone in a hurry.

Who now? he wondered irritably. Troy, for another film review? Or Millie, for some tips on cleaning? Then inspiration hit him, quick as a flash, like a light bulb going on in his brain. He'd hide, behind the pile of logs to the right of the kitchen. Brilliant, he thought, as he dived for cover.

He knelt down, straining his ears to the silence. He could hear nothing. Perhaps it had been the postman, he thought, his heart pounding more with fear at being discovered in this ridiculous position than it being a possible intruder. He heard a faint exhalation of air as though the person was disappointed not to find anyone home, then the sound of footsteps, this time heading in his direction, again a sigh, then, 'Bother!'

The voice was female, English perhaps. Strange, he thought, suddenly curious. But he couldn't reveal himself now. How would he explain himself appearing from behind a log pile? He'd look ridiculous.

'Bother!' she said again. 'Perhaps I should wait?' Then the sound *flip flop, flip flop*. As she passed his hiding place heading towards the bench that he had himself so recently occupied, he caught a whiff of her scent. It smelt familiar to him. He had to see who it was, which is why, against his better judgment, he decided to sneak a look.

Raising himself on his haunches, he peered round the side of the log pile. All he could see from this angle was a pair of lovely ankles with feet to match in flip-flops, the toenails painted a deep pink. Young pretty feet, he thought, as he craned his neck a little further forward, enabling him to admire the smooth, slender but strong looking calves to which they were attached. Enjoying the spectacle and not in the least feeling like a peeping Tom, he took a deep breath of air filling his nose once more with the celebrated perfume, which was when he inadvertently displaced a log. It dropped to the ground from the top of the pile with a leaden thud.

'Hello! Alfie! Is that you?' called out the instantly recognisable voice.

'Stella?' he replied, springing rapidly to his feet disturbing several more logs that fell in his path, tripping him so that he stumbled rather than walked towards her.

'Alfie!' she said, smiling crookedly as the man she sought appeared from behind the woodpile, detritus sticking to his clothes. 'What on earth were you doing?'

'Hiding,' he said simply, not knowing what else to say, it being acutely and nonsensically obvious to him.

'From me?' she asked laughing uncontrollably, both hands covering her mouth as she rocked from foot to dainty foot.

'Well no, not exactly. I mean had I known it was you ... that you would pay me a visit ... or rather, should I have been expecting you I would never have felt the urge to hide ... what I mean to say is why would I do that? It's lovely to see you, Stella,' he said, wishing he didn't feel so totally absurd. 'It's not everyday you meet someone you actually know on totally the opposite side of the world to the one you're used to meeting them on ... if you see what I mean,' he added, trying hard to pinch himself, certain that he must be dreaming. But no, the gorgeous form that stood in front of him was most definitely Stella. Young, pretty, Stella Armstrong, dazzling in the Australian sunshine, standing before him in a denim sundress, beaming, her green eyes laughing, her hair shining in the sunlight like a halo. 'It *is* lovely to see you,' he repeated.

'That's good,' she said giggling, leaning her head to one side. She pointed to the house. 'You've found yourself a magnificent place here, Alfie. You must be having a ball.'

'Well .... .' he began, but stopped not knowing where to start. He hadn't seen her since the scandal. Hadn't spoken to her, explained himself, asked for her opinion, her forgiveness. She'd sent him her condolences on a picture postcard via Larry who'd forwarded the note to him. Rodin's *The Thinker*, the card depicted. A cynical message he was certain although he'd been most grateful for the gesture anyway. He'd fled without attempting an explanation. Perhaps he owed her one.

179

'Stella, I . . .' he began.

'I've brought your camera, the one you're so attached too. 'I . . . we . . . Larry and I thought you were probably missing it.'

'Thank you, thank you. Yes. Yes I've missed it very much. That's very kind of you . . . of you both,' he said, taking a step closer to Stella who had taken the camera out of her small, navy rucksack and now held it out for him to take, fighting the urge to wrap his arms around her and hold her in his arms. This was the loveliest thing that had happened to him for a very long time and yet the most tortuous. 'I can't believe you'd do this for me. I . . . I . . . I'm speechless.'

'Well that's a first,' retorted Stella in her old familiar way. She cleared her throat. 'It's just that I happened to be coming to Australia, to Queensland actually . . . to meet up with Ned . . . my brother . . . you know, he married an Australian . . . . and naturally I thought . . . I mean *we* thought I could drop in, deliver the camera, see how you're getting on, commiserate about the Oscars, maybe over a cup of tea, a glass of wine . . .'

'Stella, I'm sorry, how rude of me. Come and take a seat on the decking and I'll bring you, what, tea? Wine? What will you have?'

'A glass of wine would be perfect,' said Stella gently.

'Dry white OK?'

'The best.'

'Delicious, thank you.'

'It's not bad, is it, this Aussie wine, if you like the heavy oak flavour? They certainly know how to make a good Chardonnay. And their beer's not bad either,' he added although he really didn't want to talk about the finer points of Australian alcohol. There were heaps of questions he wanted to ask her like, how long are you visiting for, would you like to stay here, can I kiss you? 'How's Neil?' he asked lamely.

'Neil?'

'The solicitor?'

'Oh! You mean Martin? Neil was the accountant.'

'Ah! Martin,' muttered Alfie.

'Gone back to his wife as it happens. We created a bit of a scandal, actually, though nothing quite on your level,' she added with a mischievous grin that quite unsettled Alfie.

Well, she always was direct, he reasoned as he tried to contain his embarrassment. 'I'm surprised you're still speaking to me.'

'Alfie!' she exclaimed, laughing. 'I worked in PR. I'm now an agent to the stars. Why on earth would I believe what I read in the papers?'

'I . . . er . . . I guess I just assumed . . .'

'Larry explained what happened.'

'He did?'

'Yeah. He's worried about you. I have something else for you,' she said, reaching for her rucksack once again. 'It's a letter. Larry hoped it might cheer you up.'

'Thanks,' said Alfie taking the letter. He glanced down at the envelope addressed to him in a wobbly hand. 'It's from Phoebe!' he exclaimed, tearing it open.

'Larry said you'd be pleased.'

'I am. This is wonderful. Stella, I haven't seen my daughter for almost a year, barely get to speak to her. I miss her to distraction. I . . .' But he was too busy reading Phoebe's note to continue.

Helo Daddy,

I wos a farie with wings but I didint fly.

I luve you.

Phoebe X xx X

And there was a photo with it, of his four-year-old daughter dressed in her white fairy outfit, grinning broadly at the photographer, waving her wand that appeared as a blur in the picture. He stared at it for what seemed like ages in silence, fighting back the urge to kiss it, struggling to hold back his tears, still aware of Stella's presence in the chair next to his, feeling her gaze on his bowed head, wondering what she was thinking, how long he had with her, hoping she understood his pain, dying a little inside as he refocused on his daughter . . .

'She's lucky, you know,' said Stella eventually. Alfie looked up from the picture. Stella was watching him, head tilted to one side. 'To have a Dad like you,' she added, her tone serious.

Alfie said nothing, just averted his gaze to the picture once more. What could he say? Phoebe wasn't lucky. Her Dad had fucked up, packed up and buggered off to the other side of the world leaving her at the mercy of two self-obsessed, self-publicising adults.

'It's not your fault, Alfie. You had no choice,' she told him tenderly as she rose from her chair to crouch down before him, resting her right hand on his knee. She squeezed it, hoping to reassure him. Still staring at the photo, he covered her hand with his.

'It *is* good to see you, Stella,' he repeated as a tear rolled down his cheek. He made no attempt to flick it away, hoping she hadn't noticed. But then a second tear fell, followed quickly by a third and a fourth. He stood up and Stella rose with him as he flicked the fifth tear angrily away with the back of his free hand.

'Alfie!' she said, flinging her arms around him. 'It's OK. It really is OK!'

And the next thing Alfie knew was that she was kissing his tears

181

away. He could feel her soft lips on his skin, first on his cheek then his neck, his mouth, then her tongue searching out his, sweet mellifluous kisses like the kiss of an angel.

'Stella,' said Alfie, finally pulling away. 'I can't quite believe this is happening.'

'What, Alfie?' she asked anxiously.

'This. You. Me. Us,' he said, trying desperately to explain his confusion.

'Why?'

'I'm being silly! Forgive me, Stella.'

'Really? That's not like you,' she said sarcastically. She smiled again. 'Tell me Alfie. What is happening?'

' For some unearthly reason I suddenly thought you had come for me,' he replied, a little too quickly.

'Ah, I see,' said Stella frowning. Embarrassed, Alfie turned away, regretting what he'd said, wondering why he always had to open his big mouth, longing more than anything to kiss her again.

'Well that's good!' she replied, kissing the hand she still held in hers.

'Stella?'

'What now?'

'You're joking, right? It's what you do.'

'Shut up fuckwit and kiss me again,' she said pulling him towards her, hugging him. He placed his hand behind her lovely head and gently drew her face towards his own.

And then they were in his bedroom, on his bed in the middle of his room, their clothes scattered over the floor where they had fallen as they'd torn them from one another in their desire to get at each other's bodies, naked in each other's arms. They held each other close. So close, Alfie could hear her heart beating a gentle rhythm inside her chest. And she, skin soft as velvet, touching him first with her hand, now with her tongue that explored his body hungrily. Their mouths touched again. Lip upon lip. She kissed him urgently. He could taste her passion, could feel her heart begin to race. He slipped his hand between her legs and she moaned but wriggled free, her long blonde hair falling across his abdomen as she kissed him, sighing with pleasure. And Alfie stared at her, at her shoulders that looked as though they had been painstakingly sculpted. Smooth, hairless, silken skin stretched tightly across her raised clavicle, dark blonde hair glistening in the moonlit room, her slim, toned, buttery brown body, perfect, flawless.

'Come here,' he whispered pulling her onto his chest. 'And let me love you.'

Five

Alfie woke early to find Stella lying by his side, her arm hooked over his chest, her naked body half covered in a sheet. She was smiling in her sleep.

Perhaps I am still dreaming, he thought nervously as he took a fold of his skin between his fingers and squeezed hard. The pain of the pinch raced from the nerve endings in his arm to his brain and back again in a flash. Well that fucking hurt so I'm obviously wide-awake, he concluded triumphantly staring once again in disbelief at her lissom form. Christ, if it could be like this always, if I could claim Stella as my own, I would die happy. I'm not a religious man but this surely is some kind of miracle. Stella's warm body snuggled up to mine, the smell of our love on her skin.

Alfie smiled and closed his eyes. Her passion last night had been overwhelming, like a kite he was trying to fly that was too strong for his grasp and would have broken free completely had he not grabbed onto its tail. He'd hung on desperately, not letting himself go, holding on, not wanting to be left behind as it soared high above the ground, terrified of falling but happy to be led. Gorgeous, wonderful Stella, whose breasts like two golden orbs had filled the cup of his hands, her nipples hard as amber beads beneath the touch of his fingers that traced the pattern of her ribs, like the ripples of a river, to the soft pillow of her belly, up to the curved ridge of her hip, down to the warm wetness between her legs. And when she'd climaxed shortly before him, it had felt to Alfie when their bodies folded into one as though he'd absorbed her beauty and her spirit through his skin, into his bloodstream like a drug. He was hooked.

But why is she here? he asked himself as his brain struggled to assimilate the shock surprise of her arrival with the erotic images of their lovemaking. Her brother, you wally! She told you, which means she'll probably up and leave some time today. And that would be very

183

bad news indeed because right now I feel like an imprisoned man emerging from a dark cave to see reality for what it is. Beautiful, spectacular, special, more brilliant than the shadows I was condemned to watch. I've come alive again. And I thought I was happy, I honestly did, back then with Kate. But Kate was just a shadow, a poor imitation. A fake. What we had was nothing more than deep-rooted lust. It was not like this. Stella is the one to stop the sky from falling down. If only I could freeze time.

By now the early morning sun had begun to filter through the white muslin curtains casting a speckled pattern across her naked form. Alfie sighed and tore himself away. He picked up his white Calvin Klein jockey shorts that lay midway between the bed and the door, pulled them on and made for the kitchen feeling suddenly impulsive. He would prepare breakfast for her. Show his affection in an honest act of domesticity. He was pretty good at scrambling eggs. That's what he'd do. He'd make her eggs. Brilliant. And bacon, too! Crispy bacon! Only come to think of it, I don't think she's all that keen on meat, he thought, replacing the bacon in the fridge and pulling out a large carton of fresh Millaa Millaa orange juice.

'If you could see your face Alfie,' Stella said, smiling at Alfie as he kicked open the door bearing a laden tray, decorated with a single white rose. She was sitting in bed dressed in one of his shirts – the sleeves rolled up, the top three buttons undone, hair tousled – unintentionally provocative and indescribably beautiful. 'How you spoil me, Macbeth. Breakfast in bed. Nobody has ever done that for me before. White roses are my favourite. Oh, Alfie I could get used to this.'

'Good. Then you shall,' declared Alfie, placing the tray carefully on her outstretched legs. Stella took a mouthful of the steaming eggs.

'Delicious!' she exclaimed. 'Don't tell me you're a top chef too.'

'I think you've seen my limit,' said Alfie sheepishly. 'I'm afraid my culinary talents begin and end with scrambled eggs. I'm glad you like them.'

'It's wonderful, thank you,' she said pressing his hand.

'I just want you to be happy. Are you happy Stella?' he asked uneasily.

'Don't tell me the great Macbeth lacks confidence?'

'I'm concerned,' he answered seriously.

'Oh!' she said, holding a forkful of egg in front of her mouth. 'Why?'

'I'm concerned that you are going to get up, pack up and go home.'

'I see,' she said staring at Alfie directly, her smile gone. Panicked, Alfie began to gabble.

'Was I gentle enough? Er ... I mean am I too old? No, what I meant to ask you ... Can you bear to stay? Do you like bacon?'

From Stella, not a word. Deep in the pit of his stomach Alfie felt a weird sensation as though his insides were on the spin cycle of a washing machine. He stared at Stella, terrified. Solemnly she stared back.

'Shit!' exclaimed Alfie, without meaning to. Stella began to laugh.

'Yes. Yes. Yes and yes,' she said. She pushed the tray aside, picked up a pillow and swung it at Alfie's head, once, twice as he tried to grab it. Leaping from the bed she faced him, dealing him a final blow with the pillow around his legs before he caught it and yanked it away. But she was quick. She ducked the swinging pillow now in his hands, dived at him and grabbed his jockey shorts. With a terrific jerk, she had them round his ankles. She laughed, uncontrollably, tears streaming down her cute round cheeks and he laughed with her as he tried to catch her but his legs got tangled in his shorts and he fell over. Stella leapt at him, smothering him with her spread-eagled body and began to cover him with kisses until he responded. And they made love together, there, on the floor.

'No more. No more, please,' said Stella.

'Oh please, just one,' implored Alfie.

'No. I'm putting my foot down. It's too uncomfortable.'

'Wimp!'

'Bully!'

'Smile!'

'I can't. Not any more.'

'But the light is just right. Hang on. And s-m-i-l-e. Brilliant,' said Alfie beaming.

'Oh Alfie, I'm in terrible pain, Alfie.'

'Nonsense! You're a natural. Now if you'd care to remove ...'

'Alfie! I'm over-exposed as it is!' she shrieked and ran off toward the house. Alfie watched her, amused. He picked up his camera and focused on the view. It was nearing sunset. Just one more photograph. Perfect. He shut the camera, put it back in his case and made towards the house.

'Aargh!'

'Got you!' said Stella, jumping out from behind the wall armed with the garden hose. She giggled. 'You're drenched! Serves you right.'

'Give me the hose, young lady,' said Alfie, with mock anger as he placed his camera under the chair on the decking. 'Right now or I'll ...

'You'll what?' she asked, ducking behind an oleander bush. 'Ooh Alfie, I'm scared. I really am.'

She poked the hose through the bush, took aim and soaked him with the freezing cold water a second time, then turned and fled, Alfie in hot pursuit. Stella was pretty quick. She was fit and had youth on her side but Alfie was no slouch. He caught her ankle as she attempted to climb the rope-ladder that hung from one of the branches of a tall eucalyptus tree at the back of the house. Climbing up her leg as she held onto the ladder, he gripped her round the waist, wrenched her free, turned and hoisted her over his shoulder, Stella giggling as he headed down an overgrown track into the trees, beating back the thick undergrowth with his free hand until they reached the lake.

'Let this be a lesson to you!' he said as he hurled her into the cool, clear water from which she resurfaced, seconds later, spluttering and protesting in unison with the family of ducks. Fully clothed, he dived in after her.

Later, they lay side by side, hand in hand, naked on the grassy bank beside the lake, their clothes beside them drying in the sun. It was the third day they'd spent together, magical days still with the dreamlike quality of the first night. And Stella had not once mentioned leaving.

So, pondered Alfie, staring at the tiny white stripes of cloud that seared the blue sky above them, will she up and leave at any minute? I mean, why would she stay? What could possibly be the attraction of a disgraced and ageing film director to a twenty-two-year-old girl? Her life's stretched out before her like a bright white canvas. At twenty years her senior I'm not a particularly scintillating prospect. I'm old, a has-been, a one-time master of the silver screen reduced to this – a recluse, a fugitive, dried-up and deserted. *My* canvas is tatty, old and covered with botched brushwork. Who, in their right mind, would want a part of that?

One of the ducks, infuriated by his brothers, began to quack loudly, interrupting his thoughts.

'Larry told me you're writing a screenplay,' said Stella suddenly, releasing her hand from his and propping herself up on one elbow, perfect naked skin, smooth as stone, settled as if for a long conversation. He forced his eyes away from her deliciously pert, round caramel breasts and sighed.

'Yes, I am,' he answered tentatively.

'How's it going?'

'Good. I plan to be finished by June. At least that was the case, before I became distracted.'

'Does it have a name?'

'Yeah. At the moment I'm calling it *Killing Fame*.'

'Sounds like a thriller. What's it about?'

'Retribution, mainly,' he said, frowning slightly before abruptly changing the subject. 'I want to teach you to sail, Stella,' he told her lifting up his arm to stroke her hair. He loved her hair, it's straightness, the way it fell across her shoulders when she inclined her head. 'And scuba dive and water-ski. You'd be good at those. We'll buy a boat.'

'That's what you're into, is it?'

'Yeah. I love all that. Since I was a kid and lived by the sea. And I had a devoted father. That helped. He taught me to sail.'

'Ah. A role model. Every good man should have one of those. Was this in Africa?'

'Yes,' replied Alfie with pride, lying back on the grass and tucking his arms behind his head. 'I was seven. We were living in Kenya at the time, in Nairobi. When it got too hot we used to escape to the coast. Mombasa. It was cooler there.'

'How lovely,' she said softly.

'Our boat was an old wooden skiff with a tatty red sail that doubled as a fishing boat. We'd spend hours in it, sailing, sometimes fishing. My father would tell me stories of his life and my mother, well she would always tell me what a skilled little fisherman I was,' he told her, as the time-worn image of his mother smiling, hugging him to her aproned waist drifted into his mind.

'It sounds like your childhood was very special, Alfie.'

'Yes ... it was ... until my mother died suddenly of a stroke. I was fourteen. My father did his best to disguise his grief but I was old enough to see it for myself. He always did his best for me, even without my mother. He tried his best to cope and to hide his tears from me but he was in pain. I knew he was because I was too. And the crazy thing was we were both trying so hard to protect one another we couldn't share our grief. We cried alone.'

He stopped talking and turned his head to look at Stella who was still propped up on one elbow and staring at him intently. How fresh, how beautiful, how special was Stella? he thought.

'Just before my father died he gave me a camera.'

'The one I brought you, the one you use all the time?'

'Yes. He told me to treasure it always and to take lots of pictures. That way I'd always remember the things I've done.'

'And you have, Alfie,' she said touching his arm lightly with her free hand.

'Two weeks later he was dead. I believe he died from a broken heart. And I was left alone with my camera. I tried to console myself with the thought that my parents were united in death.'

'So you went on and conquered the world,' said Stella. She sat up, leant over him and kissed him gently on the lips. Alfie smiled.

'I still can't quite understand why you came, Stella,' he asked her at last, hoping that she would not notice he was shaking.

187

'I came for you, Alfie, at least to see if you would have me. Is that so odd?' she answered, flatly and honestly. Alfie was taken aback and sat up with a jerk.

'But what about your brother? You're here to visit him, right?'

Stella frowned, screwing up one eye and for a while said nothing. Alfie picked up her hands and squeezed them. 'Not exactly no. I wasn't totally honest about that,' she told him, staring down at their clasped hands. 'Sorry!'

'I don't understand,' said Alfie worried. 'Tell me, please.' Stella took a deep breath.

'In actual fact I've already seen Ned. I thought as I was here I may as well pay you a visit.'

'So?' he asked her, his voice anxious, rushed. 'What next?'

'Well that depends . . .'

'On what?'

'Look Alfie, this is very difficult,' she said, leaping to her feet. She grabbed her shirt and put it on, turning her back on him.

'Why? Do you have to go? What Stella, tell me please?' begged Alfie, rising also. He went over to where she was dressing, placed his hands on her shoulders and turned her round to face him. She stamped her foot.

'Ugh! Sometimes Alfie Macbeth, you can be damned irritating.'

'I'm sorry I . . .' said Alfie helplessly.

'I'm obviously going to have to ask *you*, aren't I? . . . Seeing as how an invitation to stay has not been forthcoming.'

'You mean you want to stay here . . . with me?'

'Y . . . e . . . s,' said Stella slowly as though she were talking to a remedial.

'I can't believe it,' said Alfie, pulling her towards him as he tried desperately to assemble this latest piece of good fortune.

'Why?'

'Where do I begin? I'm old. Old enough to be your father.'

'Only just,' she interrupted laughing.

'Easily!' he corrected. 'Then there is my history, my womanising . . .' He paused to think. Was he doing the right thing, confessing all? 'The accusations!'

'Ah, the accusations,' she repeated solemnly.

'Well you haven't asked me anything about them, Stella. The press crucified me. They accused me of assaulting Kate.'

'I didn't ask you because like I said Larry told me what actually happened. And anyway I think you've suffered enough already,' she concluded.

Alfie breathed a silent sigh of relief. 'Thanks, Stella.'

'For what?'

'For having faith in me. Of course you can stay here, my darling,' he told her pulling her towards him. 'No better than that, you must. I won't hear of your going.'

'But there is the small matter of your hairy back,' she added, teasing.

'Ah, yes, my hairy back. Tricky, very tricky.'

'And the grey hair.'

'Hmm!'

'On the other hand there's your enormous wallet to think about,' she added, putting her finger to her mouth. 'All that money is quite appealing to a young girl with nothing to her name.'

'Quite!' agreed Alfie laughing. 'I understand your point exactly.'

'Then of course your notoriety, this ranch, and ...' She paused and looked down at her hands. Alfie watched intently, waiting for the next quip. 'Because I think I love you.'

Strunned by this quiet and unexpected admission, Alfie stared at her dumbly. Seconds passed, neither spoke or moved.

'Stella I have been such an idiot,' he said, breaking the silence. 'You know I love you, have loved you for a long time. It's just ... well ... it's quite simple actually ... I really can't believe that you could love me.'

Stella pulled his arms towards her. He wrapped them round her slender body while she buried her head in his chest so that when she next spoke her voice was muffled, barely audible.

'I tried hard not to. I fought and fought against it. I just ... all those times we spent together ... then ... it was horrible when the press laid into you.'

'Stella, I've loved you from the moment I first set eyes on you.'

'Alfie, don't.' She lifted her head to face his and placed a finger to his lips.

'I just need to know that you will always stay with me,' he whispered while his mind screamed not to let her go, not now, not ever, this girl who seemed to exist on a higher plane.

'Let's just take one day at a time.'

Six

At first Troy wasn't at all certain that Stella was the right girl for Alfie. Sure, he reasoned, she looked like sex on legs with her slim, toned body, fabulous breasts, fantastic long straight hair and weird green eyes, but she seemed not quite good enough somehow. Too young, he wondered? No, that wasn't it. Young was good. Fresh, energetic, innocent but totally lacking in experience, such a girl would be eager to discover life's enigmas, wasn't that what he'd read in last month's *GQ*? Well if it wasn't her age perhaps it was just that she was too ordinary. Who was she, where had she come from and what had she done with her life? It seemed to him that she was a nobody from nowhere, just like him. How on earth had she ensnared a man of Alfie's wealth and reputation? It beggared belief, it really did. Unless, he pondered as he scratched his testicles, she has hidden talents.

The other matter that was giving him cause for concern was the conversation he had had with Alfie just before they left for the Cape.

'Your mother is very sweet. She told me Stella was a breath of fresh air.'

'That's good,' he'd said, secretly appalled by his mother's cliché.

'Yeah. It's your Dad I'm worried about.'

'Oh?'

'I'm worried he sees me as some sad old Humbert craving my Lolita.'

'Really,' Troy had replied as sagely as possible.

'My only hope is that he hasn't read any Nabakov.'

Lolita, Nabakov, thought Troy. A book! There's a film called *Lolita*, black and white, starring James Mason. I'm certain although I haven't seen it so I'm not quite sure where Alfie's coming from. I must remember to hire the video, he'd decided as he made a mental note. Then he'd smiled and had said with great confidence, 'I'm sure he hasn't. My father only reads agricultural journals.'

That had made Alfie laugh and ruffle his hair. He's always doing that, ruffling my hair, Troy had thought, irritably. And actually it's quite annoying, like he thinks I'm a kid, which I'm not.

And then they'd gone away for a holiday to Cape Tribulation. They'd been gone two weeks and he'd missed Alfie's company. Perhaps that was the problem. Perhaps he resented Stella. After all she had arrived as if by magic carpet, totally unexpected and unannounced and Alfie has been totally distracted by her presence. He'd even confessed as much the day he left for the Cape.

'I have to confess, my attention has been totally grabbed.'

'You mean you're rapt,' Troy had translated.

'I mean I'm in love,' he'd replied without trace of embarrassment. Troy had squirmed. 'And you know what, Troy, I've never felt this good. Even the pain of being separated from my daughter is bearable now that I have Stella.'

'Beaut!' Troy had replied, sick to the stomach.

The fortnight had passed, slowly and uneventfully. He'd managed to drag himself out on the farm to help his Dad with the cows to pass the time until their return. And then today Stella had called inviting them all to join her and Alfie for a barbie. It was a shame that all the other neighbours would be there but that couldn't be helped. Troy was sure Alfie would be pleased to see him, especially if he arrived with a slab of beer. Well, perhaps not quite a slab, his allowance didn't run to that but a few tinnies, nonetheless.

*

The trip to Cape Tribulation had been a revelation. Stella, every inch the ravishing savage of Alfie's fantasies, had excelled, cooking on a campfire, sleeping under the stars. With tender encouragement Alfie had taught his eager companion to sail, water-ski and scuba dive.

Not only was he *in love* with her, he loved her also. He felt liberated, set free from his past existence to live out his life with a girl who seemed able to fulfil his dreams effortlessly. For Stella was equipped with an uninhibited enthusiasm for life and she was game for anything.

Now, back home, he was aware that it was time to kick-start his writing. That morning at breakfast he had muttered something about getting back to work.

'I wondered when you were going to,' remarked Stella.

'I promise not to be boring about it,' he reassured her.

'Alfie, I think it's a great idea. Pick up your pen, though why you don't use a computer is totally beyond me. Unless, of course, you don't know how!'

'Hmm!' said Alfie, ignoring the jibe. It was true he hadn't mastered keyboards yet. And even if he had he'd probably still write in longhand. It was a method that suited him, allowed him time to think, to plan. 'I think I'll begin tomorrow. I want to make some radical changes to the script. It's going to take me far longer than I'd anticipated but I'm up for the challenge.'

'So why not begin today?'

'Well I couldn't help noticing the wind is perfect for a sail. I thought we could take the boat out.'

'No! I won't be held responsible for coming between you and your work!' she exclaimed, holding up both hands.

'You won't. I promise I'll start tomorrow when the wind has died down!'

'Come on, Alfie,' said Stella frowning. 'We've had a great time, a real holiday. Now it's time to get back to work.'

'But won't you get bored without me to amuse you?'

'I doubt it. There's plenty for me to do, here.'

'Oh yes? What exactly?'

'Well, to be truthful . . .'

'Aren't you always?' he interrupted, raising his eyebrows.

'I could get a job!'

'No. Don't do that!' said Alfie, far too quickly.

'Now why did I guess you'd say that?'

'Couldn't you just wait a bit? See how things pan out. We may up and leave in six months.'

'How presumptuous you are, Mr Macbeth.'

'Yeah, you're right, Hollywood will probably hate it,' replied Alfie, mournfully.

'I'm sure Hollywood will love the screenplay, but what makes you think I'll follow you to the States?'

'Er . . .'

'The words cross, bridge and when we come to it have suddenly sprung to my mind,' she said quickly, smoothing the waters. 'But now work!'

And if Stella is a distraction to me, she is just as much an attraction to the neighbours, though in varying degrees and on different planes, thought Alfie as he geared himself up for this long overdue morning of work, his plan being to stop at lunchtime and spend the afternoon on the water. If I'd had it my way I wouldn't have introduced her to any of them. First of all there had been Jesse's reaction to Stella.

'A pretty spiffy Sheila,' she had announced. 'Though far too young for a bloke of your age to have a naughty with. And that's why I feel compelled to tell you I find it a bit peculiar, Alfie.'

'You've spent too long in the outback, Jesse!' Alfie had told her.

'I'm just thinking of the Sheila!' she'd replied, knocking Alfie's conscience, forcing him to wonder *Is Jesse right*? for one long sleepless night until Stella had forced it out of him and told him not to be so stupid, that she had a mind of her own which she was quite capable of making up without help and advice from interfering busybodies like Jesse.

Of course the Thomases had been very kind, neither Millie nor Harry referring to the age gap. And considering Stella is only four years older than Troy, that's pretty good to be getting on with, thought Alfie happily.

Troy, however, had gone glassy eyed on meeting her.

'Sex on legs,' Troy had assured him. 'You lucky old bugger!'

Was it just his imagination or had Troy been spending more time than usual at his house since Stella's arrival? And could he really be sure that Troy had been staring at her breasts when all three of them shared a beer together the other night? In my opinion, he mused, as he tried to switch off his thoughts to concentrate on his work, Troy has taken more than a healthy shine to her.

Alfie pulled back the undone cuffs of his shirt and glanced at his watch ... 6.30pm! It was evening already. Time, it seemed, had evaporated as he scratched away at his screenplay. He hadn't expected to spend quite this long at the kitchen table. And Stella had not interrupted him once.

'God bless that girl,' he said, feeling guilty and embarrassed. Selfishly he hoped, as he stumbled over a large pile of shopping heaped in brown paper bags by the front door, that she wouldn't feel neglected, that she'd understand.

She wasn't on the front deck but he found her out the back cleaning the barbeque in the fading light, in an apron and a pair of bright yellow marigolds.

'I've been shopping at Tobins.'

'Ah yes, J.T. Tobin and Sons Variety Store. Where else but Australia can you buy a rib of beef while being fitted out with a pair of strides as you chose the material for your bedroom curtains?' he asked her, kissing the soft hair on the back of her head.

'The bags are stacked in the front porch. I didn't want to unpack them in case I disturbed you.'

'That's unbelievably thoughtful of you,' he told her, hugging her

from behind as she continued brushing furiously at the metal grill with a
long-handled stiff wire brush.

'I'm just so pleased it went well. Now stop mauling me and help me
get ready. I've asked the neighbours round for supper.'

'Oh great!' said Alfie, his heart sinking. That was not what he'd had
in mind at all. 'Wouldn't you prefer to be alone with me and . . .?'

'It can't just be you and I forever, Alfie,' she scolded.

'Why not?' replied Alfie, who still hadn't let go. He squeezed her a
little harder and began to kiss her neck.

'Because . . .' began Stella, before Alfie silenced her with a kiss.

Over the past few weeks Troy had noticed that Jesse Buchanan made
Alfie feel uncomfortable. He had seen how, when she opened her mouth
to speak, Alfie's body would stiffen involuntarily as if in dread of what
she might say. At other times he appeared to ignore her by concentrating
his attentions on something else, as he seemed to be doing right now.

'She irritates you, doesn't she?' he asked.

'Who? What?' said Alfie distractedly, busying himself turning the
steaks on the grill.

'Jesse!'

'Jesse? What makes you say that?'

'She has this annoying habit of sticking her very ample nose into
everybody's business.'

'Indeed,' said Alfie stealing a glance in Jesse's direction. She was
clucking around Stella like a mutant mother hen.

'But she's harmless really,' said Troy hoping to reassure him. Alfie
smiled and ruffled his hair. Troy grinned back although this mussing of
his hair every five minutes was getting beyond a joke. Perhaps he
should say something.

'So when does Jack arrive, Jesse?' he heard his mother ask, clapping
her hands excitedly.

'Oh not Jack again!' muttered Alfie under his breath.

Troy laughed, his consternation concerning his hair forgotten.

'Next week, so he says.'

'That's great, Jesse, you must be really excited.'

'Reckon!'

'Who's Jack?' Stella asked Harry as she handed him another beer.

'Jesse's youngest. He's been overseas a while. Jesse hasn't seen him
for ages. He's finished his degree, graduated and now he's coming
home.'

'He's an artist,' explained Alfie from the barbeque.

'Really?'

'Staggering, isn't it?' replied Alfie, grinning.

194

Troy watched amused as Jesse did a double take and Stella shot Alfie a meaningful look to which he mouthed *sorry* just as the phone rang.

'I'll get it,' said Stella breezily.

'Have another beer, Alfie,' suggested Troy, flicking the top off a bottle of Victoria Bitter and handing it to Alfie.

'Thanks, Troy.'

'How's the screenplay?' he asked as Alfie took a long and satisfying swig from the bottle.

'OK,' he replied, wiping his mouth with the back of his hand. 'I've still got a lot of work to do.'

'Who did it?' he asked, nudging Alfie.

'The person you'd least expect, of course.'

'*Killing Fame*,' whispered Troy. 'I like that. It has a sinister ring to it. What's the murder weapon?'

'Wait and see.'

'I guess a single bullet through the brain,' said Troy conspiratorially. 'Or a knife. Hmm. Lots of blood.'

'I refuse to be drawn,' said Alfie flatly.

'But you will agree to be pictured?' joked Troy, picking up Alfie's camera from the table.

'Careful with that,' said Alfie as Stella came out of the house, her face ashen.

'Strewth Stella, youse seen a ghost?' bawled Jesse. But Stella ignored her. Instead she went over to Alfie and whispered something in his ear that Troy could not hear. Alfie took a step back.

He seems stunned, thought Troy worriedly as Alfie untied his apron, put down his tongs and retreated into the house. 'Is something wrong?' he asked Stella.

'Not now, Troy, please,' she said, picking up the tongs.

'Has something happened back in England?' he pestered. 'Is it his daughter? Is there something wrong with Phoebe?'

'It's Raul, OK!' answered Stella tersely, hoping to shut him up.

'Raul Mendoza! The film star?'

'Well done Troy,' said Stella dismissively.

'Isn't he . . .?'

'Yes,' interrupted Stella. 'Now leave it Troy.'

Shit, thought Troy.

'My daughter's coming to stay.' A delirious-looking Alfie, who had reappeared and was dancing down the garden, was singing his marvellous news.

'Oh darling!' exclaimed Stella, smiling with relief. 'Oh I'm so pleased for you. What wonderful news.'

195

'I know. I can't believe it. Kate's in Alaska filming, her mother's away and by chance Raul is filming in Australia. Kate told him to ask me to look after Phoebe for two, maybe three weeks.'

'Wow! That's fantastic,' said Stella who seemed delighted at the prospect of seeing Alfie's daughter.

Now that really was impressive. She must be mad about Alfie and that somehow makes it all right, thought Troy approvingly. He looked over at Jesse expecting to see her bursting with emotion, because Jesse loved kids, but she wasn't celebrating. She had sucked in her cheeks and folded her arms. Very odd, he thought, his mind now firmly focused on the celebration that would inevitably follow such news.

*

It was warm rather than hot and yet Alfie's clothes were sticking to him. This was the uncontrollable, uncompromising sweat of fear. He knew that, had felt it on his return from Thailand, could recognise the signs. It had begun as a light prickle in his armpits, the palms of his hands, the back of his neck but had sped across his body like a virulent rash until he felt slightly damp all over. And that was not all. The unsettling sensation of a butterfly flitting frantically from his stomach, through his small intestines to his colon and back made him think he wanted to open his bowels again which was exasperating given that he'd visited the lavatory three times before he'd left home.

It was all very well his being feverish with excitement at the prospect of seeing Phoebe again but he couldn't help wondering what it would be like if she didn't want to see him. Perhaps she had grown to resent his absence, had grown fonder of Raul or was missing her Mum. Would she recognise him? Did she really understand that she still had a living, breathing father?

'There she is,' said Stella suddenly, surprising him.

'Oh my God,' whispered Alfie, his pulse racing, as he gazed at his daughter. There was a familiarity about her, a Phoebeness that was instantly recognisable, although she had changed in appearance since he'd last seen her. She was taller, had lost some of her toddler chubbiness and this made her look even prettier than he remembered. Her dark brown hair had grown long and she was wearing it in a high pony-tail tied with a pink ribbon. She had inherited her mother's dark beauty except that her smile was wider than her mother's, her eyes a deeper brown. She was holding a tattered scrapbook in one hand, he noticed, and Raul's hand in the other, because the moment she spotted him she dropped both and sprinted towards him, into his outstretched arms, whooping with joy. At that moment Alfie was truly grateful to Stella for having accompanied him.

'I'll look after Raul so you can concentrate on Phoebe,' she said, stepping in front of Alfie and his daughter. She introduced herself to Raul, who responded by grabbing her hand with a magnificent flourish and the words, 'bella, bella'. Five minutes later he gave Phoebe a kiss goodbye, slapped Alfie on the back with an 'I'll call' and was gone.

'Well that went swimmingly,' said Stella happily.

'Yes, thanks to you.'

'My book, my book!' cried Phoebe. 'It's lost.'

'What book, darling?' Stella asked her.

'She was holding one when she came through the barrier. A tatty scrapbook or something like it.'

'I'll go look.'

'Don't worry,' Alfie told Phoebe, 'Stella will find it.'

'Who is Stella, Daddy?' asked Phoebe, forgetting her book for a moment.

'She's a very special friend of your Daddy's,' he said, stroking her head, delighting in the easy immediacy of his daughter.

'Your girlfriend,' she told him, as he caught sight of Stella behind Phoebe, brandishing the book.

'That's right!' he said. 'And she's found your book.'

'I like Stella,' said Phoebe taking the book from Stella and holding it to her heart.

'And you obviously love that book,' Stella said smiling. 'What is it?'

'It's my Daddy book. Uncle Larry gave it to me. Look!' She opened it proudly and thrust it at Alfie. 'It's all about you.'

'That's how you recognised me,' whispered Alfie, dumbfounded as he flicked through the pages covered in snapshots of him, newspaper pictures, articles that she was yet too young to read, invitations to his premières, lists of awards, innumerable bits of memorabilia that charted the life of the father that Phoebe, in Larry's wise opinion, must not be allowed to forget. In essence it was simple – a collection of pictures, cuttings, scraps of paper. In substance, however, it was a life. His life. Sprung from the raw imagination of a good man.

'Larry, you are one of life's true diamonds,' Alfie told him on the phone that night.

'Have you been taking those happy pills again, Alfie?' replied Larry. 'I've warned you about them before. They're very dangerous not least because of the side-effect that induces extreme euphoria in the patient.'

'I'm talking about the book, Larry.'

'Book? What book?'

'Phoebe's *Daddy Book*. She brought it with her.'

'Oh that,' said Larry dismissively. Then, 'Did she?'

'Yes she did. You see I think it means as much to her as it does to me, which is why I want to tell you that I love you Larry.'

'Steady!'

'I do, Larry. It's the God's honest truth. Phoebe could have forgotten me.'

'I doubt that, Alfie, I doubt that very much. Believe me, you are infinitely memorable. But I'm pleased you both like it. As a doting godfather, it was the very least I could do because, Alfie, I did it for her, not you! How's the lovely Stella?' he asked, swiftly changing the subject.

'Gorgeous, wonderful, everything I'd ever dreamed she would be,' he said quietly because his old friend Guilt was slapping him softly on the cheeks again, cold and clammy like a wet fish.

'Good,' said Larry quickly. 'I'm glad.'

'You must come and visit us. We'd love to see you.'

'Yes I must. I'd like that. Yes, yes.'

'Larry?'

'What?'

'I'll take good care of Stella. I promise.'

Seven

Jesse was preparing the welcome home party of the century for her long lost son, Jack. She had decorated her house with streamers, balloons, lanterns and a large banner tacked to the staircase that read WELCOME HOME SON. Stella was not amused when Alfie suggested they insert the word prodigal, unlike Troy who laughed excessively, confusing Alfie who thought it was for Stella's benefit.

'That boy is gaga about you,' he whispered in her ear.

'Rubbish, Alfie. He's simply trying to impress you. Can't you see the poor boy is in total awe of you?

'Really?' said Alfie pleased. 'Do you really think so?'

'Definitely!' she laughed as she led Phoebe to where Jesse's grandchildren were fussing over a Jack Russell puppy.

Phoebe's visit had been a revelation. She had slotted into their life the past ten days like a link in a chain. She was easy going and was content to spend her days searching out the indigenous animals on the ranch. She would stare for hours at the possums, mesmerised by their enormous eyes and bushy tails. She chased the wallabies and hunted tree frogs. Even the ugly bush turkeys held her spellbound. Her favourite, however, was the duck-billed platypus. Every day she'd persuade Alfie and Stella to take her to the lake in the hope that she'd see them. She'd spend hours happily paddling in the shallows, talking to herself and the ducks that quacked as she splashed.

She'd scared them both one day by falling in, disappearing under the water for long enough for them to realise she couldn't swim. Alfie, fully clothed, had dived in and fished her out, his heart racing fit to burst.

'Tomorrow I'll teach you to swim,' Alfie had told her as he covered her in kisses.

'Good,' Phoebe had replied, totally unconcerned.

At bedtime she'd insisted he read to her, 'like you used to Daddy,' surprising Alfie with the much-thumbed copy of the *Just So* stories he had read to her as a toddler.

'I think she's very intelligent.'

'I'm sure she is,' Stella had replied, laughing.

'I'm serious, Stella. She can read extremely well you know.'

'I know. And it's wonderful.'

But now her visit was coming to an end. Alfie was under no illusions. Phoebe would leave a big hole in his life. And then there was the conversation he'd had with her last night. That had been most unsettling.

'If you married Stella, could I come and live with you?'

'Phoebe, it's more complicated than that,' Alfie had replied, shocked.

'Why? Why can't I live with you?'

'Because ...'

'Don't you love me, Daddy?' she'd cried.

'Darling, I love you more than anything in the world. I want to wake up every day and see your smiling face, watch you grow. It breaks my heart that you are on the other side of the world. Every day I miss you, Phoebe, and it hurts. You must understand that. I love you very much. But Mummy loves you too and ...'

'No she doesn't. She's always busy. I don't want to go back. Don't make me go back.'

Why not? Alfie had wondered, panicking. What's happening at home? And how do I explain to a four-year-old girl that her Daddy is not allowed to look after her even though he wants to, even though he hates the thought of giving her back. How could she possibly understand?

'But you'll have a lovely time,' he'd said, desperately trying to reassure her. 'Maybe your Mummy will have bought you lots of presents because I'm sure she has hated being away from you too.'

'Has she?' Phoebe had asked innocently. 'Has she bought me a hamster? I really, really want a hamster.'

Oh Christ, now what had he done? He really couldn't see Kate looking after a hamster.' I'll write to Mummy, OK. I'll ask her for you. Now it's really time for little girls to go to sleep.'

'One more story. Per-lease!'

'One more story and then sleep!'

He watched her now playing contentedly with Jesse's grandchildren who were patiently trying to teach her the rules to kick the can. He sighed, thinking again how much he'd miss her when she left in two days time, then wandered into the kitchen to grab himself a beer from Jesse's well-stocked fridge. He peered into the cold chasm.

'You must be our new neighbour?' said a voice from behind his shoulder, startling Alfie who bumped his head on a shelf as he backed out of the fridge, feeling like a minor criminal, a can of Victoria Bitter in hand. 'And you like beer, that's good!'

'In England we call it lager,' said Alfie, not knowing quite what else to say. Get it together Alfie, he told himself offering his hand. 'I'm Alfie ... and you must be Jack?'

'That's right, Jack Buchanan. Pleased to meet you,' he replied with a massive grin. He shook Alfie's hand warmly. 'Chuck us a tinnie, Alfie. It's so much better than the warm stuff you poms drink. Wouldn't you agree?' he added as he ripped off the ring pull, still grinning, his clear aquamarine eyes twinkling mischievously beneath the curtain of his floppy blonde hair. He was tall, about 6'2' and had a broad well-defined jaw although his cheeks were fleshy, which made him appear younger than his twenty-four years.

Almost cherubic, thought Alfie, astonished that this handsome man could be a product of the gargantuan Jesse! 'I certainly wouldn't disagree with you Jack, though there's nothing like a pint of warm ale on a cold winter's day,' he said, warming to the young Australian.

'Here he is, darlin',' said Jesse, marching Stella into the kitchen in her usual military manner. She pushed Stella who was flushing with painful embarrassment toward Jack. Stella peered up at him barely able to look him in the eye. Alfie was irritated but said nothing. 'See, I told you she was a beauty!'

'Hi, I'm Jack,' he told Stella breezily, ignoring his mother and sensing the awkwardness of the situation.

'And this is Stella,' said Jesse, unabashed.

'Would you like a drink, Stella?' Jack asked her, once again ignoring his mother. Alfie was impressed.

'Thank you. White wine would be lovely,' she answered politely.

'Let me tell you, Stella,' continued Jack as he poured her a glass of Chardonnay, 'I am quite bowled over meeting Alfie like this. It's not often you entertain a legend in your own kitchen.'

At this comment everyone seemed to relax. Stella smiled and turned to Alfie, who laughed loudly, flattered by this unexpected remark.

'So the English press haven't turned the whole world against me, then?' I still have one fan ... two if you include Troy. Er, that is if I may count you as a fan?'

'Absolutely,' said Jack grinning again, a skill he seemed to find effortless as well as enjoyable. 'Although that's what I hate about the British tabloids. They build a bloke up burdening him with praise, luring him into a false sense of security while they wait for him to make a mistake, then bang! It's all-out attack until they bring the poor man down, much to the public's surprise who rush to the stalls to buy the papers and sales go through the roof. It's like all you celebrities are the journalist's puppets. You dance while they pull the strings.'

'I agree with you I really do but when a celebrity courts publicity, what can he expect?'

'That's incredibly generous of you, Alfie, especially since they've driven you out of your home.'

'I should have shunned the limelight. Others manage to.'

'So when are you going to stage a return?'

'Are you being serious?' asked Stella crossly. Her eyes had narrowed to a furious glare. Alfie shuddered. He hadn't seen that look for a while. Neither had Jesse, it seemed, who was watching Stella, her cavernous mouth hanging open in shocked surprise at her unprecedented outburst. 'It would be a bit difficult, don't you think?' she added, her voice heavy with sarcasm.

'Er . . . yes . . .' said Jack awkwardly.

'Stella,' Alfie said, taking her hand. 'There's no need to take it out on Jack. He didn't mean any harm.'

'Well I disagree. I think he's being a bit insensitive seeing that he's been living in England the last five years!' exclaimed Stella indignantly, letting go of Alfie's hand to flash her eyes in the artist's direction.

'Stella! Don't be silly,' whispered Alfie, stroking her back.

'Don't be so bloody patronising,' she muttered under her breath, her cheeks reddening in anger.

'Hey, I'm sorry guys,' said Jack, holding up his hands. 'All I meant was it just seems a terrible waste.'

'It's not a problem, Jack. Don't worry,' Alfie said, raising his beer to Jack with one hand, disguising his concern at Stella's outburst. 'Tell you what, let's drink to the future. Who knows what it may bring?'

'Good onya!' said Jesse, who had regained control of her jaw once more. She picked up a can of Victoria Bitter and poured it into a pint glass. 'Let's blow the froth off a few of these and get stuck into some good honest Aussie tucker off the barbie.'

'Great idea,' said Alfie.

'Excellent,' agreed Jack.

Stella, on the other hand, said nothing. Worried but unsure what to say, Alfie leant over to her, kissed her lightly on the cheek and smiled at her. For a while she stared ahead, her face set but when he kissed her again, this time on the neck, she relaxed a little, turned to him and managed a half smile.

Troy was outside in the backyard watching the kids playing kick the can.

'Hi Troy. Penny for them.'

'Crikey Stella,' said Troy startled.

'Sorry. Did I make you jump?' she asked him.

'I was miles away.'

'Anywhere nice?'

'You know what. I think you and Alfie are good together.'

'Why thank you Troy. I'm so glad we've earned your approval.'

'Yeah. Well. I just felt you should know. It can't be easy bunking up with a guy as famous, brilliant and handsome as Alfie.'

Stella laughed. 'I love a man who speaks his mind,' she said, kissing him on the cheek. Troy grinned mawkishly. For a while they stood in silence watching the kids at play. 'Phoebe's great isn't she?'

'Yeah. A diamond,' agreed Troy.

'Alfie is going to really miss her,' said Stella quietly. She stopped, shivered, folding her arms across her chest to warm her up.

'You cold?'

'A bit. It's quite chilly tonight.'

'Have you got a jumper?'

'No. Silly of me.'

'Do you want me to go to yours and get you one?'

'You'd do that for me?'

'Course,' he said grinning. 'By the way, have you met Jack yet?'

'Yeah,' she replied, rolling her eyes.

'I take it you weren't enamoured then!'

'Should I be?'

'Well he's a good-looking bugger apparently. Girls go wild over him. Something about his eyes.'

'Really?' intoned Stella sarcastically.

'Really!' confirmed Troy with a chuckle. 'Can't see it myself though. I'll be back in about 30 minutes. Any particular jumper?'

'Just grab my denim jacket. It's hanging just inside the front door.'

'I know.'

'Do you want to take the Toyota?'

'I've got the keys to Mum's,' he said pulling a bunch out of his jeans' pocket as he headed off in the direction of the front yard where his mother's white Ford Falcon was parked. 'See you later.'

He got into the car feeling happy to be of use, turned the key in the ignition, revved up the car, hit the accelerator hard and skidded out of the driveway in a cloud of dust. The road was bumpy and driving at speed soon became uncomfortable in a car that had been spent of suspension. He reduced the pressure on the accelerator and the engine quietened allowing the sweet tones of Simon and Garfunkel to infiltrate the car.

'I think we can do better than this,' he said flicking open the glove compartment and rummaging with his free hand. 'Frank Sinatra! No. *Les Miserables*! No. God Mum, have you absolutely no taste in music at all?' he said as his hand chanced upon a tape by Queen. Hmm. That's about as good as it's gonna get, he thought, chucking Simon and Garfunkel on the front passenger seat, ramming the Queen tape into the deck. He cranked up the volume filling the car with the booming beat of *We Will Rock You.*

It was dark at The Rocks, save for one solitary light outside the front door. He got out of the car, slamming the door behind him, lifted the terracotta pot to the right of the door, picked up the large iron key and put it in the lock. It was stiff, so he had to use both hands to force it round. He was concentrating heavily, leaning to the left when he felt a hand on his shoulder. He sprung upwards in terror, bumping his head on the chin of the stranger behind him.

"Ouch! Is that how you greet visitors down under?' asked the man in a deep, heavily accented voice.

Speechless, Troy spun around in alarm, fists raised and clenched, terrified that he was going to have to protect himself against an intruder and at the same time wondering how Alfie would feel if, as a result of his incompetence, his house was burgled.

Fuck, shit, fuck, why do these things always happen to me? he asked himself as he turned, panic-stricken, to face the intruder – a tall, dark, stranger who looked somehow familiar. He was frowning at Troy and rubbing a chin that looked as though it had been chiselled from granite.

'Don Juan?' he whispered almost to himself. 'Awesome. Er . . . can I . . . can . . . I . . . er . . . can I help you,' he stammered, suddenly coy.

The man frowned again. 'I'm looking for Alfie Macbeth. And Phoebe. They live here.'

'Yeah, they do.'

'Well can you tell me where they are?'

'Yeah, I can,' said Troy idiotically, staring up at the man, totally awestruck.

'Well?'

'Don Juan,' repeated Troy like an imbecile.

'Raul Mendoza,' replied the man, impatiently.

'Reckon!' said Troy, wide-eyed.

'Alfie Macbeth!' repeated Raul.

'Fancy a coldie?' he asked, grinning inanely.

'I . . .'

'C'mon. I'll take you to Alfie.'

Jesse was hovering amongst the gathering like a Queen bee. From time to time she would chivvy one of her sons into action or herd a guest towards food, using her body as though it were a trampoline, deflecting people off the spare tyres of her girth towards the destination of her choice. She laughed all night, the rolls of flesh that disguised her double chin rippling with the vibrations of her monstrous guffaw. She was wearing a sun-dress which barely contained the obese folds of her flesh, many of which had spilled over and broken free.

Please, please don't feel the need to speak to me, thought Alfie as he watched her lolloping in his direction like a giant dumpling, her gait lumbering as she heaved her massive frame across the floor straight into Troy Thomas and . . . Raul Mendoza.

Raul? Was he seeing things? he wondered, peering at the tall dark figure on the other side of the room. Hell no it is him, goddamn it. Horrified, Alfie's heart began to sink. The smarmy, muff-diving Dago isn't due to arrive until tomorrow. And why is Troy looking so damned smug? He stared as Jesse grabbed a now petrified looking Raul's hand and shook it so vigorously that his jowls wobbled. Now that is amusing, thought Alfie despite his frustration. Unattractive, overweight, middle-aged women are definitely not Raul's speciality. Phoebe! he thought suddenly, aware that the precious time he'd spent with his daughter was coming to an end. I must find her.

'And this is my mother, Millie Thomas,' said Troy, leading the hapless Raul toward his mother. 'Mum, this is Raul Mendoza

'My goodness,' said Millie blushing. 'How incredible.'

'Bella, bella!' crooned Raul, suddenly animated. He leant forward and kissed the blushing housewife on both cheeks.

'She's an absolute total fan of yours,' Troy added triumphantly. 'Loves everything you do.'

'Troy!' scolded Millie, embarrassed still further, staring down at her shoes. Amused, Troy dug his hand in his trousers and brought out a ten-dollar bill.

'Would you make her day and sign this for her?'

'It would be a pleasure,' said Raul.

Amazing how a bit of a massage to an ego can placate a man, thought Troy.

'You want to watch out, Alfie. That Spaniard's got Stella in his sights,' said Jesse, grabbing onto Alfie's arm.

'Don't be ridiculous.'

'He's been staring at her since he got here.'

'Who is Jesse talking about?' piped up Phoebe.

'No one darling,' he said sweetly. 'Go and get an ice cream, Phoebe. I'll come and find you in a minute. I just need to get hold of Stella.'

'If that Spaniard doesn't get her first, eh Alfie?' taunted Jesse, laughing.

'Stella has more sense!' he replied dismissively, scanning the room but Stella was nowhere to be seen. Raul, he noticed, was now attempting a conversation with Harry.

'He's a bit of a spunk that one,' continued Jesse, nudging Alfie painfully in the ribs.

'If you like them greasy,' countered Alfie.

But Jesse wouldn't let it lie. 'Mate of Stella's, is he?' she asked him, obviously unaware herself of Raul's credentials.

'He's my ex-wife's husband!' replied Alfie, bored of the conversation.

'Strewth!' exclaimed Jesse, her mouth dropping open a second time. A minor victory, thought Alfie, feeling rather smug.

Troy came over, a glazed star-struck expression on his face. 'I found him at your place, Alfie and brought him over,' he explained eagerly. 'Hope you don't mind?'

'And what were you doing at The Rocks?'

'Stella asked me to fetch her jacket. I think she was getting cold. I found him there on the doorstep.' He smiled, leant toward Alfie and in a conspiratorial whisper said, 'It's *the* Raul Mendoza.'

'Not a lot gets past you, does it?' he mumbled irritably, his eyes firmly fixed on Raul. 'Do me a favour, will you Troy? Find Stella for me.'

'No worries,' said Troy chirpily.

God I hate that expression, thought Alfie.

'She's over there,' said Troy, grabbing Alfie by the arm.

'Where?'

'Behind Raul. Bloody hell, he just pinched her bottom!'

'I'll kill him,' muttered Alfie under his breath as he walked toward his old adversary, the arch-seducer. Raul, unaware that he was being watched, grabbed Stella's face in both his hands and smothered her cheeks in kisses, his eyes filled with blatant Latin lust. 'I'll kill him. One day I swear I will.'

Saturday 12 May

I have heard it said that when the angels cry in heaven it rains down here on earth. It's a quaint and evocative image, child-like in its fairy-tale simplicity yet bordering on the insane. Or so I used to think because it rained the day she left me and she cried.

I was glad to have known her. Am honoured to have called her my friend. That I loved her takes my breath away. That she once loved me, a miracle. And she was the only one for me, my wife, my love, my life – irreplaceable, irretrievable. A long lost treasure, a fading picture, a confusion of thoughts and feelings that I have committed to my memory. And I promised that I would love and honour her always. I loved her when she left me, I shall always love her.

It's strange to think that I have walked the path of evil. By all accounts I was the sweetest child born to kind and loving parents. The streets down which I roamed were paved with gold, the world eager to receive me in its open arms. And I was hungry, took everything that was offered to me, devoured it voraciously. And how I lorded it up there high above the teeming throng. But now I wish I hadn't climbed so high a pedestal. It was such a long, long height from which to fall.

And as I lay beneath the rubble of my life I formed a plan. A simple case of retribution. I would lure him into the water and lose him. I excelled in the water. Triton, well that was my middle name. I dived deep and he followed as I swam hard into a current. I waved bye-bye as it swept him away. The plan was working. I surfaced, got into my boat, turned on the engine and motored off at full throttle. If he didn't drown then the sharks would get him.

I had been shark bait once myself. I had been fed to them, a failure, to do with as they pleased. As I bled, so at first they nibbled, their teeth like pin pricks on my skin that turned to agony as they sunk their jaws deep into my flesh to gorge themselves. And when their hunger was satiated they spat out my remains, broken, humiliated.

In fact the sharks did get him. It must have been a tiger shark, maybe two or three. His badly mutilated body was found washed up on Palm Beach three days later. And his severed head, with one eye missing, was netted by a fisherman the same day.

Now at last, my enemy was dead. Dead as the coral that was washed up on the beaches of the Great Barrier Reef. Dead as my career had been when I lost my first wife. Dead as the parents who had nurtured me in Africa, who had given me a magical childhood by the sea. What child could ask for more? A perfect life turned sour.

Still, at least I now had her all to myself.

Eight

'Do you believe in God?' Phoebe asked him.

What, you mean the Christian God?' Alfie replied, stroking her long raven-coloured hair, gripping her hand tightly as he lay beside his daughter, propped up on pillows in the small, bright hospital room, his camera that she'd brought him on the cabinet beside his bed. She'd stopped crying now, had calmed down, although her eyes were still red, her cheeks stained and blotchy. That she had reacted angrily had not surprised him although it had hurt him to watch her banging her fists on the walls, the bed, tearing at her hair. And all the time she kept on repeating the question, 'Why?'

Her voice, rising to a scream, had attracted the attention of the nurse. 'I should give her a valium to calm her down,' she suggested to Alfie when her attempts to mollify Phoebe with kind words had failed.

'There's no need,' Alfie told her. 'She'll settle down in a moment or two.'

Having vented her rage and realising that her father was too weak for the type of ordeal she had presented him, Phoebe had climbed onto the bed and sunk into his outstretched arms, unaware that he was broken-hearted, torn-apart by his daughter's pain.

'Any god,' she answered with a loud sniff.

'Why? Do you think I'll need one?' he answered jokingly.

'I doubt it,' she countered, 'But I will.'

'Phoebe, darling, darling Phoebe!' He held her close, desperate to find the words to take away her pain.

'You still haven't answered my question,' she continued, ignoring him. Alfie sighed.

'Who was it who said *one man's theology is another man's belly laugh*?'

'Dad!'

'Sorry Phoebe! Well, yes, as a matter of fact I do, though not the Christian God with all his rules and regulations.'

'A First Cause, then,' she whispered.

'Uncaused,' he added, laughing. 'Can I get away with that?'

'Of course you can, dopey,' said Phoebe with a smile. 'You've just described the Cosmological Argument.

'Have I?' said Alfie, giving Phoebe a big hug as he buried his head in her hair. 'Clever me!'

'I'm going to miss you so, so, *so* much,' Phoebe said hugging him back, crying a little again.

'Larry will take care of you. You know how much he adores you. And Kate, Mum, she'll be here.'

'And that's supposed to make me feel better,' said Phoebe with a sneer.

'Yes, Phoebe, it is. She loves you very much. You know that.'

'She's vain, weak, mean and totally self-centred.'

'She's had a tough life,' said Alfie gently. He'd made his peace with Kate years back. It had not been easy for her. When Raul had disappeared she had felt bitter and deserted. And if that wasn't trial enough her nine-year-old daughter was begging her daily to leave her maternal home to go and live with her Dad. She had finally relented, Phoebe had moved out and Kate had reached for the bottle. Even now he still felt guilty about it. 'She never got over Raul upping and leaving her like that,' he added softly.

'And that explains her third marriage I suppose,' said Phoebe scornfully. 'Running off with a wannabe pop star ten years her junior. What was she thinking of?'

'But she's going steady now. She seems happier with Charles.'

'Well he's a vain old actor like herself. They're perfectly suited.'

'Phoebe, that's unfair. You misjudge your mother. She's not that bad.'

'Just a bad mother you mean! She drinks all the time, cries, lies around. Ugh! She drives me mad!'

'But she does love you Phoebe.'

'Like you might a diamond ring, you mean? She loves and cares about herself a whole lot more!' She'd stopped crying again, revived by anger – her usual reaction to any mention of her mother.

It's such a shame, thought Alfie, because Kate has got a lot of love to give if only Phoebe would let her. Perhaps my death will provide the catalyst . . . But he let the thought trail off. He had not adjusted to that idea himself yet.

'There are rumours going around that Stella is in England,' said Phoebe suddenly.

'Really?' asked Alfie, coughing a little in surprise.

'Larry thinks it's all nonsense.'

'Well he would.'

'I only hope he's right,' said Phoebe. Alfie winced. 'Yeah. The press are having a field day. They're bringing up all sorts of aspects of your life including the suicide of your old friend Abe. Why did you never tell me about that Daddy? It must have been awful.'

Oh my God, thought Alfie and closed his eyes. Not that again. Although by now, he should have learned never to be surprised by the machinations of the press. However many years passed, his public persona would forever be scarred by the less savoury events of his life. No matter that he'd moved on, made good, led a quiet, hard-working life, he would always be reminded of his mistakes. And now Phoebe had been dragged through the mire. What was it about fame that gave the press the right to open old wounds as and when they liked?

'I didn't tell you because I couldn't see the point in raking up the past. It was terribly sad. I wish it hadn't happened and yes I blamed myself.' He stopped as a razor-like sting of pain overcame him causing him to gasp for breath.

Frightened, Phoebe sat up. 'Daddy? Are you OK? Should I call the nurse?'

Alfie's eyes were squeezed shut, his mouth stretched into a grimace. He shook his head as the pain peaked violently before it slackened its grip on his now taut body and began to slowly fade. He smiled weakly and opened his eyes.

'It's a funny thing Phoebs, I've been feeling pretty awful,' Alfie began, his voice faint and husky. He paused to clear his throat. 'But now that you're here I have begun to feel a whole lot better.'

'Daddy, don't. I'm all grown up now. You don't need to protect me anymore,' she said, flicking away another tear.

'I don't know what you mean.'

*

Larry stared through a window at the top of the hospital that looked out onto the street below. The handful of journalists had swelled to a small crowd. From this height they looked like a band of busy ants in search of food, scuttling in frenzied circles around one another as they attempted to garner information. But he was in a safe house here in the hospital, no journalists allowed and no mobile phones. There was a certain sanctity about his situation. He had always been so readily available. In switching off his mobile he had severed himself from reality.

Sometimes I have to ask myself why on earth I do this job, he thought ruefully, when what I seem to do is feed the beast. Why is this character, this so-called journalist, this Thomas Slater so convinced that Alfie is a murderer? It's like he's obsessed with Alfie. What is the connection between them? This morbid interest, this obsession with an imagined dark side goes way beyond the normal enquiring mind of your average journo. Hopefully someone at *The Evening News* will put a stop to all this soon. I have no doubt that when Alfie hears about this he'll take the paper straight to court. What the man is doing is slanderous and prejudicial. He should be slung into a secure unit ... And yet I have to admit having met the man I would be hard pushed to proclaim him mad. In fact he seems frighteningly sane which makes his actions all the more reprehensible. Now he claims that Stella has been sighted a second time. In Soho of all places. Well, I'm sure if she'd been in Soho she'd have come and seen me. Certain of it. And Audrey swears there's been so sign of her. That's how ludicrous that assertion is!

And how on earth am I going to keep all this from Phoebe, damn it? She's got enough on her plate having to cope with the news that her father's very ill, that is if this smear campaign doesn't kill him overnight. I really cannot understand how Slater can get away with printing such a pack of lies unless ... Larry turned round and leant wearily against the wall dropping his head into his hands. It was unthinkable but could there be some truth in Thomas's accusations? Could Alfie have killed a man? Could Alfie have killed Raul?

There really was only one thing to do. He'd find out! He could start off by asking Kate although it was unlikely she'd know where he was. But there was Raul's agent, his family, friends who might know. If all those contacts failed, he'd send someone into Northern India to find him personally.

Christl This latest witch-hunt is getting to me! I'll go and see Alfie, check Phoebe is OK and then I'll make some calls, he decided passing the hospital shop's newsstand. He glanced absently at the papers sorted into trays more or less by force of habit rather than professional interest. The headline of the latest edition of *The Evening News* leapt out at him like a mugger in a dark alley: *IS THIS A DAGGER THAT I SEE BEFORE ME?*

'Oh for heaven's sake,' he said out loud, picking up a copy. Beneath the headline Alfie's face smiled handsomely back at him. 'This is grossly unfair.'

*

'Smile please, if you can!'

'Alfie, honestly,' said Larry. The last thing he needed right now was to pose for Alfie's camera.

'What's the matter Larry?' said Alfie, snapping away anyway. 'You look like you've seen a ghost!'

Perhaps I have, thought Larry startled, still mentally mulling things over. First of all he was alarmed to find that he'd missed Phoebe who, the nurse had told him, had gone in search of a shower to freshen up a bit. Secondly he was finding it very difficult to get the image of Raul Mendoza bleeding to death in a pool of his own blood, a dagger lodged in his heart, out of his head. 'Sorry, Alfie. I'm just a bit shocked, that's all.'

'Well, as you can see, I am still alive.'

'Why must you insist on joking at a time like this, Alfie?' asked Larry, perplexed.

'Because, my dear friend, I am scared shitless, that's why.'

The frankness of this comment jerked Larry's mind into the present for a moment. He focused on his friend. 'Jesus! I'm sorry Alfie.'

'Don't be. Just promise me you'll look after Phoebe. She's distraught.'

'Of course. That goes without saying,' he said with a sigh.

'I've been a terrible burden over the years, haven't I?' Alfie replied, misinterpreting the sigh. 'Still, it'll all be over soon. I'll be dead and you can begin to live a life of normality for the first time in thirty odd years. Why Larry, with me off your hands you might even have the energy for marriage.'

'Right!' said Larry, absently yanking at his signet ring.

'OK. Spit it out.'

'Eh?'

'Come on Larry. I'm not stupid,' said Alfie as a stab of pain overtook him, causing him to cry out involuntarily.

'Alfie? Alfie! Are you OK?' asked Larry alarmed. He bent his head toward Alfie's face. 'Shall I call the nurse?' he asked him loudly.

Alfie waved his hand weakly in response, too breathless for words, then shook his head, fiddled with a switch on his pain-relieving tube and closed his eyes. Terrified but uncertain what to do next, Larry stood over his friend for a fretful five minutes, holding his hand, listening to the rapid bleeping of the heart monitor.

'Blimey, that really takes the wind out of a man's sails,' panted Alfie, prising open his eyes, smiling weakly. But Larry was too shocked by the experience to respond. 'Christ, if the pain doesn't get me, then you're sure as hell going to. You look like death warmed up!'

'I ... I ... I'm sorry Alfie. For a moment there I felt utterly helpless, seeing you in so much pain. I ...'

'There's something bothering you, Larry and I think I know what it is.'

'The ... there is? Y ... you do?' stuttered Larry, surprised at how quickly Alfie could concentrate his mind.

'Phoebe told me. It's ... ah ... ah ... Stella isn't it,' he said adjusting his position in the bed.

'Can I help?' asked Larry.

'No. That's better. It's just ... sometimes ... I get a bit uncomfortable. Stella. She's been spotted apparently.'

'Yeah. Funny, isn't it?' he asked flatly.

'Why do you say that?'

'Well. She disappeared, years ago, into thin air.'

'Ah!' replied Alfie quietly. 'So she did.'

'Well didn't she?' challenged Larry.

'Not exactly, no,' replied Alfie cautiously.

'So what happened? You've never said.'

'You've never asked? Until the other day ... at The Ivy.'

'I didn't think I should. You were so beaten up and broken, it was as though something or someone had destroyed you,' said Larry with a shudder.

'Almost. It almost destroyed me. But as you can see for yourself I am still here. For the time being anyway.'

'So will you tell me now?' continued Larry. He'd got this far. Now he needed answers.

'Why Larry? Why the sudden interest?'

'I don't know,' he said bleakly. What could he say? It wasn't like he could just come right out and ask *did you murder someone*? No. He couldn't do that. Not now. Not here. Not with Alfie strung up to all these tubes like a fly caught in a web. It wouldn't be fair ... would it? He shook his befuddled head and blinked, slowly. 'The press, I think. They're getting to me.'

'Really. Well that must be a first.'

'So are you going to tell me what actually happened?' He felt helpless, his chances fading. It was a desperate, hope-filled question.

'I can't believe you can't guess.'

'Well I imagined she left you for someone else,' he began tentatively. 'At least that is what I'd always presumed ... until now.'

'Well you'd be right. Now there's an end to it.'

'Could it be Stella?' asked Larry directly. But Alfie had had enough. He closed his eyes.

'Can we talk later? I'm exhausted.'

'Yeah. Sure. Let's do that,' said Larry disconsolately as he turned to leave, totally dissatisfied. He was none the wiser. Alfie had successfully hedged his questions. What could he conclude from that? That Thomas

Slater was right? That Alfie in a fit of pique had killed the lover his second wife Stella had left him for? Or was it far worse than that? Perhaps it was not impossible for Alfie to have killed Stella as well. Or maybe, just maybe, Alfie was too ill, too tired to be bothered with such trivialities. Have I taken leave of my senses? Stella and Raul? Alfie Macbeth a murderer? I don't think so Larry.

*

Stella and Alfie had married in their back yard under an arch of white roses. Phoebe had been a bridesmaid. She'd worn an ankle-length, ivory dress made of raw silk with an enchanting headdress of woven ivy dotted with daisies. She'd looked like a beautiful six-year-old flower fairy, recalled Larry who was sitting in the small relatives' room the kind nurse had offered him as a refuge, waiting for Phoebe.

Stella had worn a long, sleek dress of duchesse satin that had fitted her body like a glove to the knees, flaring at the back into a short fish-tail train that had floated behind her as she'd made her way to where he and Alfie stood waiting, mesmerised. She'd worn daisies in her hair under a diaphanous veil, studded with tiny white pearls and had looked more beautiful that day than he could remember, smiling radiantly with laughing eyes, happy and content.

It was the stuff of fairy-tales, this story of theirs. A wealthy, successful film director falls in love with a pretty young agent who is savvy enough to spurn his advances. Fate steps in, deals him a contemptible hand, and his life, like a pack of cards, collapses around him. He flees to Australia to nurse his wounds. Outraged by the injustice of it all, she follows hims and falls zealously and absolutely in love with him. Off they ride, astride his fabulous white steed, into the sunset, Alfie transformed from outcast to loving husband and hero. And so was born the tear-jerking opening scenes of *Killing Fame,* thought Larry with a wry smile.

The door creaked open and in walked Phoebe crying openly, supported by a nurse, carrying a newspaper. Seeing Larry, Phoebe prised herself from the nurses grip, dropped the paper and flung herself at him, pummelling his chest with her two clenched fists.

'Why didn't you tell me? Why didn't you tell me?'

'What on earth is going on Mr Woods?' asked the nurse sternly. She picked up the paper. 'The newspapers are full of dreadful stories. I am very worried about the affect this is having,' she added, motioning to Phoebe with her thumb.

Larry took a deep breath. 'Nurse Mitchell,' he said, reading the label on the nurse's uniform, 'Would you be kind enough to leave us alone for a few minutes? After which I promise that I will do my best to explain the fervour that seems to be gripping the British media by the throat.'

'That is a very welcome suggestion,' she said, retreating hastily.

'Who is he meant to have murdered?' demanded Phoebe, still beating a painful rhythm on Larry's chest. He grabbed Phoebe firmly by both wrists.

'I'm sorry, Phoebe, but how could I tell you before you'd seen your father. I couldn't. I had no choice.' Phoebe didn't appear to be listening. She was trying hard to free herself from his grip, yanking her arms this way and that. 'Ssh! Stop this, Phoebe. Calm down. We need to talk.'

'What's there to talk about? First some creep says he's seen Stella. Fine! Then same creep accuses Dad of killing a man. Next, creep is spotted outside hospital jerking off! Would someone please explain?'

'I'm as much in the dark as you are on this my darling girl,' said Larry, pulling her to his chest. This seemed to mollify her a little bit because she stopped her ranting and bawled into his shoulder.

'What has Thomas Slater got against my father?' she finally managed to ask once the fit had passed. 'Where did Stella go when she left my father? And why now, dying in hospital, does Dad want me to bring him the painting of Stella that has been hanging in his room inexplicably for the past fifteen years?'

'He wants the painting?' Larry asked bemused.

'Yes, he does,' said Phoebe desperately. 'He still loves her Larry, after all she's put him through. She broke his heart, left a hole in his being, a deep, bottomless hole and it hurt him Larry, almost destroyed him. Well I hate her. I hate her. And I blame her Larry. I blame her for this, this cancer, this terrible silent disease that is eating away at his body. It found a way into that hole, don't you see? Stella is responsible. If it hadn't been for her he'd still be fit and well.'

'Phoebe, darling Phoebe, that's not entirely true. Your Dad and Stella had almost three years of very real happiness together,' he said, lifting up her face to his.

'If she dares so much as show her face in here I will throttle her,' said Phoebe through gritted teeth.

Not before I have a chance to ask her what the hell went on back then, thought Larry grimly.

'Oh, Larry, I can't believe he's going to die. I can't believe he's going to leave me,' cried Phoebe and, forgetting her other troubles, she collapsed into Larry's outstretched arms.

Nine

The night Raul Mendoza had appeared on his doorstep had set Troy's imagination racing. For the next few weeks he'd fed the fantasy that visiting film stars would become a regular occurrence in Millaa Millaa. Two years later when not one celebrity had graced the Tablelands with their presence, Troy was finally coming to terms with the frustration he felt at Alfie's continued determination to distance himself from Hollywood. It was not unreasonable, he thought, to assume that Alfie had famous friends. After all he had been one of the world's greatest directors, a legend in his own lifetime. OK, so he'd upped sticks to a fairly quaint and remote part of the globe but that shouldn't deter these people, these *stars* who owned private jets and shot films all over the world, from dropping by.

The most likely visitor he now realised, having scaled down his expectations, would be Katherine Katz. It was not irrational to assume that she might choose to see where her daughter Phoebe spent a month's holiday each year. She'd stop to chat with Alfie over a glass of wine, he'd drop by and before long the pair of them would be reminiscing to Troy about life in the spotlight.

Just thinking of Katherine Katz caused an incredible ache in Troy's loins. He could not begin to imagine what it would be like to meet her although he *could* imagine her flesh. Katherine Katz's flesh! He could picture it now, his little fella nuzzling up to her creamy white buttocks. Now that was an inspiration for a sex-starved twenty-year-old.

Raul, in Troy's opinion, was a very lucky man. He really could not believe the garbage he'd read in *The Australian* about their marriage being under strain just because Raul hadn't made any decent films recently. The newspaper had printed a picture of Raul rolling around in the gutter. Poor bloke was obviously just having a couple of drinks with a mate when some arsehole with a camera had crept up on him, thought Troy angrily.

He'd sat and thought about the story for a while until he'd reached the conclusion that if they really did have problems then Katherine was more likely than ever to pay Alfie a visit in Millaa Millaa. She'd need a strong, sturdy shoulder to cry on and Alfie, seeing as how he was totally infatuated with Stella, would call on him to step in and provide that very shoulder. She'd be touched by his sympathy, grateful for his boyish affection and as a reward she'd take him to bed and teach him everything he'd ever need to know.

His creativity had ended there and reality had kicked in. There were no film stars and there was no Katherine. Alfie was utterly immersed in his screenplay and when he wasn't writing he was totally absorbed with Stella.

When, six months ago, Alfie and Stella had returned from a day's sailing, sunburnt, exhilarated and engaged, Troy had been in raptures. Wedding meant party and Alfie Macbeth's wedding meant big over-the-top party with loads of famous guests. Even the words *close friends* and *family* had not dampened Troy's excitement for the forthcoming ceremony. Alfie was bound to have heaps of close celebrity friends, none of whom he could bear to omit from his invitation list.

The disappointment Troy had felt on discovering that the only close friend on the invitation list was a guy named Larry Woods, had been profound. He had been as unimpressed by his profession as his name and had referred to him as *that daggy shirt-lifter* to his cousin when he'd returned to university. He'd half made up his mind not to bother showing up for the wedding but his mother, who had been most excited about the whole pathetic affair, had insisted. It had been typical of her and it had seemed to Troy that the only reason she had been put on this planet was to embarrass him at every opportunity. He'd moaned to his cousin that his family were running amok but instead of sympathising with him as Troy had hoped he would, his cousin had begged him for an invitation.

*

Writing in an environment of total equanimity had had a remarkable effect on Alfie. *Killing Fame* was complete and Alfie, placing down his pen triumphantly that Friday afternoon in September, was confident that he had another potential commercial success on his hands. It helped that he had chosen as a bride an optimist whose cup was always half full no matter what obstacles were placed in her path. Living side by side with Stella, sharing her every waking moment, it was obvious she was a person who was inexhaustibly happy, could find the positive in any given situation. When he told her how much he admired her outlook to

218

life, she would laugh and tell him that she was born lucky, that nothing bad ever befell her, unless you counted her mother leaving her when she was a child. And really that hadn't been such a bad thing, she would reason, because she'd been a pretty awful mother and Stella had been inexorably better off without her.

She was lovely, she was tender, she was beautiful, but it was her enthusiastic appreciation of her own good fortune that appealed to him the most. For years he'd been accused of being lucky, that fame had simply landed in his path, that he'd led a charmed and easy life and for a while he'd believed that was true. Stella had changed all that. To watch her live her life with such unparalleled eagerness and with no regrets, Alfie had come to realise that luck was something that a person forged. There was no earthly reason why Stella should rejoice in prosperity. Her path had, to date, been tough. But Stella was equipped with the determination, daring and courage a person needed to succeed in life. Success and happiness was about making the right choices and Stella, the lucky optimist, had done just that. It was a talent, it was awe-inspiring and it was infectious. His script was finished, now all he had to do was sell it.

'Oh Alfie, I'm very, very pleased for you,' said Stella, shrieking and pirouetting with delight. After a short search around the house he'd found her on the wooden decking at the front putting out some food for a wallaby who'd taken to visiting.

'Thank you my darling, but I could never had done it without you,' replied Alfie brimful of happiness.

'That's nonsense. And you know it,' laughed Stella, still twirling.

'It's true Stella. You inspire me,' said Alfie, grabbing hold of her and pulling her toward him. She flung her arms around his neck and kissed him.

'If thinking that makes you happy, then fine,' said Stella, prising her lips away from his and playfully punching him in the ribs.

'It does Stella, my angel, it does.'

'Me, an angel?'

'Yes. Yes. Of course an angel.'

'If I'm an angel, where are my wings?' retorted Stella. 'And besides, as any self-respecting adult knows, angels happen to be male!'

'Ah apart from one. You. My angel.'

'Excuse me while I throw up,' said Stella pulling a face. 'My God, you are full of shit today, Alfie!'

'Stella! Stella! Out of the mouths of angels even such words as shit sound heavenly.'

'You're starting to annoy me, Alfie!'

'Am I darling? I'm sorry. Let me make it up to you then,' he said grabbing her by the wrist, spinning her round in a dance as, with his other hand, he dragged her into the hallway.

'Hmm!' said Stella, pursing her lips.

Alfie laughed. 'Come upstairs and let me show you how much I ...'

'Hi! Anyone at home?'

'Oh no, it's Jack!' said Stella, unable to disguise her disappointment.

'Ssh! If we're quiet he might go away and then ...'

'Hey you guys,' said Jack. He had wandered into the hall but was standing in the sunlight that streamed into the house so that all Alfie could see was the silhouette of a well-proportioned figure standing in the doorway.

'Jack!' said Alfie a little too quickly. 'We didn't hear you.' Stella giggled and wriggled free.

'Er ... I'm not disturbing anything am I?' asked Jack, squinting in embarrassment.

'Not at all,' said Stella who'd managed to pull a straight face.

'Fancy a beer?' Alfie asked him, putting his arm around Jack's solid shoulders, desperately trying to put him at ease.

'Only if you're having one,' replied Jack, his sun-bronzed face breaking out into a grin.

'I was just on my way to the kitchen to get him one,' interjected Stella breezily. 'He's just finished his screenplay. Isn't that great?'

'Congratulations, mate,' said Jack, slapping Alfie on the back. 'You must be stoked.'

'I'm pretty pleased, I must confess. When I made the decision to write I hadn't appreciated quite how hard it was going to be. But I'm lucky. Stella has been incredibly supportive and, well, confident in my ability I suppose and that spurred me on. Although I shouldn't be celebrating at all, of course.'

'How do you figure that?'

'Well it's one thing writing the damn thing. It's going to be quite another selling it,' he said, exhaling loudly as the memory of his encounter with Michael Fenning when he was trying to sell *Nausea* to Panama Pictures sprung to mind. The road before me is a long and most definitely rocky one, he thought as he sank into one of the red cedar wood seats, gesticulating to Jack to do the same.

'But you've got to give it a go,' said Jack.

'Have I?' answered Alfie. He wasn't sure if he was ready for another public bashing and was thinking that perhaps it would be better just to sit back and enjoy the spoils of his former existence with his beautiful, sensible and practical second wife.

220

'Beer boys,' said Stella. 'And olives from Corfu, via the wonderful Tobin's, naturally. They are delicious.' Jack took one and smiled mawkishly. 'Why the long face, Alfie?' asked Stella who'd expected Alfie to throw in a quip about the Cephellonian olive being the best he'd ever tasted, but he was silent, staring into the middle distance.

'He's just realised he's got a hit on his hands and that he's duty bound to make it happen,' said Jack, winking at Stella.

Alfie grunted and looked at Stella who was trying her hardest to respond to Jack's wink with a smile. However hard he tries poor Jack gets nowhere with Stella, thought Alfie, pleased to be distracted from his dilemma. She's never told me that she doesn't like him. She's always polite and courteous in his company. Smiles, mainly, when he's being amusing and that's what gives it away, her reaction to him and the absence of words. It's not Stella. She just isn't like that. She says what she thinks. Politeness doesn't come into it. All those times she used to cut me to shreds with her barbed asides, it was because she liked me, felt I was worth the effort. I wonder if Jack has cottoned on?

Since his triumphant return, Jack Buchanan had taken up permanent residence in his family home. It seemed that the life of an artist was not to be his future. His intention, he'd told his delighted mother, was to assist his father farming sugar cane. The news that Stumpy had a successor had flung Jesse into such a wild state of total, uninhibited and shameless abandon that Alfie had avoided her for weeks.

Alfie, too, was pleased. He liked Jack, enjoyed his laid-back steady approach. Jack was a man totally at ease in his own company, full of energy and effusiveness for life. Life in the country suited him. He'd ride around the acreage on his Palomino with its striking white mane and tail, his gun slung over his shoulder. He was an expert marksman and had conveyed his skills to Alfie.

'The secret is to lean into the gun, get your weight on the front foot, as you squeeze the trigger,' he'd told Alfie, as he'd stared down the barrel, his eyes focused on the tin can that acted as a target for Alfie's shooting practice.

'And now I'd like you to teach me to shoot a camera,' Jack had said the day he'd pronounced Alfie an expert with a gun.

'I don't believe Alfie is driven by duty. It's more about ambition and nerve,' replied Stella tartly.

'I guess that's what I meant,' said Jack slowly and with a wry grin. 'I'm not so good with words.'

'Well!' said Stella, smothering her irritation at his riposte with the brightest of smiles. 'There you are.'

'I'm dying to read it, Alfie,' added Jack. 'I adore thrillers. Is it gruesome or psychological or both?'

'I'd have to go with the latter.'

'What's the plot?' persisted Jack.

'I've been trying to get him to tell me that for ages,' said Stella. 'I always presumed that he was waiting to finish it. Surely you can tell me now.'

'Tell you what, I'll let you read it,' said Alfie. 'It's such a lovely sunny day, I don't want to darken it with morbid tales of murder.'

'You'll go to the States?' asked Jack, 'For backing?'

'I think so. That's where my contacts are. Fancy a trip to Los Angeles darling?'

Stella screwed up her nose. 'Ooh! I think I'd get in the way.'

'Nonsense. I'd be lost without you.'

'Cooee!'

'Troy,' said Stella smiling, leaping to her feet. 'I swear that boy can smell a beer a mile away.'

'Not so much a boy now Stella,' said Alfie, raising his eyebrows as he watched his wife dancing down the track to meet him.

'He must be back from university,' said Jack.

'Yes. It's been wonderfully quiet without him,' added Alfie. Fascinating, he thought as he watched Stella greet Troy with a kiss on both cheeks, that he should turn up at our place the moment he returns home. Ah and with a companion, I see.

'Any chance he's found himself a girlfriend?' Alfie asked Jack.

'Oh Alfie, you have no worries there,' replied Jack, laughing. 'It's you Troy worships.'

'That's what Stella always says,' groaned Alfie.

'And I think his companion though slight is actually a young man.'

'Shame!'

'Hey Alfie!' yelled Troy as he bounded onto the deck and grabbed Alfie by the hand, jumping as he shook it causing Alfie's vertebra to creak in protest. 'Stella's told me the news. It's fantastic, tops. I bet you're . . .'

'Stoked,' interrupted Alfie resignedly. 'Yes I am.'

Behind Troy his thin companion smiled eerily, revealing a set of small pointed teeth.

'This is my cousin,' explained Troy proudly. 'He's at university with me.'

'Pleased to meet you,' said Alfie offering his hand.

'He's actually far brainier than I am,' confessed Troy.

Alfie glanced at Troy's relation. He might be brainy but, poor sod, he was not blessed with good looks. He was skinny, his sallow skin dotted with acne and his slit-like eyes set too far apart.

'G'day Mr Macbeth,' he said as his eyes opened a fraction. The whites of his eyes were as yellow as his skin. 'I'm Millie's nephew, Tom Slater. Very pleased to meet you too.'

Ten

'YOU NEVER TOLD ME HE WAS A FUCKING JOURNALIST,' screamed Alfie, his voice echoing around the large hallway. Troy could feel the blood draining from his head as Alfie, whose blood appeared to be rising, took a purposeful step towards him.

'Well he isn't,' replied Troy foolishly, retreating a couple of steps until his back was touching the front wall of the house. To the right of where he stood he could hear the rain lashing at the large window-pane, and beyond that the sound of it hammering the decking outside. Inside the room was dark.

'Oh isn't he?' growled Alfie, his eyes narrowing. He took a couple of steps closer.

'No, definitely not,' stammered Troy. 'Not yet.'

'NOT YET YOU LITTLE FF . . .' bawled Alfie, his voice reverberating in Troy's ears he was that close, face to face, at boiling point, his cheeks glowing crimson. Troy pressed his body into the wall and closed his eyes but jumped and opened them again as a clap of thunder rent the sudden silence of the room. Alfie leant forward and put his mouth to Troy's left ear. 'So tell me Troy,' he whispered. 'Why have I've just had the picture editor of *The Cairns Post* on the telephone?'

'I . . . I . . . I . . . d . . . d . . . don't know,' stuttered Troy, closing his eyes again. With Alfie's incarnadine face barely a breath away from his own, it helped.

'Because they want a recent photograph of me to accompany the article submitted to them today by none other than your lovely cousin, Tom Slater.'

'How did he get your number?' asked Troy incredulously, opening his eyes in wonder.

Infuriated by Troy's naivety, Alfie drew back his fist. Troy ducked.

'HE'S A FUCKING JOURNALIST, TROY, BUT THAT'S HARDLY THE POINT HERE IS IT?' He slammed his fist into the window frame to the left of where Troy had been standing. The lightning flashed illuminating the room and the fear in Troy's eyes.

'No, Alfie. I'm certain it isn't.'

'Did you know that he intended to study journalism?' Alfie delivered the question slowly and quietly in as controlled a manner as possible.

'Well, yes. He's made no secret of his intentions,' said Troy matter-of-factly, confident that this was a situation where the truth mattered. He balked as Alfie shut his eyes and inhaled a long and painful lungful of air. The thunder cracked, distracting Alfie who wandered over to the front door and opened it as another bolt of lightning seared the darkness of the room. Relieved not to be feeling like an insect pinned in a case anymore, Troy shook the tension from his body and relaxed a little.

'And yet you, Troy Thomas with your average IQ, didn't think it might be wise to tell me this?' continued Alfie, spinning round to fix him with another more ferocious glare.

'I . . .'

'Or Stella. Jack even. ANYONE!' said Alfie, his voice reaching a crescendo as the thunder rolled.

'I didn't think it was important.'

'You didn't think it important. HE-LLO! Is there anyone there?' Alfie strode towards Troy and lifted up his hair to stare into his right ear. 'Anyone with the tiniest bit of common sense who knew what had happened to me would have at best warned me, at worst steered the conversation well off my screenplay. You see, Troy . . . it's unbelievably simple. I do not wish to be cannon fodder for the press again. Do you understand? Or are you, as they so delicately put it here in Australia, *not the full quid*?'

'I've been a total dill, Alfie. I'm sorry, I really am. The last thing I want to do is bring you trouble.'

'Yeah, right,' said Alfie, calming down at last.

Shame-faced and humiliated Troy turned to look out of the window, away from the intensity of Alfie's scrutiny. The rain was pummelling the dry earth like a plough. 'Will you sue?' Troy asked him queasily.

'What? No,' said Alfie quietly, almost light-heartedly, thought Troy. He turned round. Alfie, who had backed away, threw him a half-smile. 'There's no need.'

'Oh?'

'I demanded to speak to the editor, naturally and suggested he pull the article, which he agreed to do without debate. You see, Troy, it's only a local rag. It really couldn't afford to be sued.'

'Oh that's great news, Alfie,' said Troy tentatively although it did appear that his ordeal was over.

'Don't tell me, you're stoked,' Alfie replied, smiling effortlessly now.

'I'll never let you down like that again, Alfie.'

'I'm sure you won't,' said Alfie, laughing now and ruffling Troy's hair. For once Troy didn't mind.

'I mean it Alfie,' he said with startling intensity. 'I know I'm not the brightest card in the pack but I promise you, I will never ever embarrass you again.'

Alfie opened his mouth to speak but what he intended to say Troy would never know because he was halted by a sonorous rapping on the front door that caused the pair of them to jump involuntarily.

'That's either the big, bad wolf,' said Alfie, composing himself, 'or Jesse.' Troy laughed, a relief for Alfie. 'Before I open it Troy, do you want to hang around 'til she's gone and have a beer?'

'Thanks Alfie, but I'll be getting back if you don't mind,' he mumbled.

'Another time then?' said Alfie, now regretting his outburst.

'Yeah. Later,' replied Troy.

Alfie opened the door and Jesse who looked as though she were entirely covered in tarpaulin, bustled in. Troy inched past her.

'See you Troy,' said Alfie winking at him. Troy, managing a bleak smile, raised his hand in a limp farewell salute then, head-bowed in the rain, disappeared into the storm.

Bugger, thought Alfie as he watched him go, I have really upset him. If only I could learn to control that temper of mine. And now I've got Jesse to contend with when what I'm really concerned about right now is Stella. Why on earth did she choose to go walking on a day like this? I only hope she's found some shelter, he thought as he turned his attention to Jesse. Christ, what is she wearing, he wondered in alarm. It looks like the local marquee.

'G'day Alfie, me old mate,' she said, dragging him to her voluminous breasts.

'This is an interesting fashion statement,' said Alfie, wresting himself free.

'Why thank you Alfie,' she said proudly. 'I made it myself as it happens, out of an old tent belonging to my boys. I'm glad you like it.'

Oh here we go, thought Alfie resignedly. 'So what can I do you for?'

'Happens I was doing a bit of sewing, Alfie. And I don't want to big-note myself but I've made a load of cloths for the table and I thought to myself, I know who'd appreciate one of these.'

'Er . . .'

'Not you, mate, Stella' she said, digging him playfully in the ribs.

Where is she?' She paused to scan the room just in case Stella was lurking in the shadows. 'Is she crook?'

'She's gone for a walk'

'Shocking weather for walking.'

'That's what I told her,' said Alfie, realising that perhaps this was the first time he'd agreed with Jesse on anything and felt a sudden warmth towards his outsized neighbour who stood in his hallway, rain dripping from her canopied form. 'Mind you, Jesse, if you don't mind me saying, it looks like *you* walked here.'

'Bit of rain never hurt a tough sheila like me,' she said, throwing back her head to laugh. 'Oh Alfie,' she said wiping her eyes, 'I still can't get over an old bloke like you being hitched to a child-woman young enough to be your daughter.'

Fortunately, at that moment, Stella burst through the door, water trickling rapidly down the brown, waxed Drizabone that she wore, the rim of her Akubra hat brim full of rain.

'Still raining then,' said Jesse with a loud guffaw.

'I should say,' said Stella grinning. 'Now don't look at me like that, Alfie. I know you were right.'

'Hmm!' replied Alfie frowning. 'I shouldn't think either of you encountered any other pedestrian traffic on your journeys.'

'He he. Not me,' said Jesse, slapping him heavily on the back. He lurched forward a couple of steps before regaining his balance.

'Actually I did see someone,' said Stella. 'Though I don't think I was meant to. He was hiding in the bushes and I swear he was trying to photograph me.'

'Bloody paparazzi,' groaned Alfie. 'They've finally found me.'

'No, Alfie, I don't think it was. I'm sure I recognised the photographer.'

'Really?'

'Yes. I got a good look at him when the lightning flashed. I think it was Millie's nephew, that Tom whatever his name is.'

'Slater,' muttered Alfie under his breath.

'Oh, that shonky mongrel's back is he?' asked Jesse with a shake of her head. 'Will Millie never learn?'

'Oh?' said Alfie, intrigued.

'He's a no-hoper that one. Ever since he was an ankle biter he's been causing trouble for those Thomases. No mother, y'see,' explained Jesse.

Stella and Alfie exchanged looks. 'So, he's bad news?' Alfie asked her.

'Reckon. Nasty little sneak that one.'

'Troy seems to like him.'

'Can't for the life of me understand why. Made Troy's life a misery as a nipper, always bullying him, telling tales on him. Guess he's frightened of him.'

'Poor Troy,' said Stella.

'I think it's time I had a word with Millie about her nephew. Or better still with Tom himself,' said Alfie, drawing his body up to its full height.

'Oh he won't like that,' snorted Jesse. 'He won't like that at all. Hates criticism that one, reacts very badly indeed to criticism.'

*

Alfie was not in the mood for getting wet. He'd dashed from the porch to his Toyota Landcruiser like a 100 metre sprinter to the tape. His intentions, unlike the visibility on the rough roads that led to the Thomases, were transparently clear. Tom Slater had severely tested his patience and it was high time the snivelling little sewer rat knew it.

He could hear the mud splashing against the battered paintwork of the four-wheel drive as he drove at a furious pace down the pot-holed track to his neighbour's farm. He flung open the door, slamming it behind him as he strode with intense purpose toward the house. He had no idea what he was going to say, had no speech prepared, he only knew that until he had vented his spleen on Tom Slater he would not rest easy.

It was Millie who answered his knocking. Noticing he was upset she said little as she led him to her kitchen to the left of the house. A sumptuous smell of roasting lamb greeted him as he entered the room that was, as usual, cluttered with piles of kitchen crockery, pots of utensils, bundles of herbs hanging from the ceiling, baskets of vegetables on the floor, piles of paper on the formica surfaces, dishes drying on the draining board.

'Terrible weather, isn't it?' she asked him shyly. 'Can I get you some coffee? Beer?'

'No thanks, Millie. I'm not stopping. I just wondered if I could have a word with your nephew.'

'Is there something wrong?' she asked nervously. Alfie grunted. 'Has Tom been bothering you?'

'I should say!'

'Oh dear,' said Millie. 'I'm very sorry Alfie. Of course, I'll get him straight away.' And she left, her skirts rustling as she bustled out of the room.

Alfie stared at the chaotic scene glumly. This room that he usually found homely and comforting today felt restrictive and unwholesome.

'Alfie!' sneered Tom as he slithered into the kitchen, catching him off guard. 'Good of you to pay me a visit.' He had about him an air of casual self-assurance and spoke in a voice laden with cynicism and superiority that enraged Alfie.

'You've got a bloody nerve,' he began, repulsed by Tom's proximity.

'How so?' replied Tom, his thin lips stretched into a grotesque imitation of a smile.

'I think you know what I'm talking about,' growled Alfie, desperately trying to smother the anger rising deep within him, determined to stay in control. Tom snarled and turned his pupils skywards, giving Alfie the impression that he was scanning his brain.

'No. I'm sorry. I have no idea,' he replied, his pupils returning to their natural place in his face, his mouth still set in a grin. Alfie felt threatened. Why wasn't this kid frightened? How dare he not admit his crimes?

'Now look here you low-life,' he said angrily, taking a couple of steps towards Tom, jabbing him in the chest with his index finger as though it were a knife. 'People like you are scum, do you hear me? Eh? Eh?'

Tom laughed and shook his head. 'Really? And I suppose adulterous cheats like your good self are top of the tree.'

'OK, OK, seeing as you don't understand YOU BASEBORN, PLUG-UGLY GUTTERSNIPE,' he yelled, boiling with indignation as his temper spilled over, stabbing Tom in the chest with his finger again. A flicker of fear crossed Tom's face but he stood his ground as Alfie continued, his voice at full volume, the vein at his temple throbbing. 'I'll spell it out for you ... You bodged together an exclusive interview I apparently gave you and sold it to the local rag in a revolting and tawdry attempt at journalism ... tabloid journalism. Presumably the next part of your vulgar plan was to hawk this story elsewhere which is why you have been spotted skulking round our house, hiding in the bushes, hoping for a snapshot of me.'

'It's a free country, Alfie, this land of mine.'

'But it's not lawless. Trust me on that!'

'There is no law against free speech.'

'But there are laws against trespass. So let me tell you Tom Slater, should this article appear in any paper in the world I will have you done for trespassing, threatening behaviour, dangerous driving, sexual harassment and anything else I choose.'

'Yeah right. I'm terrified, Alfie, I really am. Let's be serious for a minute, Alfie. You're running scared. You've fled your home. Who's going to listen to a sad old fugitive like you? The press destroyed you Alfie, I hardly think they'll listen to you now.'

'Be under no illusions, Tom Slater,' said Alfie menacingly. 'I have had your article pulled. The editor, Matt Marsh I believe his name was, was overtly apologetic. And I am telling you, if you mess with me not only will you never become the journalist you aspire to be, you will face public humiliation on a scale that will amount to life-long ruination.'

'Are you threatening me?'

'Yes arsewipe, I am.'

Eleven

It was hot, about 34 degrees, a perfect day for a trip to the coast. It would have been tragic to spend the morning ensconced in the house, talking long-distance, had it not been for the outcome. It was a long shot but Alfie's aim had been to try and get in contact with David Palmer, his mentor of old who had recently been appointed head of Panama Pictures. He hadn't even expected to get as far as Palmer's PA and had almost fallen off the kitchen chair when he was put through to the great man himself. It seemed that Palmer had been eager to speak to him too, excusing himself from a lunchtime meeting to take the call on his mobile outside the restaurant.

He launched your career, Alfie reminded himself as he talked the fascinated producer through the synopsis of his screenplay. He would be interested.

'How soon can you get here?'

'As soon as I can get a flight!'

He dialled Qantas and booked a first class ticket for the next day. Feeling elated, he was on his way to find Stella to tell her the good news when the phone rang again.

'Hola, Alfie! How's it going, sport?'

'Raul?!' replied Alfie, staring into the receiver in total disbelief.

'Yes. How d'ya guess? No. Don' tell me. Issa charming Spanish accent.'

'What do you want, Raul?' Alfie asked through gritted teeth.

'I'm in Austr . . . Aus . . . Oz, filming.'

'Really! Is Phoebe with you?' he added hopefully, remembering the last time Raul had called.

'No! No! Phleebe's at home wizza gorgeous Katie. The worl juss carn get enough of Katie, eh?'

Great! He's drunk.

'Iss pretty fuckin' lonely near this red rock. I tho' I'd take a break, maybe zrop by and see you and the totally gorgeous Stella.'

231

'You are joking?' said Alfie, who was struggling to see the funny side.

'Iss zis film. Iss fuckin' crap, Alfie, thass what it is.'

'My heart bleeds for you Raul, it really does. Now piss off.'

'I'll zrop . . . oops . . . I'll zrop by very soon.'

'No you fucking won't,' he said slamming down the phone. Has Raul gone mad? Has he forgotten why I'm in Australia in the first place? he wondered incredulously.

Just over three years had passed since Alfie had been unceremoniously stripped of the last vestiges of his dignity. In many ways his life had taken a turn for the better. He was blissfully happy with Stella and tomorrow he was set to re-launch his career but still he felt he would be pushed to describe his life as complete. Raul's phone call served only to highlight that fact. He felt rattled. This was the man responsible for his public execution by media. He hated Raul for that. Despised him. But that was not reason enough. Rather it was the swift, cold-hearted way he had taken Alfie's place as father to his daughter, a fact that lingered menacingly, like a cancerous growth, at the back of his mind and which sickened him to the core. He'd heard from Larry that Raul's career was fast disappearing down the can and that his marriage to Kate was under intense strain, but neither of these facts provided him with adequate compensation for the loss he'd suffered at his hands. When he thought of Raul he felt homicidal.

Forget him, he told himself furiously. Don't let the greasy dago ruin your day. Go and find Stella and tell her your good news.

*

The last couple of days had been very difficult for Troy. He had been embarrassed and upset by a series of events that, to all intents and purposes, had been kick-started by him. His mother told him that he was being unduly harsh on himself. Introducing his cousin to Alfie had been very neighbourly of him. No more no less. It was ludicrous that he should take responsibility for a situation that somehow had gone badly awry. It was a clash of characters that nobody could have forecast, she told him. He must stop worrying and leave it to Tom and Alfie to sort out. Judging by the heated conversation in their kitchen the other night that they could not help but overhear, Alfie had done just that.

Troy, however, knew better. He knew Alfie's history. He had known of his cousin's desire to become a journalist. And he had acted naively. Why? Because he wanted to impress the cousin whom he had looked up to all his life and an introduction to a friend who just happened to be a famous film director was as about as impressive as you could get.

Now everything had changed, he thought miserably as he lay on his bed that hot, sunny morning, his curtains drawn. He'd fallen out with Tom, told him he never wanted to speak to him again. It had been no idle threat. He had meant every word, however difficult it was going to be to actually carry it out. And he had fallen out with Alfie. He was sure of that because however much Alfie had tried to make light of his outburst the fact remained, he had been heart-stoppingly angry. And he had had every right to be because some stupid little undergraduate had let him down. Nothing would ever be the same again. Any modicum of respect he had garnered over the last couple of years was gone to waste. Alfie would forever treat him like the loser he was. And that was the very worst thing about this whole sorry business. Why had Tom betrayed his trust like this? He knew that Alfie was a friend. Is this how Tom intended to make his name? When Tom had first mentioned that he wanted to be a journalist, he'd assumed he'd want to be a news reporter or better still a war correspondent.

'This sneaking around writing stories, spilling secrets, this is the work of the paparazzi, Tom,' he'd told him before he'd severed all ties.

'So named by Fellini,' Tom had replied.

'Eh?'

'That's what he named the photographers in *La Dolce Vita*. Paparazzi. Zooming around Rome on their Vespas, snapping stars without any regard to their privacy whatsoever. It's Italian for buzzing insects.'

And Tom had grinned as he said it as though he were proud to be placed in the same bracket.

Troy shivered. You think you know a man, the way he feels, the things he does, the colour of his boxers and then he goes and acts out of character and stuns you. I've known Tom longer than any other living being. He was two when I was born but I'm sure I can remember his face, pramside. I know we were different but I looked up to him. He was cleverer than me right from the start. He knew things. When he was ten years old he made a go-kart. He understood Shakespeare. Even though I was younger, he hung out with me. I remember the day he introduced me to the cinema. From that moment on I was hooked on films. It's down to him that I know so much because his knowledge, well it's encyclopaedic. He's a walking talking *Halliwell's*. I can't compete. Well none of that matters any more because he's out of my life. Now all I have to do is think of a way to make it up to Alfie.

He groaned and covered his eyes with his hands. The situation was hopeless. Stella and Alfie were probably only too pleased to see the back of him. Wait a minute, he thought suddenly, sitting up with a jolt. Stella. That's it. I'll go and talk to her.

*

Troy clambered up the wet rocks beneath the waterfall with the assured dexterity of a man who'd achieved the feat many times before. About a foot from the top he sidestepped the flowing water and heaved himself up the last rock so that he was standing just above where the waterfall cascaded into the pool below. Stella was splashing about in the water beneath him, laughing hysterically.

'You'll never do it,' she screamed, though her voice was all but drowned out by the resounding rush of the water.

'You wanna bet?' Troy asked her with confidence. This was a stunt he'd tried with great success many times. Stella was bound to be impressed and while she was praising him for his skill he'd steer the conversation onto Alfie.

'Yeah. I bet you 50 dollars you'll die.'

'Very funny!'

'Stop it, you idiot!' yelled Stella who had realised that he actually intended to jump. 'You'll kill yourself.'

'But you bet me,' retorted Troy, feigning disappointment.

'Yeah. So admit defeat.'

Troy grinned and raised his arms.

'No, don't. Troy, no,' she shrieked.

Troy laughed. 'Watch out,' he said as he leapt off the rock, hugging his legs to his chest to perform the perfect bomb, knowing that his entry would cause a thunderous splash.

'Bloody hell, Troy,' Stella said as he resurfaced, grinning broadly. You're a total maniac.'

'That'll be 50 dollars, thank you Stella.'

'Right, you've asked for it.' With both arms, she began to spray him with wave upon wave of water, blinding him so that he did not notice Alfie's arrival on the bank in front of him. Only when she ceased her tormenting and the curtain of water subsided did he notice the upright figure of his idol standing on the small sandy beach, waving at them with a look of utter bemusement on his face.

Shit, thought Troy, frowning.

'Wassa matter, scaredy cat?' taunted Stella.

'Alfie,' said Troy, jerking his head toward her husband. Stella turned round.

'Stella,' called Alfie, still waving, trying to attract her attention. 'I thought I'd find you down here.'

'How did it go?' she asked him as she waded towards him.

'Very good,' said Alfie excitedly.

Stella sprang naked from the water. 'Stella! Troy!' exclaimed Alfie alarmed, rushing over to collect her towel that was draped over a nearby rock. Further down the beach and feeling something of a gooseberry, Troy exited the water.

'Hi Alfie,' he said quietly.

'Playing silly buggers again,' mocked Alfie.

Troy blushed. 'Cooling off,' he said sheepishly.

'Right!' said Alfie, raising one eyebrow. 'Well at least you're dressed,' he added staring at Troy's baggy blue, flowery Bermuda shorts.

'Don't be mean,' said Stella, now draped in a towel. 'You're embarrassing him.'

'Nonsense,' he said, slapping Troy on the back.

He seems to be enjoying my discomfort, thought Troy, managing a faint laugh as he stood there, his bare, slim, hairless sun-tanned torso, glistening in the sun. Feeling awkward he crossed his arms and shuffled off in the direction of his towel.

'So? How did it go?'

'Brilliant. Superb,' said Alfie, in reply to Stella's question. 'I leave tomorrow.'

'That's fantastic. Oh Alfie I am so pleased for you,' Troy heard her say as he gathered up his clothes, wanting only to vanish. As he scurried off into the undergrowth feeling every inch the injured animal, he took one last glance over his shoulder to see Stella smothering Alfie in kisses. Was it his imagination or did Alfie shoot him a filthy look out of one half opened eye? You've got to lighten up Troy, he told himself sadly, depressed that his mission had failed. You're becoming paranoid.

*

'Why don't you come with me, Stella?' Alfie asked her as he set about packing. 'I could phone Qantas and have you booked on the flight in seconds. I can't bear the thought of leaving you behind.'

'I'll be all right.'

'I don't doubt that for a second. I'm not so sure I will be.'

'Don't make me laugh, Alfie. You've managed fine on your own so far!'

'What can I say to convince you?'

'Of what, exactly?'

'How much I love you.'

'I love you too, darling, but I think this is something that you would do better on your own. Besides, I hate the thought of the United States press corps hunting us down then taking pot shots at us. I'm sure my presence would be like a red rag to a bull. It was brilliant keeping our marriage out of the papers. My presence by your side would change all that.'

'The annoying thing is that you are probably right as usual.'

'In this case, I know I am. You don't want to have to go through that again and anyway, I would most certainly distract you,' she said, winking mischievously.

'Oh Stella, you have made such a difference to my life,' he said, pulling her towards him. She laughed as he hugged her, burying his head in her hair.

'You certainly know how to make a girl feel good about herself,' she joked. 'I'll have to be careful or I'll start believing you.'

'Just promise you'll be careful while I'm away.'

'I promise.'

'No daredevil stunts.'

'Like what exactly?'

'You know, high-diving, dangerous sailing, scuba . . .'

'Alfie, I'm not a child.'

'That's exactly what frightens me.' Stella hit him hard on the biceps. 'Ouch!'

'Oh I am sorry. Did I hurt you?'

Alfie said nothing, just pulled her body closer, slowly breathing in her sweet familiar smell, and kissed her. 'Raul phoned,' he said suddenly, breaking away. 'He said he was going to visit.'

'Oh! With Phoebe?'

'No. Apparently he's filming some shite-awful movie at Ayer's Rock. Said he was bored to tears and would drop by soon.'

'He wouldn't.'

'He might, so be warned. Oh and while you're being vigilant, watch out for that Troy.'

'Why? What's up with him?' asked Stella, struggling to keep up with Alfie's train of thought.

'I'm sure he's infatuated with you.'

'I've told you before, Alfie, it's your attention he craves.'

But Alfie wasn't listening. 'I realise he's far too young for your refined taste but he's a good looking guy, loaded with testosterone.'

'You used to say he reminded you of yourself at his age,' said Stella in a lightly mocking tone.

'I did . . . and that's exactly what I'm afraid of.'

'Really? And what devilish acts did you get up to? Do show me.'

'I intend to, Stella, the moment I get back from Jack's place. Fancy a trip to the Buchanan establishment?' Stella frowned. Alfie smiled and kissed her furrowed brow. 'I'd be happy knowing they were looking out for you, especially if Raul turns up. Jesse's a bit of a loony but Jack's a sensible guy.' Stella groaned. 'Go on, it would make my day.'

'That's blackmail,' said Stella, her eyes narrowing.

'Fantastic,' said Alfie, laughing. 'I just knew you'd say yes.'

They found Jack in his studio, a rickety old wooden shed at the back of the farmhouse. He was standing at his easel totally absorbed in a painting.

'A goddess,' said Alfie approvingly.

Jack jumped and turned around. 'Christ, Alfie. You nearly gave me a heart attack!' He was wearing what had once been a white T-shirt, ripped in places, and splattered with paint like a Jackson Pollock masterpiece. It was a little too small for him, the material slightly strained across his chest. 'Hello Stella,' he said politely.

'Hi Jack!' she replied, staring at the canvas.

'Sorry, mate,' said Alfie amused. 'Had I found a door I would have knocked.'

'No worries!' He flicked a few loose strands of blonde fringe out of his eyes with a paint-covered hand, leaving a streak of magenta on his cheek.

'So who is this?'

'Hebe,' said Stella, surprising everyone. 'Feeding Hercules nectar from a gourd.'

'That's right,' said Jack, impressed.

'It's very good,' said Stella quietly.

'Thank you. I had excellent models to work from. They kept very still,' he said modestly although he was grinning broadly.

'You should pose for him Stella. As an angel, maybe, with large white wings made from swans' feathers,' said Alfie. Stella glared at him. 'I'm joking. Honest.'

'Of course, I'd be delighted to paint you anyway you liked,' said Jack courteously, as he picked up a cloth and wiped the brush he was holding.

'So speaks a true gentleman,' said Alfie hurriedly. 'Anyway Jack, the reason we dropped by was to tell you my news.'

'Oh? Good news, I hope?'

'I hope too. I'm taking my film to LA.'

'That's terrific.'

'I hope so,' said Alfie who at the mention of his film felt inexplicably anxious, as though his stomach was playing leap-frog with his colon.

'Good luck, mate, although I'm sure you won't need it,' said Jack, cleaning his paint-stained hands on an equally grubby cloth. 'This calls for a celebration. Let's go and blow the froth off a few lagers.'

'Excellent idea.'

'Cooee! Alfie, Stella!' It was the loud salutation of Jack's mother.

'Hi Jesse,' said Alfie, his heart sinking. Stella, he noticed, just smiled.

'What's youse three up to? Hatching plans?'

'We were just going to have a beer, mother,' said Jack, winking at Alfie.

'Ah! Celebrating the way youse dealt with young Tom Slater,' said Jesse forming her own conclusion.

'How . . .' began Alfie, somewhat taken aback.

'I'd like to offer my congrats too, Alfie. A ripsnorter of a dressing down, so I gather. And not before time.'

'Alfie was just acting in self-defence,' explained Stella, blushing. She had been alarmed at the violence of Alfie's reaction to Tom Slater's plotting.

'Er, yes,' said Alfie, feeling uncomfortable.

'I don't care what he was doing, that dunny rat has been begging for a roasting since he was a nipper. Alfie done well, that's all I'm saying on the matter.'

Twelve

'I'm coming with you, Phoebe. The painting is far too big for you to manage on your own.'

'You don't have to, really,' Phoebe assured him. 'I'll be fine.'

'Phoebe, I won't hear of it. I simply will not allow you to be on your own,' Larry replied firmly. Instead of frowning at him as he had expected, Phoebe managed a watery weak smile that seemed to say *thank you*.

Worn out by the expenditure of so much raw emotion, Phoebe sat beside her godfather in the taxi, her head resting on his shoulder, silent and unblinking. Larry, his arm around Phoebe and feeling wearier than he had ever been, was well aware that there was nothing that could be said. Words, his words, sugar-coated, calculated, sympathetic, would be as little use to Phoebe as fairy stories right now.

It was 7pm. Darkness had descended casting the wet, grey city into blackness. With heavy heart and spirits sinking still further in the sombre gloom, Larry and Phoebe traipsed up the stone steps to Alfie's Chelsea home.

'We'll get the painting, jump in the taxi and go back to my place,' Larry told her as she fumbled with the keys.

'No. No. We'll get the painting and then I'll take it straight to the hospital. Dad needs me there.'

'Yes he does,' said Larry gently, taking the keys from Phoebe and opening the large black door. 'But you will only be of use to him after a good night's rest. You are exhausted, Phoebe. You need some sleep. Come home with me tonight and we'll go back to the hospital bright and early tomorrow morning.'

'I . . .'

'Phoebe, no argument. Trust me on this.'

'OK, OK,' she agreed wearily.

'Damn!' said Larry, skidding on something. 'Where are the lights?'

'I'll get it,' said Phoebe, flicking the switch. Four pieces of paper lay, in no particular order, on the marble floor, scattered like unwanted leaflets.

'Junk mail,' commented Larry, picking up the papers. He glanced a distinterested eye over them. 'Blimey,' he chuckled. 'It seems he left something behind. That's not like Alfie.'

'What are they?' asked Phoebe.

'A few pages of the screenplay of *Killing Fame,*' said Larry amused. 'He must have been reading it, reminiscing before his operation and dropped these.'

'But they weren't here yesterday. I stopped by to pick up his camera and it was immaculate.'

'Well the cleaner probably disturbed them.'

'But he keeps it in his desk,' continued Phoebe, flushing. 'Locked away.'

'Well maybe he'd left it in a pile on the hall table over there and you disturbed it when you shut the door,' suggested Larry unconcerned. 'Wait here while I dash upstairs and get the painting.'

'OK,' said Phoebe frowning as Larry attacked the stairs two at a time, eager to get this over with, determined that Phoebe be in bed by 9pm. He opened the door of Alfie's room and without turning on the light, lifted the picture off its hook on the wall opposite the bed.

'Larry!' screamed Phoebe so suddenly and so violently he almost dropped the painting. Carefully, he leant it against the wall of the bedroom then dashed down the stairs. His goddaughter was standing ashen-faced and open-mouthed in the middle of the sitting-room, like the character in a whodunit discovering a body.

'Somebody has been in here, Larry. And I don't mean the cleaner. Things have gone.'

'What do you mean? What things?'

'I don't know.'

'Phoebe, little one, you are not making sense,' said Larry perplexed.

'I know, I know, I'm sorry but over there on the coffee table, see, well the books have been disturbed. And on the desk in the corner, the top drawer has been forced. Look Larry, the lock. It's broken.'

'Are you sure, Phoebe?' he asked, walking warily over to the desk, half-expecting Professor Plum to leap out from behind the sofa, brandishing a candlestick.

'Absolutely certain. Dad's been burgled. Somebody has broken in. Why, Larry? Why would they do that?'

'I don't know,' replied Larry quietly sliding open the draw. He slid his fingers under the casing. The wood was splintered. The lock had been forced.

'Maybe Alfie forced it open,' he suggested calmly.

'Why?' demanded Phoebe.

'Lost his key, perhaps.'

'No!' said Phoebe flatly. 'Someone has been in here.'

This is ominous, thought Larry. If Phoebe is right and someone has forced an entry then that same someone, the burglar, seemed to know exactly what he wanted and where to find it. 'Right. We go home. We sleep on this.'

'We call the police,' insisted Phoebe.

'In any other circumstance I would agree with you but think about it Phoebe, there's a maniac in the press accusing your Dad of murder. If we report this to the police we might ignite a fire.'

'You think it's a trap?'

'No Phoebe, I don't. I'm guessing.'

'Who would do a thing like this?'

'I don't know,' said Larry solemnly, taking his terrified goddaughter by the hand. But I have a bloody good idea, he thought. Only what exactly has he taken?

*

It was 6.30am when Larry was woken by the sharp snap of his letterbox. There was no need of his brain to remind him that the newspapers had arrived. The noise of the iron spring recoiling was like a bell to Pavlov's dogs. His reflexes had become conditioned to the sound. It heralded the morning. It was time to get up. In a state of semi-consciousness he padded across his bedroom carpet to his bathroom, shedding his pyjama bottoms as he went. He turned on the shower, waited a few moments, adjusted the temperature to warm, stepped into the cubicle and stood passively under the heavy jet of water as it drenched him totally. Only then did cognisance kick in.

Papers! Alfie! Thomas Slater! Quick!

His heart pounding, he jumped out of the shower, grabbed a towel and began to rub his body vigorously. Clothes. Clean ones definitely, he thought, flinging open his wardrobe and whipping out a clean white, cotton poplin shirt, khaki chinos and dark blue linen jacket. He struggled with his socks, straining to pull them over feet that were still wet, then ran into his brown loafers, picked up his mobile phone that seemed to be permanently turned off these days and made for the stairs. He raced down them, half-running, half-falling in his haste to reach the front door and the papers.

There was *The Daily Mail.* He picked it up and flicked through the pages but found nothing. Unsure whether to be disappointed or relieved he set upon *The Guardian* but the pages were empty of stories about Alfie Macbeth.

The Evening News, screamed his brain, it'll be in that. Christ! He slapped his forehead in dismay. The first edition won't be in the shops until 10am. I've got three hours to wait.

'Hello Larry,' said Phoebe as her wan face appeared at the kitchen door. She was fully dressed, apart from her feet – hair brushed, teeth cleaned.

'Hello sweetheart,' he said, desperately trying to appear calm and collected. 'Did you sleep well?'

'Better than expected,' she replied yawning. 'I must have been exhausted.'

'Sit down and I'll make us both some coffee,' he said jumping up, pleased to have something constructive to do. He picked up the kettle, filled it with water and turned it on.

'So are we going to phone the police?' she asked him, pulling out a chair.

'No, not yet,' he said slowly. He took the cafetière out of the cupboard and filled it with the ground coffee that he kept in a tin by the kettle.

'Why, Larry? Why not?'

'Because . . .' He paused. The kettle boiled. He filled the cafetière.

'Because what?' she demanded.

Without answering, Larry fetched two mugs and some milk, which he poured into a small jug. He carried the coffee to the table, pushed the plunger down, poured them both a mug, sighed and said, 'Because I want to see *The Evening News* first.'

'Why?' asked Phoebe patiently. She took the coffee from Larry and added some milk. 'Do you think this has something to do with Thomas Slater?'

'Possibly.'

'But you told me you've never heard of him.'

'I haven't, but he *is* Australian.'

'Which means?'

'Look Phoebe, I'm guessing here but it's got something to do with the time your Dad spent in Australia.'

'You mean when Stella left him?' Larry nodded. 'Dad was broken-hearted, that's what happened.'

'I know. I know he was.'

'It was the second time it had happened to him.'

'Yeah, I know,' said Larry, his mind refocusing on Raul. He really had to find the time today to make some calls. He'd get Audrey onto it. He had to find Raul.

'You're not saying you actually believe he could have killed Stella's lover.'

'Phoebe, I'll be honest with you, I have no idea what happened. I don't know whom Stella ran away with. I didn't know the people over there. I met them at his wedding, fleetingly. And afterwards I saw no reason to get in touch with them. This thing, these accusations, were not being flung around back then.'

'Exactly, because they're all made up. Thomas Slater is insane. You have to believe in Dad's innocence, Larry. He's not a murderer.'

'I know that Phoebe.'

'Well it doesn't sound that way to me,' she said, her voice rising, her cheeks flushed red.

'I promise, once I've seen the *The Evening News* we'll go to the police. Phoebe. Trust me on this,' he said, placing his hand on hers.

'Ugh! OK. But only because . . .' but her voice trailed off.

'Come on,' said Larry. 'Let's go see your father.'

*

'It's a brilliant likeness, don't you think?' Alfie asked her.

'It's OK,' she replied noncommittally.

'He was a brilliant artist.'

'Who?'

'Jack Buchanan. Do you remember him?'

'Vaguely,' said Phoebe disinterestedly. 'Blonde, with ice blue eyes.'

'Exactly! Ha!' said Alfie thrilled.

'You seem a lot better today,' said Phoebe, smiling for the first time.

'I am. The pain has died down a bit. You're here and I have my picture. My nurse told me yesterday that Florence Nightingale believed that variety of form and brilliance of colour have a powerful effect on patients. Translated I imagine that means this splendid oil painting of mine will aid my recovery. If I stare at it long enough I will be cured,' he added mischievously.

'Well if it gets you well I'm very happy that it's here,' said Phoebe, kissing her father on the forehead.

'You've never liked it have you?' he asked her quietly.

'It's just . . . I can't understand why you want to be reminded of her, that's all. She treated you very badly, Dad. I'll never forgive her for that.'

'Not even for your father.'

'I . . . I . . .'

'It would mean an awful lot to me if you did,' he continued. Phoebe stood before him, uncertain, chewing her bottom lip. 'Is there any more news about her?'

'Stella? Er . . . no,' said Phoebe, now biting her fingernail. 'Dad?'

'Yes, Phoebe. What's troubling you?'

'Dad. I think someone broke into your house.'

'You think?'

'I know. They broke into your desk, stole your screenplay of *Killing Fame* and other things.'

'What other things?'

'Dad, I don't know. I don't know what you keep in your desk apart from the script.'

The nurse bustled in, obviously flustered.

'Good morning Nurse Mitchell. How are you today?' asked Alfie breezily, picking up his camera. 'Smile for the camera.'

' Er . . . Mr Macbeth, Miss Macbeth.'

'Alfie and Phoebe,' interrupted Alfie. 'And I'd much prefer it if you smiled. You do have such a lovely smile.'

'I'm sorry. Mr . . . .Alfie, you have a visitor.'

'But he's not supposed to have any visitors,' said Phoebe crossly.

'I know, I know and I am very sorry but she was most insistent.'

'She?' said Alfie noticing, at the mention of the visitor's gender, a look of alarm on his daughter's face.

'Yes, *she*,' answered the instantly recognisable voice as the well-heeled legs of an elegant woman strode into the room. Father and daughter stared at each other in shocked disbelief.

'Kate!'

'Mum? What on earth are you doing here?'

*

It was 10am and Larry was waiting outside the newsagents a couple of hundred metres down the road from the hospital when the van pulled up. He waited a few moments for the driver to unload the papers before he entered the shop.

'That'll be 40p exactly,' said the newsagent smiling broadly, taking Larry's change.

'Thank you,' mumbled Larry robotically, staring at the headline.

'Nasty business about that Alfie Macbeth,' said the newsagent, clicking his tongue. 'Another shocking story today and what with him

244

in hospital and all. I always thought he was a top bloke meself, but a murderer? Who would have thought it?'

'Terrible,' muttered Larry under his breath as he turned to leave. He didn't want to get into a conversation. He only wanted to read the print. But not here. Where? The hospital? No. A cafe, he thought, catching sight of a Starbucks. He staggered towards the counter and ordered a latte. The paper, folded under his arm, felt heavy like an unwanted burden that seemed to hold him in its evil power. What had Alfie done? he wondered miserably as the assistant handed him his coffee. He took it mumbling his thanks and slumped down at the nearest free table, laid the paper out in front of him and smoothed it with the flat of his hand.

THE FILM, THE DIRECTOR, HIS WIFE AND HER LOVER, declared the headline. The introduction was short and accusatory, Thomas Slater's words stinging his reason like poisonous venom. The point he was making that life had imitated art. In real life as in his film *Killing Fame,* the heroine, in this case his second wife, Stella, had left him for another man. In a fit of pique, Alfie had murdered her lover. The proof was to be found in a diary, Alfie's diary, an excerpt from which followed:

Sunday 13 May

The hardest thing of all was actually planning the murder. I had to get him to our ranch under false pretences. It's not like we were the best of friends. I couldn't just ring him up and say, 'Hi, how are you? Come and stay for a few days.' Although, I dare say our hatred of one another was mutual.

Once I had lured him to the ranch, the murder would be relatively simple. The man loved a drink. Well, didn't we all? All I had to do was serve him a drink laced with the poison of my choice. You see that was the method I eventually decided on. Poisoning. The only difficulty now was deciding which poison I should use. There is a huge range to choose from, you know – belladonna, carbolic acid, arsenic, prussic acid. Hell, the choice is endless.

Death from poisoning is not pleasant. It doesn't take much time but it can be ugly, is often painful. He drank, smiled and then his eyes began to flicker. And as the truth began to dawn on him his grin turned grimace as he clutched his throat. That was when I noticed the little bubbles of saliva forming at the right hand side of his mouth like the froth on a beer, though obviously not as pleasant, because he grabbed his stomach, bent over double and groaned. And still he stared at me in wide-eyed agony, unable to speak save for the guttural expostulations that he spat from his mouth.

After a while he fell to the floor. It would have been a huge relief had he not begun to writhe around on the decking, moaning and whining. It was a wonder the neighbours didn't hear.

'Shut up,' I said. 'Shut up and die, will you?'

He didn't reply, he just gurgled insanely. Then he vomited. He retched and retched. The contents of his gut spilled out of his mouth onto my nice clean decking, though I was thankful it was only vomit.

Inevitably he died. He died with one hand outstretched as though he were pleading with me, begging me to pull him back from the abyss. I stood and stared. What, me save him? After all he had put me through.

'I don't think so,' I said as I stamped on his hand.

Now I had to dispose of the body. I had to if I wanted to keep Stella. I had to destroy the evidence. It wouldn't do for Stella to return home and stumble over the corpse. She would be suspicious. She might even think that I had poisoned him.

Of course, I already knew what I would do. I would bind him, weight him and throw him in the lake. I have said so before and I will say so again.

So, thought Larry horrified as he buried his face in his hands, that is what Thomas Slater stole. A diary. Alfie's diary as he quite clearly claims and if he's printed it word for word then it looks certain to incriminate him. Now the shit will really hit the fan. Phoebe's right, I must go to the police. Thomas Slater must not be allowed to have it all his own way. He pulled his mobile phone out of his trouser pocket and turned it on for the first time in ages. It rang immediately.

'Audrey!' he said reading the name. 'Hi! What's up?'

'It's Raul,' replied his secretary. 'Shall I tell you over the phone?'

Thirteen

'It was funny Raul turning up last week.'

'Hilarious!' muttered Stella under her breath as she pulled a pile of plates out from the kitchen cupboard she was cleaning. Troy smiled. 'Careful with those. I think they're considered the best ones,' she said as she staggered to her feet and handed them to him.

'He was in a bad way,' said Troy. He took the plates and placed them carefully on the kitchen table. The image of Raul, uncharacteristically dishevelled and drunk, was proving difficult to erase from his mind. 'Not to mention aromatically challenged,' he added, screwing up his nose at the memory. 'When I saw him lying on your decking I really thought he'd carked it.'

'I bet you did,' she said as she knelt down in front of the cupboard again.

'Until he groaned. That's when I realised he had a gutful of piss.'

'Troy. That's disgusting.'

'I mean he was drunk. Reckon he'd been drinking with the flies.'

'Flies?'

'Alone.'

'Thank you. Here, some more plates.'

'You were brilliant taking him in like that.'

'What else could I do?' she said frowning. 'Chuck me the sponge.'

'Sure.' Troy off-loaded the plates onto the table then headed towards the sink. It was typical of Stella, he thought as he ran the tap, to be so matter-of-fact about a situation many others, including his mother, would find awkward and upsetting. She was kind and she was capable. He rinsed out the sponge, squeezed out the excess water, turned round and hurled it in Stella's direction.

'Thanks,' she said as she deftly caught the sponge in her left hand then bent down, her head and upper body disappearing into the cupboard.

The more time he spent with her, the more he understood what it was that held Alfie so enthralled. One in a million, that's how you described a person like Stella. Pretty, fearless, straightforward and undeniably fit. Oh yes, Stella was fit. Especially dressed as she was today in a skimpy pair of denim shorts and a pale pink vest that rode up her back as she leant into the cupboard to reveal a very pleasing amount of suntanned skin. He glanced down and stared in fascination at the white strip of her G-string that had appeared as a result of her shorts being pulled downwards while, bent double, she worked the sponge vigorously, intent on her task. It's OK to look, he reasoned, just important not to touch. And to think that Alfie once had the run of Katherine Katz's body, he thought neatly returning to Raul again. 'Did Katherine give him the flick? Did he say?'

'No he didn't.'

Sad, thought Troy, that Raul, one of his childhood heroes, should be reduced to this. Seeing him laid out cold, saliva dribbling down his chin, had shattered an illusion.

'Thing is Troy, it's all about egos,' explained Stella matter-of-factly as she re-emerged from the cupboard. She leant back onto her ankles. 'They need a lot of feeding, especially when they are the size of Raul Mendoza's. And it just isn't happening at the moment.'

'But he must have felt so much better after a night with you,' said Troy warmly. Stella's eyes narrowed.

'I'm sorry, I didn't mean . . .'

'Well think before you speak then,' said Stella crossly.

'You miss him, don't you?'

'Who?' asked Stella tetchily.

'Alfie of course.'

'Pass me those plates,' said Stella, ignoring him.

'I know you miss him. You've been different these last few days.'

'Different?' asked Stella, frowning. 'What do you mean?'

'Well, quiet and withdrawn, I suppose. And then all this cleaning, well it's because he's on your mind.'

'Who is?'

'Alfie,' repeated Troy, patiently.

'Oh yes,' said Stella absently, picking up the sponge.

'He'll be back soon.'

'Any day now.'

'And you're certain he's forgiven me.'

'Troy we've been over this several times this last fortnight,' she said irritably, rising to her feet.

'I know and I'm sorry. It's just that he didn't seem to have forgiven me before he left.'

'He was angry, he lashed out and now he's probably forgotten all about it.' She untied her apron. Troy watched as she hung it on the back of the kitchen door. She turned round, tucking a few loose strands of hair behind her ear, smiled suddenly then walked over to where he was standing, held his face in her hands and kissed him on the cheek. 'Thanks so much for helping me out today, Troy, but now you'll have to excuse me, I've got to go.'

'I was just about to go myself,' he said, returning her smile with affection. She's trying hard, he thought, as he waved goodbye, but it is obvious by her erratic behaviour that she is lost without Alfie.

*

The drive from Cairns up the Gillies highway to Millaa Millaa would take him about an hour and a quarter. That meant 75 minutes until he was in Stella's arms again. How he had missed Stella. These last two weeks spent apart from her had opened his eyes to the fact that he loved Stella more than he thought it possible for one human to love another. His devotion to his wife bordered on the religious, were it not for the dreams They were far from spiritual. Every night he dreamt of her: her warm breath caressing his face as she slept, the lightness of her touch as she explored his body, the absolute perfection of her form, her flawless skin, the softly rounded curve of her naked hip as she lay, head resting on one arm, listening to him after they had made love, the freckle under her right eye, her smile as warm and radiant as the rosy morning Australian sunrise they would often watch in awed silence through the open curtains of the French windows as they lay in bed.

Then one night he dreamt he woke to find her standing silently in the shadow of the corner of their room. He got up and tried to cross the dark to touch her but he could not reach her no matter how hard he tried. She looked at him with desperation in her sea-green eyes as she began to cry. So he tried again, harder this time, willing his body to reach this unfathomable place that seemed to exist, right there, in front of his eyes, but still he could not get to her. He could feel the tears of his frustration pouring down his cheek as, with all his might, he took a running jump and landed right in front of her. Barely able to believe his sudden change of fortune, he held out his hand to touch her but as her ran his hands over the outline of her body he was horrified to discover that he could feel nothing. She stopped crying, smiled at him, then disappeared leaving him alone in the darkness. He woke in a cold sweat, shaking, terrified until his conscious mind kicked in, his bearings returned and he realised that, though vivid, it had merely been a terrible but meaningless dream.

The next day as he sat in David Palmer's office signing the deal in the presence of lawyers, he made a mental note that he would never allow himself to suffer the agony of such pain and anxiety again. Time and space had imposed a temporary but nonetheless aching void in his life. And even though he had phoned Stella daily to allow himself at least the luxury of the sound of her voice, there could be no substitute for the physicality of her actual presence.

He laughed, happy to be on his way home. Any minute now he would be driving down the dusty track to the house that he shared with Stella. He'd kiss her as he picked her up to carry her to the bedroom where he'd gently place her on the bed and carefully remove both their clothes . . .

'Nonsense, Alfie,' he said, interrupting his thoughts. 'You haven't seen her for two weeks. Self control? I don't think so. You'll find her, rip the clothes off her, and take her right there on the floor.

'Troy?'

'Yes.'

'Hi, it's Alfie.'

'Alfie. Great. Where are you?'

'I'm at home.'

'You're back. Brilliant. How did it go?'

'Very well.'

'You mean they bought it?'

'Indeed I do.'

'Wow. You must be stoked?'

Alfie laughed, resigned to the inevitability of the reply. 'I am.'

'When do you start? Filming, I mean.'

'Hopefully in about three months, after I've rewritten the ending.'

'Oh? Didn't they like it?'

'Well we're talking Hollywood here. They believe in happy endings and mine, well let's just say it was dark. Very dark indeed.'

'Do you mind?'

'No. Not really. At least not enough to baulk the project.'

'Cool.'

'Exactly,' said Alfie with a sigh. As lovely as it was to talk to the effervescent adolescent, there was another reason for his call. Stella. She hadn't been at home when he'd arrived two hours ago and now, having unpacked, he found himself sitting, twiddling his thumbs, staring idly at the idyllic view. The suspense was killing him. He'd rung the Buchanan's first but there had been no answer. The only other port of call was the Thomases. If Millie didn't know where Stella was, he was certain Troy would. Troy always seemed to know what everyone was doing. Interested to the point of voyeuristic was how Alfie viewed his inquisitiveness into their lives. But Stella was adamant and had convinced him as much before he left that Troy was simply in awe of him. His infatuation was a direct result of the esteem in which he held one of the greatest film directors the world had ever known. And he was hurting also because he felt he'd let Alfie down with the Tom Slater business. He had to do something to put that right but as yet he wasn't sure how.

'Troy, I don't suppose you know where Stella is? I've rung the Buchanans and there's no answer.'

'She's been very busy recently.'

'Really? Doing what?'

'I don't know but don't worry, Stella's a sensible girl. She'll be fine.'

'Troy,' said Alfie, slowly, as he tried to contain his irritation. 'I'm not worried about her, I'm just keen to see her.'

'Oh yes. Sorry. Of course. You would be. Sorry. I can't help you. I haven't a clue where she is.'

'Not to worry,' sighed Alfie. 'How are things with you?' he added as an afterthought.

'Great. Really good.'

'Excellent. And I trust you looked after Stella while I was away.'

'I tried but she doesn't need much looking after.'

'That much is true. She's very capable, Stella.'

'You should have seen the way she handled Raul,' he blurted out.

'Raul?!' exclaimed Alfie, stunned by the mention of the name.

'Yeah, I know, freaky or what?' continued Troy fatuously. 'He was in a shocking state.'

'What do you mean?'

'He'd had a gutful . . . He was drunk. Drunk as a skunk in fact. Smelt like one too. But Stella didn't bat an eyelid. She just asked me to help her get him into bed.'

'Bed?'

'Yeah.'

'Why?' he asked limply. It seemed to him that his world was spinning, that Troy's words were distant noises, nonsensical, imponderable and yet vitally important.

'Because it was night, I guess, and . . . well . . . he couldn't walk.'

'And you stayed with him, right?' asked Alfie as he struggled to rationalise his thoughts.

'Nah. Stella looked after him for the night.'

252

'Stella?' repeated Alfie breathlessly. 'On her own?'

'It was incredibly good of her, don't you think?'

'Incredible,' said Alfie, his mind a mess of uncompromising images. Stella, naked in the shower the following morning, easy prey for Raul's priapic eyes, bloated with desire, fixed with lascivious intent on her erect, pale fawn nipples. Could she? Would she? No, no of course not. Stella had more sense, didn't she?

'Alfie? Are you still there?'

'Yes, sorry. Jet lag. Listen, I've got to go and unpack. I'll catch you later.'

'OK. Bye,' said Troy breezily.

Alfie put down the receiver and stood stock still, frozen by fear. Raul Mendoza. Was the man to be a regular feature of his life turning up all the time, despair and destruction following in his wake? Did Raul have some sort of fixation with him that he had to shadow his life, haunting him like some crazed zombie?

'Alfie?'

'Stella,' responded Alfie, starting at the sound of his wife's voice. He rushed into the hallway, heart thumping, the image of Raul sneering, arms folded like a smug politician, in the forefront of his mind. 'Stella,' he repeated hesitantly on sight of her. With eyes wide but fearful, he stood before his wife, desperate to hug her but holding back, unsure. And Stella stood motionless, struggling under the weight of a large package wrapped in brown paper that she clutched to her body, frowning slightly.

'Can I help you with that?' he asked her, shocked at how formal he sounded, appalled at the six foot gap that separated them, not knowing how to bridge it.

'You can do better than that,' she said with the faintest of smiles. 'It's for you.'

'Me? Why?'

'It's a present.'

'But it's not my birthday, our anniversary.'

'It's not for anything in particular, just a present because I thought you would like it,' she said, frowning again. She took a step closer to him. 'Here, take it.'

He took the parcel from her, held it and stared at it for a while. 'Shall I open it?'

'You may as well,' she said, her smile twitching at the corners of her mouth as though it were a mask she were trying to wear that didn't quite fit. Quietly, methodically, he removed the paper recalling how, little more than an hour ago, he'd anticipated ripping not paper from a gift but the clothes from her body. Beneath the layers of paper peel was a painting. A magnificent painting of Stella, naked, lying, back arched, one hand raised above her head, relaxed, sensual, her glassy eyes staring at him, smiling. 'Do you like it?'

'I'm overwhelmed,' he replied, exhaling loudly.

'Well that's better than being underwhelmed,' she replied quietly.

'Stella, it's stunning, a masterpiece,' he said, glancing first at the painting and then at Stella. 'It's beautiful. I mean you are beautiful. I had forgotten quite how beautiful you are, seeing you again ... this picture ... after endless nights spent dreaming of your image.' He put it down, flat on the floor, then stepped towards her and kissed her. All the questions he wanted to ask about Raul could wait. He didn't care a jot. Stella was his and his alone. Without saying another word he turned around and, leading her gently by the hand, began to climb the stairs.

Fourteen

It was three weeks since Alfie had returned from the States but Troy had seen very little of him, preferring to keep out of his way for fear of falling foul of his temper once more. He'd kept a low profile, busying himself with his holiday work, helping his Dad with the cows and trying to avoid thinking about the problem of how he would cope with the imminent visit from cousin Tom – until today. He was lying on his bed mulling over the conundrum as the smell of baking bread meandered from its source in the kitchen to his bedroom above in a heady stream. He loved baking day. He always had. But the delicious aroma and the sound of *Burt Bacharach Movie Tunes* seemed at odds with the contradictory stance his mother had taken in allowing Tom back into their house. She had been appalled at his behaviour, embarrassed by the way her nephew had treated her revered neighbour and this she had conveyed in no uncertain terms to her sister. So why on earth had she changed her mind? Did she realise the strain she was placing on her own son?

The phone rang. He could hear his mother talking in muffled tones. What was it about mothers that caused them to behave so randomly? Why was it always one rule for them, another for their kids? Could they not see the total absence in logic surrounding every decision they made? If I ever decide to get married, he told himself as he squeezed his eyes shut in abject frustration, I will study the mother's reasoning powers before committing to another life of irrational thinking. He heard the sound of her heels clicking on the stone floor of their hallway.

'That was Alfie, darling,' she called up to him. 'He's invited you over. There's something he wants to ask you and it's too personal apparently to do over the phone. Troy? Can you hear me?'

'Yes mother,' said Troy who had leapt to his feet as if called to attention by a sergeant-major.

'I told him you'd be over right away,' she said, then turned and pattered back to the comfort of her kitchen and her music.

It had to be good news, reasoned Troy as he dashed down the stairs, to have to be told in person, didn't it? The great Alfie Macbeth calling on him, twenty-year-old Troy Thomas. He had lost count of the number of times Stella had told him that Alfie had forgiven him but this was the first time he really felt he could believe it.

The wheels of his mother's Ford Falcon barely touched the tattered tarmac as he skidded and bounced his way to The Rocks. As the car oscillated precariously up the dirt track in a cloud of dust, he didn't immediately notice the presence of Jack Buchanan's jeep. It wasn't until he turned on the windscreen wipers to clear the dust that was settling in an opaque grey film on the white car that he saw it. Damn, he thought as his heart sank. This request of Alfie's obviously wasn't as exclusive as he'd concluded. Trying hard to smother his disappointment he got slowly out of the car, the spring in his step replaced with a dragging apprehension, and plodded up the wooden steps to Alfie and Stella's front door.

There was no answer to his knocking but still he waited far longer than was necessary before trying the door. As expected, it was unlocked so he stepped into the hallway, recalling as he looked around at the large light, wooden-floored space, how ominous this place had seemed the night of the storm when, as a result of his own incompetence, Alfie had vented his rage on him. He shivered and folded his arms, his confidence of 20 minutes earlier evaporating entirely in the heat of his memories.

'Hello? Troy? Is that you?' called Alfie from the kitchen.

'Hi!' replied Troy feebly.

'Come on through, we're out the back.' His spirits lifting a little, Troy shuffled through the hall and into the kitchen where Alfie greeted him with a warm shake of the hand and a vigorous slap on the back.

'Can I get you a beer? Jack and I are both having one?' Alfie asked him, pulling out a six-pack of ice-cold VB from the fridge.

'Cool!' replied Troy, a little tentatively. Alfie pulled one free of its plastic casing and handed it to Troy.

'Excellent,' he said with a huge smile.

Infected by Alfie's apparently unbounded bonhomie, Troy beamed back then followed him through the French windows into the backyard.

'Hi, mate,' said Jack, raising his tinny in welcome. He was sitting on a teak chair beside a table under the shade of a gum tree. Troy grinned and raised his back. 'Dad given you the day off?'

'Something like that,' said Troy sheepishly, wishing he could avoid the small talk.

'I gather you've been a real help to him this vacation,' continued Jack in his usual, pleasant way.

Troy nodded but said nothing. He knew he was being rude, that he should ask Jack how things were over at his place. He was unusually pale and had black circles under his eyes that made him look tired. Troy had heard from his father that Stumpy had been ill so that was probably why. Anyway, right now he couldn't concern himself with trivialities like that. He wanted only to cut to the chase. It was all he could do to stop himself asking Alfie what he wanted.

'He won't like what I've got to ask you then,' said Alfie with a mischievous grin. 'Suddenly I am thinking perhaps I shouldn't put you in the position of having to make a choice.'

'A choice?' asked Troy, intrigued. He glanced at Jack as if for clues but he had pulled a handkerchief out of his khaki combats and was wiping his brow, a preoccupied expression on his face.

Alfie noticed. 'Are you all right, Jack?'

Damn it, thought Troy in desperation.

'Oh, I'm fine,' said Jack dismissively, who looked far from that. 'Just a little hot.'

'You might be going down with something,' said Alfie, distracted. 'I was thinking how erm . . . clement the weather was today. Wouldn't you say, Troy?'

'Er . . .' stammered Troy.

'Pleasantly warm,' translated Alfie.

'Oh, yes. It's much cooler than it has been. Perhaps you've caught the flu,' he added as helpfully as he could.

'Bound to have,' said Alfie, winking at Troy. Flummoxed, Troy stared blankly back. 'Troy, I'm sorry,' said Alfie laughing. 'You're standing there at odds and ends with yourself, wondering why the hell I've asked you here.'

'Well . . .' began Troy, embarrassed that Jack might think he was unfeeling.

'I shall get to the point,' said Alfie, holding up his hand. 'I've invited you over to ask you whether you would consider being a runner on the set of *Killing Fame*.'

'Are you serious?' whispered Troy, not quite believing this latest turn of events. Just like that. Totally out of the blue. Wham, bam thank you ma'am. Well, put like that how could a guy refuse? The answer could only be yes. Yes please, in fact. It really didn't need saying.

'Well Troy?'

This question meant that Alfie actually did need an answer and was patiently waiting for one . . . only not the one Troy gave him, which he

257

would later blame on his mother's taste in music. It popped out of his mouth before he could stop it.

'What's it all about, Alfie?' sang Troy.

'Ha, ha, very funny. I've never heard that before!' he said as Troy silently castigated his mother for daring to infiltrate his brain on such an important day in his life. *The* most important day of his life he swiftly corrected himself.

'I mean, are you serious?'

'Deadly so,' replied Alfie. 'Obviously it would mean missing a term of university, a decision that should be given some thought.'

'I know but it's such a huge opportunity.'

'It's an opportunity,' said Alfie. 'But that is all. If you are as keen on forging out a career in the movies as you claim to be, then acting as a runner would give you an insight into the making of a film which could prove useful in the future. It will be an experience, not a means to an end. And the pay is dreadful.'

'I'd love to,' confirmed Troy reaching out for Alfie's hand that he clutched and shook with such rapidity he spilled the beer he held in his other. 'Thank you, thank you, thank you.'

'I have to confess, Stella gave me the idea.'

'THANK YOU STELLA,' shouted Troy. He let go of Alfie's hand, spun around and showered Alfie with the remains of his beer.

'Calm down, Troy,' said Alfie good-naturedly. 'She won't be able to hear you.'

'Why? Where is she?' asked Troy a little disappointed not to be able to share this moment with her.

'Oh, she's at the doctor's,' replied Alfie casually.

'What's wrong?' asked Jack, his pale blue eyes like two shards of ice narrowing in concern.

'Don't worry, Jack. You won't have caught anything from her.'

A wave of colour washed across Jack's pale face. 'I'm sorry, I was just concerned. For Stella, that is.'

'Women's problems, so she says,' said Alfie, amused at Jack's embarrassment. 'Although I think she's worried about my return to filming. She's been acting a little strangely since my return. It's hardly surprising, really. I'm a little worried myself.' He shrugged his shoulders then turned his attention back to Troy. 'So you'll talk it over with your parents?'

'Yes,' said Troy. 'But you can count me in.'

'I'm going to leave you two to chat,' said Jack rising from his chair. Alfie got up, to wave him off. 'Sit down, Alfie. I can see myself out. And good luck to you both.'

'Thanks Jack. Take care of yourself now. Perhaps you should pay a visit to the doctor.'

'Maybe,' replied Jack with the faintest of smiles. With a slight wave of his hand, he turned and left.

'Been working far too hard,' said Alfie to Troy. 'What with Stumpy being ill and all the painting he's been doing.'

'Yeah,' said Troy, though he was barely listening. This was his dream come true. A chance to work in films. He didn't want to talk about Jack, he was happy just to sit and relish the moment.

'He painted Stella you know, while I was away. It's a work of a very talented artist. I think he's missing his vocation. He's wasting his time and his talents working on his father's farm. I see that now. Not to mention burning himself out.'

'That's great Alfie,' said Troy, glossing over Jack's misfortunes once again. He'd like to see the painting but he couldn't ask. Not now he'd found a way back into Alfie's confidence. And he really didn't want to spend the rest of the day discussing the vagaries of Jack Buchanan's oh so boring life. 'When do we start?'

'Keen as mustard,' said Alfie ruffling Troy's hair. 'That's excellent.'

Monday 14 May

*My angel. My Stella. Stella Maris, Star of the Sea, star of my life.
Stella, Stella, Stella, how sweet the word Stella.*

*I loved you, Stella and you alone: the cadence of your voice, the
gently sloping line of your hair that fell across your shoulders as you
inclined your head to kiss me, sweet mellifluous kisses from honeyed
lips.*

*When I close my eyes I can recall every detail of your face, the small
gap between your front teeth, the shapeliness of your form, your
sculpted clavicle, the softly rounded curve of your hip, every grain of
your silken skin – buttery-brown, taut as a drum, flawless save for the
freckle under your right eye, your angel eyes. The nights we spent on
the soft, feather bed in the centre of the white room, the white muslin
curtains blowing in the slight breeze, the endless sunshine days of our
eternal paradise when I lived in your heart and you in mine. I was
bound to you by this telluric love, caught up in knots, meticulous and
strong, knots that no earthly being could untie. Indefinable,
unparalleled love, to such a passion I was honoured to be a slave.*

*But you . . . You were not so tied. You slipped your bonds, rose up
and walked away. From me, our life, my inspiration.*

*I know you could not lie. You never did, not once in all the time I'd
known you. But how I wish this once you could have managed that at
least. That's all I wanted, one small, white lie to paper over the tiniest
crack in the wall of our life.*

But you couldn't lie.

It was not your style.

*I sharpened the blade of my knife, rusting, grooved, the one I use for
gutting fish, as you confessed to me. I think we both knew what I
intended to do with it. But still you were calm when you told me that
you loved him. I remember your face, the physical paradox of the tear
on your cheek, the smile on your lips. Can still recall the antipathy of
your voice, the inflexions of hope, the monotone of despair.*

*You weren't at all frightened of the knife, Stella, though you closed
your eyes all the same. And I knew that you were trying to ignore its
existence but would you be able to ignore the pain?*

*'To kindness and knowledge we only make promises, but pain we
obey.'*

But maybe, just maybe you hadn't read any Proust.

*You smiled at me with angel eyes as I thrust my knife into your heart.
That was when I saw your wings for the first time. They were much*

260

bigger than I had expected. Weighty, powerful, the pure ivory feathers had an eagle's span. On your head, a golden halo. You wore it at a jaunty angle. I liked that. It suited you. A blaze of light emanated from the silver gown that caressed your body, sensually, like a lover's touch. I had to shield my eyes to protect them from its incandescent glare. When I dared to look again, you were hovering over me, hands clasped in prayer.

But before you flew away you alighted beside me one last time and let me put my arms around you, as a father might do to his daughter. I wondered, as I stroked your gorgeous, smooth, shiny hair and breathed in your scent, if that was how you had always perceived me.

And all the time my heart was breaking. I could feel it, an abhorrent agony, a deep, protracted, aching pain that just went on and on.

'Stay with me, Stella. I'll look after you. I'll make it better. It will be good again.'

I held you still. It would be the last time I ever held you. I did not want the closeness to end. I did not want to let you go.

Then you flew away on your cloud of gold, leaving me alone. I felt a stabbing pain in my heart as I descended, deeper and deeper, like a falling stone into the fiery darkness of hell.

My shell had now truly been broken.

Fifteen

'Alfie! You look dreadful! What on earth's happened to you?'

'It's lovely to see you too, Kate. How are things?' said Alfie with a wry smile. Still the same old Kate, he mused – indignant, insensitive, no smile or hello, worse, no kiss for her daughter. In fact she barely acknowledged Phoebe.

'What's all this nonsense about cancer?' she asked thrusting some large, white lilies in his general direction while simultaneously ignoring his question.

'It's not nonsense Mother,' interjected Phoebe who had stepped forward to intercept the flowers. Unable to further ignore her daughter's presence, Kate turned to her, raised her head and looked down her nose at Phoebe with unequivocal scorn.

'Excuse me young lady but I was talking to your father.' She turned her exquisitely coiffured head in Alfie's direction. 'What strange little game are you playing this time?'

'It's not a game Mother and you are not helping. Dad is seriously ill,' answered Phoebe, her voice not far off a shout. 'He is going to die.' And with that retort, flung the lilies on the chair in the corner.

'We are all of us going to die,' said Kate theatrically, rolling her eyes in Phoebe's direction. 'Alfie, please, I insist you tell me what is going on.'

Alfie's heart felt heavy. However much he tried to persuade his daughter otherwise, Kate had grown more impossible with age. Elegantly dressed in a Prada trouser suit, a stunning pair of Manolo Blahnik shoes on her feet, she looked almost as marvellous in the flesh as she did in the many air-brushed photos of her that still appeared all too regularly in colour magazines. She was beautiful, selfish and she was vain, but above all else she appeared to be in control. And here he was lying in a hospital bed, helpless before her. He took a deep breath to muster up the energy required to bring Kate into line. If only he didn't feel so emasculated.

262

'Kate!' he barked sternly and was amused when Kate jumped backwards in surprise. 'Curb your tongue. Phoebe's upset. It's true. I have been given weeks to live. For once in your life try to focus on someone other than yourself,' he said as his voice trailed off into little more than a wheeze. Damn it, he thought, I haven't the strength to get angry.

'You might have told me.'

'I was going to. I only discovered the information myself yesterday.'

'And yet I read it in today's papers!' snapped Kate.

'Don't be ridiculous,' said Alfie weakly. 'The press had no idea.'

'Larry!' said Kate with a sneer.

'He would never act without instruction,' responded Alfie.

'But don't you see, he's protecting you again.'

'Mum! Don't,' said Phoebe, stamping her foot.

'What, Phoebe? What's going on?' asked Alfie, appealing to his daughter.

'Tell me it's another one of your games,' demanded Kate. 'Because, frankly, I resent being questioned at length by the Metropolitan Police.'

Phoebe groaned.

'The burglary?' asked Alfie confused by information that was being hurled at him from all directions. 'Why on earth would they question you?'

'Burglary? I know nothing of a burglary,' said Kate.

'Dad, the press have gone mad, that's all. It's nothing really,' persisted Phoebe, managing a shaky smile. She walked over to her father, sat down on the bed, and picked up his hand. Alfie was not fooled but he said nothing. 'They think they've spotted Stella, that's all.'

'The poisonous little slapper,' muttered Kate under her breath. Then louder, 'Where are you hiding *her?*'

'Oh for heaven's sake Mother, that's idle speculation,' said Phoebe angrily. 'You of all people should know not to believe what's written in the papers,' she added with a withering stare.

'So you mean that ghastly, common, gold-digging whore is not about to walk through that door,' said Kate venomously.

'That's enough Kate,' ordered Alfie, closing his eyes. 'Now spit it out one of you. What's been going on?'

'No,' said Phoebe forcibly. 'You're too ill to heed the nonsense of a demonic journalist.'

'The police wanted to know when I last heard from Raul,' said Kate exhaustedly, as though she were explaining a ludicrous plot line. 'They wanted to know where he was living, what he was doing. Naturally I told them he was a practising Buddhist, ensconced in the protective bosom of the Dalai Lama, in North India. Dharamsala, to be precise,' she added facetiously.

'What's he done now?' asked Alfie, irritated.

'It's not what he's done,' scoffed Kate. 'But what you've done to him.'

'I haven't done anything to him,' said Alfie with a laugh, barely able to believe what he was hearing. 'I've been in hospital.'

'Mum!' hissed Phoebe, glaring at Kate, willing her to stop.

'Darling,' said Kate patronisingly, turning to Phoebe. 'If the police are accusing him of murder then I am afraid to say he has a right to know.'

'Murder?' croaked Alfie. Had he gone mad or was Kate saying what he thought she was saying and, if she was, she was making no sense at all, to him anyway. He looked at Phoebe whose face had turned the colour of milk. 'Phoebe, did you know about this?'

Realising that it was useless to protest further, Phoebe simply nodded at her father.

'And the press are writing about it?'

'Yes, but it's nonsense Dad. We know that. It's just some journalist making trouble.'

'Who am I supposed to have murdered?'

'Well, judging by the line of questioning, Raul,' said Kate with a snort. 'Fifteen years ago, according to *The Evening News*. So I told the police if Alfie Macbeth has killed Raul, it certainly wasn't fifteen years ago.'

'You what?' asked Phoebe incredulously.

'I haven't spoken to Raul for two years. For all I know he could be lying dead in a lake,' replied Kate sarcastically.

'Don't tell me you believe this rubbish?' asked Phoebe angrily.

'Lake?' repeated Alfie faintly. 'Can I see the paper?'

'Be my guest,' said Kate. She took a copy of *The Evening News* out of her Louis Vuitton bag, walked over to Alfie and dropped it on his lap with an air of triumph. 'I think at the very least you owe us both an explanation.'

'Nurse Mitchell,' said Phoebe, alarmed.

Startled by his daughter's tone of voice, Alfie glanced over Phoebe's head toward the door. A very nervous nurse Mitchell was hovering in the doorway and standing behind her were two burly men in suits that he did not recognise at all.

'I'm sorry to intrude Miss Macbeth, Ms Katz, Mr Macbeth but DI Marshall and Sgt Fawkes are intent on speaking to you.' She smiled a watery smile in Alfie's direction. 'Five minutes, gentlemen, that is all.'

*

Larry marched, with all the purpose of an errant soldier way off course, down the Fulham Road towards the hospital. He needed answers and he needed them fast, although he was hard pressed to admit he knew what the questions were. His mind, like an untidy drawer, needed organising.

Thomas Slater ... Tom Slater ... Slater, he repeated to himself as he trawled his gridlocked brain for some memory of the name but there was nothing. This vendetta he's launched against Alfie has to come from somewhere, he reasoned. For a man to pen such poison against another suggests that Slater is out to seek revenge. Poison so incriminating Alfie could end up in jail. What's incurred this man's wrath? What did Alfie do? Could it have something to do with Raul? Perhaps Thomas Slater is a friend of his. Think, Larry, think, he pleaded his subconscious. I have to be clear in my own mind. I can't just rip the hell out of that slimy git. I need facts.

By now he was close enough to the hospital to be able to see the confusion of journalists huddled outside. What had begun as a small but resilient group had swelled overnight into a tumultuous media circus. Audrey had phoned him that morning to tell him that Thomas Slater's story had featured in every newspaper and on every news programme across the land. Speculation was running out of control. Radio disc jockeys were inviting members of the public to phone in their opinions on the matter. Chat show hosts were deliberating Alfie's innocence with their celebrity guests. Larry was comforted to hear that not everyone thought he was guilty. The public, Audrey had told him, seemed to be viewing the claims as a vile and slanderous smear campaign. It was, they told the presenters, a sorry example of our time, that newspapers could run amok, tearing into the life of an innocent man just to increase sales.

'We've been inundated with calls since the story broke, from journalists demanding exclusives, the truth, dirt, photos and the more naive, Kate's telephone number and Alfie's room number at the hospital,' Audrey had told him. 'Hysteria has gripped the nation.'

He's lived by publicity now he'll probably die by publicity, thought Larry sadly. We'll have to move him. He's not well enough to cope with this level of intrusion. He'd reached Limerston Street and was on the outskirts of the vociferous, heaving mass of journalists, paparazzi, sound technicians and cameramen who were spilling onto the road as they jostled for the prime position nearest the lobby. Even some curious on-lookers, fascinated by the media scrum, had been caught up in the action. As a result of all the mayhem the traffic had come to a complete standstill, the jam of cars tailing back down the Fulham Road. The frustrated motorists hooted their horns angrily.

It was pandemonium, deafening disorganised chaos. The upside, however, was that Larry arrived without being recognised. He knew the luxury of anonymity would be fleeting. The moment he was spotted he would be besieged. His plan, if he could call it that, was to find Thomas Slater, extricate him from the tangled rabble, pull him into a taxi and then interrogate him.

It won't work Larry, his psyche told him. You know it's impossible. First of all a taxi won't be able to get near the place and secondly, to extract Thomas without being noticed will be as difficult as removing *The Mona Lisa* from the Louvre.

For the first time in his media-led life he wondered whether it wouldn't be better to give up and go home. He was about to turn round and walk back down the Fulham Road when he caught sight of Thomas Slater, a worn grey canvas bag slung over his shoulder, walking towards him from the left, down Limerston Street. Trying not to do anything that would attract attention, he walked head bowed towards Thomas, grabbed him by the tricep before the journalist could protest and guided him back down the Fulham Road for about a hundred yards, weaving through the motionless traffic to the other side of the road into The Pitcher and Piano.

'Larry! To what do I owe the honour of an early lunchtime drink?' he sneered as he allowed himself to be led to a table at the back of the pub, an area that was poorly illuminated.

'I'll get you a beer, don't worry,' he said through gritted teeth.

'I'd sooner a whisky if that's all the same to you. I can't stand the warm piss you Poms call beer.'

'A Guinness and a single malt,' Larry asked the barman who had stepped over to clean the table. 'Could you bring them over?' he added, flashing a tenner.

'No problem, mate,' replied the barman amiably. Larry thanked him and turned his attentions back to his companion.

'I have some questions for you,' he said gruffly.

'Fire away,' replied Thomas with a malevolent grin.

'The diary. How did you know about that?'

'I didn't,' replied Thomas, still smiling. 'It just happened to be there.'

'So you admit you did break into Alfie's home.'

'It doesn't take an Einstein to work that much out,' scoffed Thomas.

'So if you weren't after the diary, what were you after?' asked Larry perplexed.

'The screenplay, of course. I figured he'd have a copy of that.'

'*Killing Fame*?'

'Right on, Poirot!'

'So you're making this up, then. Why?'

'Nope!' replied Thomas, pursing his lips.

'Oh for God's sake man. Why the subterfuge. There's no truth in what you're claiming. Why don't you hold up your hand, tell the world whatever it is Alfie has actually done to you and go home?'

'Your drinks gentleman,' said the barman, placing the drinks in front of them. 'And your change sir.'

'Keep that,' said Larry, waving the man away.

'Think about it Larry,' taunted Thomas who was beaming broadly now, enjoying every second of Larry's obvious discomfort. '*Killing Fame*, Alfie Macbeth's Oscar winning thriller. It's a dark story, albeit with a happy ending, of an older man's infatuation with a sexy young girl. An infatuation that turns a successful, happy-go-lucky film director into a raging, jealous tyrant intent on revenge when his bride leaves him for a younger man. Unbeknown to his wife, he shoots his rival at point blank range. It is a simple, swift, cold-blooded murder that rids him of his problem, instantly. He is free to love and be loved again providing his wife never finds out why or how her lover mysteriously disappeared. All he has to do is figure out where to hide the body, a place where no one will ever find it. He puts it in a black polythene bag that he weights with stones, binds it and throws it in the lake and – hey presto! – our hero gets away with murder.'

'But he was writing the script before Stella left him,' said Larry exhaustedly.

'So! The film didn't come out for another three years.'

'And your point is?'

'There was a lake at The Rocks, the house that Alfie lived in at Millaa Millaa. That's where the body is. He says so in his diary time and time again.'

'So you knew him then?' asked Larry aghast. Horrified by what he was hearing he fell backwards in his chair.

'Well done!' said Thomas licking his lips with his snake-like tongue. He took a gulp of his whisky, spilling a little so that it trickled unattractively down his chin. He wiped it away with the back of his hand then reached into his canvas bag and pulled out a book.

'Is that the diary?'

'Two out of two.'

267

'Whose body?' asked Larry. Ignoring the jibe he stared at the odious man.

'Bodies,' corrected Tom, who was now no longer smiling. 'Look.' He opened the black leather notebook and flicked over a few pages. 'Here. Read this.'

Larry took the book that was offered to him and peered down at the script. The entry, which was written in an untidy scrawl, was simply titled *Monday 14 May.* The words Alfie had written were frightening and nonsensical. He could feel the flesh creeping from his bones as he read the description of a deranged maniac calmly stabbing his wife with a serrated fishing knife. He turned back a few pages scanning each chilling entry for clues. Murder. It ran through the pages like blood through a vein, every entry describing a merciless killing in hideous detail, a different weapon for each foul crime. And the underlying reason for each murder was always the same. Retribution. It was definitely Alfie's writing, though not his voice. That was bitter, twisted and evil, unrecognisable as the man he knew and loved. And, as Thomas Slater had so succinctly pointed out, the depiction of a heart-broken, cuckolded lover who kills his rival was synonymous with the central theme of his film.

'But you claimed to have seen her,' he said looking up from the book that contained so much damning evidence. 'You claimed she arrived on a Qantas flight from Brisbane four days ago. You took her picture,' added Larry as he tried manfully to find an escape route for his friend.

'I took that fifteen years ago,' snorted Tom. 'And *the great man* wasn't very amused even then.'

But Larry wasn't interested. He did not want to listen to the gloats of a man intent on revenge. 'This is nothing more than the rantings of an insane man. It's quite obvious that Alfie was out of his mind when he wrote this.'

'Exactly. He wrote this diary just after Stella left him.'

'Well, quite. He was upset. Distraught. I know that.'

'Mad!'

'So it seems.'

'And are you saying sad, mad people don't commit murder?'

'No ... I ...' stuttered Larry.

'Isn't that exactly when a lot of murders happen? A spur of the moment thing borne of rage and insanity.'

'But no one knows what happened. That's my point.'

'You're wrong, Larry. I know what happened. I was there.'

268

Sixteen

'I'll deliver your tickets in the next few weeks. I also have to find out if you will need an equity card. But Troy, you must speak to Millie and Harry first. I don't want you just upping and leaving without your parents' approval, OK?'

'Sure, Alfie.'

'I mean it Troy. I have no intention of allowing you on the plane without it. And after you have told them I shall talk to them and try to put their minds at rest,' he assured him. He could understand the young man's excitement but he liked the Thomases and had no wish to upset them. Troy was just the sort of lad who'd do a bunk rather than suffer the anxiety of negotiations. He was enthusiastic, an asset that would stand him in good stead during the rigours of filming, but he was also impetuous.

'Aw, Alfie. I'm not a kid anymore.'

'Then don't act like one,' he advised him. 'Your parents know how keen you are on movies. If I remember rightly it was the first thing your mother told me when we met. Once they have got over the shock I am certain they will support your decision.'

'I hope you're right.'

'Well the only way to find out is to go home and set the ball rolling. But remember, be patient, don't rush them. Adults need time to mull things over.'

Troy sprung to his feet as if the chair he was sitting in had ejected him.

'You're right Alfie,' he said, an expression of sudden and total cognisance stretched across his face. 'So I had better get going.' He handed Alfie his half drunk can of beer and was about to sprint to his car when he noticed Stella, pale and tired, standing at the French windows, unsmiling.

'Hi Stella,' he said bouncing over to her. 'Alfie's just told me the good news. Thanks a million for putting in a good word for me.'

'How did it go at the doctors?' asked Alfie walking over, worried by her sudden, quiet reappearance. She looked unwell, the skin of her face that was usually flushed with good health was colourless, her normally bright eyes, dull and abstracted as though she were staring at objects that no other human eye could see. 'Sit down, darling, you look white as a sheet,' he said, putting a protective arm round her sun-tanned shoulders.

She shook it off, frowning. 'Troy, would you mind leaving us alone,' she said flatly, staring in Troy's direction although at a place some inches above his head.

'No ... er ... course not. Matter of fact I was just leaving anyway.' Without the spirit of a few moments earlier and with a concerned glance in Alfie's direction, he turned and walked slowly towards his mother's car.

Alfie did not fully understand why it was that he'd begun to shake. A slight tremor that vibrated throughout his body leaving him flushed with heat yet icy cold. It was the vacant and distracted gaze that disturbed him the most.

'What's wrong Stella? Are you ill?'

For the first time since she returned home, Stella's eyes now focused solely on his own. Clear, green, dancing eyes that now looked bloodshot, swollen, loaded with tears, which Stella refused to shed. And still she said nothing.

'If it's something serious, we can sort it out ...'

Stella laughed suddenly, a horrible haunted laugh. 'I'm not ill, Alfie,' she said as a single tear trickled hesitantly down her cheek.

'What then? Are you worried about me going away again? Because don't be. You know I want you to come with me. Troy's coming. Well you know that already. The boy's *stoked*, to use his own expression. That was a great idea of yours, Stella,' he said, aware that he was gabbling.

'Alfie, stop,' said Stella shrilly. She flung her hands over her eyes, bent her head forward and began to tremble. 'Something awful has happened ...'

'What Stella?' Blood was thumping at his eardrums. He could barely hear her, so he placed both arms around her and pulled her to him.

'Something awful,' sobbed Stella, her voice muffled by his shoulder into which she spoke, her hands still covering her eyes.

'What Stella?' he coaxed her, trying his hardest to remain calm, hoping to slow down the electricity that shot round his body like the spring-loaded metal ball in a pinball machine, banging at his heart, his lungs, his stomach.

'I can't explain. I can't.'

'Try, Stella,' he begged her, lifting her head towards his own. 'Please. I need to know.'

Slowly, hesitantly, Stella removed her hands from her face and lifted up her eyes to his. 'I'm pregnant,' she said after a time, her voice so soft it was barely audible.

'But that's great. It's fantastic.' The relief he felt at this unexpected news made him want to laugh with joy.

She shook her head, 'You don't understand.'

'Stella, you're not making any sense. A baby is a good thing. OK, we haven't discussed it but I am delighted at the news. It's fantastic. The best thing that could possibly happen to me ... to us. Stella, it may all seem strange and frightening now but I promise you, you will get used to the idea once you've got over the shock.'

'No. No. You don't understand,' she insisted.

'Well help me then,' said Alfie good-naturedly.

'I don't want to hurt you,' she whispered, tugging at her hair.

'I've got a hind like a rhinoceros. You know that.'

'And I don't think you'll ever forgive me, not that I'm asking for your forgiveness. I wouldn't do that.'

'Stella, you're not making any sense,' he said, his terror growing.

'Everything has gone wrong.'

'No, Stella. You're pregnant that's all.'

'I've let you down.'

'How so?'

'I felt all along that you thought I was perfect.'

'You *are* perfect, Stella.'

'Only now you have to discover the awful truth. I am just like everyone else. I'm loaded with faults. I'll list them for you, there are so many,' she said, her voice rising.

'Shh, Stella. You are tired and emotional. Your hormones are all out of kilter. Sit down and I'll make us both a cup of tea.' He spoke the words aware how futile they sounded.

'I think you put me on a pedestal, Alfie,' she continued, ignoring his offer.

'Nonsense!'

'And boy has it hurt me falling off that pedestal.'

'You're shocked, Stella, that's all.'

'Yes I am. I'm shocked because I really believed I could live up to this vision you had of me. I so desperately wanted to. You made me feel so good about myself.'

'You do. You have. I love you Stella. You know that,' he told her trying his hardest to reassure her as his gut twisted and turned in panic.

'Everything is falling apart,' she cried, the tears spilling over her lower, red-rimmed lid. 'Alfie . . . I'm . . . leaving . . . you.'

'What?' Alfie, who had been struggling to make sense of any aspect of the situation, recoiled in horror at this bombshell

It's not your baby. It's . . .'

'I'm not interrupting anything, am I?'

'What!' exclaimed Alfie, turning to face the speaker. He was disorientated, his mind reeling as he looked straight into the jaundiced eyes of Tom Slater.

'What the hell are you doing here?'

'Millie sent me over to apologise,' said Tom self-righteously.

'How long have you been standing there?' asked Alfie, distracted from his misery by his repugnance at the proximity of this low life.

'Ooh. I don't know,' said Tom, raising a finger to his lips. 'Two, maybe three minutes.'

It was enough.

'Go. Go NOW,' roared Alfie, taking a step towards Tom.

'I'm going,' he said, holding up his hands as he retreated to the drive, his lips pressed together in a thin, angry line.

But Alfie couldn't concern himself with Tom Slater. Not when Stella was behaving so strangely. 'It's not my baby?' He delivered the question quietly, reasonably though he felt physically distressed.

'No,' she replied, dropping her head in shame.

'And you are leaving me?' he asked as if by repeating her words he could assimilate and process the information in his reeling mind.

'Yes.'

'For the father of the child?'

'Yes. I am. Yes.'

'But I love you Stella,' he pleaded.

'I know. I know and I love you too but . . .'

'But what, Stella?' he asked with a howl.

'This is awful. I feel so dreadful. I . . .'

'Tell me it's not true,' begged Alfie.

'I can't, I won't lie to you. I'm leaving, Alfie. I'm sorry . . .'

'Stay, Stella,' cried Alfie, grabbing her by the arms. 'I love you more than you will ever know. I can't live without you. Say you're making this up, tell me you love me too.' It was a last ditch attempt.

'Alfie don't,' she said, trying to break free from his grasp.

'But does *he* love you?' Alfie beseeched her, not letting go.

'Yes Alfie, he does,' replied Stella.

'Who, Stella. Who is it?' he asked helplessly, relaxing his grip though he did not want to let her go. Not now. Not ever.

'Alfie, no.'

'Tell me Stella, I have a right to know,' he implored her as, like a pane of glass hit with a hammer, his heart shattered into a thousand pieces, no way of fixing it – like the glass, just broken.

Seventeen

A heavy silence had filled the room anaesthetizing its occupants who could only stare open-mouthed at the two plain clothed policemen. Everyone that is except Kate who, arms folded, head to one side, smiled knowingly.

'I presume we are not witnessing the great efficiency of the Metropolitan Police's response to a break-in,' said Alfie, finally breaking the silence. One of the men, Sgt Fawkes, glanced down at his shoes. The other man, DI Marshall, raised his hand to his mouth and coughed importantly.

'You may or not be aware, Mr Macbeth, that the recent articles that have featured so prominently in *The Evening News* and *The Daily Mail* have generated what can only be described as national hysteria.'

Kate gave a derisory snort. Phoebe flashed her a furious glare.

'I wasn't aware of this until about five minutes ago,' said Alfie, pausing to catch his breath, which was coming in short bursts. His chest had tightened and he felt a pain in his left arm. Phoebe noticed.

'Dad. Dad. Are you all right?' she asked him, grabbing his hand.

'I'm fine, sweetheart,' he whispered, closing his eyes to help him ride the pain.

'Shall I call the nurse?'

Alfie shook his head and opened his eyes. 'Why didn't you tell me?'

'I couldn't . . . I didn't . . .'

'I would like to stress that at this stage we have absolutely no concrete evidence that you have committed any crime,' interrupted DI Marshall tactfully.

'So why are you here?' burst out Phoebe. 'Can't you see my father is sick?'

'Shh, Phoebe,' said Alfie, recovering his composure. 'Let the poor man speak.'

'We received an anonymous tip off this morning that there is a body

274

lying at the bottom of a lake somewhere in Queensland. I reiterate there is no concrete evidence to support this. However when someone makes such a claim then we are obliged to make certain enquiries.'

'Right,' said Alfie wearily.

'I would like to take this opportunity of telling you that I have been a fan of your work for the past thirty years.'

'That's awfully decent of you,' said Alfie politely.

'And your good self of course, Ms Katz,' he added, nodding at Kate who was quietly fuming in the doorway. DI Marshall cleared his throat again.

'We have spoken to Ms Katz already and after talking to you we will be hoping to make contact with the journalist concerned.'

'What, you mean he isn't still skulking around outside,' retorted Phoebe.

'No. Mr Slater is proving somewhat elusive at the moment.'

At the sound of the name, Alfie started. What? Slater? Could that be Tom Slater? He glanced down at the copy of *The Evening News* that Kate had handed him and stared in disbelief at the headline, THE FILM, THE DIRECTOR, HIS WIFE AND HER LOVER by Thomas Slater. How trite, he thought, girding himself for an explanation.

'I know this man,' he said simply. 'Please give me a moment to read the article and I will endeavour to explain.'

*

Troy sat at his computer staring at the flickering screen in a trance-like state. He had no idea how long he had been sitting like that but he was aware that, at some point, night had fallen. He knew this to be the case because the birds were no longer singing. He was certain of this. Still focusing on the screen, he strained his ears. Nothing. All around him was silence. The birds outside the room had gone to bed. Pleased at his discovery, he began to tap away at his keyboard.

He felt happy here in his room. Safe, secure like a baby in a womb. He stayed here most days much to his mother's dismay, his curtains drawn, the heavy blackout fabric that he had insisted on obliterating all traces of natural light. He had no faith in sunlight. Its rays lent clarity to all things. And Troy had no need for clarity. Not only that, on the rare occasions that he ventured out in it, it burnt his eyes. He hated that. Lamplight, that was OK as long as it was dimmed. He could be inconspicuous that way. And that was important because he had no wish to be found. Not by *them*, anyway. *They* were always looking for him. He had to hide from *them*.

But his mother couldn't understand that. But then she couldn't understand that her food tasted funny these past twelve years. He'd tried his hardest to explain why this should be, that *they* had been tampering with it in order to poison him, but she just shook her head, or cried, tears dribbling through the fingers she held before her eyes as she ran out of the room. And he would worry about her for a little while, fearful that *they* might suddenly decide to get her, catch her unawares.

And she was unhappy when he laughed. He often did that though he couldn't say that he was happy. He just laughed. For ages, sometimes. She would beg him to stop, tell him that he was scaring her. Don't laugh! Eat! Go outside! Get some fresh air! This was her mantra these days. If he wasn't so tired he'd worry about her, he really would. And he was very, very tired. So tired, in fact, that he could barely focus on the screen.

Some time back she had insisted that he try and get a job. Did she not realise that he had spent the last fifteen years training to be a film director? And not just any old director. Oh no. He was set to be the best. The very best. Like his old mate Alfie Macbeth. He'd won an Oscar. Quite right too, in Troy's opinion. It was a brilliant film, *Killing Fame*. Terrifying in places. It would have been far, far scarier had Hollywood not insisted he changed the ending. Not many people were aware of that but then not many people would be considered a friend of Alfie Macbeth. He was. Troy Thomas. He was a good friend of Alfie Macbeth. He was to have been a runner on that film, *Killing Fame*. Yup. If it hadn't been for Stella. Stella Armstrong. That woman was truly evil. He knew that. He had been told by a reliable source. Now there was another friend to be proud of. Not too many people could boast of a phone line to God. He agreed with Troy. Stella had ruined everything. Him, his dreams, his life, Alfie, everything. If there was one thing he hated more than *them,* it was *her*. And now Alfie was dying.

That's what he'd been doing, he remembered, pleased that he was on the ball. He'd been scanning the British newspapers on the internet as he did almost everyday for stories about Alfie. Only Alfie was very ill. He'd told him so himself when he'd rung about a week ago. He was going to have a serious operation. It was very upsetting knowing that he had cancer. Perhaps he should phone the hospital. Yes. That's what he should do. He'd call the hospital.

Something else was bothering him, though. What was that? Something else about Alfie. He'd read it today. It had been headlines in a newspaper called *The Evening News*, a publication that had dark, satanic overtones, he could vaguely recall. That's what he'd been reading, he realised triumphantly, focusing his eyes on the screen. *THE*

FILM, THE DIRECTOR, HIS WIFE AND HER LOVER, he read as his agitation returned. He began to panic. Clutching his throat as he gulped for air, he jumped to his feet before crumpling to a sobbing heap on the floor. Tom Slater had written the article. Good old Tom, his cousin, the only person who continued to visit him. But wait a minute, didn't Tom work in Sydney on *The Australian*? But this paper, *The Evening News*, was a London paper. How had he managed that? Was he in London? No, he couldn't be, he'd visited him last week. And he wouldn't write stuff like this. Not anymore. He'd promised Troy. He was good now. But how could he be? These articles suggested that Tom was one of *them*. And that worried him. Had he told him something he shouldn't? Had Tom forced something out of him? No, he would never give anything away. He'd promised. But if Tom *was* one of them the only way he could have got anything out of him was by sticking a needle in him, injecting him with some drug. Yes. That was it. That's what he'd done. Oh God. He had to warn Alfie. He had to help him.

*

'Don't say anything, Alfie,' said Larry bursting into the room, fully aware of the police presence. 'There's no need. Raul Mendoza is very much alive and well and actually, is planning a return to the silver screen.'

Ten eyes drilled into Larry standing in the doorway, hair akimbo, shirt tail hanging outside his chinos, suede loafers soaking wet, a distorted grin hanging on his crimson face.

My God, it's mad Tom escaped from Bedlam, thought Alfie, startled by the dishevelled appearance of his great friend. 'Raul,' he said calmly, belying the shock he felt following his conversation with the police. 'I really am supposed to have murdered Raul Mendoza?'

'Yes. I mean no,' said Larry, grimacing wildly. 'It depends on how you look at it.'

Kate groaned. 'The man's gone nuts,' she muttered under her breath.

'You're not getting nearly enough sleep,' said Alfie, bemused by his friend's wacky behaviour.

'Daddy knows Thomas Slater,' interjected Phoebe, fighting back the tears.

'Time's up gentlemen,' ordered Nurse Mitchell, storming into the room so rapidly she caused a breeze. 'Five minutes, that's what I said. And as for you sir, you should be ashamed of yourself forcing an entry like this and with the police here,' she said focusing her attentions onto Larry.

'Sorry,' he apologised shamefacedly.

'Just one last question Mr Macbeth and then Sgt Fawkes and I will leave you in peace,' said DI Marshall hurriedly. 'If the Australian Police dragged the lake on what used to be your land in Millaa Millaa, would I be right in assuming they will not find the remains of a body, male or female, murdered fifteen years ago?'

'That is correct,' confirmed Alfie.

Eighteen

The pale-green room was quiet now and filled with the scent of expensive flowers creatively arranged by Nurse Mitchell in the hospital's cheap, chipped vases. Muttering something about the perils of fame, visiting hours and privacy, she had ushered the small gathering out of Alfie's room, scolding them as if they were young kids.

Relieved to have at last cleared up some of the mystery surrounding Tom Slater's claims, Larry, who had regained most of, if not all of his usual bonhomie, had left Phoebe in the care of Nurse Mitchell to escort Kate, who was sounding off about the injustice of Alfie's continued fame, out of the hospital. The teaming hordes of journalists, excited to see a star at last, pounced on her hurling questions, thrusting microphones and cameras at her from every direction. It was all Larry could do to prevent them being crushed. It was an ugly scene, the media representatives like vultures feeding on carrion, an experience he wouldn't wish on his worst enemy.

But Kate surprised him and shone like the star she had once been. Evidently delighted to be in the spotlight once more, she answered question after question, politely and succinctly, posed for photographs, spoke into the camera. No, she did not believe that her ex-husband Alfie Macbeth was a murderer. Yes she had spoken to Venetia Johnson about Alfie's aggressive behaviour. No, she had not claimed that he was a rapist. Venetia had twisted the facts. Yes it was true, she hadn't spoken to her ex-husband Raul Mendoza for two years but a reliable source had told her that he was alive and well and preparing for a return to the Western world, possibly even a comeback. Yes, she was happily married, and yes her career was going well.

'And is Alfie Macbeth dying of cancer?'

'He's very ill, yes.'

'And has his second wife visited him?'

279

'I have no idea,' replied Kate, brushing the question aside like a stray hair.

Larry was amazed. It had been a consummate performance. Kate had behaved with decorum. One or two less committed journalists, happy at last to have garnered some material, began to pack up their equipment, their job completed.

'As you are probably aware,' said Larry, keen to tie up any loose ends with one last announcement, 'DI Marshall of the Metropolitan Police has been making inquiries into the claims surrounding Alfie Macbeth. He will be issuing a full statement on tonight's TV news. Thank you for your time.' And with that he led Kate by the arm and placed her in a taxi.

'Thanks,' he told her. 'Though I have to ask why?'

Kate snorted and stuck her elegant nose in the air. 'Well don't,' she said dismissively.

It was 7pm. Alfie had been asleep for the last five hours. Sitting in the waiting room, flicking through the pile of old magazines on the table, staring vacantly at the modern art on the walls, Larry and Phoebe waited patiently for permission to return to Alfie's bedside.

At last a nurse, whom neither of them recognised, appeared in the waiting room to tell them Alfie was awake and asking for them. Night had fallen and the room, lit by a single lamp, seemed calm and quiet, the smell of antiseptic drowned in the sea of fragrant flowers. Opposite the bed, Jack Buchanan's painting hung on the wall. Only the gentle bleeping of Alfie's heart monitor disturbed the absolute peace and tranquility.

'Just before my father died he gave me a camera,' he told them as they wandered into the room, pronouncing the words, slowly, carefully, intent on giving them their full meaning. 'Take lots of pictures he told me . . .'

'. . . so you'll always remember the things you have done,' said Phoebe completing the sentence, taking up her position on his bed. Larry smiled and sat down on the chair.

'Well done, Phoebe. You remember,' he said squeezing her hand. 'So you see, I have measured out my life in photographs.'

Larry laughed.

'When I die . . .'

'Daddy, don't.'

'I will die, Phoebe. Not even I can escape that fate.' Larry grunted. 'When I die, I want you to have these photographs to treasure Phoebe and maybe make some sense of my life.'

'There's a lot of life left in you, old chap. Of that I am sure,' said Larry, sensing Phoebe was close to tears.

'Yeah, yeah,' said Alfie, winking at him.

'But before you do decide to leave us,' continued Larry in the same lively banter. 'Perhaps you could do us the honour of explaining your relationship with that lizard-like creature that calls himself a journalist.'

'Tom Slater.'

'Indeed.'

'Well let me begin by telling you that our hatred of one another is mutual. He was my Australian neighbour Millie Thomas's nephew. Troy Thomas, Millie's son, used to visit Stella and me often. He was a movie enthusiast, energetic and inquisitive.' He paused to catch his breath, closing his eyes. 'I liked Troy. He was going to be a runner on the film but I had my breakdown then relocated to England.' He stopped, opened his eyes and coughed quietly. 'It wasn't that I forgot to ask him if he was still interested, it was just that I thought seeing him would open old wounds. Not enough time had elapsed. I wasn't ready for physical reminders of Stella. And Troy was a good friend of Stella's. It's been bothering me recently that he might have been disappointed. I rang him just before I came into hospital. As luck would have it he was staying with Millie.'

'And was he?' asked Larry.

'What?'

'Disappointed?'

'No. Far from it. He sounded thrilled to speak to me. He told me that he'd kept up with me via the internet, then he asked me if I was planning a trip to Australia. I felt so guilty to have lost touch with him I told him the most intimate thing I could think of.'

'That you had cancer,' said Larry quietly.

'Exactly.'

'But you hadn't told me,' said Phoebe indignantly.

'I know and I'm sorry about that. It was guilt-led and he was a million miles away.' Alfie sighed. 'Stella always said that Troy was infatuated with me. I felt I owed him some honesty in the end.'

Phoebe smiled and squeezed his hand.

'And Thomas Slater?' asked Larry.

'He was an avid film buff which is why Troy introduced him to me. Troy had no idea that he would write an article on me. I was in hiding. The last thing I wanted at that time was for the world to get wind of the fact that I was trying to write a screenplay. Tom wrote an article and tried to sell it. Unfortunately for him, having tried to take a covert picture of Stella, the picture editor rang and asked me for a photo. I stopped the article immediately, threatened to sue the paper, you know the type of thing.'

281

'Which is why I'd never heard of him,' said Larry.

'I came down heavily on him. Humiliated him. Sent out a defamatory letter to the Australian press. Threatened him. He did not like that one little bit.'

'But he says he was there when Stella left you.'

'Yes he was, the miserable little sneak. He said he'd come to apologise.'

'So how come he never reported that?'

'I presume he had no idea what happened to me. And I believe he was scared.'

'Scared but very, very bitter.'

'Bitter perhaps and also full of hatred. I believe Tom despised me. And I guess he's been waiting for the right time to seek his revenge. With me being ill in hospital, too ill to fight back, this was the perfect time.'

'He must have known you were ill,' said Larry.

'Of course he did, though I don't know how.'

'Troy. Obviously. They were cousins after all.'

'No way. Troy would never have done that to me. He learnt the hard way. He swore he'd be forever loyal and I believe him.'

'OK if you say so, but it would have taken one hell of a foraging job for Tom to find out any other way.'

'But don't you see Larry? He was bent on revenge. Why else would he break into my house? When he found the book he must have thought he'd struck oil.'

'Book? You mean the diary, Alfie?' said Larry, clearing his throat. 'It's full of descriptions of the most gruesome murders.'

'You've seen it?'

'Thomas took great pleasure in showing it to me.'

'That piece in the paper?' said Phoebe. 'I thought he'd made that up.'

'I know,' said Alfie with a sigh. 'You see I broke down shortly after Stella left me, mentally and physically. Troy's father Harry found me about a week after Stella left, bearded and unwashed, staring at a blank wall. He had me admitted to a psychiatric unit in a Sydney hospital where I stayed for three months.'

'He told me that you'd taken Stella on holiday,' said Larry.

'I couldn't tell you, Larry. I was too proud.'

'But I was a friend. We'd been through so much together.'

'I know that Larry, I know, but I was ashamed and only wanted to forget the whole sorry business. I needed a focus in my life and that was Phoebe. It was important that I was strong for her.'

'But the diary,' said Larry.

'In my deranged state I kept a record of my thoughts in a book. The book Tom stole. I suppose you could call it a diary although it was fuelled by my anger. I don't really know why I kept it. Perhaps I thought it might keep me sane. You see I have never stopped loving Stella though I have long since ceased hating Jack.'

'Jack?' said Phoebe, sitting bolt upright. 'It was Jack she left you for, not Raul.'

'The artist?' asked Larry incredulously. 'The guy who painted that?' He pointed at the painting. 'You kept it after all he'd done to you.'

'It's a beautiful painting.'

'And that's meant to aid your recuperation?'

'It's a beautiful painting,' repeated Alfie.

'That's hardly the point. He stole your wife,' said Larry horrified.

'Yes I know and it almost destroyed me.'

'I'd have burnt it or taken a knife to it,' said Larry. 'I really cannot understand why you've kept it all these years.'

'Jack Buchanan was a very dear friend of mine. It's funny because from the moment she met him I was convinced that Stella hated him. He seemed to irritate her in some way. But when I went away to Los Angeles to meet with David Palmer she approached him to see if he would paint her as a surprise for me on my return. Well, of course, he said yes. Who wouldn't?'

Phoebe pursed her lips but said nothing.

'What resulted was a beautiful life painting of the woman I loved and the start of a passionate love affair that culminated in the conception of a child.'

'Stella got pregnant,' burst out Phoebe, astonished.

'It bound them together, sealed their fate. Jack was a kind and very beautiful man. I understand why Stella fell for him.'

'How can you be so forgiving?' Larry asked him mystified. 'Stella meant the world to you.'

'And that is it in a nutshell. She left me without asking for a penny of my fortune, wracked with grief.'

'Grief? What did she have to be sad about?' asked Phoebe angrily.

'Her own guilt,' explained Alfie. 'I understand that now. It was her life. She couldn't stay with me just to see me happily through mine. She had to leave me to live her own, albeit with the legacy of guilt. I used to dream that one day she would return but I have long since given up thinking that he would bring her back to me.'

'Thomas Slater was certain that life had mirrored art,' said Larry who was surprised to find that he was fighting back tears. 'He kept on and on about the similarities between your life and your thriller, *Killing Fame.*'

'Well there are some pretty terrible parallels,' said Alfie with a smile. 'But alas, no happy ending for me.'

By now Phoebe had surrendered to her emotions. Large tears rolled down her cheeks, though she smiled bravely all the same.

'Come here, you,' said Alfie pulling her towards him. 'I have so much to be grateful for. A life lived to the full, a stack of films made. I won myself an Oscar, made great friends but best of all, better than anything else, I have a clever, stunning and talented daughter whom I love to pieces. What man could ask for more?'

'Here, here,' agreed Larry, stroking his goddaughter's long, dark hair.

'I'm sorry to intrude,' said Nurse Mitchell popping her head round the door.

'Come in gorgeous,' said Alfie, cheerily.

'Stop it, Alfie, you old flirt, you know she's mine,' said Larry. Nurse Mitchell obliged them both by turning a deep shade of scarlet.

'Ignore them,' said Phoebe, smiling through her tears. 'They're just a couple of overgrown kids.'

'It's lovely to see things have settled down,' she said, her face fading back to its usual rosy colour.

'Quite so,' said Larry.

'However, there is a woman outside who is insistent on seeing Alfie. She says it's important and I . . . well . . . I believe her.'

'A woman?' said Larry, raising both eyebrows. 'Sounds like your lucky day.'

'Who is it?' asked Phoebe.

'She says her name is Stella Macbeth,' said the nurse, blushing again.

'Stella?' all three repeated.

'Yes. That's right.'

'Send her in,' said Alfie breathlessly. 'She's right, it is important.'

Nineteen

Troy was lying on his bed in his darkened room trying to make sense of it all. And that was difficult because inside his head a battalion of soldiers were marching row upon row, their boots pounding across the soft cortex of his brain as they prepared for battle in the thick, grey fog. Like him they were on a mission. It was bewildering though. How could they fight when they could barely see? Really, he should help them. He knew that. Show them the way. He could do that. It was a path he trod often, undercover, out of sight, whenever he went in search of *them.*

Four days had past since the awful truth had dawned on him. He'd worked it out, fitted the pieces together. Tom was one of *them.* Now that he knew this to be the case he would make sure that he was prepared for any funny business. When Tom was visiting he would be extra vigilant. Tom was a dirty player, underhand and devious. Now that he thought about it, he had suffered years of unpleasantness at his hands – the lies, the deceit and lately, the injections. Some kind of truth drug, he was certain of that, but his mother kept on insisting that this was not the case. What did she know? *She* couldn't hear the voices. Of course she couldn't. *She* wasn't connected. The idea was ludicrous.

What he hadn't realised was that Jack Buchanan was also part of *their* gang. Oh yes, everyone in Millaa Millaa knew that Stella had run off with the blonde haired, blue-eyed boy. Oh yes, little boy blue went and blew his horn and Stella came running. Pathetic, that's what it was and yet his mother and father still saw them regularly. Millie was always telling him how they had done this and they had done that. But it was because of Jack that Alfie had kept away. Couldn't his mother see that? And Jack was the reason her own son hadn't made his big break. It was all Jack's fault. Alfie's cancer, too. That was obviously down to Jack. Jack was one of *them.*

That was his mission. He knew what to do, what weapon to use. He had been given a sign. He'd do it for Alfie. That way Alfie would never forget his good friend Troy Thomas ever again.

*

'Stella! Stella! Is it really you?' he asked, staring wide-eyed and disbelieving at the beautiful apparition who stood nervously before him.

'Yes, Alfie,' she said, her voice barely above a whisper, her glassy green eyes focused directly at Alfie's own. They sparkled even in the lamplight as they always had. Fifteen years had passed and yet she appeared the same although her hair seemed fairer, truly blonde. Thick, glossy hair, it framed her elfin face, falling to her shoulders where it lay in a perfect line. Under her right eye a freckle, the only blemish on a face that now was etched with the finest of lines beneath her eyes, at the corners of her mouth.

'So you didn't marry Jack then?'

'No,' she answered simply.

'But you had children?'

'Yes. Three beautiful blonde children,' she said it prosaically and without further explanation.

Alfie smiled and pressed her hand. Jack Buchanan, blonde hair, blue eyes. 'Ah. A trio of cherubs born of angels.' He sighed.

Stella laughed and touched his face with her fingertips. 'Still the same old Alfie.'

'And you love him?'

Stella said nothing, just crinkled up her nose and bit her lower lip.

Of course she does, you sad old man, he told himself. I would have thought that was obvious because she looks a million dollars. Don't go and ruin the occasion. She looks awkward enough already.

'So you've come to say goodbye to the old devil have you?' Stella winced and lowered her eyes. Her hair swung forward, obscuring her face as it always had. Alfie smiled. 'I feel as though I shall be able to die now – now that I have seen you again,' he told her, picking up her hand. 'In my dreams I've seen you, a thousand times or more, but somehow dreams never quite live up to a person's expectation. It's incredibly frustrating when you wake up and find yourself alone.'

Stella lifted her eyes to his, frowned slightly but did not reply.

'I can't quite believe you're here and I have no real understanding of why you came. All I know is that when I go to sleep for the last time, I think I shall be forever happy.' He smiled and closed his eyes, content to wallow in the corporeal pleasure her presence allowed.

For a moment Stella sat beside him, silently holding his hand. After a while she squeezed it affectionately then let it go to run her fingers down the grooved line of his cheek, once, twice, three times, across the raised vein on his left temple, then softly, gently across his dry, closed lips. He opened his eyes and held her by both arms as she kissed him lightly on his mouth.

'Will Phoebe be OK?' she asked him after some time had elapsed.

'Eventually and with time. Larry will always be there for her.'

'She's very beautiful.'

'Yes. She is.'

'You must be proud of her.'

'Yes, Stella, I am,' said Alfie taking her hand again. 'It was brave of you to come.' Stella shrugged. 'But then you always were the brave one,' he added with a laugh. 'I'm very pleased that you have not changed.'

'I'm sure I have. I'm not quite as impetuous these days. Responsibilities can temper such things,' she said, smiling again.

How he loved to see her smile, the way it eased across her cheeks in tiny lines, like a flickering torch to her clear, green eyes that shone and sparkled, radiating happiness. It was the light he used to live by all those years ago. There was so much he wanted to ask her, so much he wanted to know about her life that he knew she wouldn't tell him. It was just her way. It always had been.

'How's Jesse?'

'She's fine. A real help with the kids.'

'I bet she is.'

'She's looking after them while I'm away.'

'And does she approve of your visit?'

'Hmm,' said Stella, refusing to be drawn.

Alfie smiled. He really wasn't interested to hear about Jesse but there were other things he'd like to know. No harm in trying.

'Is Jack good to you?'

'Alfie!'

'Do you still see Troy?' This question proved a little more successful in that it received an answer, though not the one Alfie was expecting.

'No, not for ages. No one does.'

'Oh?' asked Alfie. 'Why's that?'

'He's mentally ill,' replied Stella flatly. 'Schizophrenic, Millie says.'

'No! That's dreadful!' exclaimed Alfie. 'Is he able to work, lead a normal life?

'No. Not at all. He lives at home, locked in his room all day, curtains drawn, surfing the internet, staring into space. He's a great worry to Millie and Harry especially when he refuses to take his medication for weeks on end. Millie's constantly exhausted. She's thinner than ever and she's aged, poor thing.'

'When did this happen?' asked Alfie, appalled at what he was hearing.

'The first signs appeared about a year after you left,' continued Stella sadly. 'He'd dropped out of university saying that he intended to make it in films. He went to loads of interviews for all sorts of jobs, catering, runner's jobs, publicity, lighting, sound, but was turned down every time. To earn his way he helped Harry on the farm. He began to lose weight and to sleep a lot, kept telling his parents that he was a failure. Initially they thought he was depressed because of the job rejections but then he stopped eating altogether and told Millie it was because he was being poisoned. When Millie offered to taste everything she cooked him in his presence he began to eat again. Then he began to laugh at inappropriate things. He became apathetic and unable to concentrate on the simplest task. But the worst thing for all of them was Troy's insistence that he could hear voices.'

'But I spoke to him last week. He sounded fine,' said Alfie, horrified by what he was hearing.

'Sometimes he appears completely normal, lucid, calm, the good old Troy that we knew and loved, which of course he still is, although in reality he is very, very ill. And he absolutely refuses to talk to me. Says I'm one of *them*.'

'Them?'

'The people the voices talk to him about.'

'God that's awful,' said Alfie. 'I still feel so guilty. The job as runner . . .'

'Millie insists that he was born with the disease but that it didn't show until his late twenties,' interrupted Stella, squeezing Alfie's hand. 'She's been brilliant with him, very patient, taking everything he throws at her calmly and with phenomenal understanding. It took them ages to persuade him to see the first psychiatrist and about six years before he was diagnosed. The drugs they prescribed him really help control the illness but as with all drugs they have side effects so he refuses to take them from time to time.'

'Poor Troy,' said Alfie who could not imagine his young energetic friend so debilitated. If only he'd known. If only he had kept in contact. A bit late now, he thought, bleakly.

'Yes. It's dreadful, horribly sad for Troy, of course, but also for Harry and Millie. Millie tells me they feel so helpless.'

'I had no idea.'

'He was thrown into deep despair when he discovered you were ill. Millie rang last week and told us.'

'Oh God!'

'If it hadn't been for him I wouldn't have known you were ill. But I didn't travel half the way round the world to talk about Troy.'

'No, you didn't,' said Alfie sadly. 'But I'm glad you did.'

'I want to hear all about you and your Oscar,' said Stella, changing the subject with typical abruptness.

'Oh c'mon. Since when has fame and adulation impressed you?'

'I loved your acceptance speech. Your modesty was most disarming.'

'You watched the Oscar ceremony!'

'Loved the suit, Alfie. Who put you in Armani?'

'No idea,' he said with a laugh. 'Larry arranged all that.'

'I was pleased to see you refused to button up your cuffs.'

'Not much gets past you!'

'I half expected it to be on display,' she joked looking around the room until her eyes alighted on Jack's picture on the wall. She gasped, covering her mouth with her hand.

'Don't worry,' he said reaching out for her arm. 'There's nothing sad about it. I happen to like the picture. And anyway, it's no bad thing not to want to forget.'

'Alfie!'

'You see I can understand what happened, how I fell short of your dreams.'

'Alfie, don't.'

'But it's true, Stella. You know that. I could not be what you wanted, needed. Whereas Jack . . .'

'Don't try to second guess. Not now.'

'He's a good man, Jack, one of the best.'

'Alfie.'

'I didn't always see it that way. I have to confess there was a time when I would have quite easily destroyed your happiness by . . .' He stopped. 'But you know that too.'

'You had a right to be angry. I let you down.'

'As I let you down. I smothered you with affection, wrapped the heavy mantle of perfection tightly around you until you could not breathe. You were a free spirit, I knew that and still I gilded the cage that bound your life to mine. I should never have tried to contain someone as free. I never should have done that.'

'You didn't. It wasn't like that. I loved you like crazy. We were happy together.'

'Until the day . . .' he said, his voice trailing off. He glanced at Stella, at the tear that rolled down her lovely cheek. 'Where did he paint you Stella? That's all I want to know.'

'By the lake,' she whispered. 'He painted me by the lake.'

'That's where it all began. By our lake?'

'Yes,' she whispered, lowering her eyes.

'And had I known you were coming and that it would upset you, I would have taken the picture down,' he added, stroking her hair. 'Now come here and let me hold you, one last time.'

*

'Miss Macbeth, Mr Woods, come quickly,' said a nurse, bursting into the waiting room as professionally as her emotions would allow.

'Alfie?' asked Larry, springing to his feet in alarm.

'Yes.'

'Oh God,' screamed Phoebe, running from the waiting room to her father, Larry in close pursuit. Phoebe pulled open the door.

'What's happening?' she asked the doctor, who was standing by Alfie but seemingly doing nothing while a nurse placed an oxygen mask on his face. To the left of Alfie the heart monitor buzzed angrily, the line it traced, erratic. Stella stood by the bed holding Alfie's hand, petrified and horrified by what she was witnessing, tears running in a silent stream down her sun-tanned cheeks.

'Ventricular fibrillation,' explained the doctor. 'His heart's electrical activity has become disordered. His ventricles are fluttering rather than beating which means the heart is pumping little or no blood around his body.'

'You'll be needing a defibrillator then,' said Phoebe.

'Will he?' asked Larry astounded, momentarily forgetting her veterinary training.

'I am afraid Alfie Macbeth has suffered a massive heart attack,' explained the doctor now addressing Larry. A touch too matter-of-factly, thought Larry, who was feeling as though he had walked into a pathology lab, Alfie's body, already the corpse, laid out on the slab.

'Where are the crash team?' asked Phoebe desperately, rushing to her father's side. 'Shouldn't they be here by now?' Without acknowledging Stella, who tactfully stepped aside, Phoebe picked up her father's hand and held it to her mouth, kissing it furiously as though this affectionate yet futile gesture would somehow resuscitate him.

'Is he still alive?' asked Larry hesitatingly, thinking that his friend looked far from that.

'He is still breathing, yes,' confirmed the doctor.

'But surely there is something you can do,' insisted Larry angrily. 'You surely aren't just going to stand there and watch him die.'

'This is what he requested, should he suffer a heart attack or stroke,' explained the doctor. 'I truly wish that wasn't the case but I am duty bound to respect those wishes.'

'Oh Daddy, Daddy, please don't die,' cried Phoebe, laying her head on his emaciated belly, a little child again.

'Yes but surely his daughter's wants are a bit more important at this stage,' continued Larry, flailing his arms in desperation, feeling totally incapacitated.

'Larry,' whispered Stella. Moving across the room she took hold of his arm, desperately trying to impart some strength she could not feel. 'Think of Phoebe,' she implored him, appealing to him with those unforgettable green eyes, her strange yet familiar face, normally so cocksure, today rigid with fright, hanging on to his arm in reassurance as well as support. He shook his head in despair, put his arm round her and pulled her towards him, fighting back the tears.

'Daddy, Daddy, don't die. I love you Daddy. Don't leave me. Not now, not after all we've been through. Please Daddy, please,' sobbed Phoebe, overwhelmed with grief, oblivious to those around her.

Behind her, Larry watched also, horrified, willing his friend to wake up, crack a joke, anything but die. But Alfie was breathing in short, shallow bursts, the colour draining from his face, flesh-coloured to blue to dull grey.

'Don't die, Daddy. Don't die. I'm here,' wailed Phoebe now kissing her father's pale cheeks, drenching them with her tears as, with a final exhausted murmur, Alfie Macbeth breathed his last. The heart monitor gave out a resounding bleep as the line flattened.

'No, no,' sobbed Phoebe hopelessly. 'No. Don't go. Don't leave me, Daddy. I couldn't bear for you to leave me.'

'I'm very, very sorry, Miss Macbeth,' said the doctor before turning to his nurse. 'Time of death 21.12.' The nurse nodded and wrote it down.

'Oh my God,' whispered Larry, covering his mouth with both hands.

'No, Daddy, no,' cried Phoebe.

'He's gone, Phoebe, he's at rest,' said the nurse kindly, placing her hands on Phoebe's shoulders.

'But I didn't get to say goodbye,' she wailed, burying her head in her father's shoulder as she desperately clutched his lifeless form. 'I didn't tell him how much I loved him. Didn't tell him that he was the best father in the world. He can't die. I haven't told him.'

'Phoebe ... he ... knows ... darling,' said Larry who was sobbing openly now.

'But I didn't say goodbye,' repeated Phoebe, not letting go.

'I'm sure he heard you,' said the nurse, calmly.

'Yes he did,' affirmed the doctor. 'He was still alive when you came in and would have heard every word you said.'

'But I don't want him to die,' cried Phoebe.

'None of us do ... sweetheart,' said Larry, stroking her hair. 'We all of us loved him.'

'I won't be able to live without him.'

'You're hurting,' said Larry.

'That's right,' said the nurse. 'You are in shock. The pain will lessen over time.'

But Phoebe could not understand. It was painfully obvious to Larry that she felt as though her world had ended. The father whom she had adored, with whom her world had begun and ended, now lay before her, dead. Nothing and no one could replace his love, the pride he felt for her, the joy, the triumph and the concern. The bubble of security in which she had grown-up and excelled had suddenly and tragically burst, leaving her vulnerable, terrified and alone. Of course, in time, she would learn to carry on in spite of his death, and knowing Phoebe it would quite literally be *in spite*. But nothing anyone said or did right now could help her through this most immediate, insufferable and enduring pain.

'I wish I had done more,' said Phoebe, suddenly turning to Larry. 'I wish I had given back as much as he gave. He was totally selfless, you see. The love he lavished on me, completely unconditional. If I asked him to walk across hot coals for me, he would have done it without batting an eyelid. You know that Larry, don't you?'

'You were his daughter, Phoebe, and he loved you.'

'Yes but he was no ordinary Dad,' said Phoebe, crying again. 'He would have died for me. Larry, you know that. You were there.'

'That's right, Phoebe,' murmured Stella. 'He was all those things and more.'

At the sound of Stella's voice, Phoebe stood up and glared at her.

'GO AWAY,' she screamed. 'This is all your fault. If it hadn't been for you he would still be alive.'

'Phoebe,' said Larry gently.

'It's OK. I understand. I'm leaving,' whispered Stella unblinking, tears pouring down her cheeks.

'Good,' said Phoebe, unconcerned for any pain Stella might be feeling. 'Because you are not welcome here.'

Stella turned, head bowed, and walked quietly out of the room.

'Come away, Phoebe,' said Larry gently as he valiantly fought the urge to scream and shout at the injustice of it all. He felt heavy, overloaded with a grief that seemed to smother him, sucking the optimism from him as he stood by helplessly watching the tragic scene.

'No. I'M NOT LEAVING HIM,' Phoebe yelled as the tears continued to fall. 'GO AWAY, ALL OF YOU. LEAVE US ALONE.'

'It's all right,' said the nurse to Larry. 'We'll leave her be for a while. Let her say her goodbyes.'

The night that followed Alfie's death, thought Larry, was without doubt the worst night of his life. Phoebe had clung to her father for a full two hours more before Larry had finally managed to coax her away. Alfie's body had gone cold, his skin waxy, his spirit long gone when he had prised his distraught goddaughter away and, with the aid of Nurse Mitchell, who was now back on duty, put her into a bed in a private room and persuaded her to take some valium. He had sat with her until, at last, she fell asleep.

Afterwards he had gone in search of Stella and found her all alone, pacing the floor of the waiting-room, her face swollen, stained with tears. He had a hundred questions that he wanted to ask her to try to make sense of the tragedy of fifteen years before. He wanted to tell her how angry he had been and yet how much he loved her, but the moment he saw her alone, injured, heart-broken, he simply opened his arms to her. She ran into Larry's outstretched arms as if they were the safest refuge in the world and they clung to one another like a pair of lost shipwrecked survivors terrified of drowning, sobbing together unselfconsciously for the next half hour. Worn out and emotionally drained, they eventually sat down on adjoining chairs and fell asleep, their bodies leaning into one another, Stella's head resting against him, his arm around her shoulder.

At around 6am Larry woke to a gentle knocking on the door. A nurse entered followed by a weary and apprehensive looking DI Marshall. His neck was stiff and his head throbbed and the last thing he needed was another chat with the well-meaning detective. Stella had been roused by the noise too, and was yawning.

'Who is that?' she asked Larry.

'DI Marshall, madam,' said the inspector holding out his hand.

'Stella Macbeth,' she replied, quietly, shaking his hand.

'I realise that the news I am about to deliver has come at the worst possible time for you and Alfie's relations but I thought it important to tell you before the press get their teeth into it,' began DI Marshall nervously.

'Don't worry, I understand,' said Larry wearily, rubbing his face with his hands. 'You're only doing your job.'

'Thank you, that's very reasonable of you,' said DI Marshall mopping his brow with a frayed white handkerchief. 'You see it has come as a terrific shock to all of us down at the yard.'

'I know, it's very tragic,' said Larry, trying desperately to bury his personal grief. 'Alfie Macbeth was a good man.'

DI Marshall coughed and wiped his brow a second time.

'Yes it's very tragic. I was a huge fan of Mr Macbeth. But what I was actually referring to was an alarming piece of evidence that has come to light.'

'I'm sorry,' said Larry, who was too tired to follow what the policeman was saying. He looked at Stella who just shrugged.

'The police were called to The Rocks in the early hours of the morning.'

'Eh?' said Larry, confused.

'Why?' enquired Stella. 'The house is empty.'

'There was an incident down by the lake yesterday,' explained the inspector. 'The police were called.'

'The lake,' repeated Larry, still not following.

'There's a lake on the land not far from the house,' Stella told him.

'That's right, madam,' said the inspector pausing to cough again. 'And contrary to expectation, my expectation that is,' he qualified, 'they've found a body beside the lake.'

'A body?' asked Stella and Larry in unison.

'That's right.'

'Yesterday?'

'Yes.'

'Someone we know?' gulped Stella, the colour draining from her face.

'At this stage I am not prepared to say.'

'Why?' she asked. By now Stella was clutching her throat, terrified.

'Because the body has not yet been formally identified.'

'Oh Christ,' said Larry horrified. Stella winced.

'But I can tell you it was suicide.'

'Oh,' said Stella with an audible sigh of relief.

'It can't be Thomas Slater,' whispered Larry. 'I was only with him yesterday.'

'And they're certain it was suicide?' reaffirmed Stella. 'How come?'

'Yes. Corroborated by the presence of a gun by the first body. And the second body they then found at the bottom of the lake.'

'Another body? A second body?' shrieked Stella in alarm.

Beside her Larry had begun to shake uncontrollably.

Twenty

His palm is sweaty. He knows this because the handle of his father's old army Enfield feels slippery, tricky to grip. And it is difficult to see his target, the fog that surrounds him dark, dank, dense. Heavy too, like a lead weight bearing down on his shoulders. Inside his head the soldiers' boots are pounding a steady beat to which he notices, with some alarm, his heart is keeping time. Thump, thump, thump, thump. The din is deafening. And now he can see it also, a red, misty curtain that hangs before his eyes and pulsates rhythmically, toneless, droning.

His hand is trembling as he points the gun. His victim shaking, open-mouthed, afraid, staring down the barrel, his ice blue eyes wide with fright. He sees that he's about to die. But he's talking. Troy knows this only because he can see the man's mouth speaking soundlessly. The muscles in his cheeks flex as he frantically works his dry lips into shapes, the blue vein on his temple angry, raised. But the soldier's boots reverberate around his brain, thump, thump, thump, thump, obscuring all sound.

He tries to focus on his task but is still distracted by his victim who is gesticulating wildly with his arms. His mouth, goldfish-like, blows a repeated single word towards him like bubbles in a stream. Thump, thump, thump. It is the same word over and over again . . . W-H-Y?

'Why? I think you and I both know why. Tom told me what you did. You are one of *them*. And I know what to do. Alfie told me. I've seen it at the movies.'

Suddenly all is quiet. The soldiers have ceased their marching and are standing to attention, watching, waiting. Troy closes his eyes and squeezes the trigger.

A loud scream escapes Jack's mouth, piercing the silence. For a moment they stand opposite one another, motionless, eyes locked, Jack's arms clutching his chest. Troy adjusts his aim and fires another shot more effective than the first. Jack crashes backwards, cracking his head on a large rock with such force his skull splits open. His brains, like jelly, spill out onto the grass.

Troy shakes his head in amazement as he tries to concentrate on the bloody, lifeless corpse less than six feet in front of him. The first bullet has gone right through him. He is surprised by that. It has entered Jack's body just below his left shoulder, ripping through his shoulder blade to splinter the wood behind him where it has lodged, embedded in the tree trunk. He takes a few tentative steps towards his victim, staring in amazement at the second, lethal bullet hole, a bull's-eye, right between his eyes, spewing blood. Behind Jack's head, a puddle of blood and brains discolours the grass. A red river of blood, tainted grey. Jack's blood. Jack's brains.

He feels calmer now as he takes the black, heavy-duty polythene bag out of his rucksack. He bought it from Tobin's earlier that day and is very glad of it now. He struggles with the body for over an hour, binding the bag with ropes, weighting it with rocks. By the time he has finished he is dirty and sweaty, the soldiers long gone.

Straining under the weight of the sarcophagus, his muscles burning with the exertion, he drags the body slowly, painfully to the lake. He is exhausted when he reaches the water. Struggling in the shallows not wanting to let go, he wades fully clothed to where the water is deeper and murkier, all but drowning in the process until finally, worn out, breathless, he releases his hold.

'He'll sink further into the middle as time goes on,' Troy tells the family of ducks who are quacking loudly, angry at being disturbed. Smiling, he turns and makes his weary way to the shore. His saturated clothes that cling to his body now drip heavily forming a puddle at his feet on the sandy beach.

'I'll be going now,' he tells the ducks as he looks down at his hands. His fingers are stained with grime and there are traces of darkened blood behind his nails. 'I've done my job. A difficult one, I have to admit, but something that I had to do.'

And with a hand that is trembling slightly, he picks up his father's revolver, places it slowly and carefully in his mouth, lodging the barrel firmly against his palate, and squeezes the trigger one last time.

THE END

296

Excerpt from forthcoming novel by Fiona Cane . . .

When the Dove Cried

1

I used to think that Adam was every mother's dream. Well-mannered, handsome, he exuded confidence and authority, which was reflected both in his manner and his clothes. He was a stylish dresser, neither dandified nor foppish, elegant rather than racy. His white cotton shirts were crisply ironed, his jackets and trousers neatly pressed and his dark brown hair, tamed of curls, was kept short in a sleek haircut, parted from the side. Everything about Adam was orderly and precise, including the way he walked. There was, however, an element of artificiality about that. It was affected, laborious as though he had practised and carefully manufactured it for hours, days, maybe weeks, one hand in his pocket, deliberate, exacting with protracted, measured strides. With the benefit of hindsight, I think, more than anything, it was his walk that gave him away.

I used to think that Adam was every mother's dream, except, perhaps, for mine. She never said anything to confirm my suspicion - well, not exactly. It was just something she asked me, the first time she met him, having chatted for an hour over innumerable cups of fragrant Earl Grey tea that she'd had bought specially for the occasion, and after several slices of her rich homemade fruitcake. It was the stickiest cake imaginable, the kind that glues your teeth together and distorts the way you talk for minutes after eating, but delicious, nonetheless. I remember Daddy was proudly showing Adam the trays of seedlings in his potting shed, and I was standing, waiting by his Mercedes, when she touched my hand and quietly asked me, *Are you sure?* I laughed and told her that of course I was, and she replied, *That's wonderful darling. I'm happy for you.* I didn't think to ask her then why she had posed the question. What was it that she'd seen behind his pale grey eyes? Had she guessed that I, too, had had my doubts? Did she know?

How different would my life have been, I often wonder, if I had. But I didn't ask her. I just smiled, kissed her happily on the soft, smooth skin of her cheek then drove away with Adam. It's only now, in retrospect, after all that has happened, I wish I had.

I had a friend called Rose de Lisle who thought of life as an exquisitely wrapped gift, refined, polished, tied with pink satin ribbon, a pretty bow on top. At least she did until that day in May when I rang her to tell her what had happened. I believe my news would have damaged her forever, had she stuck around. But what happened to me that honey-sweet spring morning, sullied forever her deodorised idea of the world. It was as though I'd shoved her head in a pile of warm manure and begged her to eat. She couldn't deal with it. She didn't want to know.

Three emotions affected me that day. Each of them catching me unawares, creeping up on me, springing their surprises on the happy innocent, all of them harrowing in their own particular way.

First of all I felt fear. I was frightened by the presence of a police car in our drive. Had Adam sent out a search party? I was terrified how he would react on my return - his violent anger, the bruises, my consequent shame. This was followed some time later by guilt. Guilt that I hadn't been at home waiting, although I'd had no reason to expect him. Guilt that my absence had occurred on the only night he'd probably ever needed me. Guilt at where I'd been.

It wasn't until the sun went down that I experienced the third emotion, more terrible in essence than the other two. Pain, like a piece of shrapnel entering the body, found its way to my heart. It was an atrocious pain, searing and sharp, haemorrhaging despair, denial and grief indiscriminately as it strangled forever any glimmer of hope of a rosy, antiseptic world.

It was the day the dove cried. Finn Costello's dove. A balmy day in May. The buttercup sun beamed brightly in an aquamarine sky devoid of even a wisp of cloud and the racemes of sweet-smelling wisteria hung, like bunches of dusty blue grapes, from the gnarled rope-like branches that covered our house. DI Taylor, a solemn-faced but courteous man met me by the back door, led me inside and politely advised me to sit down, which I did, at the kitchen table. *We believe your husband Adam is dead,* he told me carefully. And I thought, well that explains his humourless expression. A *body was found on the bridle path by the river. We believe he was murdered,* he continued calmly.

The bitter paradox of the situation wasn't lost on me. Outside the sun continued to shine.